For Martha

This book had a lot of help from my big sister Martha, who was like no other woman I know. She was extremely social, the glue that held family and friends together, and yet chose to spend the last part of her life living in a beautiful but isolated log home. She hunted her own land and was as independent and stubborn as Olivia. She gave to me generously – love, friendship, encouragement, insight, too much fabulous food, and just enough alcohol. I miss her every day.

Acknowledgements

Special thanks are owed to my friend and "overseer" Jane Abramowitz, who never fails to go the extra mile for her friends. I also received invaluable support and feedback on the books in this series from Tina Foley, Rasana Atreya, Carol Kean, Linda Scharaga, Mark Thomas, Michael Greenberg, Bobbi Dekay, Erik Cross, Michal Weissman, Yvonne Schumacher Strejcek, and Henry Tobias.

Olivia, Mourning

Book 1 of the Olivia Series

Yael Politis

Olivia, Mourning

Cover photo by Yulia Kazansky
Cover design by Tatiana Vila

Olivia, Mourning

Chapter One

Five Rocks, Pennsylvania – January 21, 1841

In the 19th century a wagon couldn't cross Pennsylvania without circumventing the worst of the Ridge-and-Valley Appalachians. Despite the breathtaking beauty of the lush green mountains, travelers gave a prayer of thanks when they finally made it past the Allegheny Front. There the plateau fell to the lowlands, into what some folks still called Westsylvania. Flat ground had never looked so good.

Some of those wagons later took a wrong turn and clomped across a charming covered bridge. *Thank the good Lord Almighty*, those drivers thought. *Nice bridge like that, there must be a town ahead.* And there was – Five Rocks. It offered one of everything they needed – Livery, Feed & Grain, General Store, Saloon, Doctor, and Lawyer – along with a choice of three churches. But none of these accidental visitors (for no stranger came to Five Rocks by design) stayed for more than a night. On their way out they clucked their tongues and wondered what on earth had possessed those folks to build their homes on what seemed to be the only ugly patch of ground in all of Pennsylvania. The few trees were gnarled and bent over, and not even weeds thrived in the hard-scrabble gray dirt.

Olivia Killion's father, Old Man Seborn Killion, was the owner of Killion's General in Five Rocks. She and her two older brothers, Avis and Tobey, lived with him in one of the eight "rich folks' houses" on Maple Street. Olivia had attended the one-room schoolhouse until she was past fifteen, when her father's illness put him in bed for good. She knew it was her place to stay home and care for Old Seborn.

Since then, for two long years, every morning had been the same – heat up water and fight past his flailing arms to bathe some part of him, while he hollered that she was trying to give him pneumonia. He was more cooperative while she fed him his breakfast. Afterwards she sat staring out the window while she listened to him complain. In the afternoons Olivia read to him and did her best to put off pouring the shots of whiskey he demanded. When he began drifting in and out of sleep she passed the time reading or trying to dredge up memories of her mother. In Olivia's imagination Nola June floated up and down the staircase, always draped in a flowing garment of warm colors, her head topped with a mist of blonde curls. It was her mother's face Olivia couldn't remember.

Olivia had come to see her life as a never-to-end procession of such days, until a cold morning in late January 1841. Carrying a pitcher of hot water and a clean towel, Olivia nudged her father's door open with her hip, wondering how bad he was going to be. Some water sloshed onto the floorboards, and she prepared herself for one of his looks. His tiny yellow eyes had a way of glaring that was worse than yelling.

She knew he was gone without looking at him. The room was silent and smelled of the waste he had evacuated. She set the pitcher and towel on the bureau and turned toward the bed. He lay with his arms at his sides, under the blanket, as if he had tucked himself in. His head was thrown back, his mouth hanging open and revealing tobacco-stained teeth. At least his eyes were closed.

She dried her hands on her apron and stared at him, shamed by the first thought that rushed to mind – no more baths. And no more washing out the green and brown lumps he spat into china teacups. Or helping him onto the chamber pot. She searched her heart for grief, but was unable to think of a single reason to wish him back alive. Not for his sake, and not for hers. Not that she hated him. There wasn't anything about him to hate; but neither had there been much to love, even before he got sick. And he had taken such a dreadful long time dying. Olivia yanked the window open and went to the top of the stairs to call her brother Tobey.

Tobey stopped at the foot of the bed and stood rocking back and forth on his heels as he said, "Well, we're orphans now. That's what we are." Then he went down to tell the housekeeper, Mrs. Hardaway.

"Why on earth do you got that window open?" he asked when he returned. "It's snowing out there."

"You're supposed to leave a window open when someone dies. For at least two hours, so their spirit can go free. That's what Mammo Killion said when Uncle Scruggs got killed."

"Well, I don't think it's necessary to give double pneumonia to the spirits of the living," he said and slid the window shut.

Mrs. Hardaway waddled into the room and put a hand on Olivia's shoulder. "There, there. Thank the good Lord for taking him peacefully in his sleep. Tobey, you go get Doc Gaylin. And stop by the store to tell your brother. He'd better bring a load of eats back with him. You're going to have a mess of folks coming in to pay their respects." Olivia glanced at Mrs. Hardaway in surprise, having forgotten that death was a social event.

"I'd better get him cleaned up," Olivia said, bracing herself.

Mrs. Hardaway squeezed her shoulder again. "Let me do that," she said quietly. "You go wait in your room. I'll call you if I need help turning him. Soon as the news gets around some ladies from the church are bound to be in to help."

Olivia put her arms around the housekeeper and nearly cried with gratitude, which she knew was mistaken for grief. She had been dreading this final task. Not the stench of the filth; she could stomach that. But she had never seen Old Seborn naked. She'd always

3

handed him the cloth so he could wash himself "down there," under the covers.

"There, there." The housekeeper patted her back. "You been such a good daughter all this long time. Don't you worry no more. The church ladies will come get him ready for laying out. I'll just make him presentable. Why don't you go cover the mirrors?"

By the time Mrs. Hardaway finished cleaning Seborn up and removing the soiled sheets Tobey had returned. He and Olivia pulled chairs to the bedside and waited for the doctor and their brother Avis. Olivia slipped her hand into Tobey's.

"You feeling alright?" he asked.

"Better than I should. How about you?"

"Mostly glad it's over, I guess."

"Me too. And ashamed of feeling that way." Olivia stared at the floor.

"Can't help what you feel."

She squeezed his hand and put her other palm over it. "I guess you're the only person in the whole wide world that I really care about. I wish it weren't true, but I guess it is. Since Uncle Scruggs died anyway."

"Thing you like best about me is I'm not Avis," Tobey said.

Olivia turned her gaze back to their father. "He looks real old, doesn't he? More like a grandfather than a father. Doesn't seem right. I felt so much worse when that horse kicked Uncle Scruggs in the head."

"Can't help what you feel," Tobey repeated.

The stone chimney ran through their father's room, so it was the warmest in the house, but they could still see their breath. Olivia couldn't blame her father for never wanting her to wash him, but now that all the busybodies were going to be parading around him, whispering and shaking their heads, she wished he didn't look so neglected. Olivia thought about giving him a quick shave, but the impulse didn't manage to evolve into action. She felt as if a heavy mantle of exhaustion had settled over her. The next four days, until they lowered her father into his grave, passed in a blur.

After the funeral Mr. Carmichael, the town's attorney, came to the house to read the will. There were no surprises; the store and house both went to the oldest son, Avis. Olivia sat and listened, slowly beginning to comprehend her new situation.

The next morning she rose early and slipped out the front door, hoping to be unseen. A thick layer of ice covered the porch steps and she clutched the wooden handrail. Clumsy in her thick-soled boots and heavy black coat, she plodded up Maple Street through the deep snow. She was relieved to see that no one was stirring; the January cold seemed to be keeping the nosy neighbor ladies under their quilts. She hoped that none of them were spying from behind their parlor curtains, tsk-tsking about Old Man Killion's daughter. "What is that girl up to now, traipsing around all by herself, not a day since they put her father in the ground? Never did know how to behave, that one."

Olivia had heard the good women in the pews behind her all through her father's funeral service, a flock of pecking hens in winter poke bonnets. They lowered their voices, but not enough; she heard their opinions of what that Killion girl ought to do. Or not do. Just what was wrong with her and how it ought to be fixed. "But what can you expect, what with that mother of hers. Never was right in the head."

Olivia turned left onto Main Street, toward the row of weathered clapboard shops and offices. The smooth white crust of snow was not perfect – a few lonely trails of footprints had disturbed it – but it managed to make the dingy little town picturesque. Five Rocks had not benefited from the talents of a town planner; structures went up wherever any of its 768 residents chose to put them, and the slipshod façade of Main Street was one of the unfortunate results.

As she trudged along Olivia silently scolded Old Seborn. *So what if Avis is the oldest son? What about Tobey and me? There's no law says a man can't leave anything to his younger son and daughter. Did Avis spend the last two years taking care of you? I'd like to see him try giving you a bath, the way you batted your arms around, like I was trying to kill you. I'm the one with the bruises. Parents are supposed to take care of their children. All their children. Don't expect me to feel guilty for looking out for myself. If I don't, who will? Not you, that's for sure.*

She stopped for a moment and listened to the silence, the only sounds her labored breathing and the muffled clop of horse's hooves. She felt herself growing clammy inside the thick coat, more from anxiety than the exertion of the walk. She'd never had a conversation with Mr. Carmichael and felt suddenly shy. What was she going to say to the lawyer? Why had she come so early? He probably wasn't even in his office yet. But when she looked up she saw curls of smoke rising above the tin roof. She hoped he was alone, no busybody in there to go blabbing about her coming to see him. She stared at the trails of footprints – two leading toward the office and one away from it – and hoped they had been made by Mr. Carmichael and a client arriving and the client leaving.

She paused before stepping up onto the wooden sidewalk, afraid of tripping. The drifts were so high she couldn't tell where the boardwalk dropped off, so she lifted her coat and skirt and kicked at the snow until she could see the edge. In the process she managed to get a boot full of snow, which quickly melted and soaked her already frozen foot.

A pang of self-pity stabbed through her and she thought, *why do I have to do this alone? Why am I always alone?*

For a moment she imagined the forlorn figure she

must present – draped in black, stark against the glare of the snow, with the rust-colored splash of Tobey's wide-brimmed felt hat on her head. She remembered the heavy oil paintings that hung in the public library over in Hillsong and could imagine a similar one of her, its neatly lettered caption reading "Orphan in Snow." She clenched her jaw tight and stepped onto the walk, determined that no one was going to go around feeling sorry for her. If she couldn't get that land, she'd just have to get a job. Seventeen was old enough. She ran her favorite refrain through her mind – *There's no reason why things have to remain the way they are.*

She unwound her scarf and removed the floppy felt hat, feeling defensive about her choice of headgear. *Well so what*, she thought. *A man's hat might be inappropriate for a young lady, but who wants to traipse around in a woolen bonnet when it might snow? You can't go five paces before it gets all stinky and itchy, like wearing a dead possum on your head. And a poke bonnet? Bosh. Horses don't like having blinders on them. Why should women?* Some men used those stupid bonnets as an excuse for saying women ought not to be allowed outside alone, lest they get run down in the road. Almost as bad as the way the Chinese purposely crippled those poor women Miss Evans had taught them about, hobbling around on their bound feet.

She tried to clear her mind and compose her thoughts. She wanted the lawyer's advice, not disapproval or pity. She folded her scarf, removed a glove to run her fingers through her dark hair, and rapped on the door. Inside a chair scraped and the door was opened by a young man of Olivia's age, wearing threadbare overalls and a bulky blue sweater. He smelled of tobacco and a body badly in need of washing.

"Billy Adams. Hullo. What are you doing here?" Olivia knocked the snow from her boots and wiped

7

them on the rag rug before entering.

She cast curious eyes around Mr. Carmichael's simply furnished office, having expected it to be grander. Chairs sat behind and in front of a large wooden desk. In the corner stood a bookcase and an iron stove, with two more chairs in front of it.

"Hullo, Olivia," Billy said, backing up a few steps. "I come here to use Mr. Carmichael's books." He turned and nodded at the thick volume that lay open on the desk. "I'm going to be an attorney, just like Mr. Carmichael. I been clerking for him, and he lets me use his books in exchange."

"Don't you need schooling for that?" She tugged at the fingers of her other glove as she moved closer to the warmth of the stove.

"Not if you can pass the examination on your own." Billy reached for the straight back chair that stood in front of the desk and pulled it out for Olivia. "And Mr. Carmichael's gonna help me get ready for it. He oughta be back pretty quick. Went to get some paper signed. Guess it was too confidential for me to take."

Olivia kept her coat on and sat down, while Billy reclaimed his seat behind the desk. She stared as he ran stubby fingers through his greasy blonde curls. He had never joined in with the other children when they made fun of her mother so she bore him no ill will, but, even so, resentment rose in her.

I was always the best pupil in class, she thought, *and this blockhead, who didn't even learn his letters until he was ten, is the one who can become a lawyer. It isn't right. It just isn't right. I can yap my jaw as good as Billy Adams.*

Feet stomped on the sidewalk and the door opened, letting in a fresh gust of cold air. Mr. Carmichael entered, enfolded in a wide black coat and carrying a cracked leather case.

"A good morning to you, Miss Killion," he said, one eyebrow raised. His voice always took Olivia by surprise. It was deep and warm and didn't seem to go with his sharp features and awkward gait. Neither did his kind eyes, which now held Olivia in their steady gaze. "How may I be of service to you?"

He was tall and so thin and pale that Olivia thought she could just about see through him. Whenever he walked past the schoolyard, elbows and knees protruding in all directions, the children shrieked, "Ichabod Crane, Ichabod Crane," and fled in mock terror.

He set his case down, hung his coat on a hook, and removed his top hat, revealing the dull black curls that framed his receding hairline and long white face.

There was something comforting about his presence and Olivia no longer felt shy. She glanced at Billy, who closed the book and stood up. He wordlessly pulled on his coat and disappeared out the door.

"I wanted to ask you something about my father's will," Olivia said.

"Certainly." Mr. Carmichael seated himself behind the desk, moved the book Billy had been reading aside, and unlocked a drawer. He removed a sheaf of papers from it and looked up, waiting for Olivia to continue.

"But first, I wanted to ask, is it true you have to keep anything I tell you secret?"

He put his palms together and brought his fingertips to the end of his long nose. After a moment he lowered his hands flat on the desk. "Yes, that's right. Seborn was my client and you have inherited his right to confidentiality."

"I wanted to ask you about the land," Olivia said.

"All right." He leafed through the papers. "Yes, here it is." He began reading. "Forty acres of farmland in Culpepper County, Kentucky – the deed to which is attached to this document – which were left to me by my dear departed wife, Nola June Sessions Killion, are to be inherited by my firstborn grandson. If there is no grandson –"

"No, not that," she said. "I meant the other land – the farm out in Michigan that Uncle Scruggs left him." She leaned forward, watching him turn the pages.

Mr. Carmichael moved his finger down the text and then read in a steady drone. "My wife's brother, Lorenzo Scruggs, left me eighty useless acres in the swamp known as Michigan, near a Godforsaken place by the name of Fae's Landing. This worthless piece of wilderness shall be inherited by whichever of my offspring is fool enough to claim it and try to put in a crop. If neither of them does so within two years of my demise, the land is to be sold and the proceeds divided between my two sons." The lawyer stopped reading and looked up at Olivia.

"That's what I thought," she said, raising her forefinger. "When it talks about who can claim that land it says 'my offspring,' not 'my sons.'"

"And?"

"Well, I'm sprung off him just as much as Avis or Tobey."

"Am I to understand that you wish to make a claim on this land?"

"Yes. I do. The way I see it – when he says 'offspring' and 'neither of them,' he's talking about me and Tobey. I mean, he knew perfectly well that Avis was going to get the house and the store, so he decided to give Tobey and me a chance at that piece of land."

Mr. Carmichael read the paragraph again, then put his hands back in their praying position and thought before replying. "Well, not a soul would agree with you on the face of it," he pronounced. "Anyone reading this would assume that the entire paragraph refers to your brothers. I have little doubt that you also believe that to have been your father's intention. However, the ambiguity of the text could make for an interesting court case. You are correct. One could argue that his specific reference to 'my sons' in regard to the proceeds from a sale could be taken to suggest that he was *not* referring to those same sons when he said 'my offspring.' Hence, the different terminology. Of course, if it ever came before a judge the opposing counsel would say it was obvious that the entire paragraph refers to your brothers, and I've no doubt the judge would rule in his favor."

"But I could make a claim?"

"Anyone can make a claim to anything. Winning the case is another matter. Do you think your brothers would challenge such a claim?"

Olivia tilted her head and stared at the wall behind him while she considered his question. "No. I mean, there's a good chance they wouldn't. Neither of them cares two cents about having that land and once I got going farming it I could pay them back the money they'd have gotten if they'd sold it. But them wanting the land for themselves is not the problem. The problem is, they'd never in a million years agree to me going out there to claim it. That's the reason I wanted to know if you have to keep this conversation a secret."

The lawyer's jaw dropped. "You can't be thinking of going to a wild place like Michigan on your own!"

"No." She shook her head. "I know I could never work eighty acres by myself. I'd have to get a partner or a hired man. I figure I can get a room in the town, in that Fae's Landing place, and my partner can live on the farm. The will doesn't say I have to live there; all it says is that I have to try to put in a crop. *Try.* I don't even have to actually grow anything."

"How old are you, Miss Killion?"

"Near on eighteen."

He puckered his lips and leaned back. "Well, there are no legal obstacles to you holding property in your own name, as long as you are not married. And if neither of your brothers contests your claim, you certainly could inherit that land. But a young woman like you can't just go off without a husband."

"Well, I don't have one of those, do I? I'll just have

to figure out something else." She thanked the lawyer and rose.

He came around the desk and reached the door in time to open it for her. Turning to face her, he stared into her eyes. She saw sadness in his, but when he spoke his voice was dry and matter-of-fact. "I'm very sorry about your father and your situation. But that's just the way the world is."

Chapter Two

A blur of lacy snowflakes greeted Olivia when she left Mr. Carmichael's office. She put her head back and opened her mouth to capture some of them, like she used to do when she was a little girl. Snow on her face was one thing she loved about winter; another was the crisp air, free of the hot weather stench of horse manure and outhouses. She heard the faint tinkle of bells and saw a woman come out of Killion's General with a basket on her arm. *Good*, she thought. *Avis has opened the store and won't be in the kitchen to ask me where I've been.*

Before turning homeward Olivia paused at the corner to look up and down Main Street, at the town she was so anxious to leave. She was mostly oblivious to its shortcomings, having almost nothing to compare it with. Every year on the Saturday before Easter their father used to rent a buggy and take them for a drive to Hillsong – the only other town Olivia had ever visited. Two things always made Hillsong seem like paradise to Olivia. The first was a library – two whole rooms lined with books up to the ceiling. Olivia loved to climb the tall ladders and browse through the volumes. If only she could breathe in all that knowledge. All those stories.

Her father always left her there for a few hours, while he and his sons tended to "men's business."

Olivia would still be high up on one of the rolling ladders when her brothers came bursting in to get her. They could never resist pushing the ladder back and forth between them, Olivia laughing and shrieking, until the librarian chased them out.

The second marvel of Hillsong was an ice cream parlor that stayed open as long as the ice was holding. They had fancy chairs with hearts carved into the backs and served dishes of vanilla ice cream topped with wild berries and whipped cream. They even gave each customer a thin slice of bread to wipe their hands with.

By contrast, Five Rocks had the Reading Room, where people tossed the books and periodicals they had no use for. It was in a rickety shed in back of the post office, which itself was nothing but an old store room behind the Brewster house. As for ice cream, a few times each spring Mrs. Monroe over at the boarding house froze up a batch. The children lined up outside her back door, each clutching three pennies and their own dish and spoon. Olivia had no friends to come whistle for her, so she was usually last in line, but Mrs. Monroe always made sure there was a scoop left for her.

When Olivia arrived home from Mr. Carmichael's office she found Mrs. Hardaway working the pump handle over the kitchen sink. The housekeeper was a big, even-tempered woman, wide and solid, with a plain square face. A few strands of graying brown hair had escaped the bun at the crown of her head.

"Oh, there you are, dear," she said as she turned. "Tobey said he thought you'd gone out for a walk. Awful cold out there. You'd better sit yourself down and get something hot in you." She nodded toward the kettle humming on the iron stove.

"No thank you, maybe later."

Olivia removed her boots and soggy socks and put on the colorful house slippers Mrs. Hardaway had knitted from leftover bits of yarn. Then she went up to her room, where she closed and latched the door. She pulled a heavy flannel robe on over her dress and tried to blow some warmth into her cupped hands. Then she removed a battered knife from the top drawer of her bureau, got down on her hands and knees, and opened the tiny door that led into the small attic under the eaves.

She crawled in, batting cobwebs from her hair and face and blowing them out of her mouth. Feeling in the dark, she shoved a canvas satchel aside, used the knife to pry up two loose floorboards, and retrieved a red velvet bag. She backed out and sat on her heels, beating small flurries of dust from the bag. Then she took it to her bed and poured out a stream of gold coins. Three years ago, before a horse kicked him in the head and killed him, her Uncle Scruggs had shown Olivia where he kept the red sack hidden, tacked to the bottom of his overstuffed chair.

"That money will always be there waiting on you, Olivia," he'd told her more than once. "When my time arrives, I want you to come get it, before the buzzards swoop down and clear this place out. Please. You always been my favorite – nearest thing to a child of my own. No one else knows about it and there ain't no reason for you to tell no one. I been saving it for you, and it ain't nobody's business but yours."

Since Uncle Scruggs' death Olivia had kept the coins hidden under the floorboards. She hadn't spent a penny and checked every few months to make sure they were still there. Then one evening Tobey had knocked on the door while the money was spread on the bed, and she'd let him in and told him where she'd gotten it.

Now she wondered if that had been unkind. Uncle Scruggs had given this money to her, and their father had left all his property to Avis; only Tobey had received nothing. She frowned, thinking, *I should give*

14

half of this to Tobey. That's only fair.

She sorted and counted her inheritance. They were all there: thirty $10 Eagles, thirty $5 Half-Eagles, and sixty $2.50 Quarter Eagles. Six hundred dollars in all. She'd use it to pay for tools and seed and a hired man. She frowned again, thinking that she shouldn't give Tobey his share just yet. She'd invest it in the farm, and a few years from now she'd have a much larger sum to share with him. Shivering with cold, she scooped the coins back into the velvet bag and returned it to its hiding place.

Maybe I can get Tobey to come to Michigan with me, she thought. *Why should he have to work for Avis? Truth is, as soon as Avis marries old boss face Lady Mabel, Tobey will feel like he's working for her. What kind of life is that? He needs something of his own. We'll start with Uncle Scruggs' land, and use the money we make to buy more and more land.*

It seemed a perfect plan until she tried to imagine her brother – with his thin white arms, thick glasses, and constantly running nose – felling trees, plowing furrows, and harvesting fields of wheat. Even more than he lacked the physical strength, she knew he lacked the ambition.

She remembered the conversation they'd had the day before, after Mr. Carmichael finished reading the will. Olivia had dragged Tobey up to her bedroom to complain about being left dependent on Avis.

"You could teach school," Tobey suggested. "Teach some white kids to read and write for a change."

A long time ago, when Olivia was just a little girl, she'd taught her only friend – who happened to be colored – to read and write. She couldn't believe the way people *still* talked about it, as if she'd done something wrong. Olivia bristled at Tobey's remark, but held her tongue, not wanting to change the subject.

"That way you'd have your own money, if that's what's so important to you," Tobey continued.

15

"You know teachers don't get paid hardly anything." She wiggled her backside to get more comfortable, jostling the mattress and making her layers of petticoats rustle. "You think I want to be like Miss Evans? She gets passed around like a bag of week-old fish, has to go live with a different family every month. Some of them make her help with the housework after school and still act like they're doing her a big favor."

Tobey sighed and patted her thigh. "People do all kinds of things, little sister. What's it matter anyway, Livvie? It's only until you get married." Olivia saw her brother wishing he could suck those words back the moment they were out of his mouth.

She'd never had any gentlemen callers. Not a one. No one ever said it out loud, but Olivia could see them all thinking it – she was going to be difficult to marry off. She might not be a great beauty – her face was too thin for that – but she was pretty enough, slight of build, with dark wavy hair, smooth skin, and bright blue eyes. Way prettier than most of the married women in town. But she seemed to lack some essential quality that caused a man to come courting.

Tobey changed the subject. "You know Avis will let you work in the store, if you want."

"Puh." Olivia expelled a quick burst of air and shook her head. "Now that father's gone, Mabel Mears is going to drag Avis to the altar quicker than two licks. And then she'll be all over everything, like tar. Just you wait and see. I'd as soon go to Massachusetts and slave in one of those textile mills as be bossed by her. And how come you're so calm about it? Why don't you care?"

"Don't see how me caring is going to make a whit of difference. Father left the store to Avis; it's only natural for his wife to have a hand in running it. No point getting all fired up about it."

Olivia rose from the bed and stood facing him, her fists on her hips and a scowl on her face. "Well, that's just fine. Next thing I know, you're going to be telling me to simmer down."

Tobey smiled sadly and shook his head. That was what their father had always said whenever one of them displayed a definite sign of life – "Now simmer down. Just you simmer down there."

"No, I'm not going to tell you to simmer down. But it is true that you're a young lady now and can't be going down by the river to throw rocks and holler like a banshee every time something isn't to your liking. You got to start trying harder to fit in. Mabel's got that nail hit right on the head. And you got to learn to take things like they come. You like to think you can change everything if you want to bad enough, but you can't."

"I know I can't change everything. I'm not stupid. I know one person can't change hardly anything at all." She paced to the window and back. "But you can try to fix some things in your own life. How do you think the world gets to be the way it is? If everybody lay down and lapped up whatever flowed down the road, our grandparents would never have come over here. There wouldn't even be any United States of America to come to. We'd all be back in Ireland, bowing down to the Queen of England, or doing whatever they did before some fool got all fired up. We'd be living in caves or mud houses, is what we'd be doing."

Olivia sighed and started down the stairs. *No,* she thought, *Tobey is not going to come to Michigan with me. Doesn't have it in him. What's the word? Gumption. He doesn't have the gumption. So who? Who can I get to come? No one is who. I'll have to go by myself, to that Fae's Landing place. Find someone to hire when I get there.*

But the prospect of traveling alone made her queasy. Even more frightening than taking a stage to Erie and a steamboat to Detroit was the problem of how she would get from Detroit to Fae's Landing. Buy a

17

wagon in Detroit and drive through the woods all alone, no idea where she was going? She wouldn't know how to go about buying a wagon, let alone how to replace a wheel or fix a broken axle. She tried scolding herself. *Shame on you, how do you think you're going to run your own farm, if you're too lily-livered to even get there?* It didn't help. She'd ridden horses and gone hunting, but always with her Uncle Scruggs. She'd never driven anything, not even a little one-horse buggy, and had no idea how to handle one of those big farm wagons.

She went to the kitchen, poured herself a cup of the bitter black coffee Mrs. Hardaway kept on the stove, and sat at the table, chin resting on the heel of her hand. She felt despair creeping over her, which Mrs. Hardaway mistook for sorrow.

"There, there." The housekeeper set down her bowl of biscuit dough and washed her hands so she could pat Olivia's head. "It's so hard losing our loved ones. Takes it a while to sink in." She launched into a long tale of the death of her own parents.

Olivia half-listened, nodding her head at appropriate intervals, as she sipped the burnt coffee. Then she shook herself and asked Mrs. Hardaway if she needed any help. The housekeeper went to the window and pulled back the red and white checkered curtain.

"Well, I would, but I hate to ask you to go back out in this. It's coming right down again."

"I don't mind snow," Olivia said, rising. "A walk would feel good. What do you need? Something from the store?" She reached for her coat.

Mrs. Hardaway shook her head. "I got a pile of pot handles need mending. Been putting it off, but now that darn oven door has got loose again, about ready to fall right off. I got to be able to keep food warm, what with all the folks coming to call. You think you could go scare up Mourning Free? I believe I seen him working over to Ferguson's Livery this week."

Mourning Free. Olivia felt like giving Mrs. Hardaway a hug.

Why didn't I think of him? Olivia felt like shouting out loud. She turned away from the housekeeper, thinking, *Mourning would be perfect. The way he's worked everywhere in town, he knows how to do everything – fix a wagon wheel, raise a barn, put on a roof, clear a field, shoe a horse. Even knows how to cook – sometimes makes breakfast, dinner, and supper for the boarders at Mrs. Monroe's. Won't expect to be paid as much as a white man either. And, most important of all, if ever there was a soul in need of a new start in life, it's Mr. Mourning Free.*

Chapter Three

Olivia told Mrs. Hardaway that she would be glad to go fetch Mourning Free. "But I think I'll wait until after dinner," she said and returned her coat to the rack.

She would be glad for an excuse to flee the house after the noon meal – when more flocks of women could be expected to climb the Killion's front porch, each carrying a covered dish or pie as the price of admission. No one wanted to miss what might be their last chance to snoop around Old Man Killion's house. Yesterday Olivia had caught one of the church ladies in his study, going through the drawers of the desk. What made women so nosy about the inside of other people's houses? Olivia could see nothing interesting about theirs. It was a regular wood frame, clapboard house. It may have been larger than most others in town, but there was nothing fancy about it. She did, however, understand why they were so curious about her father. Since she was a child Olivia had known that – according to the busybodies – her father "had hardly buried that crazy wife of his before he started carrying on with that Place woman."

19

But avoiding those women with their stew pans was not the only reason Olivia chose to wait. She didn't want to be in the middle of explaining her proposition to Mourning Free and have to go home to eat. It might take a while to convince him that going to Michigan was the best chance he'd ever have to make something of himself. She could imagine the way he'd look at her when she first told him her plan – like a horse must have kicked her in the head. But eventually she would make him realize what a great opportunity this was, even more so for him than for her.

She moved about the kitchen, setting the table and slicing bread, her face set in a frown as she composed the arguments she would present to him. She acknowledged her brothers' arrival home with no more than a nod of her head and listened to nothing of what they said during the meal. When she rose to clear away the plates, a smile finally crossed her face. There was one argument for which Mourning would have no response: "What do you have to lose?"

Olivia had heard all the stories about Mourning Free's parents. Willis and Rosie Jackson had been runaway slaves who stumbled into all-white Five Rocks late one night, more than half frozen and starved. One of the local abolitionists found them and wrapped them in blankets. He left them stoking a fire in the stove of the Great Friends Meeting House while he ran from street to street, knocking on the doors of his co-religionists. Within an hour they had convened a meeting, eager to offer shelter to the Jacksons. They were, however, worried by the fact that Five Rocks had no "Bottoms" or "Nigger Town" for them to blend into; it had no negro residents at all. Even so, Mr. and Mrs. Brewster, founders of the local seven-member Anti-Slavery Society, offered the fugitives the use of the shed behind their house, the same structure that would later become Five Rocks' modest Reading Room.

No one had a better suggestion. The men spent the

next few hours clearing out the shed and moving in the furnishings that other Quakers donated. By morning the dazed Jacksons had a home, of sorts. Mrs. Brewster brought their meals on trays, always with a pudding or special treat for Rosie, who was most obviously in the family way. Each time Mrs. Brewster left she paused in the doorway and warned them to stay out of sight. "There might be some a them slave-hunters chasing after you and you two stick out around here like a couple a purple elephants."

The first thing the Jacksons did was change their family name to Free. The anti-slavery people tried to talk them into choosing something else, saying it was far too obvious, but Willis and Rosie were set on being called Free. Sadly, they enjoyed only a few months of liberty before Willis succumbed to the influenza. Then a few weeks later Rosie died giving birth to Mourning.

The orphaned black baby was taken in by Alice and Goody Carter, who lived a two-hour walk away, in "The Bottoms" of the town of South Valley. They already had four children but hadn't the heart to turn away the fondling in Mrs. Brewster's arms.

Goody spent most days in Five Rocks, doing odd jobs for whoever needed him. When Mourning was six he began working alongside his foster father. The boy had a natural aptitude for fixing things and did whatever was asked of him without complaint. He was soon well-known to all of Five Rocks' merchants, who often quarreled over who was most in need of Mourning's services that week.

Not long after Mourning's ninth birthday Goody made up his mind to go west and try farming. Mourning refused to go with them, insisting that he could stay in Five Rocks and take care of himself. He would go right on doing what he had been for years, working at Killion's General and the other businesses in town. He could sleep in the loft of Ferguson's Livery or the storeroom of the Feed & Grain. He often did that anyway, to save the long walk home and back.

But Goody was having none of it. "You gonna have folks saying we ain't treated you right."

The day the Carters finished loading up their wagon, Mourning sneaked into Killion's General and hid behind the bolts of fabric in the storeroom. Seven-year-old Olivia watched as Goody Carter picked him up and dragged him out to the wagon. Mourning fought hard, kicking wildly and yelling, "I ain't gonna go, I ain't gonna. You can't make me. I ain't yours. I ain't none a your business." The white customers stepped aside in dismay, the women's bonnets bobbing, but no one felt inclined to interfere.

A few days later Olivia walked down to the bank of the Saugauta River. It was a warm day in May, the sky a startling blue, the fields dotted with yellow and purple wildflowers. She spread a red and white checkered tablecloth over a patch of clover and knelt on one corner of it. A gentle breeze played with the cloth, so she anchored two other corners with her rag doll and picnic basket. She was humming "Mary, Mary, Quite Contrary" to her doll when she heard someone slosh out of the river. She looked up, amazed to see Mourning Free climbing up the bank, his scrawny chest bare and his trousers dripping. He was carrying his shoes in one hand and a brown shirt and blue cloth bag in the other.

"Hullo, Mourning," Olivia said, eyes wide.

"Hullo to you, Livia." He walked over and tossed his belongings to the ground.

"Did you fall into the river?"

"Nah. Been gettin' cleaned up. Heard someone come and thought I'm a have to hide down there. Then I hear it just be you, talkin' to your stupid doll."

"Do you want to have a tea party with us?" She reached for her doll and pulled it back to her lap, making room for him to join her on the tablecloth.

"You got any food ain't make-believe?"

She opened the picnic basket and arranged chunks of cheese, a few slices of bread, and two apples on a white linen napkin. Mourning sank to his knees, making large wet circles on the cloth, grabbed some cheese and bread, and filled his mouth.

"Ain't et nothing for two days," he mumbled, cheeks bulging.

"Who were you hiding from?"

"Everybody." He swallowed and reached for more bread and cheese, but hesitated, glancing at his hostess.

"It's okay," Olivia said and leaned away from the food. "You can have it all. I thought they took you away."

He bit into a chunk of cheese and sat back on his heels. "That right. But I run away from 'em. Been walkin' for three days."

This announcement left Olivia frowning. She watched him eat for a few moments before asking, "But who's going to take care of you?"

"Me." He jerked his thumb at his bare chest. "I can take as good care a myself as them Carters ever done."

"Why, were they mean to you?"

He tilted his head back and grinned. "That what Goody think folks gonna say." Then he looked straight at Olivia, his expression serious. "No, Goody always give me a good tanning when I got it comin', but they ain't never treated me bad. But they got four kids without me. That be crowd 'nuff in one cabin."

Olivia studied the horizon, still frowning in bewilderment. "How did you find your way home?"

"Followed the river back. Minute I seen it, I know that be my chance to run."

She hugged her doll and stared at this amazing boy, somewhat frightened of him. "You can have the apples too." She pushed the plate toward him.

They sat staring at the sunlight on the river while they listened to the distant buzz of honeybees and breathed in the sweet smell of clover. Mourning chomped on the apples, leaving nothing but the stem and seeds.

"Why were you hiding?" Olivia asked.

"I don't think they be lookin' for me." He tossed the tiny remains of the last apple away and lay back in the warm sun, hands behind his head. "They be just as glad I gone. But I gonna stay out a sight a few more days, just in case." He lifted his head to look at Olivia. "Once they be gone west for good, ain't nothin' no one can do with me."

"But you don't have a mommy or a daddy," Olivia said in a small voice, feeling cruel the moment she said it.

"Don't need 'em. I can sleep in the loft over at the livery. Or in Smithy's back room. In someone's barn. Wherever I be workin'."

"Oh." Olivia imagined having to sleep in a pile of hay and started to get up, anxious to be home and safely away from Mourning.

"Tonight I'm a sleep in that old barn, 'cross from Mrs. Place's. You could bring me some food over to there, you felt like."

"You already ate all the food."

"Can't you get no more?"

"I don't know," she said, tilting her head toward a shrugged shoulder, afraid of getting in trouble. "What kind of food?"

"Kind you eat."

She stared at him, her bottom lip sucking the top one. "I don't know." She began putting things in her basket. When she reached for the tablecloth, he stood up too.

"Bread be good, you ain't got nothin' else."

She packed her things as quickly as she could.

"Blanket be good, too. Get cold at night."

"You can have this." She held out the tablecloth, which she had been folding. It was hers, for her picnic basket, and Mrs. Hardaway would never notice it was

24

gone.

He took the cloth and fingered it. "Thanks. But a blanket still be good."

"Okay," Olivia said, remembering an old gray blanket in the linen closet she didn't think anyone would miss. "But you've got to promise to teach me to skip stones on the river the way you do."

He nodded and grinned, then turned to frown at her. "And you ain't gonna tell nobody 'bout me bein' here?"

"No. I won't tell. Cross my heart." She made a large X over her chest with her right hand. "I have to go home now." She picked up the basket.

"See you later," he said.

"Bye."

She started walking away, then stopped and turned around. "Mourning?"

"What?"

"How come you didn't hide from me?"

He stared at her for a few moments. "Don't know. Just dint think I had to."

She hadn't planned on going back. She couldn't take things from home without asking permission; that would be stealing. But back in her room she couldn't stop thinking about how cold it had been last night. Finally she got the gray blanket, threw it out her window, and ran downstairs and outside to hide it in the bushes at the back of the house. She felt terribly guilty until she remembered the time she had heard the grown-ups talking. They said the slave-catchers called the abolitionists thieves because they helped slaves get away. But Mrs. Brewster said that wasn't stealing at all, that was a very good deed; they were helping poor black souls who were escaping from vile evil-doers. So somehow Olivia mixed it up in her mind and exonerated herself. Mourning was, after all, poor, black, and running away. So taking things to help him wouldn't really be stealing.

Once she began her spree of crime, she was surprised by how easy it was. She simply waited until Mrs. Hardaway was hanging laundry out back and filled her basket with apples, bread, and small amounts of smoked fish and venison. When she thought of Mourning all alone in the dark she added some candles and matches. Then she stood by the front door, waiting to hear Mrs. Hardaway come back in. When the back door banged Olivia fled with her picnic basket, ran behind the house to retrieve the blanket, and set off to find Mourning.

Since it was still light she didn't think he would have gone to the barn yet, so she returned to the river. The breeze had picked up and a ribbon of gold shimmered across the water. She gave a loud whistle and then began singing "Mary, Mary, Quite Contrary," in case Mourning might be afraid to come out and see who was whistling.

He emerged from behind a stand of bushes. She handed him the blanket and held up one of the wooden flaps of the basket to show him the food. Then she pulled out her slate, which she had added at the last minute.

"What that for?" He nodded at it.

"Well, I got to thinking, about how you've never gone to school," Olivia said. "You know, a person can't do much in life without knowing how to read." She quoted Miss Evans. "So I'd better teach you your letters. One every day. We'll start with 'L' because it's a real easy one. In return you've got to teach me how to skip stones like you promised. Five whole skips."

Mourning survived on Olivia's pilfered offerings for four days. Then he finally showed himself on Main Street. In a town like Five Rocks, in which nothing ever happened, his reappearance was cause for much excited discussion. Everyone expressed shock and concern for what would become of the poor boy, but Olivia could see that most of them were overjoyed to

26

have him back. Every day since Mourning had been taken away, Reverend Dixby had come into Killion's General Store complaining that he couldn't find anyone to sweep and scrub the floor of the Congregational Church.

Now the good Reverend lost no time in calling a town meeting to be held in his un-swept and un-scrubbed church. The Mourning Free situation must be discussed. Olivia and Mourning hid outside, beneath one of the open windows at the back. Reverend Dixby started it off by speaking at length about their Christian duty to pitch in together to ease the situation of this poor orphan. He thought the best solution would be for the whole town to take care of him. Mourning was right; he could go back to working like before. Whoever he was working for would give him his dinner that day.

Mrs. Brewster was the first to respond. "That's ridiculous. Saying everyone will take care of him is the same as saying no one will. I don't know how people who call themselves Christians could even consider such a thing. He isn't even ten years old."

"All right then." A male voice called out from the back of the church. "How 'bout you adopt him? Tuck that Nigra boy between your clean white sheets every night?" This evoked a wave of snickering.

Reverend Dixby raised his voice. "Gentlemen, please, we are trying to have a serious discussion, in a Christian spirit."

"That boy's been taking care of himself long as I remember," another man said. "Tell you one thing – he'd survive on his own better than you would, Dixby." Several men hooted and women hushed them. "Besides," the man continued when the laughter had died down, "the negro race is used to that kind of thing."

"What is that supposed to mean?" Mrs. Brewster asked.

"Look at all them slave children get sold away from

27

their parents and get along just fine. And them tribes over in the jungles of Africa don't know which children belong to which parents any more than them monkeys do."

"What can you possibly think you understand about the suffering of slave children torn from the arms of their mothers?" Mrs. Brewster retorted. "And I've no doubt the hitching post knows more about Africa than you do. You couldn't find it on the map for a dollar." This drew even louder laughter.

"So what do *you* think we ought to do with the little darky?" a different voice called out.

"There are plenty of good negro families over in South Valley," Mrs. Brewster said. "I'm sure we could find one willing to take him in."

"What makes you think he won't run again, just like he done from Goody Carter's good negro family?" A voice Olivia recognized as that of Mr. Bellinir, the owner of the Feed & Grain, spoke. "If he's wantin' to stay here so bad, why not let him? I can pay him wages for a few days a week. Give him his dinner on the days he works for me."

"I can do the same," Mr. Sorenson, who owned the brewery and saloon, piped up.

This led to a chorus of indignant male voices: "Just hold your horses, who says you get him? . . . I got more work for him than you do . . . No, you don't and I been paying him more than anyone else . . . You don't got no loft he can sleep in . . . ."

Olivia stood on her tiptoes and peeked in the window, just in time to see Mrs. Brewster grab old Mr. Vance's cane and pound the floor with it, commanding silence. "Shame on you all! Fighting over who gets first right to exploit the poor child. Give him his dinner, indeed. So is he to go without breakfast and supper? And on Sundays and days when he has no work, he simply will not eat at all?"

Mrs. Monroe spoke up. "If he wanted to learn to

help me with the cooking for my boarders, I could give him a plate out in the kitchen whenever he's not working anywhere else."

"And where's he supposed to sleep?" Mrs. Brewster pressed.

"I could let him stay in that storage shed out back," Reverend Dixby said. "Won't even charge him anything. He can stay there in exchange for a few simple chores each week."

Olivia and Mourning turned to look over their shoulders at the windowless shed. It hadn't been used for years, had no stove, and looked ready to blow over in the first good wind.

"That won't be necessary," Mr. Carmichael said. "The boy is welcome to sleep in my office."

"That wouldn't be right," Reverend Dixby retorted. "How could he afford to pay rent?"

"Who said anything about charging him rent?"

"Then what do you want of him?"

"As long as he cuts his own firewood, he is welcome to the warmth of my stove. I'll ask nothing of him in exchange."

"And what if he gets sick?" Mrs. Brewster pressed. "Who's going to care for him?"

"Isn't that what you Christian ladies are good at?" The rowdy voice from the back broke in again.

"If he's set on staying, why not give him a chance?" Mr. Carmichael spoke and no one dared interrupt him. "Those good negro families in 'The Bottoms' aren't going anywhere. I understand your concerns, Mrs. Brewster, and they are real ones. I'd like to believe that if the boy fell ill, we would all find it in our hearts to help care for him. If he requires the services of Doc Gaylin, I will commit myself to bearing the cost of those services."

"You don't have to worry about that," Doc Gaylin said. "There will be no charge."

Reverend Dixby soon brought the discussion to an

end. He affirmed their collective responsibility for the boy and sent them home smiling. Allowing Mourning Free to stay in Five Rocks and earn pennies doing the menial jobs they didn't want to do for themselves was the Christian thing to do.

That night Olivia lay awake, staring at the ceiling and thinking how awful it was for a child to have no parents to stick up for him.

After that meeting Olivia went looking for Mourning every afternoon and pulled him aside for his lesson. If they had time and it was sunny, they went down by the river. Otherwise school was held in the storeroom of Killion's General, using the pickle barrel for a desk. One day Mrs. Monroe peeked through the open door while Mourning was studying what Olivia had written on her slate. Then they heard her lodge a loud complaint with Olivia's father.

"I heard that girl of yours was teaching him to read."

"What of it?" Seborn growled.

"Well it's nothing to me, but folks are saying it ain't seemly. She ought not to keep so much company with a nigger."

"They are children," Seborn said. "He's only a boy. A boy with enough troubles of his own, I might add, without all you good women piling more on."

Olivia listened with her head cocked. It was the kindest thing she had ever heard her father say.

Mrs. Monroe ignored the insult and persisted. "Well, I fail to see what need a colored boy has of book learning."

"Way I see it, make life easier all around," Seborn replied. "If he could read, whoever he's working for could leave him a note, tell him what he's wanted to do."

"Well, all I know is that back East women who open schools for darky children go to jail. It said so right in the newspaper," Mrs. Monroe said, before the tinkle of the bells on the door announced her departure.

"That Mrs. Monroe don't know nothin'," Mourning said. "Colored man need to know how to read more than any white man."

"That doesn't make sense." Olivia frowned at him.

"It surely do. What if I tell you 'bout some slaves what escaped off a plantation all the way down in Virginia. For weeks they's goin' north."

Olivia never pointed out his grammatical errors. When Billy Adams or any of the other boys at school said things like "don't know nothin'" or "ain't got" Olivia rolled her eyes and repeated the correct phrase in a show of great superiority. But Mourning's voice flowed into his pattern of speech with such warm resonance, it sounded as if the words were meant to be put together just that way. Olivia was more tempted to imitate him than correct him, but knew how ridiculous she would sound.

"They ain't got nothin' but their feet," Mourning continued. "And they be walkin' all night and hidin' in the woods when the sun be shinin'. Don't got nothin' to eat but bark and berries. Just about starve straight to death. Can't hardly stand up. Can't hardly see where they goin'. But they keep on, walkin' all night. Walkin' and walkin'. And walkin' some more." He stopped to dip a cup of water from the barrel and drink it.

"So what happened to them?"

"Finally they be here in Pennsylvania, in the snow. Walk all the way from Virginia. And then what you think happen to them? Them slaves be losin' their direction and turnin' 'round the wrong way. They be spendin' the next few days walkin' smack back toward that slave state what they come from. Smack toward the slave-catcher what's chasin' after 'em. You know why? Cause of they can't read no map and can't read no road sign. So that show you." He stabbed a finger at the air in front of Olivia's face. "Person got to know where they be in this world. Specially a person what can get sold if he be in the wrong place."

31

"So what happened?" Olivia asked. "Did the slave-catchers get them?"

"No. Luck from the Lord, they pass by a field where a colored man be workin'. He set them back on the right way. They find their way to Five Rocks in time for her to birth her baby."

Olivia stared at him for a long moment, hand cupped over her mouth, slowly absorbing the realization that the slaves in Mourning's story were his parents.

"Well, you don't have to worry, Mourning Free," she said at last. "You already read way better than most of the blockhead white kids around here."

Ten years had passed since then and Olivia seldom saw Mourning any more. They were agreeable to one another whenever he worked at Killion's General, but he spent most of his time at the Feed & Grain, Ferguson's Livery, or Smithy's – all places Olivia seldom had cause to visit. When the weather was mild he was often gone for months at a time, working outside of town on someone's farm. By now he was nearly a stranger to her.

Olivia put on her coat and boots, picked a wrinkled cellar apple from the bowl on the table and put it in her pocket, wrapped a scarf around her ears and mouth, and opened the back door. She felt like laughing when an image formed in her mind – her trying to drag a kicking and screaming Mourning Free into a wagon headed for Michigan.

Chapter Four

Olivia was glad to see it had stopped snowing. She loved the steel blue haze of the afternoon light in this kind of weather. The sun had begun to drop in the sky and the town wore a veil of mystery, the houses casting gray shadows and the church steeples stark against the muted sky.

For a moment she grew melancholy. With her father gone she was an orphan too, just like Mourning Free. She didn't have anyone to stick up for her either. But she shook herself silently. *Oh, woe is you. So get going and start sticking up for yourself. That's the way the world is.* She found herself taking more comfort in Mr. Carmichael's plain hard statement of fact than in all the damp condolences that had been heaped upon her by sobbing women.

She raised her chin and forced a blank expression on her face before starting up Main Street in search of Big Bad, the broken-down workhorse no longer worth his feed that Mourning had bought a few years ago. When he moved from place to place he packed all his worldly possessions into two small leather bags and threw them over the back of Big Bad's saddle.

Olivia spotted the horse tethered in front of the Feed & Grain. "Hullo there, old boy," she said, offering him the apple and stroking his neck while he chomped. "Poor old thing. If that back of yours gets any more swayed, your belly's going to start scraping the ground." The horse turned its brown eyes on her and moved its head up and down, as if agreeing. "Guess your daddy must be in there." She patted his warm neck good-bye.

When I have my own farm, she thought, *I'm going to get a nice old horse like Big Bad. Well, not that old, but calm and friendly like him. I'll ride him everywhere – into town, over to visit the neighbors – and not sidesaddle either. Anyone has a problem with that, it's just too bad. But they'll be glad to see me coming, because I'm going to learn how to bake pies and cakes and always take one along when I go to visit. And I'll have a big golden dog who'll go everywhere with me, running along beside the horse, snapping at butterflies. That's how it will be in the beginning anyway, before I have a family. Then I'll*

33

have too many children to fit in a buggy; I'll have to get a big farm wagon and put extra seats in the back. When the dog gets tired of running, he'll bark and jump up there with them.

She entered the Feed & Grain and found it empty of customers. Mr. Bellinir was bent over the counter, writing in a ledger. Olivia greeted him and asked if he knew where she could find Mourning Free.

"Out back." He jerked his thumb.

Mourning was working alone in the cavernous storeroom. His back was to the wide doorway, so he didn't see her standing there and she watched him for a few minutes.

This man could be my salvation, she thought. *Now all I have to do is make him realize that I could be his.*

He plucked a sack of feed from the heap in the center of the room and heaved it onto the top of a neat pile, making it taller than he was. He paused to shake his arms, then counted the sacks in the stack and turned to write on a piece of paper that lay on a wobbly wooden table.

Olivia waited for him to finish before saying, "Hullo Mourning."

He glanced over his shoulder and said, "Day to you, Livia," in an off-handed way. Then he stiffened and turned to face her, looking at his toes while he mumbled, "I sorry . . . 'bout your father."

She nodded. "Thank you for saying so. Mrs. Hardaway asked me to come get you. She needs you to mend some pot handles and the door of the oven."

"Early tomorrow okay?"

"Sure," she said. She moved closer to him, stopping three feet away, and lowered her voice. "But I . . . I wanted to talk to you about something else. In private."

He stared at her and said nothing.

"It's about a business dealing."

His face broke into a grin. "Who you be doin' business with, that old rag doll or your teddy bear?"

34

"I mean it," Olivia said. "I'm serious. It's a chance for both of us to change our whole lives."

His expression went blank again.

"But it's sort of secret. I need to talk to you about it in private."

"You must be in a confusion. Ain't nowhere near April Fools' Day." He turned away and picked up another sack of feed.

"All right, if that's the way you want to be. I'm not fooling around, but suit yourself. Pay me no mind. If you don't want to have your own farm, your own land, I can't force you to." She turned to leave.

She was at the door when he asked, "What land?"

She spun around, her face lit up. "I knew you'd do it!" She managed to keep her voice low, though she felt like shouting.

"I ain't said I'm a do nothin'," he said as she approached.

"Oh you will, once I explain. But that might take a while and . . ." She paused and nodded toward the front room of the store and Mr. Bellinir. "He knows I'm back here with you, so I shouldn't stay too long." She frowned. "I thought maybe we could meet down by the river, but it's so cold. How about in the Congregational Church? Reverend Dixby doesn't keep it locked, does he?"

"Nah." Mourning shook his head. "But you don't wanna be talkin' 'bout nothing secret in there. Reverend Dixby got a nose what way too big. He see you goin' in there after me, take him 'bout three and a half minutes to call a town meeting on us. But I got a place we can talk. Nice and warm, too. I got the key to Mr. Carmichael's office and he gone over to Strickley. Ain't gonna come back till late at night. I'm a go there first, through the back door, and get the stove lit up. Then you come knock on the front door and wait a bit 'fore you let yourself in. Anyone see you, they gonna think him or Billy Adams be in there and hollered out

35

for you to come in."

"How long should I wait before I come?"

"Don't matter. Few minutes."

"Is it all right for you to leave work now?"

"No mind to him when I be doin' this, long as it get done. I'm a tell him I gotta fix your stove. Poor old Mrs. Hardaway can't cook nothin' – door keep fallin' on her foot."

Olivia nodded and turned to leave. From the middle of the store she called over her shoulder, "I'll tell Mrs. Hardaway you'll be right there," and then said goodbye to Mr. Bellinir. He barely nodded, his attention focused on his ledger, though Olivia suspected he paid more mind to what went on around him than he let on.

She paused outside Killion's General, glimpsed Mourning coming out onto the sidewalk, and slipped into her brother's store to wait. This was the most excitement she'd had in years. She nodded to Avis and milled around the shelves, helping herself to some of the peppermint candies he kept in a glass bowl on the counter. When she went back outside wisps of smoke were curling from Mr. Carmichael's stovepipe. Olivia did as Mourning had told her to and found him sitting on one of the two chairs next to the stove. She settled opposite him.

"Okay," he said. "What land you got to give away?"

"You remember my Uncle Scruggs, don't you?"

"Lorenzo? What used to be the Post Master?"

"Yes."

"Yeah, I ain't never gonna forget him. I been standin' right behind him the day that horse took into his head. I seen it all."

"Well, maybe you don't know that before he came back here, he was a farmer. He and his wife Lydia Ann had a place – eighty-acres. Right on the bank of a river with good fresh water. He dug a cellar, built a cabin over it, put up a barn, even set a springhouse over the river. It's a beautiful place. He never would have left

36

except Lydia Ann died of the fever and he lost his heart for it. So he came back to town, but the farm still belonged to him. When he died it went to my father and now it will go to me or one of my brothers – whichever one of us wants to claim it and put in a crop. Neither Avis nor Tobey is interested. I am. All I need is someone to help me." She paused. "That's why I need you to be my partner. To do the farming."

He tipped his chair back, balancing on the hind legs. "I see how that gonna get you a farm. All I see it gettin' me be an aching back."

"I haven't finished yet –"

"Sides, farming take more than land and one skinny nigger you think be dumb enough to work it for you. You gotta have money. Gotta buy seed. Gotta eat for a whole year –"

"I have six hundred dollars of my own money. In gold coin. You won't have to pay for anything. Once a crop is in, I'll inherit the land. That's all we have to do. But you could keep working it. I don't know how long it takes to make money farming. You can figure that out better than I can. But whatever we lose, it's my money. Whatever profit we make is yours. You keep it all, until you have enough to buy your own eighty acres. Maybe even your own quarter section. But you don't have to work my farm that long if you don't want to. The deal is, you go there with me, make the cabin livable, clear a few acres, and put in one crop. Then you can quit any time you want and I'll pay –"

Olivia abruptly stopped talking and listened as heavy footfalls clomped on the wooden sidewalk. What would they do if someone knocked on the door? Everyone knew that Mourning was allowed to stay in Mr. Carmichael's office, but should she hide under the desk? The footsteps continued on without stopping, but she swallowed hard, facing what she knew was the biggest problem in her plan – the two of them being alone together. If she were to go off with a white man

37

who wasn't her kin, even if he was old and decrepit, tongues would never stop flapping. And a young colored one?

Well, that's just another reason why it's going to be a secret, she reminded herself.

But she knew the problem was real. She and Mourning would have to travel together, spend days, weeks, and months alone together on Uncle Scruggs' farm. She stared at Mourning for a moment, wondering how well they would manage that. She still thought of him as her friend, though for years they'd barely spoken. Now he was all grown up and she didn't know much about the young man sitting across from her.

I know the most important thing, she thought. *I trust him. He is a good man. Never did a speck of harm to anyone. When he promises to do something, he does it. We'll just have to manage, figure the rest out as we go along.*

She plunged on. "I'll pay you –"

"Pay me what? How much?" He sat his chair back down on all four legs.

"Well, I guess I don't know. I guess I haven't really thought it all out. But we'll come to an arrangement that we both think is fair. And put it in writing."

He leaned forward, elbows on knees, watching her intently. "Suppose I stay on, but we ain't making no money?" he asked.

"Well, that will depend on you, won't it?"

"Me and a barrel of luck. God give you whatever kind a weather he feel like, not what kind you be needin'. And I got no say over prices or what kind a insects gonna come eat everything up."

"I realize that." She nodded. "All I know is, plenty of people make a go of farming and most of them start out with a lot less than we will. And I'll be the one taking all the risk. What do you have to lose? Worst that can happen, you wasted some time. Would you rather spend another year chasing around here, fifty people telling you what to do? I'm asking you, what do you have to lose?"

He sat perfectly still, leaning forward and studying his feet. Then he straightened up and slapped both thighs. "All right. You got a partner. Where this land be? Walking distance from town?"

"No. Not exactly." She avoided his eyes as she removed a piece of paper from her pocket and unfolded the map she had drawn. "It's out in Michigan. Right there." She held it out to him, pointing at a small dot not far from Detroit.

He took the paper from her and studied it, his mouth puckered as if he were holding a dead snake between his upper lip and nose. "Michigan? This Garden of Eden be in Michigan?" He thrust the paper back at her, stood up, and closed the damper of the stove. "You for sure off in the head. Michigan. I look crazy to you?"

"What's wrong with Michigan? It's not so far away. There are steamships right from Erie that go all the way to Detroit."

"You know I can't be travelin' with no white girl." He glared at her.

"Says who?"

"Say the world. What your brothers gonna say when you tell 'em 'bout this great plan you got?"

"I'm not going to tell them. We're going to keep it a secret. I'll leave them a note, so they won't be worried, but they won't read it until after I'm gone."

"You tryin' to get me killed? How long you think it gonna take them to come find you?"

"I'm not that big of a dolt. I have no intention of telling them where I really went." She rose and stepped toward him. "The note will say I went out east to look for a teaching job. I'll promise to write and let them know where I am as soon as I get settled. When I'm ready to claim the land, I'll come back and tell them the truth."

"Oh, so that okay then. They ain't gonna string me up till next year." He waved a hand, as if dismissing her in disgust.

"Nobody's going to string anyone up," she said. "They won't know you had anything to do with it. I'll say I got a hired man to work the land for me. That won't even be lying, really. You'll be sort of like a hired man. And we won't leave town together. You can tell folks you've heard of some distant relatives and are going to look for them. Leave a few days before I do. No one's going to think we went off together. Why would they? Especially if we're careful about not being seen with each other between now and when we leave."

He shook his head. "You got any brains? What 'bout folks out there in Michigan? How you think they gonna like this colored boy showin' up with a white girl?"

"They don't have to like it. There's nothing they can do about it. They don't have to know we're partners or anything. You're my hired man. What's wrong with that? I don't plan to live there on the farm with you. I'll get a room in town and buy a horse to ride out to the farm every day. There won't be anything for them to talk –"

"Never mind, Livia." He waved his hand at her again, sounding weary. "Stop wastin' all that air. I can't go to no Michigan, not with you and not with nobody. I gotta stay here in Five Rocks."

"Why? What's so wonderful about Five Rocks?"

"I got Mr. Carmichael here."

She looked at him blankly. "All right, so it's very nice of him to let you sleep in his office –"

"It ain't that." He moved his chair a bit closer to hers. "You know my parents been slaves?"

She nodded her head.

"So that mean, by the law, I be a slave too."

"That can't be so. You were born here. There's no slavery here."

"Don't matter. By the law, I belong to the man what

40

owned my parents. Slave-chasers 'llowed to come into free states, take back property."

"But that was so long ago. If there was ever anyone chasing after your mother and father they're probably dead by now. And even if they're not, they have no idea you exist. Don't know your name or where you live. How could anyone come looking for you?"

"You don't understand. It don't matter none to them slave-catchers. They come lookin' for a nigger they can't find, they just as glad to take one they can find. Truth is, it ain't no mind to them if I be free by the law or not. If I got nobody to stand up for me, anyone what want to can tie me up and throw me in his wagon. I do him just fine. One nigger as good as another. Out in Michigan, ain't nobody gonna stand up for me."

"And here Mr. Carmichael will."

Mourning nodded. "First night I go to sleep in his office after that town meeting he come in, say he think he gonna keep me company till I fall asleep. When I wake up the next day he still sittin' there in that chair. He give me a piece of paper say I been born to free parents, say I be a Free Man of Color. Got a stamp and his mark on it. He tell me that any time I need, he gonna stand up with me in front of a judge, swear it be so. And folks here ain't gonna call Mr. Carmichael no liar, even if they know he ain't talkin' the truth. So I don't got something to lose. I got everything to lose."

"Don't you think I'd stand up for you? I can lie as good as him. Probably better."

At least Mourning didn't say what she knew he must be thinking: "Ain't nobody gonna pay no mind to no girl." What he did say was, "Maybe so, but you ain't got no 'fficial stamp." Then he rose and opened the door for her to leave.

41

Chapter Five

Olivia trudged home, back to wondering if there wasn't some way she could persuade Tobey to come with her and share the land. *Sure, I can convince him to do that. All he has to do is change everything about him*, she thought and sighed, resigned to the fact that she would have to hire someone else. *But who?*

It had been relatively easy to imagine entering into such a venture with Mourning Free, whom she had known all her life. She trusted him. Regarded him as a person of high character, in his own prickly, stubborn way. And she couldn't imagine the two of them having man-woman problems. Olivia had seen how men could behave, as if they wanted to wrap some woman up in a big spider web. But Mourning had never looked at her in that sticky way. Even when they were children, he'd never twisted her arm, pushed her into the river, or done any of the things little boys do to get a little girl's attention. And she'd never wanted him to. True, he had grown into a tall, hard body, his skin smooth and shiny. His white teeth flashed in a lovely way when he smiled. *But that's pretty much never, ornery as he is*, she thought.

She made the unconscious assumption that the color of Mourning's skin was a brick wall between them; neither of them would dare take a hammer to it. Where was she going to find anyone else with whom she would feel that safe?

She sighed and forced herself to reconsider. Maybe Five Rocks wasn't so horrible. After all, every town must have its share of nosy, annoying women. And Avis wasn't really such a bad sort. Truth be told, he usually said and did the right thing. Olivia couldn't deny that he was a good and decent man. Most folks in town would probably say Avis was the only one of those three

Killion children that was worth a lick. Perhaps she could work in the store, but take a room in another town, get a horse like Big Bad, and ride to work. If she lived far enough away, not every single person she met on the street would know all the stories about her mother and father. Maybe now that she was grown, she could find some place to be just plain Olivia.

As she climbed the back steps she heard Mabel Mears' voice in the kitchen, bossing Avis and Tobey. Avis's beloved must be fixing supper again. Olivia closed her eyes and pressed her forehead against the icy doorframe, exhausted.

She tried to console herself. At least the food would be delicious. Olivia hadn't realized how bad a cook Mrs. Hardaway was until the formidable Mabel invaded their kitchen. With no basis for comparison, Olivia had assumed that beef was by nature dry and leathery and that there was nothing to be done with a chicken but toss it into a pot of boiling water and serve it pale and pimply, scattered clumps of pinfeathers still clinging to it. The first meal Mabel prepared for them had been an eye-opening spread of flaky biscuits, pot roast you could cut with a fork, glazed carrots, and fluffy mashed potatoes. Now Olivia smelled Mabel's fried chicken. She always got a perfect scorch on it, crispy outside and ready to fall off the bone.

"Avis, dear, come get the big platter down." Mabel's voice carried easily through wood and glass. "Tobey, you slice up the bread. Not that knife, use this one. I had it sharpened last week. Then you can ladle out the gravy. Better wrap this towel around you, save your coat. Where on earth can that Olivia have gotten to?"

Olivia increased the pressure of her forehead against the cold wood. Shivering, her head aching, she remained outside on the steps, listening to Mabel issue more commands and then demanding, "Doesn't that sister of yours know what time you have your supper? I hope everything isn't going to get all dried out because some people choose to be inconsiderate."

No. I can't do it, Olivia thought. *Anything would be better than living and working with Mabel Mears. I'll get a job in a textile mill. Go west to a logging camp and do laundry. Become a mail order bride.* Finally, Olivia could stand the cold no longer and pulled the back door open.

"Well, there you are," Mabel said. "Oh my, you'd better leave those boots out on the porch, before they leave a puddle. You boys sit down, everything's ready."

Olivia did her best to ignore her, but Mabel took the chair next to her. After Avis mumbled the Grace that Mabel had taught him and the food had been passed, Mabel leaned back and reached for a journal that lay open on the pie safe behind her.

"I know it's not good manners to read at the table," Mabel said, "but I've been wanting you to hear this, Olivia, and I don't know when else I'll get the chance, seeing as you spend so little time at home. And when you are here, you've got yourself locked in your room. Anyway, it's the most interesting article, here in my 'Godey's Lady's Book.'" She looked pointedly at Olivia before beginning to read. "A sensible woman is always aware of her inferiority. She performs those tasks that she can, but never forgets her dependence on the stronger sex and is always grateful for the support of a man. She knows that she is the weaker vessel, and it is as such that man honors her. Her weakness is not a blemish, but what endears her to man."

Olivia refrained from rolling her eyes as she wondered if the will of big, strong Avis had ever once prevailed over that of "endearingly weak" Mabel. Olivia knew where this was going – a tedious lecture about how a young lady had to behave in order to attract gentlemen callers.

Olivia hid her annoyance and changed the subject, keeping her voice calm and neutral. "I was reading something in there myself the other day. Your 'Godey's

44

Lady's Book' says it's perfectly acceptable for a woman to travel on her own, without a chaperone."

"Well, I suppose that depends on where she's going, doesn't it?" Mabel said and licked a glob of gravy off her finger before setting the journal back down on the pie safe.

"Why would it depend on that?" Avis asked. "If she needs a chaperone, she needs a chaperone. And if she doesn't, she doesn't."

"Well, dear, isn't it obvious that there's a difference between an overnight journey and, say, a stagecoach ride to another town?"

"Not obvious to me. If it's all right for her to take a stage to another town, I don't see why she can't check herself into a hotel room in that other town and then go on with another stage ride the next day."

"There is all the difference in the world. If family puts her on the stage and she's met by her hosts at the other end of the line, that's a whole different thing. She's never actually alone."

"Except when she's on the stage," Avis said and motioned for Olivia to pass the bread basket.

Mabel's impatience all but fumed out of her ears. "The driver is bound to protect her as long as she's in his coach, now isn't he? So she's not really alone."

"Well, suppose the stage makes a stop?" Avis wasn't actually grinning, but Olivia could see how much he enjoyed getting under Mabel's skin. They could bicker for hours over nothing, as if they'd already been married for about two hundred and fifty years.

Avis turned toward Mabel. "Does she have to arrange for someone to meet her and stand guard while she gets off for a drink of water?"

"Honestly, Avis Killion, I don't know why you always have to be so contrary. Obviously, the driver is responsible for her safety during the entire journey, including the stops."

"I haven't seen many stage drivers I'd entrust with

the safety of a woman I cared much about." Avis wiped up gravy with a piece of bread.

Olivia closed her eyes, imagining night after endless night of this.

"Can you pass me those mashed potatoes?" Tobey broke in. "Your gravy is as good as ever, Mabel. You'll have us all busting out of our britches. Anything interesting in the Pittsburgh paper?" he asked Avis.

"They caught that gang was robbing all the banks, so I guess it wasn't anyone we know." Avis seemed to be waiting for a laugh, but no one obliged.

"I'd like to please be excused." Olivia wiped her mouth and put her napkin next to her plate.

"Why you haven't hardly eaten a thing," Mabel protested.

"I'm full. It was delicious, Mabel, but I'm tired."

"Some people might think a young lady could spend some time with her family." Mabel frowned.

"Leave her be, Mabel," Avis said softly and Olivia pushed her chair back.

Mabel's hushed voice followed Olivia to the stairs. "Honestly, you don't have to make it sound as if I hound the poor girl. You know as well as I do that she lacks the guiding hand of an older woman. And you know I care for her just like I was her big sister."

Olivia went up and flopped onto her bed, pulling the quilt over her. She shivered, wishing she had stopped to take some hot stones from the shelf under the stove. She plumped the pillow and her hand touched the guidebook she had found among Uncle Scruggs' things. It was the kind they printed up for folks planning to make the journey out west, over the Mississippi and across the plains. Olivia had gotten it out of the attic and all but memorized it, reasoning that if she prepared herself for everything it talked about, she would certainly be able to manage the much simpler journey to Michigan. The guidebook explained what was needed to set up a farm, how to survive in the outdoors, how to make medicine from various plants, and how to preserve different kinds of foods. It even listed the quantities of flour, sugar, coffee, beans, cooking oil, whale oil, soda, baking powder, and salt that a family needed to survive for the first year. She sat up and started thumbing through it again, but shoved it back under the pillow at the sound of a soft tap on the door.

"You feeling okay?" Tobey asked as he peeked in.

"No worse than usual. You feel like going for a walk?"

"A walk? It's starting to get dark and it's freezing out there."

"I thought we might go down to the cemetery," she said. "Lay some green branches on father's grave." She knew it was unfair to use that excuse to drag him out of the house, but felt desperate to get away. The constant drone of Mabel's voice downstairs made her feel like a prisoner in her room.

Tobey sucked in a deep breath and pursed his lips. "Okay, I guess, but just there and back."

When they came down and reached for their coats Mabel raised an eyebrow. "I thought you were so tired," she said.

Olivia trumped her with, "We're going to visit Father's grave," thinking that ought to shut her up.

She and Tobey trudged through the snow toward the eastern side of town, where Main Street curled around on itself, forming a cul-de-sac that everyone called "The Circle." Jettie Place was the only one who lived down there. Her small red barn sat close to the road. The front half of it had been converted into her bakery shop; the large ovens and workroom occupied the back. Mrs. Place's house stood to the left of and slightly behind the barn, on the curve of "The Circle." She didn't have any neighbors and that seemed to suit both her and the town just fine. The sign over her bakery said "Jettie's Place," but none of the townswomen called it that. That would have sounded

47

too friendly. Mrs. Place's bread and pies were too good for them to be able to boycott her establishment, but they sniffed their noses whenever they mentioned "that woman's bakery."

Now, as they passed Mrs. Place's house, Olivia watched out of the corner of her eye, trying to take in every detail of the house and bakery without turning her head. She had often gone into the shop to buy bread and cookies when she was a little girl and Mrs. Place had always been kind to her. She used to tuck extra treats into the bag and call Olivia "you sweet child."

Olivia couldn't remember how old she had been when she first heard one of the busybodies say it outright – call Jettie Place "Old Man Killion's whore." But she had been old enough to have a vague idea what that meant. Her father and Mrs. Place must get in a bed together and do whatever the horrible thing is that husbands and wives do. Olivia had gone into "Jettie's Place" a few times after that and stood staring up at "the whore" – a tired-looking woman with bright yellow hair and rouged cheeks and a laugh that was too quick and too loud. It was difficult for Olivia to imagine Mrs. Place and her father sipping a cup of tea together. Removing their clothing? Impossible.

Not that Olivia minded the idea of her father having a connection with another woman. Her mother had died a long time ago, so there was no reason to mind on her account. Olivia simply failed to understand. Why on earth would anyone want to be in the same room with her father when he didn't have his clothes on? Olivia had seen his drooping potbelly and spindly legs. He hadn't exactly been a sparkling personality either. He spent all day in the store, took short breaks for his meals, and then did the accounts or read for a few hours before retiring. Saturday nights he played whist with friends. At least so he told his children. That must have been when he did his fornicating with the woman who called herself "Mrs." although Olivia had never

48

seen any evidence of a Mr. Place, dead or alive. She wondered if her brothers had heard the same whispers about their "carrying on." They must have, but Olivia had never spoken to them about it. Not even Tobey. Not until the day before her father died.

Now, as they neared the cemetery, Olivia slipped her arm through Tobey's. "I'm already forgetting him," she said. "I've been trying to remember what his laugh sounded like, but I can't."

"We didn't hear it all that much," Tobey said. "Except for when he'd say that one thing he used to repeat all the time, until one day Mrs. Brewster got after him."

"What thing?"

"Don't you remember? Whenever Avis or me started acting smart, he'd elbow us in the ribs and say, 'Well, I guess you're a pretty fart smeller, aren't you?' Then he'd laugh."

Olivia forced a smile and they walked on in silence.

"Have you seen *her* since that day?" Olivia nodded ever so slightly back toward "Jettie's Place."

"No. You?"

Olivia shook her head. She didn't know if her father had loved her mother and she had no idea what he might have felt for Mrs. Jettie Place. She did know that the rumors about him carrying on with "his whore" were true. He'd left them no doubt of that. The day before he died Seborn had ordered Tobey to bring Mrs. Place to him.

Chapter Six

The last morning of his life Old Seborn had been wheezing and rheumy-eyed. After bathing him, Olivia asked, "Are you needful of anything else, Father?"

He retched, spit an enormous gob of brown phlegm into a blue and white porcelain teacup, and nodded toward the bottle of rye whiskey on the dresser. Olivia poured a shot into a clean cup and watched him take a sip and cough.

"Yes, I am most needful – of having Mrs. Jettie Place brought to me. Tell Tobey to go fetch her."

Olivia expressed no objection. Once she recovered from the shock of this request, she was more curious than anything else. Excited. At last something to relieve the numbing boredom. The past two years had been one long, dull blur of caring for her father, going to the store, and walking along the river bank alone.

Tobey was unpacking stock in the back of the store when Olivia touched his arm. "Our father wants you to fetch a visitor for him."

"And who would that be?"

"Mrs. Place."

He blinked and froze for a moment, then continued unloading the crate. "Would that be right now?"

"Yes."

"Well, then I guess I'd best go fetch Mrs. Place." He stood up straight and removed his apron. Olivia need no longer wonder if Tobey had heard about their father and Mrs. Place; the sharp edge of resentment in his voice left no question.

"Am I hearing you correctly?" Avis's head bobbed in the doorway. "Are you intending to bring that woman into our mother's home?"

"Father asked for her," Olivia said, not about to let Avis spoil the show.

Tobey put on his coat, while Avis continued to protest. Mabel Mears also appeared, hands on her hips, poised to oversee the commotion. She placed a soothing hand on Avis's arm and told him there was no choice but to obey. You could not deny a dying man his last wishes.

"Take her in the back door," Mabel said, now grasping Tobey's arm, issuing her instructions through clenched teeth. "Carry a box with you, so if anyone does see you, they'll think she's making some kind of delivery." Mabel marched back out to the front counter. Resigned, Avis trailed after her.

"The way she swishes those crinolines, it's a wonder she doesn't set herself on fire," Olivia muttered.

"Would have expected her to howl louder than Avis," Tobey said as he patted his pockets, looking for his gloves.

"She's no dummy," Olivia said. "You think she's going to get herself on the wrong side of our father now, while he can still change his will?"

He pulled his hat and gloves on and went out the back door. Poor Tobey. He had a hard time making small talk with the customers. Olivia tried, and failed, to imagine the conversation in which her brother and Mrs. Place might engage. When Olivia got home and opened the back door she could already hear Seborn's bell clanging and went straight upstairs.

"So, has he gone for her?"

"Yes, Father." She turned to leave the room.

"No. You stay here. I'll be needing a witness." He nodded at the rocker that stood next to the bed. "You can read to me till she gets here."

Olivia obediently sat down and picked up "Gulliver's Travels." She read until they heard the front door open and Tobey's voice at the bottom of the stairs. "Up there, second door on the right." Unfamiliar steps tapped hesitantly up the stairs, followed by a tentative knock on the open door.

"Come in, come in," Seborn rasped.

Though Mrs. Place wore a thick red woolen coat, she shivered as she stood in the doorway, looking as if she expected to be arrested, if not shot. Olivia set the book on the bed and rose to face her.

Mrs. Place visibly steeled herself before she spoke. "Good afternoon to you, Mr. Killion. It's good to see you looking so well. Afternoon to you, Miss Killion." Mrs. Place nodded toward Olivia's chair, but avoided looking

51

directly at her. "Did you want to place some kind of special order from the bakery?"

"No need for play-acting," he said, his voice hoarse. "Do you suppose the world is full of fools? I didn't raise any, I can tell you."

Olivia took a few awkward steps toward Mrs. Place and stuck out her hand. "It's a pleasure to see you again, Mrs. Place," Olivia said, astounding both Jettie Place and herself. That kind of social grace wasn't in Olivia's nature. She always felt like the most awkward person in any group, not the one who helped put anyone else at ease. Mrs. Place paled, but took Olivia's hand and smiled.

"Set yourself down here." Seborn nodded at the rocker Olivia had vacated and Mrs. Place did as told. Olivia edged around to the other side of the bed, to a vantage point from which she could observe both their faces. His showed no emotion, as if he were performing a task to be checked off a list. Jettie Place looked both nervous and resentful.

"Look here, we both know I won't be getting out of this bed."

"Please don't talk like that." Mrs. Place put her hand on his, uneasily tracking Olivia out of the corner of her eye. Olivia thought she had never seen a worse liar.

"I'm only saying what's true. And here's something else that's true – you may have cultivated expectations over the years, but there's not going to be any mention of you in my will." He paused and coughed. "So I want to do right by you now, while I'm still breathing. And I'm not saying that Avis might accuse you of tricking me out of that money, but there's no harm in having Olivia here as a witness."

"I'm sure you don't owe me anything, sir." Mrs. Place took her hand off his and averted her face.

"You've been good to me. Kept me a man. Until now." He looked at the pitifully small mound his frail body made under the covers and shook his head. "And

52

you're a woman, aren't you? Woman always thinks a man owes her the world and a half."

Mrs. Place's face collapsed, as if all the flesh were melting off.

He waved his hand toward Olivia with a dismissive motion. "Don't worry about her. It's time she knows the things go on between men and women," he said. "She'll take a husband soon enough."

Olivia turned her back to them and stared out the window, but her gaze returned to her father when he broke the thick silence that had engulfed the room.

"This is for you," he said, wheezing as he leaned over to remove a thick white envelope from the drawer of the nightstand and hold it out to Mrs. Place. "Cash money. No waiting for the blasted lawyer. I had to have Avis get it from the bank for me and you can bet he's going to want to know where it disappeared to." He stopped to cough again. "That's why Olivia is here, so no one will be able to say I didn't give it to you of my own free will, or that you put an evil spell on my poor senile mind. You can trust her. She's got her share of faults in her character, but it's her bad luck that lying ain't one of them."

Mrs. Place stood up and arranged her skirts. "Well, thank you Seborn. I can assure you, I'm most grateful to you." She slipped the envelope into a deep pocket and chattered about the cake she was going to go right home and bake for him.

He cut her off with a wave of his hand and closed his eyes. "You'd best go now. Good-bye, Jettie."

She paused for a moment before she moved to his side and bent down to plant a kiss on his cheek. "I'll be seeing you, Seborn. You get yourself all better. You hear me?"

Eyes still closed, he made another impatient gesture with his hand.

"Let me show you out, Mrs. Place," Olivia said after a moment's silence. Mrs. Place followed her out to the

53

hall where they heard voices downstairs – Tobey, Avis, and Mabel arriving home for their noonday meal.

"Perhaps you'd like to step into my room, take a moment to collect yourself before you go down there," Olivia said. Mrs. Place had been looking down the stairs as if they descended straight into hell.

"Yes, I would. You're awfully kind," she said, suspicion creeping into her voice.

"Come in." Olivia opened the door. "Why don't you sit over there on the window seat? I could fetch you a pitcher of water, if you'd like to freshen up."

"No. That won't be necessary." Mrs. Place walked quickly to the window and seated herself, suddenly the picture of composure.

"He never talked much about you." She looked Olivia over with a cool eye. "Always griped about Avis the conniver and Tobias the spineless weakling, but I can't remember any complaints about you. I'd see you in the shop, of course. You were always such a sweet little thing."

Olivia suddenly realized that her father's mistress was as curious about her and her brothers as Olivia was about her.

Mrs. Place removed the envelope from her pocket and turned it over. "Wondering how much is in here? I suppose you think it's rightly yours." She sighed and gave Olivia a tired smile. "Don't worry. It can't be much. He always was tightfisted. Never even gave me a present. Not once, all these years. He cost me money, if you want to know the truth. There he was, Old Man Killion, my rich fancy man, with the big house on Maple Street, but all he ever did was come over and grant me the privilege of serving him a meal. At my expense, of course. I did have to borrow from him a few times, but he always let me pay him back."

"So why did you ... why were you ... his friend?" Olivia sank to the bed, shocked by the audacity of her question, but too curious to keep her mouth shut.

"Oh, I don't know." Mrs. Place leaned back. "I suppose because no one else was there – and he was. Let me feel like maybe someone thought about me once in a while." She suddenly stood up and moved toward the door.

Olivia was reluctant to let her go. "Did he ever talk to you about my mother?"

"Nola June, the saint?" Mrs. Place stopped and turned to face Olivia. "Just all the time. She was so frail, so pure, so righteous." Then, after a pause, she put a hand on Olivia's shoulder and added softly, "He truly cared for her. Loved her with all his heart."

Olivia knew she was supposed to be angry with Mrs. Place. Despise her. But she felt nothing like that. She was too busy being amazed by this woman who broke all the rules. "You're awfully strong," Olivia blurted out.

"Now that's something you don't never want to be saying about a woman, not if you like her even one little bit." Mrs. Place shook her head and smiled sadly at Olivia. "People will forgive just about anything in a man, except being too weak, and the one thing they absolutely cannot forgive in a woman is being too strong."

She nodded good-bye to Olivia and stepped into the hall. The voices had drifted to the kitchen at the back of the house and Mrs. Place quietly slipped down the front stairs and let herself out.

When Olivia and Tobey arrived at the cemetery they followed the path to their parents' resting place. Seborn's headstone wasn't ready yet; a piece of wood with lettering in black paint marked his grave. Nola June's was of intricately carved marble.

Seborn Killion
July 6, 1794
January 26, 1841

55

Nola June Sessions Killion
September 26, 1800
February 3, 1829

"I was almost six when she died," Olivia said. "Seems like I ought to be able to remember more about her."

She stared at the graves and felt nothing, thinking something must be wrong with her. Nearby were two more headstones. One belonged to her little brother, Jason Lee. He had died of the fever when he was two and Olivia was four. She had no recollection of him at all. The other grave was that of her Uncle Scruggs.

"It's so sad that Uncle Scruggs is buried all alone here, while his Lydia Ann lies out there in Michigan. They ought to be together," she said.

Tobey said nothing. He clapped his arms around himself and Olivia knew it was his way of saying he was ready to turn around and go home.

"Remember how Uncle Scruggs always liked to show us the deed to his land, brag about how it was signed by President John Quincy Adams' own hand?"

Tobey nodded with obvious disinterest. "Where were you planning on getting green branches to lay on the graves?" he asked.

Olivia ignored the question. "He was so proud of that wooden floor he put in their cabin, all hand-planed lumber, so smooth you could run your fingers over it and never know there was a trap door to the cellar."

"Can we get going?"

"And he built a stone fireplace and chimney –"

"Olivia, can we talk about this at home?"

"I like remembering the way he –"

"I know, I know. It was a magical paradise, wild strawberries as big as your fist, corn higher than a house, trees taller than the birds fly, and trout that leapt out of the river into his frying pan. The forest was so green it hurt his eyes to look at it. Oh, I forgot, Lydia

Ann had to go out every morning and bang on a cooking pot to chase the deer away from her laundry tub. Just enough curious bears, sly wolves, and cunning-but-noble Indians to keep life interesting. Can we please go home now?"

"Wouldn't you like to go see that land some time?"

"Why would I want to do that? Everyone knows there's no good farmland out there in Michigan. And all he built was a little one-room cabin. Chopped down trees and piled the logs up on each other, bark and all. And it's been out there rotting for twenty years."

"Thirteen."

"There's probably nothing left standing."

Olivia turned to face her brother. He was wearing the thick winter coat that made him look like a little boy, his arms sticking out to the sides. He removed his foggy spectacles to wipe them on his sleeve, but fumbled and dropped them in the snow. She bit her bottom lip as he bent to retrieve them.

"You're going to spend your life working in that store, aren't you?" she asked with a sigh.

"Seems so."

Sweet Tobey. He would never fail to disappoint. She looked up at the stars coming out, feeling small and alone under the endless sky.

"Okay, let's go." She slipped her arm through her brother's and they walked in silence for a while.

"Are you coming to work in the store tomorrow?" he asked.

"No, I don't think so. Mourning Free is coming over to fix some things for Mrs. Hardaway and I want to be there. I have to show him exactly what needs to be done."

Chapter Seven

The next morning Olivia sat at the kitchen table drinking coffee, while Mourning banged on the oven door. She silently admired the way he worked, his movements quick and sure. The only thing he might not be good at was shooting a gun, but Uncle Scruggs had made sure Olivia knew how to do that. She had only taken aim at empty milk tins, but unfailingly blasted them from fifty paces. Sometimes even a hundred. She had also gone hunting with her uncle. Though she had never actually shot at an animal, she had helped follow a blood trail and so felt sure she'd be able to put meat on the table. And did it really matter if she couldn't? Mourning must know how to fish and she could keep chickens in the yard.

Mrs. Hardaway had gone out the back door with her shopping basket, leaving Olivia and Mourning alone in the house. Olivia said to Mourning's back, "You know there are over a hundred negroes out there in Detroit, Michigan. I can show you where it says so, right in a book. And there's a town called Backwoods, not so far from Fae's Landing, with a whole lot too." The last statement was a stretch of the truth. The book did mention the existence of a negro community in Backwoods, but didn't say of how many.

Mourning ignored her and grunted, clanging his tools.

"You should have heard Uncle Scruggs talk about that how beautiful it is out there. And Fae's Landing is only about forty miles from Detroit, where they have markets and railroads and boats on the river. So it would be easy to sell whatever you grow." She paused and waited for him to respond, but he continued banging on the oven door.

She took a breath and continued. "You know, people

who want to get ahead in life have to move with the times. And the ones who get farthest ahead are the ones who stay a step ahead of the rest. Now's the time to go. With that Erie Canal open ten steamboats are docking in Detroit every day, full of people looking to buy land. Pretty soon there won't be any left. It says right here," she said, pointing at the almanac on the table in front of her, "that in 1830 there were only about 30,000 people in all of Michigan. How many do you think they counted last year?" She paused before answering her own question. "Over 213,000." She repeated the number, emphasizing each syllable.

He stood up and turned to face her. "I told you why I can't go."

"Why would some old slave-catcher come poking around my uncle's farm? They don't even have slavery in Michigan. Outlawed it four years ago."

"Maybe they ain't got slavery, but they got plenty a runaway slaves. Probably even more than Pennsylvania. That underground railroad go right through Michigan on the way to Canada. So they be plenty a slave-catchers chasin' after 'em." He set the hammer down, rose from squatting in front of the stove, and took a seat across the table from her.

She got up to pour him a cup of coffee and set it in front of him. "Well, if the underground railroad goes through Michigan, that means there are plenty of white people out there willing to stand up for a black man. You'll have Mr. Carmichael's paper, you'll have me, and you'll have all those abolitionists. Before we leave you can ask Mr. Carmichael to make another copy of that paper. I'll hold on to one of them for you, just in case you ever lose yours. Once we're there we can find a local judge or attorney, someone like Mr. Carmichael and give him a copy for safe-keeping. Michigan isn't some wild territory. It's been a state for four years. They've got laws there, same as here. "

She did not, however, tell him everything she knew

59

about those laws. After Uncle Scruggs returned to Five Rocks he had continued to receive the Detroit Gazette by post. Olivia had found a bundle of yellowing issues, each four pages long, the first three in English, the last in French. From them she learned that Michigan had the same laws against negroes that they seemed to have everywhere. Whites and negroes were forbidden to marry. Public schools were not required to accept negro children and if they chose to do so were allowed to provide separate facilities. In Michigan, however, they had another terrible law that she had never heard of before. She learned of it from an article that had appeared on the front page of an issue published in 1828:

"A much-needed amendment to the law for the regulation of negroes has finally been passed. As we have already informed our readers the original law passed in 1827 requires all negroes to carry a valid, court-attested Certificate of Freedom and to register with the clerk of the County Court and file a $500 bond guaranteeing good behavior. The new amendment enables sheriffs and constables to evict non-complying negroes."

A letter to the editor in the next issue complained that:

"Not hardly a one of these dark bipeds has obeyed the law. This unfortunate species not equal to ourselves roams our towns and cities unsupervised while the men we pay to uphold the law choose to ignore their disregard for our legal system. For this sorry state of affairs we can thank the niggery abolitionists who are deviants and favor the social integration of these inferior creatures."

60

Her conscience shouted at her to show that article to Mourning, but she couldn't bring herself to destroy whatever chance there may be of him coming with her. Anyway, didn't the horrible man who wrote that nasty letter complain about nobody obeying the stupid law? And the sheriffs not caring that they didn't? And Fae's Landing probably didn't even have a sheriff. Anyway, maybe the negroes didn't have to give them $500. Maybe filing a bond meant that a person signed some paper promising to pay $500 if they went and robbed someone or did some other bad thing. Mourning would never do anything like that.

Mourning said nothing and Olivia leaned forward and pressed on. "Please, Mourning, you've got to think it over again. Mr. Carmichael isn't going to be around forever. You've got to make a life for yourself. I know you could run a farm better than anyone. You'd know how to buy a wagon and a team of oxen, wouldn't you?"

He stooped his shoulders and slowed his speech to a drawl, the imitation of a groveling slave he had begun doing when they were children, any time she got bossy and annoyed him. "Far's I 'member, Miz Olivia, you be wantin' to buy something, you be handin' over yo' money and then you be takin' that thing home."

"Oh stop being ornery, you and your 'Miz Olivia.' You know what I mean. Would you know how to pick out a good pair and what you should pay for them?"

"Spose so."

"You listen to me, Mourning Free. You can be as cantankerous as you want, but you know you can trust me. And I don't mind telling you, I haven't been able to think of anyone else that I would want to do this with. You've got to think about it. You'll never have another chance like this. It's true that you'll be the one doing most of the hard work, but I'll help with whatever I can. You can boss me. I surely know you'd like that."

He grinned. "Boss you? That sound like the hardest part a your plan."

"Seriously, Mourning, I'll do the cooking and the laundry. Milk the cow when we get one. Raise some chickens. Just like a regular farmer's wife. Like I said, you can use whatever money we make to buy your own land, until you've got forty acres of your own. After that, if you want, I'll pay you a fair wage to keep on working mine. Or at least to oversee whoever I hire."

"Black man overseein' a white one. That indeed be a pretty picture. You got me bossin' white folks ever which way," Mourning said, but his easy grin turned to a look of fierce concentration and he sat silently studying the grain of the wooden table.

Olivia waited a few minutes before speaking again. This time her tone of voice assumed it was decided. "If all sorts of things do go wrong and we don't make any money ... well, you work out what would be a fair wage for each month you worked and I'll pay it to you. There won't be any way you can lose." She paused to let this idea sink in before continuing. "There's all sorts of land out there, Mourning. Once you get your own place going, you can keep buying more and more. They practically give it away. You'll have your own quarter section in no time." This was another stretcher. In fact she hadn't the slightest idea what the current price of land in Michigan was, nor how much of it there was for sale. But all those steamboats full of eager immigrants must mean something.

Finally he spoke. "I always knowed you was strange, but that some crazy idea, even for you. You best stay here in your daddy's house and read your books." But his tone of voice had changed and Olivia thought she had him.

"It's not a crazy idea, Mourning. Who do you think goes to places like that, anyway? People like us. People with nothing, looking for a chance to get something. It's not my daddy's house any more. It belongs to Avis now and I need something of my own. Look at the people around here who've got money – they're the ones whose family came when there was nothing and made something out of it. Just like all the people going to Michigan now."

"You ain't done a day's hard work in your life. You got no idea what you talkin' about. You tryin' to tell me you gonna chop firewood and haul water? Sew your own clothes? Churn butter?"

"I can do those things, Mourning. I know I can. I'm young and healthy. I know it'll be hard, but when a person wants something badly enough, they can do anything. I'll get used to whatever I have to. And we aren't going out into the wilderness. There's a town nearby, with stores. We'll be able to buy most of those things."

"What about your brothers? They gonna be comin' after me with all the rope they can find."

"No one strings up negroes in Pennsylvania. Or in Michigan. You've been reading too many abolitionist newspapers," she said in exasperation. "You know, for someone who's never set foot in a slave state and has been treated pretty decently by every white person he's ever known, you spend an awful lot of time worrying about getting lynched or sold down the river. Besides, I already told you, I'm not going to tell them where I'm going. And you don't have to tell anyone either."

He scowled at her and took a sip of the coffee. "I could sell Big Bad," he said, his voice low, barely audible.

"You don't have to do that. I told you, I've got money." She stopped. "Oh, well, I guess you would have to sell him, since we can't take him on the steamboat. But you'd keep that money. Our arrangement would be that I supply all the money and the land we start out with; you supply the strong back."

"What if you run out a money?"

"We'll think about that when it happens."

He scowled again.

"Look," she said, "I suppose if we did go broke you

63

could always get work at one of the logging camps. They operate mostly during the winter, when there's enough snow on the ground to make skid ways, so it's perfect for a farmer."

He glared.

"Well, I'd go with you, of course. I could get a job as a cook or washing the loggers' clothes. Then, come springtime, we'd go back to farming. And why start out worrying about every tiny thing that could go wrong? What's the worst thing that can happen to us? We fail. And you know the only thing that's worse than failing? Being afraid to try. Stop rolling your eyes. Clichés get to be clichés by being true."

They heard Mrs. Hardaway's heavy step on the back porch and both grew silent. He rose, set his coffee cup on the counter, and began gathering up the pots she had set out for him.

"Day to you, Mrs. Hardaway," he said as she came in. "I get these back later this afternoon," he said.

"That will be just fine. Thank you for coming so quick," she replied and set her basket on the table.

After the noonday meal, Olivia went behind the post office to the Reading Room and spent an hour working through the dusty stacks, picking out every book and journal she could find that had anything good to say about Michigan. Then she went looking for Mourning again and waited until no one else was around before shoving *Morse's Geography* under his nose.

He again rolled his eyes and acted as if he were humoring her. "What now, someone find diamonds on your uncle's place? Or maybe Moses been sighted wanderin' there? Or maybe them Michigan farmers started growin' gold 'stead a corn."

"No, no gold or diamonds. But they do have trails that are wide enough for a wagon and they go to all these cities: Chicago, Port Huron, Saginaw, and Grand Rapids." She pointed to each one on the map and Mourning's eyes followed her finger. She left the book

64

and clomped out.

The next morning she found him again and pulled a copy of the *Journal of the American West* from under her coat. "There's a whole article in here about Michigan – about how it isn't true what people used to say about it being a big swamp. That was all a big fat lie told by Mr. fancy pants millionaire John Jacob Astor and his fur company because all they wanted in Michigan was lots of bears and foxes, not settlers. So they made up a report about Michigan being no good for farming."

"And now who say different?"

"There's a government report that says so – from twenty years ago. They sent a bunch of men called the Cass Expedition to go canoeing all over Michigan. Those men came back swearing that all the farmers had to do was clear away the trees and they'd have fine farmland."

Olivia kept up her campaign, but it wasn't reading material she was counting on to win him over. The bossy, annoying women of Five Rocks would do that for her.

A body can live with anything, as long as they believe they have no other choice, she thought. *But once he's convinced he does have one, he won't be able to stand those busybodies for one more minute.*

One day in February Mourning finally asked, "Just where it be, this land we gonna farm? Show me on the map."

Olivia felt as if he had kicked her in the stomach. She wasn't prepared for it. She was so busy convincing him, she forgot to convince herself. But there it was, him saying it out loud, agreeing to go with her. For a moment she stared at him, stunned. Then she had to restrain herself from throwing her arms around him. In the end, all she did was point at the map and say, "Well, now that that's finally settled, we can get down to planning. From now on we have to be extra careful not to be seen together."

Olivia went through her father's desk and found the deed to the land and a copy of both wills – Uncle Scruggs' and Seborn's. She took them upstairs and slipped them into a thick envelope that she hid under her mattress. Then she began pouring over her guidebooks again, underlining important points and making neatly printed lists. When she next met with Mourning she caught him studying her when he thought she wasn't looking. *He must be wondering if I'll really go through with it,* she thought. *Same as I'm wondering about him.*

They would buy most of what they needed in Detroit and so planned to carry as little as possible – only their clothing, a few personal belongings, and Mourning's heavy case of tools, which he called his Most Precious Belongings. As far as Olivia could see, it was pretty much his only belonging. Olivia would also bring the double-barreled shotgun Uncle Scruggs had given to her and she planned to relieve Tobey of the flintlock Hawken rifle and flintlock pistol that had been birthday presents to him from their father. Tobey never touched them. They had been under the eaves collecting dust for as long as Olivia could remember.

Olivia and Mourning both wrote down everything they thought they needed to buy when they got to Detroit and compared lists. The necessities – lanterns, whale oil, matches, soap, rope, washtub, bedding, pots, pans, water barrel – seemed endless. There was always something else.

"You forgot feed for the oxen," she reminded Mourning one evening.

"Ain't forgot," he said. "We don't gotta be buyin' no team. We can hire us a wagon in Detroit to take us to your uncle's place. Farmers don't buy no team when they just startin' out. Ain't none a them can afford to. They pull their own stumps and push their own plows."

"Well, we *can* afford to," Olivia said. "Do you have

any idea how many stumps are going to need pulling? And if you think you're going to call me out and hitch me to the plow, you can think again. You save on buying oxen and we're likely to miss a season. That's poor man's thinking," she quoted her father. "Save a penny and lose making a dollar."

"Cost a lot a money to feed 'em."

"I know that. But we can offer to rent them out to other farmers for a few days a week to help pay for their keep and soon enough we'll be growing whatever they eat."

"Bet they ain't no corn-crackers out there what got any cash money to be rentin' oxen."

"Then we'll barter. For butter and eggs or whatever they do have – or for work. It will be worth it in the long run. My father always said: you have to spend money to make money."

"You say so. It your money."

She relentlessly planned and ticked off items, but lay awake most nights, terrified. What if the boat sinks? Catches on fire? The engine explodes and kills us? Could slave-catchers really drag Mourning down south? What about Indians? Robbers? The only way she got any sleep was by reminding herself that they weren't really going to go – Mourning was sure to back out at the last minute.

Chapter Eight

For Olivia the hardest part of preparing for life in the Michigan woods was trying to decide how much of what type of clothing to take. The guidebooks warned that there would be nothing else to wear until the women had begun shearing sheep, spinning wool, weaving yarn, and sewing clothes. Olivia had no intention of performing any of those chores. Fae's Landing must have a dressmaker and a general store

67

that sold fabric. She decided to pack six dresses – two for Sunday best, two for work in the summer, and two for winter. On second thought, perhaps she'd better take three winter work dresses. There was no telling how long it would take clothes to dry in winter, in front of a fireplace in a small cabin. Or out in the barn where they would turn to ice.

Olivia was glad Mabel Mears had nagged Avis into putting in a small stock of the new factory-made dresses. She waited to do her shopping until Monday afternoon, when she knew Mabel would be at her knitting circle. She had no desire to hear Mabel's opinion of a girl wearing bright colors when she should still be in mourning.

She loved the first summer dress she pulled off the rack. It was soft cotton – a simple print of wispy blue flowers on ivory, with a narrow white collar and sleeves that cuffed below the elbow. The dark blue apron – front and back panels that tied together at the sides – had deep pockets.

Avis was busy behind the counter up front and paid her no mind. Finally, she took a deep breath and strode over to him. "I'd like to take this dress home," she said, draping it over the counter. "And look for a few others."

"Mmmm..." He hardly glanced at it.

"Well, aren't you going to say anything?"

"What do you want me to say?"

"Well, is that all right with you? Do you want me to pay for it?"

"Pay for it? No, I don't want you to *pay* for it. But I will praise the Lord that maybe you're finally going to try to look like a young lady. You been wearing that brown sack so long, looks near ready to fall off. Take all the dresses you want. By all means." He seemed embarrassed and turned to flee into the storeroom.

Why do I always expect the worst of him? she wondered. *And then when he surprises me by being nice, I think he's doing it for the wrong reasons. But* she couldn't help suspecting that he considered it an excellent investment – spruce Olivia up a bit, maybe some poor man would take her off her brother's hands.

She picked out three more dresses – two of which she knew would have to be taken in – but it was the one of a deep royal blue that she couldn't wait to try on. She hurried home, stepped into it, and stood in front of the hinged oval mirror in her room, beginning to understand why women fretted so much over their clothes. She looked like a whole different person, all grown up. Elegant. She still wore her dark hair like a young girl, cut blunt and shoved behind her ears, but now she swept it up with both hands and could imagine herself a real lady, all done up, with ringlets and ribbons in her hair.

Under the eaves she had found two large rectangular wicker baskets with lids that lifted on hinges. One of them had been half-filled with her mother's clothes and Olivia wondered who'd packed them away after she died. Their father? Mrs. Hardaway? Good thing Mabel hadn't been around back then; she'd have hung them in the store. Olivia cleaned the baskets and practiced packing: two velvet winter bonnets; two pairs of mitts; four cotton day caps; a corset; four chemises; a pile of stockings, garters, and extra white collars and cuffs. Then she started with the petticoats she so hated – three flannel, three muslin, three calico, and only one crinoline. She still had to fit in her dresses, an umbrella, a parasol, a heavy winter coat, and whatever she was going to wear on her feet.

Her guidebooks advised going barefoot as much as possible during the summer, in order to save shoe leather for cold weather. They also said one should save on scuffing by always, winter or summer, removing shoes when riding in a wagon. She had no intention of doing that either.

Mourning happened to be in Killion's General the day she confiscated three pairs of work shoes. They were all the same, with cloth uppers, squared patent leather tips at the toes and heel sections, and laces at the inner ankle. That week, when they met near Uncle Scruggs' grave to compare lists, Mourning asked why he had seen her carting off a barrel full of shoes.

"I'll need them."

"Ain't nobody need no three pair a shoes."

"If you want to risk having to run through the woods barefoot, that's your affair, but I want to be sure to have enough sturdy work shoes. I'm only taking one pair for Sunday."

"You mean them three ain't all?"

"I can't very well attend church in work boots."

"I bet all them farmers wives out there do. If they even got a church."

"It's just one little pair of Roman sandals."

"Roman what?"

"They're real pretty." She purposely annoyed him. "Black kid, cut low, with ribbons that lace right here across the instep and tie around the ankle. I got some clogs, too, with wooden soles and canvas straps, to wear over them, protect them from the snow or mud."

"Now I know why you be needin' a team of oxen."

"Believe me, I wish I could go off with just a few shirts and trousers like you," she said wistfully and this was the truth. "I didn't make the rules about what women have to wear. But a person is better off decently dressed than not. Especially when that person is going someplace new. We'll have to depend on other folks now and then and it's best they don't start out with a bad impression."

Olivia owned few items of sentimental value. One of them was her mother's hairbrush. It was wooden, with an intricate pattern of scrolls carved into its back. Every evening when she brushed her hair, she wondered what Nola June would have thought about her daughter running off. Was she up there in heaven horrified? Or cheering her on? Olivia couldn't help but wonder if her mother's state of "not quite right in the head" hadn't been simple boredom.

One evening in mid-March Olivia knocked on Tobey's door. He was lying on his bed, thumbing through a catalog of dry goods. He sat up and swung his legs over the edge and she perched next to him, holding out the wooden brush.

"Do you remember this?"

"Am I supposed to?"

"It was our mother's. She gave it to me one Christmas. Told me Gram Sessions gave it to her, when she was my age."

She ran the brush through her hair and then held it in her lap.

"Can't say I do recall it." Tobey blinked at her.

"What do you remember about her?" she asked.

"What do you mean?"

"I mean what do you remember about her?"

He thought for what seemed like an awfully long time.

"She used to knit a lot."

"She did?" That took Olivia by surprise. She couldn't understand how anyone had the patience to fool around with all those balls of yarn. All that knitting and purling and you had to take it on faith that anyone would want to wear what turned out. But it especially surprised her to hear that about Nola June. She couldn't imagine her mother sitting in one place long enough to finish a row. In Olivia's imagination Nola June never stopped moving.

"Oh yeah, she did. Hats and mufflers."

"What else?"

"Oh, I don't know. Maybe she made a sweater now and then."

"No, I mean, what else do you remember about her, besides knitting?"

"Well, let's see. I remember her planting a lot of

71

stuff out back. It's all overgrown now, but when she was alive she kept it all trimmed and nice. Used to keep a real colorful flower garden. And she liked lemonade. I remember that. She was always pounding lemons on the kitchen table and mixing up big pitchers of it, so sweet even a kid could hardly drink it. She planted mint leaves out by the pump, so she'd always have some to add to the lemonade."

"Can you remember her voice?"

He thought for a moment. "Not really. She was soft-spoken. I do know that. Never heard her raise her voice. And Father always spoke real gentle-like when he was talking to her."

"I remember her brushing my hair with this brush. She'd sit me between her knees and brush and brush. That's the only touch of hers I remember. The only thing at all. Except for her humming. In my mind she always seems to be humming. I've got her watch too," Olivia said.

"Yeah, I do remember that. The gold one you can open up and put a picture in. Has a little gold pencil on the same chain."

Olivia nodded. "Gram Sessions gave her that too. Do you think our father ever gave her any nice presents?"

"I don't know, but I wouldn't imagine it too likely. Wasn't his way."

She rested her head on Tobey's shoulder and felt like crying. "I just hate it that I don't remember her at all. I wish I had one clear memory. Just one. One thing that I knew was me truly remembering my mother and not a story I heard, or something I dreamed up."

Tobey patted her knee and she rose to leave. Back in her room she searched for Nola June's watch in the top drawer of her bureau and her fingers brushed something hard under a neat stack of handkerchiefs. Her mother's combs. She'd forgotten about them. They were not for combing one's hair, but the kind women use for decoration, a narrow row of seven or eight teeth, six inches long. One was of tortoise shell, the other two of bone. Bright red, green, and yellow stones sparkled at their crowns.

Suddenly Olivia's mind opened to an image of Nola June, the way she had worn her hair every day, pinned up with simple hairpins, sometimes with a length of ribbon or flowers twined through it. Then she saw her mother descending the stairs on Christmas Eve, something shiny draped over her shoulders and two bone combs extruding from an intricate pile of hair. A princess. She was *not* a crazy lady. People only said those horrible things because they were so jealous of how elegant she was, the way she moved in an aura of light. Nola June would have hated Mabel Mears.

Olivia sighed and set the watch and combs on the bed next to the brush. She didn't want to take them with her, for fear of losing them out in the wilderness, but neither did she want to leave them behind. She frowned for a moment, then returned one of the combs to the drawer and rolled the others up, together with the watch and hairbrush, in a flannel petticoat and tucked it into one of the baskets.

Later, when everyone was asleep, she lit a candle and slipped downstairs to take her Bible from the bookshelf, moving the other books farther apart, to hide the empty space. The writing on the inside cover, noting all the marriages, births, and deaths in the family, was in Nola June's delicate hand. Olivia had added the deaths of her mother, Uncle Scruggs, and now her father. She took the Bible upstairs, wrapped it in a petticoat, and tucked it into the basket next to the money bag she had sewn. It was a cloth belt, from which four long pockets hung, that she planned to tie around her waist, under her skirt and petticoats. She would keep ten dollars emergency money in her stockings and the rest of the heavy gold coins in those pockets.

On the first of April she went to meet Mourning Free under the old covered bridge and handed him two five dollar coins.

"Safest thing would be to keep one in each boot," she said. "So no matter what, you've always got some money. And you'd best collect any wages owing to you. I'd say we're ready to go."

Chapter Nine

Two weeks later, in the middle of May 1841, Mourning drove a wagon up Maple Street to collect Olivia's wicker baskets. She'd waited until her brothers left for the store and Mrs. Hardaway was back in the kitchen humming. Then she'd dragged them down the front stairs, one at a time. They were heavy and made a loud thump on each step, but Mrs. Hardaway's hearing was bad. Despite misgivings, Olivia did as Mourning had told her – set the baskets on the other side of the front hedge, hidden from the house but in plain sight of the nosy neighbors across the street. Olivia thought she should try to conceal them in the bushes. Mourning snorted his disapproval of that idea.

"You Killions got neighbor ladies what see what kind a spiders you got on your porch. Best way to get them ladies interested in something is try and hide it. They ain't gonna think nothin' of me picking up some junk in front of your house. All the folks in this town think they doin' me a giganteous favor, lettin' me haul away the things they got no use for. Anyways," he said, "soon enough all them ladies gonna know – Olivia Killion gone and run off. But they ain't gonna think it was with me, just 'cause I pick up your things. You only done what any of them would. Who else you gonna get to carry for you?"

The next morning Olivia woke early, her mind

74

blank. She felt exhausted, but was no longer tormented by anxiety. Things were either going to go as planned or they weren't and there was not another thing she could do about it. She didn't feel excited or scared, only impatient for the time to pass, to be on that stage and on her way out of Five Rocks. She had convinced herself not to worry about being seen. So what if someone saw her? What were they going to do? All Olivia had to do was act natural and make up some relatives she was going to visit. Anyway, Avis and Tobey would know soon enough that she was gone.

When the clock struck five, Olivia got out of bed and crept down to use the outhouse before encumbering herself in the traveling clothes she had set out on the hardback chair. She splashed water on her hands and face before putting on her new Sunday dress of soft dark gray and the black velvet bolero jacket that went over it. To save room in the baskets she had reluctantly encased herself in a corset and stepped into six petticoats. She stood in front of the mirror admiring how grown-up she looked and tucked her hair into a white day cap.

Then she reached under her cumbersome skirts to tie her homemade money belt around her waist, thinking that if men had to flounce around wearing these stupid petticoats, not much would get done in this world. The belt was heavy, but the solid weight of the gold coins was more of a comfort than a burden. Last, she pulled the Hawken rifle from under her bed. It was too long to fit in the baskets, even on the diagonal. She slung it over her shoulder and then arranged her long black cloak around it.

She made the bed, smoothed the pink and white quilted cover, and looked around the room. All the surfaces were clear, except for the pitcher, basin, and hand towel on the dresser. She removed the note she had written from the dresser drawer and placed it on the bed. Then she reconsidered and tucked it under the pillow, not wanting to risk anyone finding it before she was safely on her way.

She picked up her tapestry bag, pulled the bedroom door shut, and tiptoed down the stairs and out the front door. It was still early and she went for one last walk down by the river, where faint rays of sun glinted gold off the placid water. The air was still chilly, but had lost its sting. She felt calm and slightly puzzled by the ease with which she was walking away from her life. She felt no sadness, regret, or sense of impending loss. Nothing but eager for a new beginning. Apparently Mabel Mears was scarier than the Indians, bears, and wolves in Fae's Landing.

Olivia skipped a few stones over the surface of the river and turned to walk back toward the post office. A stage passed through Five Rocks twice a week. Anyone who wanted to go to Erie stood on the wooden sidewalk near the Brewster house at six-thirty in the morning, though it was likely to be closer to seven before the coach finally arrived.

Mourning was not traveling with her. Mr. Bellinir from the Feed & Grain drove to the port once a month to pick up supplies and Mourning had arranged to ride with him, together with his and Olivia's belongings.

The stage soon pulled up. Olivia paid the driver, bundled herself into the backwards-facing seat opposite a young couple, and exchanged brief hulloes with them before carefully arranging the rifle, laying her head against the side of the coach, and pretending to be sleepy. As they clop-clopped out of town and over the covered bridge Olivia's peace of mind abandoned her. At last on her way, she grew damp with sweat. What if Mourning didn't show up? What if she couldn't find her way to the steamboat office? What if she was robbed?

She finally managed to doze off and by the end of the six-hour journey had regained her resolve. What was the worst that could happen? She would spend a few nights in a public house, waiting for Mourning. If he didn't come, she would just have to take the stage back home and think of a new idea. It was a discouraging thought, but no cause for panic. She alighted in Erie and stood on the sidewalk, blinking and beating the dust from her clothes. How did one transport oneself from one place to another in a huge city?

"No one meeting you, Miss?" the driver asked.

She shrugged and shook her head, embarrassed to be all by herself, an object of pity.

"Stage office is right across the street." He bobbed his nose in that direction. "They got a hotel, not too expensive, two streets over that way. Or you can hire a wagon back there, behind the livery," he said, jerking his thumb over his shoulder. He finished removing the harness from the team of horses and led them off before she managed to open her mouth to thank him and ask how to get to the steamship company.

"Excuse me." She stopped the next man she encountered on the street. He was rough looking, but removed his worn hat and hugged it to his chest while she asked for directions.

"It ain't far, Miss. Two streets down and one over. Can't miss it. You going to Detroit, there's a boat leaving in a few hours – the *Windsong*."

She thanked him, smiling. Better to spend another night on the boat than in a public house. She'd heard that in one of those places you were half certain to get robbed the minute you fell asleep.

The tinkle of the bell when she opened the door to the steamship office startled her; it sounded just like the one in Killion's General. A man in a black cap stood behind a counter selling tickets. On the wall behind him hung an enormous black slate. There it was in white chalk – the *S.S. Windsong* – departing for Detroit. What a lovely name for a boat. She went back outside to pace the wooden sidewalk and crane her neck for sight of Mourning Free. Her thoughts wandered to home, knowing that by now someone must have found the note she had left, saying she had gone to look for a better paying teaching job than she would find near Five Rocks.

Poor Tobey may have guessed the truth, she thought. *If so, part of him feels like he ought to come after me, but another part is arguing that he has no right to interfere in my life.*

For once it was a relief to know that when there was any doubt about what he should do rattling around in Tobey's mind, you could pretty much count on him not to do anything at all. A lifetime passed before Mourning came strolling cheerily up the street, hands in his pockets and whistling.

"Hullo, Mourning."

"And a good morning to you, Miss Olivia." He grinned and took off his wide-brimmed felt hat. He was wearing his church-going clothes, but they were thick with dust. He had obviously tried to polish his shoes with lard mixed with soot from the cook stove caps. They were a terrible mess, with dirt, leaves, and even an acorn clinging to them.

"Where are our bags?" she asked, thinking he was no good at pretending. She could tell he was just as scared as she was.

"Someone bringin' 'em real soon." He looked behind him just as a wagon driven by a young black man turned the corner. "See, right there."

They waited for the driver to pull up beside them and Olivia saw that her wicker baskets and Mourning's toolbox, leather case, and carpetbag were safe in the bed of the wagon. She asked the driver if he could wait for them to get tickets and then take them down to the port. He nodded agreeably and put his feet up.

"There's a boat leaving in about two hours," she told Mourning. "I'd better go pay our way."

Mourning followed her inside and they studied the sign over the ticket window that listed prices. First class to Detroit was $18. Steerage was $7.

"What should we get? What do you think steerage is?" she asked in a whisper.

"Don't know." Mourning shrugged, giving her an "I thought you so smart and know all them things" look. "I forgot to aks, last time I took a boat to Detroit," he said.

"Steerage is deck passage," a white man standing behind them said to Olivia. "It means you spend the entire trip on the deck. Will you and your boy be traveling on the *Windsong*?"

"Yes, I guess so," she said.

"That's her, down there by the pier." He nodded out the window.

The boat looked enormous, with three towering black chimneys and a forest of wooden masts. It had an upstairs and a downstairs and she could see people standing on both levels. The paddle wheels looked taller than any building she'd ever seen. Stevedores were busy loading luggage, crates, and even animals onto it. A large black stallion shook its head and refused to walk the plank down into the hold until a dockworker drew a big red bandanna out of his pocket and tied it over the horse's eyes. Olivia gazed at the scene, wondering how she had managed not to notice any of it before, while she was waiting for Mourning.

I have to pay better attention, she thought. *This is the beginning of my new life. My real life. I have to stop worrying about nonsense and remember everything.*

"She's a good vessel. A lake boat." The man showed off his knowledge. "Can't go through the locks of the Canal with that paddle, so she runs from Buffalo to Detroit. You get yourself a cabin, but your boy will be fine on the deck. This time of year it's not so cold."

"How long does it take to get to Detroit?" she asked, though she thought she knew the answer.

"Good two, two and a half days. Longer if they have

to repair machinery or stop more than once to take on coal. They usually let you off in Cleveland for a few hours. You'll take your meals in the dining room, of course, but you best buy your boy some sandwiches before you go aboard. There's always someone selling sandwiches and coffee to the deck passengers, but they charge more than you'll pay here and the coffee's more peas than beans."

"Thank you." Olivia tried to turn away, but the man was determined to be friendly and held out a hand as he said his name.

"Mabel Mears," she responded and offered a weak handshake. "Nice making your acquaintance." She nodded to the stranger before turning to her "boy."

"Come outside," she said, in what even she could hear was a bossy, annoying tone of voice.

"Yes, Miz Mabel, right away." Mourning gave her a look that could wither weeds and shuffled out to the sidewalk.

"So should I get cabins for both of us?" she asked, her voice just above a whisper.

Part of the business agreement they had reached was that he would eventually repay her for his passage, so that decision was up to him.

"They 'llow coloreds to stay in cabins?" he asked uncertainly, no longer sullen.

"I don't know. I can ask. All they can do is say no. If they do allow it, do you want to spend the money?"

"I don't see *you* in no hurry to be freezin' your backside on the deck of that boat," he said. "It gotta be cold at night, middle of all that water."

"Well, Mourning, aren't you used to things like that?" she said and he glared at her as though she were all the white folks in the world. "Well, aren't you?" she said helplessly. "Don't you go giving me that look. It's not my fault you grew up sleeping in lofts and store rooms. Anyway, I didn't say I thought you *should* take deck passage. I asked you if you *wanted* to. It's your eleven dollars."

"Right now look to me it be *our* dollars. I thought we spose to be partners. You the one said she gonna help plow fields and go wash loggers' clothes, she has to. You be spendin' money on bein' a lady, we ain't gonna make it 'round to next summer."

Her jaw fell open when she understood what he was implying – not that he should take a cabin like her, but that *she* should take deck passage like him. She turned her gaze on the boat. It was a warm afternoon and she tried to convince herself that it might be pleasant, lounging in the sun on the deck, with a nice cool breeze off the lake. But she'd had her own room all her life, never slept on the same side of a wall as family or friend, let alone in public, surrounded by strangers, on a hard wooden deck.

"I don't know, Mourning. Maybe we'd both better get cabins. Out on that deck someone could steal all our money while we're sleeping. We wouldn't get any rest at all, having to watch our things. We'd get to Detroit so tired, we'd be in no shape to buy our supplies and make the trip to Fae's Landing that same day. We'd end up wasting even more money on hotel rooms in Detroit."

"Way you got that money tied to you, ain't no one gonna be stealin' nothing, 'less you dead first. Anyway, we can take turns sleepin'. You think you gonna have a nice soft bed waitin' on you in that log cabin? You gonna sleep on good hard Michigan ground. You best be gettin' used to it. You wanna keep to your plan, you gotta get used to bein' poor folks. For a time anyway."

She stared out at the late afternoon sun on the lake and took a deep breath. He had a point. And spending two days on the deck of a steamboat could be her first adventure. Sitting all alone in a cabin would be boring. She'd never thought of it that way, but Mourning was right. By embarking on this journey she had volunteered to live like poor folks. She'd better get used to doing without, making do. But what clinched her

81

decision to sleep on the deck was her desire to wipe the smirk from Mourning's face.

I'll show him. I'm not as spoiled as he tries to make me out to be. Anyway, I'll feel safer with Mourning nearby than I would alone in a cabin.

"All right. We'll both take steerage. I can sleep on a deck every bit as well as you."

She went in to book their passage and then handed her tapestry bag to Mourning, together with his ticket. "You get our cases on board," she said. "I'll go buy food for the trip. The ticket agent said the boat will be stopping in Cleveland, so I'll buy enough for just the first day."

"Wait." He went to the wagon and opened his bag. Take these." He handed her two buckskin pouches. "Ask the folks in the store to fill them."

"Of course, I was just about to ask for them," she lied, angry with herself for having forgotten about water.

"How we gonna find each other on that boat?" he asked.

"I don't know." It seemed to have doubled in size during the course of their conversation. "You pick what you think is a good place – with any kind of privacy or protection from the wind – and wait for me to find you."

She walked a few blocks to a general store and bought bread, butter, a small pot of jam, a few slices of cheese, some salt beef, four hard-boiled eggs, four apples, and two pears. She saw a pump handle out back and received permission to fill the skins from it. It made a heavy load and she trudged down to the wharf. She took tiny steps over the gangplank to the lower deck, handed her ticket to a man in a black jacket and cap, and stepped aboard the *Windsong*.

Shoulders aching, she set her burdens down and looked around. There were all manner of people on the boat. Many looked prosperous – men in suits and top hats and women in flowered prints and bonnets – but more were poor folk in suspenders and ragged homespun. She frowned, not seeing any black faces. Flocks of seagulls cawed overhead and one of them perched on the rail next to her. She had never seen one before and stared into its cold black eyes, thinking it reminded her of a snake. Then she breathed in the fishy smell of the lake and turned to look at Erie, strung out along the shore. *Just look at that city,* she thought. *And the lake. You can't even see the other side!*

She retrieved her bundles and worked her way through crowds of people. It didn't take long to spot Mourning, standing near the back of the boat, in what she had to agree looked like a cozy spot. The upper deck provided a roof and the support beams formed a corner in which he had piled their belongings, defining a small space that was sheltered on two sides from the wind and the spray off the lake. There was only one problem.

"Here you are." She set everything down and smiled uneasily in the direction of the other passengers. Mourning removed his hat and grinned at her while she slid the long rifle under one of the baskets.

She leaned over and whispered in his ear. "Everyone back here is colored." Ten or twelve negroes were busy arranging their belongings in that part of the boat. A few tossed curious glances her way, but most were paying her no mind.

He made a great show of looking surprised. "My goodness, Miz Olivia, you right. My, my, my."

"I don't know if I can stay here," she whispered. "I mean ... maybe ... I might not be allowed."

He rubbed his chin. "Well, if you was to aks real nice ... apologize for not knowin' your rightful place –"

"You know what I mean. Maybe the white ..." She gave up, stood straight-backed, and turned toward him wearing the nastiest look she could muster. Then she leaned over again. "You know, Mourning Free, your natural self is ornery enough. There's no need for all

83

this extra effort. I didn't make the world the way it is and I didn't make your skin black. I'm just trying to get along, same as you. I suppose I'd rather have been born a man, just like you'd rather have been born white –"

"Ain't never said I rather be white." He shook his head. "Ain't never said that."

"Just stop being so ... so ... the way you're being. We're going to have enough problems not of our own making. It isn't any easier for me traveling with you than it is for you traveling with me."

He pursed his lips, looking contrite. "Guess you right 'bout that. This be the only part of the boat they 'llow coloreds, probably cause it be so noisy, right over the engine. But that make it the warmest place, too," he said cheerfully. "Maybe you got to stay in the white part."

She looked around, terrified at the idea of sleeping on the deck all alone. "Well, is there some kind of line, between the white part and the colored part? So I could be on the white side of it and you on the colored?"

"Dunno. Man just told me to come back here."

"Well, we've got to stay together so we can take turns watching our things. But there's no need to call attention to ourselves. I'll go walk around the white part until it gets dark and then put my hood up before I come back here. You keep a space for me."

He nodded.

"But first, let's go over there by the rail and have something to eat. They didn't say you can't walk there, did they? I'm near on starving to death. Here's what I bought." She handed the bags of food over for his inspection.

"All that for one day?" He made a show of collapsing under the weight of the bags. "Good thing you dint buy for a week. Sink this ship down to the bottom of the lake."

They stood on either side of a tall wooden crate that stood by the rail and used it for a table. Olivia tore

84

chunks of bread from a loaf, slapped slices of cheese onto them, and they ate hungrily. Then she looked up and saw two white women approaching them; one of them nudged her friend and nodded at Mourning. Olivia kept her chin high, stared straight at her, and gave her a sweet smile; she was surprised at how quickly the woman looked away.

Now there's a lesson for my new life, she thought. *Being bold may not always help, but it never seems to hurt.*

Soon there was a lot of noise and hustle. Steam was up, the engine chugged, sailors hauled in ropes, and the boat pulled away from the pier with a series of great whooshes. They leaned over the railing and broke into wide smiles.

"Here we go, partner." She held her hand out to him.

He hesitated for a long moment before clasping it in his and repeating, "Partner."

Chapter Ten

Olivia's stare lingered on their clasped hands for a moment; Mourning's was so dark, hers so pale. She must have touched him before, but she couldn't remember when. His skin felt so much warmer than hers and she couldn't stop staring at the physical difference that separated them.

She'd grown up around Quakers and abolitionists and occasionally slipped into the Quakers' Meeting House on Sunday mornings. It was a stark, empty room with wooden benches arranged in a square, facing one another. Whoever wished to speak stood up and did so. Most of what they said made sense to her, especially when they talked about the "colored situation." Even – or perhaps especially – as a child she had understood how appalling it was for one human being to be able to

85

buy and sell another. For her it was pure instinct and not based on a religious belief that all human beings were God's children. Olivia had yet to make up her mind on that score – whether there was such a thing as God. Her father had said all religions were a tub of eyewash. All that Christian mumbo-jumbo was nothing but a trick, so people wouldn't mind dying.

With Mourning for a friend, she knew how ridiculous it was to believe that skin color had anything to do with intelligence or integrity. She thought more highly of Mourning Free than she did of anyone else in town, with the possible exception of Mr. Carmichael. So when people talked about negroes being simple-minded, lazy, and child-like, she silently rolled her eyes. But there was one thing she couldn't argue with – colored people sure did look different. She suddenly noticed Mourning watching the way she was staring at their hands and pulled hers away.

"It ain't gonna rub off," he said with a sneer.

"I wasn't worried it would and you can please stop looking at me like that."

"You think you different from other white folks, but you ain't. You all the same. Think the world belong just to you."

She turned to look him in the face. "I don't think I'm better than you and I don't think I've ever acted like I do." She had begun speaking angrily, but her voice grew softer. "You've got to admit, though, we sure do look different." She put her hand back on the rail next to his, their forearms touching. "Just look at that."

His face relented into a grin.

"I'll tell you one thing," she ventured, cringing in anticipation of an angry response. "I can understand why the first white men who set foot in Africa thought those natives must be something way different from them."

"It ain't but skin."

"Well, I know that. But just imagine a person who'd

never seen black skin or hair like yours before. It sure would seem strange. What if we get off this boat in Michigan and everyone we see is covered with a coat of fur, like a dog, or bark, like a tree? You've got to admit, that would take some getting used to. And I bet those first white folks looked just as strange to the Africans that saw *them*. Maybe those natives would have treated the whites just as badly, if they'd been the ones holding the guns."

Mourning stared out at the shoreline, his face relaxed and expressionless.

"But there's one thing I won't argue with." She lightly nudged his elbow with hers and he glanced over at her. "White folks have sure had enough time to get used to the way colored people look. You'd think by now they'd have stopped saying all the stupid things they do."

They stood together, silently watching Erie grow smaller. The sun was still warm, but the breeze off the lake was cool on their faces. The boat didn't go far out, so the wild green shoreline remained in sight. They were still standing at the rail when the sun set over the water ahead of them. They stood on their tiptoes and stuck their heads out to admire its last blaze of color. Then they both slid down to sit on the deck, backs against the side of the ship.

"You look like a flower growin' out a one of them lily pads," Mourning said, nodding at the way Olivia's skirts billowed around her torso.

"A wilted one. And starving again. Can you reach the food?" she asked

Mourning took out his knife to slice the crusty bread and stopped making fun of her for having bought two whole loaves. They were both famished. He drank from one of the skins of water and passed it to her. Olivia was conscious of waiting until she thought none of the white passengers milling around the deck were looking before she lifted it to her lips to drink.

No reason to antagonize people, she thought, still harboring a fear of being ordered into the white section. Apart from that worry she felt relaxed and at peace, sitting next to Mourning and sharing a meal. Part of her regretted that the trip would take only two days. It was a luxury to be nowhere, no one around who knew her, with nothing to do but stretch her muscles and listen to the sounds of the lake and the steady chug of the engine beneath them.

Then she saw the two snooty white women marching toward her, this time with a man in tow. He freed his arms from their grasp, removed his hat, and bent down to speak to Olivia.

"Is this nigger bothering you, Miss?" he asked.

"No, everything is just fine," she replied with a smile. "He's just serving me my evening meal, but I appreciate your concern."

"Are you sure?" He glanced nervously at the women on either side of him.

"Absolutely sure."

"Well then…"

They went away, the women looking back over their shoulders and muttering something about white trash. Mourning said nothing; he stared at the toe of his shoe, his face a slab of stone.

"I suppose you think I should have said something more to them," she said.

He maintained his silence.

"People like that are a waste of breath. What would an argument accomplish, besides making a scene? I'm trying my best not to draw attention to us. I don't want one of those guys in the black caps coming to tell me that this section is for coloreds and I have to go over there." She nodded in the direction in which the two women and their male companion had disappeared. "I'd be too scared without you."

He turned toward her and shrugged, but she interpreted it as a friendly shrug.

88

"I'm not a fighter, Mourning. I've never wanted to change the world. All I want is to make my own little piece of it as nice as I can. We'll both have a lot more trouble doing that if all the white folks we meet get it into their heads that we're way too friendly for their liking. We're going to need good relations with our neighbors and if telling them you're my hired man – and me bossing you like you are – will keep them from getting all rankled, well so what? It's none of their business anyway. And once you've gotten to know the colored folks in that Backwoods place and you've got your own land –"

"I know." He interrupted her. "I ain't gonna make no argument with you 'bout none a that. Just seem like they need to be a whole lot a people makin' a whole lot a scenes 'fore anything gonna change."

"I'm sure you're right about that." She pressed her aching back against the side of the boat. "But there's more than one way to prove a point. I could go off and march around with those suffragist ladies, shouting and carrying on about how women don't need men taking care of them. Or I can just go ahead and do a good job of taking care of myself. You having your own land and being a better farmer than all the white folks will say a lot more about how smart and hard-working negroes are than a bunch of yelling would."

Once the sun had disappeared, the air turned cold. Before they settled in for the night Olivia took a leisurely walk around the deck, then pulled the hood of her cloak up and tried to stay in shadows as she made her way back to the colored section. She and Mourning put on their winter coats, hats, and gloves, and balled up some of their other clothing to pillow their heads. Then they stretched out head-to-toe, keeping a proper distance, with the water pouches, bag of food, and Mourning's tool case and bag between them.

They could hear other passengers being sick over the rail, but the gentle motion of the boat seemed to

89

agree with both of them. Neither of them felt like talking and Olivia enjoyed silently watching the stars light up the strip of sky that was visible between the rail and the roof. She began eavesdropping on one of the colored couples behind them.

"I don't know how I let you bring us on this perilous, perilous journey," the woman, who was dreadfully seasick, was saying. "I'm a die right here on this cursed boat and that be for the best. Might as well meet my maker here, with my children gathered round me, escape the dangers and tribulations of that wilderness you dragging us to."

Olivia smiled, thinking, *she doesn't mean a word of it. You can hear it in her voice. It's just their way.* Olivia turned her head a bit; one look at the couple confirmed that opinion. The woman's head rested on her husband's chest. He was smiling over the top of it as he held her close, stroking her hair and softly repeating that everything was going to be all right.

It's a sort of playacting, Olivia decided. *She gets to say out loud all the things she's afraid of and the more she complains, the more he gets to show how patient he is and how much he loves her.*

Finally the man spoke. "You know I'm gonna build you a great big house in the woods," he said. "Under the tallest chestnut tree you ever seen. You ain't never gonna do for no one else again. They gonna be a pump right inside the house and you gonna hang them curtains you been saving."

Olivia turned to peek at them again, feeling terribly alone. She couldn't help being jealous of that woman. *Maybe it isn't so awful to have a man who wants to take care of you,* she thought, *even if he does think that gives him the right to boss you now and then. I wouldn't mind having someone hold me like that, make me feel safe. Not if he was a kind and gentle man like that one.* She wondered if Avis ever spoke that way with Mabel. She couldn't imagine it, but Mrs.

Hardaway always said, "No one on the outside ever knows nothing about what goes on between a man and a woman."

Olivia drifted off to sleep, imagining strong arms around her and a soft voice murmuring in her ear. She was startled awake by a colored boy leaning over her, reaching for their bag of food.

"What do you think you're doing?" She batted her arms and he disappeared into the shadows.

Mourning sat up and she told him what had happened. They groped around in the dark, taking count of their belongings. Nothing seemed to be missing. Mourning found some twine in his toolbox and tied each piece of their luggage to one of their limbs. Olivia sat hugging her knees, looking miserable.

"You don't gotta be afeared," Mourning said. "It was only a kid."

"I'm not scared," she said. "I just ... I think maybe I hit him. I mean, I woke up and there he was –"

"So you feelin' bad?" He shook his head in disbelief. "You wanna feel sorry 'bout something, feel sorry you dint hit him harder. Little thief."

"But he was just a little boy trying to take some food. What if he's all alone on this boat and hungry?"

"So he coulda aksed. If he aksed, you woulda gave him some food, right?"

"Well, of course."

"So what he gotta go stealin' for?"

After they were settled back down she lowered her voice to a whisper and asked if he had heard the couple behind them talking.

"Uh-huh," he said.

"He's so nice – the way he talked to his wife. I can't imagine my father ever talking to my mother like that."

"Old Seborn loved your mamma plenty, don't be worryin' 'bout that. I never seen no man cry like him, day he found her."

"What do you mean, 'found her?' Found her

where?" she asked, suddenly shivering with cold.

The air between them seemed to have grown thick.

"Found her where?"

"We gotta get some sleep," he said and turned over.

Olivia would have shaken his shoulder, demanding he tell her, but knew it wouldn't do any good. When Mourning decided to be stubborn, he was good and stubborn.

Never mind, Mourning Free, she thought. *I'm going to have all the time in the world to find out what you meant. I'll pry it out of you with a crowbar if I have to.*

Chapter Eleven

The ship's dressing bell roused Olivia at 4:30 the next morning. She shivered with the damp, untangled herself from the twine and tried to stretch the stiffness from her limbs without disturbing Mourning. He was still asleep, his hat covering his face. She couldn't imagine how she must look and was glad that her mirror was buried in one of the baskets. She ran her fingers through her hair, but didn't bother with her day cap. It was still dark and, anyway, none of these people were ever going to see her again.

When they were planning the trip Mourning had presented her with a homemade leather purse on a belt and said, "You gotta be able to get at some money without havin' to lift up all them skirts and whatever else you got under there." Now she squeezed the soft skin, feeling the coins and assuring herself that no one had robbed her during the night. Then she stood and lifted her arms over her head for a real stretch.

Further up the deck a straggly young man was selling tin cups of coffee out of a battered pot. Olivia smiled, pleased for Mourning to be proven so clever about keeping a small amount of money accessible. He stirred and Olivia turned her back to him, trying to grant him some privacy. She heard him sit up and waited for him to speak before turning around to wish him a good morning.

"I'm going to get a cup of coffee," she said. "Are you ready for one?"

"Guess so." He leaned forward and began untying himself from the baggage.

Olivia soon returned with the coffee and perched on his tool case. They sat in comfortable silence, sipping the hot bitter liquid.

She knew it was a mistake to ask again so soon, but couldn't help herself. "What did you mean last night?" she asked. "What you said about my father finding my mother?"

"Don't know what you talkin' 'bout." He shook his head and gazed out at the lake.

Why was he lying? "You said something about the way he cried when he found her."

"I been real tired last night. Don't know what I said. Listen, if you be needin' the privy, go straight ahead. But I gotta go soon."

"That's all right," she said, blushing. "You go first."

She finished her coffee and tried to smooth her wrinkled clothing and re-comb her hair with her fingers. Then she sat thinking. He must have been referring to the day Seborn found Nola June dead in her bed. Olivia frowned as she calculated. Her mother had died in February 1829 when Olivia was not yet six. Mourning was no more than three years older than her. What on earth would Mourning Free have been doing in the upstairs of their house when he was eight or nine years old? Maybe he'd been bringing in firewood and ran upstairs when he heard a commotion? She shook her head. He would never do that. He wouldn't step up onto the porch of a house belonging to white folks, without being told to do so.

Mourning returned and it was her turn to use the

privy. There was one for men and one for women. Five-holers, so there was no privacy. When she returned they stood by the rail and poured water from a pouch over one another's hands.

Then they took turns strolling about the deck. The sky was clear and she knew the air would warm up, once the sun made its appearance. The man in the black cap and jacket who had taken Olivia's ticket when she boarded tipped his cap to her.

"Morning to you, Miss. See you've gotten your sea legs just fine," he said.

"It's lovely out here on the water," she smiled, knowing it was ridiculous to feel as proud as she did for not being seasick.

"Not always. You're having grand luck with the weather. Last trip I thought sure we was going under. Had to pull into a cove on an island right afore Cleveland. Three days we sat there shivering, hiding from that storm . . ." He went into great detail about the height of the waves and the child who was almost washed overboard, using his hands to illustrate the way the bow of the boat had bobbed forward, as if it were about to dive for the bottom.

When Olivia managed to extricate herself and resumed her stroll, she set her mind on taking in every detail of the enormous steamboat. It was quite a sight. An area of the lower deck had been roped off to serve as a pigpen and a few skinny dogs stood around it yapping. She wondered what made those pigs worth transporting all the way to Michigan. Were there no pigs to be had in Detroit? They were making their usual pig stink, so she didn't stay to wonder for long.

Everyone on the boat seemed to have something to say to anyone willing to listen, each one more expert than the next about Michigan, farming, boats, and the weather. Many of the passengers were ruddy-faced, blonde-haired people whose language made them sound like they were constantly clearing their throat.

Olivia paused to watch two majestic bay horses in their roped off stalls, wishing she had an apple in her pocket. They were beautiful animals, but jittery. Neither of them seemed to have their sea legs. She stroked both of their necks and then, feeling hungry, wandered back to where Mourning was waiting. He had already laid out another grand meal. She went to buy a second cup of coffee for each of them, sat down, and put her face up to the early morning sun, content.

She had expected to come off this boat with exciting tales for her grandchildren – storms, broken-down engines, exploding boilers, fires, or at least a threatening sandbar. But so far it seemed that their trip would be relentlessly uneventful. Later that afternoon the boat docked in Cleveland. They had only an hour to go ashore and buy more food.

Mourning became friendly with the other colored passengers and spent most of the trip exchanging information with them. Though some intended to continue farther west, most were headed for small towns in Michigan. Olivia heard someone mention a nice black community in Backwoods and nodded to Mourning as if to say, "Didn't I tell you so?"

She avoided engaging the white passengers in conversation. Mostly she sat on Mourning's tool case, with a volume of Elizabeth Barrett Browning for company. While they were sharing their evening meal, she once again tried to get Mourning to tell her what he knew about her mother, but he looked so uncomfortable that she let it go.

Once we're settled I'll just have to find a bee tree, she thought. *Make a big batch of Mammo Killion's honey wine. That stuff gets anyone talking.*

On the third morning the passengers began stirring before dawn. Olivia heard someone say they'd be reaching the mouth of the Detroit River in a few hours. By the time Olivia and Mourning had stretched their aching limbs and finished their breakfast, the lake ahead of them had begun to narrow and passengers crowded the rails. Olivia and Mourning managed to squeeze among them – on what she by now knew to call the port side of the boat – and marvel at the shoreline. It was dense with orange and red flowered shrubs of a kind Olivia had never seen.

"That be Canada over to starboard," the colored man standing next to them said.

Olivia stood on her tiptoes and looked behind her, saying, "A whole foreign country, right there! You could throw a stone at it."

"I hear in Detroit they got a ferry, take you over to Windsor," the colored man said. Then he laced his fingers together over the small mound of his belly, looking pleased with himself. "Now let me aks you folks a question. About geogurphy. If a person be going straight south from Detroit, what be the first foreign country he gonna run into?"

"Mexico?" Olivia ventured.

"Nope," said the man. "You wanna guess?" He turned to Mourning.

"Argentina? Ain't that a country down there?"

"Indeed, but that ain't the one he gonna come to. No sir. You go south from Detroit, first foreign country you gonna run into is Canada. Fella showed me on a map." He slapped Mourning on the back and moved away to ask another passenger the same question.

Olivia turned back to the rail and nudged Mourning, saying, "Just look at that," as she nodded at the cluster of islands ahead. "I can't believe how pretty it is here."

The islands were all densely vegetated and they could see a tangle of wild grape vines around the fruit trees. So Uncle Scruggs hadn't been fooling about his paradise. She looked behind her again and saw that there were more islands near the Canadian bank, which also had four windmills strung along it, their white sails tautly swollen.

"Oh, aren't they just the most beautiful things?" she

said and then turned back to the American side. "Oh look, there's one over there too."

"Captain fixin' to turn to the right," Mourning said. "Gonna go 'round that big island up there." She looked ahead and saw the lush island he was nodding at, the east bank of which was a shallow shoal littered with boulders. Mourning continued, "It called Grosse Ile. That mean Big Island in French. Shipping channel go between it and Canada."

"How do you know that?"

"Been talkin' with a fella what lives here. He say everything growin' on that Big Island be wild. Ain't no farmer planted none of it. But look at it, all in straight rows, just like God laid out an orchard. When we get 'bout past it, you gonna see a couple a real small islands. One a them be called Mammy Judy, after an Indian squaw what used to go there to fish. Past it be another one called Fighting Island, 'ccount a the Indians used to make their camp on it, fight the British ships goin' by."

Mourning was obviously proud of knowing so many things about Michigan that Olivia didn't. Olivia smiled back at him, wishing she could squeeze his hand.

"Thank you for coming with me, Mourning," she said softly. "I'm really glad you did. I know we can do this together."

He kept his smile on and nodded. He said nothing, but she thought his eyes shone with a far stronger light of hope and anticipation than even she felt.

The black woman who had been so seasick stood at the rail next to Olivia. Her husband was close behind her, his arms around her, and Olivia again felt a pang of loneliness as she wondered, *What is it about that woman that makes him feel like that? By watching her can I learn how to make someone love me?*

When they neared the northern tip of Fighting Island the ship slowed to veer around a sharp bend to the right and Olivia's mouth fell open. She counted five

97

small steam-driven boats, all festooned with colorful banners. She could read the writing on the one that was coming towards them – *Excursions to Hog Island, Picnic Lunch Included*. Farther up the river were schooners of different sizes, sails taut in the wind, flying under brightly colored flags and coats of arms. Rafts, barges, and fishing boats bobbed among them, as did dug-out canoes, with and without sails.

"You'd think they'd all be crashing into one another," she said in a whisper. "Isn't it beautiful? So romantic. Especially those sailboats. It looks like they're having a party, dancing around each other on the water."

"Water by the port been just as crowded in Erie. Cleveland too," Mourning said, sounding a bit puzzled. "Had plenty a sails too. You ain't said nothing 'bout them being so beautiful."

"I guess I wasn't paying much attention. Or here the river makes it so much more ... I don't know." She stopped and stared, unable to say out loud what she was feeling – that this was the place she was meant to be. She felt ridiculous even thinking it.

When she glanced up at Mourning his smile had grown wider. Again she wished she could touch him, just in a friendly manner. This was a moment she wanted to share.

"Maybe you like it so much cause this gonna be *our* city," he said. "We gonna come here a lot."

"Yes, that's right. It's not far from here to the farm."

"See that marsh over there." Mourning pointed to the shoreline. "That really a river. River Rouge. We gonna be comin' on Detroit now, lickety-split."

They passed a grimy cluster of grist mills, saw mills, tanneries, and small factories, but when Olivia looked past those, the city in the distance was beautiful. A pair of spires towered through the tree tops and a tin cupola glinted in the sun. When they drew near the railroad yard Olivia's jaw dropped again.

98

"Jesus, Mary, and Joseph," she whispered. "Just look at it."

Wharves well over 100 feet long jutted into the water and armies of stevedores were unloading the cargo ships at the docks into an endless row of warehouses. Between the warehouses Olivia glimpsed several sets of tracks and beyond them was a city of tall silos, mile-high stacks of crates, piles of lumber, and vats of oil.

"I never imagined anything like this," she said. "This is so ... so much."

She blinked as a lilting voice called out. "*Bonjour! Bienvenue!*" Olivia looked down and saw an enormous canoe, crammed with ten or twelve pairs of oarsmen. None of their colorful shirts matched, but their headwear was identical – bright red caps with long pointed tops that folded over and ended in a tassel, like a sleeping cap or the hat of an elf in a children's book of fairy tales. Every inch of space between them was piled high with huge bundles of furs.

"They must be some a them French voyageurs I heard about," Mourning said. "Take the trappers out and bring their furs back. This Michigan got rivers what take you just about anywhere."

As the canoe passed within a few yards of the ship, the man standing in the bow grinned up at Olivia, tore his hat off, clutched it to his heart, and called out, "*Quelle jolie fille . . . une vraie beaute. J'ai le coeur qui flanche ma belle.*"

Olivia blushed, not knowing enough French to understand what he was saying, but enough to think it was something sappy. As they whooshed past, the man turned and sang, "*Il y a lontemps que je t'aime, jamais je ne t'oublierai . . .*"

The other men in the canoe laughed and loudly joined in the song. A few lowered their paddles and turned back toward the steamboat, smiling, waving, and calling welcomes until they were out of sight.

"Guess you been right 'bout romantic," Mourning teased. "That fella like you pretty good."

"My troubles are over. Love has found me."

Soon the busy port came into sight and the man in the black cap walked past, announcing that they were ready to dock. Olivia wasn't happy to have arrived. The cold hard deck had become familiar and she was terrified of plunging into those crowds of people down on the docks. All those statistics she'd read to Mourning, attesting to Detroit's burgeoning population, had been only numbers on a page; she'd still expected to arrive at a frontier town – hovels of sticks and wattle, a cluster of log cabins, maybe a few homes built of fieldstone – not this enormous city strung along the shore.

Neither did Mourning seem anxious to disembark. They remained at the rail while the boat emptied around them. The wharves were a madhouse, the road behind them clogged with large wagons and dozens of funny one-horse buggies, most of them with only two wheels. These makeshift vehicles had a place for only the driver to sit; one or two passengers perched on a small ramp behind him, clutching the back of the seat.

"Well," Olivia said at last, "I guess if we're going to buy a wagon ... Mourning, look at that! There's an Indian down there." She pointed at a man with long black hair adorned with feathers.

"They won't do you no harm, Miss." The man in the black cap spoke from behind her. "They been living here forever. Started with the French letting 'em put up their village outside the old fort. Heard one of 'em bought one of the old French ribbon farms."

Olivia chatted with him for a short while and then turned to Mourning. "Should I stay here and watch our things while you go look for a wagon? Or do you want me to come with you?"

He looked down at the crowds on the wharf. "Can't see what help you gonna be to me."

The deck around them was empty. Mourning had made a stack of his tool box and her wicker baskets and Olivia squatted behind it to reach under her skirts for money. She stealthily pressed the coins into Mourning's palm, afraid of anyone seeing a flash of gold before he slipped them into his pockets.

"How much you give me?" he whispered.

"A hundred and fifty dollars."

They had agreed that he would try to get a team for $80, but go as high as $100, and try to get a wagon for $30, but go as high as $45. He slung one of the water pouches over his shoulder and turned to leave.

"Don't you want to eat something before you go?"

"Ain't hungry," he said and plopped his wide-brimmed felt hat onto his head.

"At least take some fruit."

She bent down for two apples and two pears, which he shoved into his pockets. Then she watched him tromp down the gangplank, praying he wouldn't be abducted or robbed the moment his feet hit the road. He didn't look back and was soon swallowed up in the general chaos. Olivia leaned against the rail, prepared for a long wait and trying not to fret about the disasters that might befall Mourning. The man in the black jacket came near again and she asked him some questions about the city.

"Tell ya, Miss, I ain't all that familiar with the business establishments. Know my way to the United States Hotel and the tavern right near it and that's about all I got need of. But I can tell you where the main streets are at. The one you see right there, running along the river, that's Atwater. Next street up is Jefferson Avenue. They probably got them kind of stores you're looking for on them."

"It looks like a real city," she said, disappointed to find Detroit so civilized. She had never seen so many brick buildings and even spotted a red and white striped barber's pole.

"Oh yeah, Michigan got settled real quick, once they opened up that Erie Canal. Half of New York and New England came pouring out here. Not to mention all them folks what don't even speak English. Couldn't put enough boats in the water. I hear they even got a new university some ways west of here. And farther past that they're building a state prison. Now there's a sure sign that civilization has arrived."

Chapter Twelve

Mourning wasn't gone nearly as long as she'd expected. She was looking idly over the rail and there he was, halfway up the gangplank, waving his hat and hollering.

"Come on down here," he called.

"Okay, I'm coming. Just a minute."

Feeling disoriented and afraid, she hurriedly checked that the fastenings were clamped tight on her baskets and Mourning's tool case. The man in the black jacket was standing near the gangplank and she asked him to keep an eye on their things.

"Come on, come on." Mourning proudly led her ashore. A wagon and a team of oxen, one black and one an orange-brown color, stood near the gangplank. "Meet Dixby and Dougan."

Olivia smiled. Mourning had named the animals after Five Rocks' Congregational and Episcopalian ministers, whom he'd always said were the most miserly of the people he worked for.

"Which one is this?" She patted the black one on his warm broad nose and received a friendly nod of his head.

"That be Dixby."

"Well, hullo Dixby," she said. As she walked around to survey the wagon, she let her hand run over Dougan's orange flank, so he wouldn't feel neglected.

"How'd you get them so fast?"

"I go in the first grain store I pass and right there be this desperate fellow, downright beggin' the owner to take 'em off his hands. Both the wagon and the team. But that storeowner, he don't want 'em. Say he just bought a team and wagon off someone else goin' back east."

"Maybe there's something wrong with them," she said as she walked around again.

"No, they ain't no nothing wrong. I checked 'em over. Them animals healthy and the wagon be in fine shape. Brakes even got skid shoes," he said. The irritation in his voice made her feel bad for not having shown more appreciation.

She gave him a smile, pranced around the wagon, and climbed up onto it. "Oh Mourning, it's wonderful. Just look at this nice red cushion on the seat. It's perfect. Where'd all that stuff come from?" In the wagon bed behind her were sacks of feed and seed, some iron tools, a large washtub, and some pots and pans.

"The feed and washtub come with the wagon. Rest I bought with part a the money what was left."

"You had that much left over? What did you pay for the wagon?"

"Ninety dollars. Not for the wagon. For the wagon *and* the team."

"Only ninety dollars! Mourning, you're a genius! You see! A lucky beginning like this is a sure sign that everything's going to be all right!" Then she lowered her voice and asked, "Did you have any problems?"

"That white man took them gold coins out a my colored hand just fine."

"See! Didn't I tell you Michigan is a grand place?"

She silently thanked God for Mourning, imagining how awful it would have been to arrive here alone. How on earth would she have found some stranger to hire? Even if she did, anyone but Mourning could have walked off with her money and disappeared. Or claimed to have paid much more for the wagon and pocketed the difference.

"Well, let's get going." Olivia's energy returned and she hurried back up the gangplank to help Mourning haul their things down. On their last trip back to the wagon she stopped to thank the man in the black jacket and impulsively planted a kiss on his cheek. "I'm going to have my own farm," she informed him, beaming proudly.

"Better you than me," he called after her with a grin.

"I already been in a few stores," Mourning said, after they finished loading their cases onto the wagon. "I seen a big difference in prices, so we gotta go 'round a few times. I been in four different stores 'fore I bought that stuff." He nodded at the back of the wagon.

So that was how they spent a long and tedious day. Atwater was the only street that had been paved with stone, so they were glad for the red cushion on the seat. A few streets were strewn with a haphazard covering of thin rounds of cedar, but when Olivia commented to one of the storekeepers on how pretty they were, he spat into a barrel and said. "Them dang things ain't no use at all. Make it bumpier when it's dry and first good rain, they up and float away."

Between checking their purchases against their lists, keeping track of the different prices as they went from store to store, and fretting about the trip ahead of them and how on earth they were going to find one tiny little cabin in all those woods out there, the day passed in a blur. They had a few arguments, as when Olivia emerged from a store and called Mourning in to carry two mattresses out to the wagon. He looked at her as if she'd gone loony.

"Mattresses! We don't got to be buyin' no mattresses. We get some canvas, sew it over double, fill it with hay."

"Really? Exactly where do you think you're going to

get hay out there?" She could tell from the look on his face that he hadn't thought of that. They both found it hard to fully comprehend – they were headed for a new home where one had to assume there was *nothing*. None of the things a person normally takes for granted.

"So we use grass or weeds. Leaves maybe."

"Look, I know you think I'm a spoiled child, but we won't be able to work very hard if we can't get a good night's sleep. I don't think two store-bought mattresses are such a great extravagance."

"Your money." He shrugged and followed her in to get them. He made no comment when she added two comforters to their purchases. She chose faded used ones and tried to hold her head at an angle that dared him to object, though she didn't see how he could. What would he suggest, that they bury themselves in leaves to keep warm? Or cuddle up between Dixby and Dougan?

When she came out of another store carrying a new broom with neatly trimmed bristles, he shook his head. "You know how long it take me to make you a splint broom? 'Bout five minutes. Know how much it cost? 'Bout nothing." Olivia raised her index finger to her pursed lips and tossed the broom into the back of the wagon.

When they were done shopping they sat on the wagon seat, gnawing on bread and jerky and no longer irritable. Olivia watched the people who passed them in the street. To her disappointment none of them looked like gunslingers or bank robbers. Apart from a pair of rough-looking, fur-bearing trappers, they looked far too much like the law-abiding, church-going folks of Five Rocks. They encountered no more Indians that day, though she was pleased to see a number of black faces.

"We best get going," Mourning said, wiping his hands on his pants. "Fella in the store said we gotta turn onto that big wide street where we seen that building with the silver dome and go till we come to a square what got some grass on it. That where we gotta turn left onto the Chicago Road. He dint remember if it got a sign on it or not and if it got one, it might not say Chicago. It might say the new name – Michigan Avenue. You got your map from your uncle's will?"

"Yes." Olivia leaned over the back of the seat to lift the lid of one of her wicker baskets and remove her precious envelope. "Yes, here it is, the Chicago Road, right here." She held it out to Mourning with her finger on it. "So we're all right? You know the way?"

He nodded. "We be all right. Don't matter none if we get lost no how. 'Mount a shopping you done, we could survive in the woods for a year or two. Feed a lot a the forest critters too."

"Are you ever going to stop griping about me buying that loaf of sugar? I'll be glad to fix your coffee bitter if you want."

Their bickering was good-natured. Everything was going well. There was only one thing left to do. Follow Uncle Scruggs' map.

Before they turned onto the Chicago Road, Olivia put her hand on Mourning's forearm. "Look at that, Mourning." She pointed at a three-story building of yellow brick. "Detroit Female Seminary," she read the sign. "That whole big building, just for girls. Maybe after we get rich I can go to school here."

"That ain't all they got in Detroit." He grinned. "This morning I been in the Black Second Baptist church. Whole congregation of coloreds, part freed slaves, part people what was born free. They got a school in there too. Haw Dixby, Haw Dougan," he commanded the team and turned onto the Chicago road. "You been right 'bout this city, Livia. They got colored dock workers and servants and all, like you gonna expect, but they also got a colored barber and I seen white customers sittin' in his chairs. They got coloreds what owns all kinds a stores and white folks goin' in and buyin' from 'em, like that ain't no thing. Even got a

106

colored saloon where white folks go to gamble."

Olivia smiled. "So I guess you're going to feel comfortable here."

"That ain't all. They got a colored doctor what treats white people and a colored man what bought hisself a steamship. Hadda hire hisself a white captain, cause they don't wanna give him a license, but it still be his boat."

Olivia kept a smile on her face, though she knew there were plenty of white people in Detroit – even abolitionists – who didn't like having negroes around. While waiting for Mourning to come out of one of the stores, she had picked up someone's discarded newspaper. An article on the front page called free colored people the "unwanted debris of an unfortunate and undesirable institution." It said even Thomas Jefferson had advocated shipping all the coloreds away, to Haiti or Liberia. Jefferson had suggested that the American government sell the land that had been taken from the Indians to pay for transporting "the whole annual issue" of black children to some far off place. The "old stock" should be allowed to die off in the ordinary course of nature. But at least, if Mourning's impressions were correct, white people in Detroit were not inclined to harm coloreds.

Ahead of them Olivia could see where the buildings ended and the woods began and suddenly felt reluctant to leave the city limits. "Maybe we should go back to one of those hotels and wait until morning to start out," she said. "It'll be dark soon."

"Best to travel at night," Mourning said. "Cooler it be, better it be for the oxen."

"Well, let's stay anyway," she said. "How much can hotel rooms cost? Tomorrow morning we could even take one of those ferries over to Windsor, see what Canada's like."

"Nah. We best be gettin' where we goin'. We don't wanna leave this load in the wagon more than we gotta.

We be comin' back to Detroit soon enough. Once we settled in, know how we gonna keep ourselves alive, we can go spend a day over in Canada. Go down *south* to Canada." He smiled.

"All right." She looked away from him. "I don't know why I'm being such a big baby. Scared of getting lost in the dark."

"Good to be scared," he said. "Make you careful. But we got lanterns and we got oil and we got guns and a wild lady here what knows how to shoot 'em. Remember the question you been aksing me all the time – What's the worst that can happen? Worst that can happen, we drive around in circles for a few days."

"When are you going to teach me to drive?"

"Not today. Gotta teach myself first. Empty wagon be hard enough. Heavy load like this, when we gotta go down hills, them brakes – even with the skids on – ain't nothing against all that weight pushin' on 'em."

"Oh." She turned to look at the load in the back, imagining them going down a steep hill and the wagon crashing over poor Dixby and Dougan, flattening them into orange and black smudges on the trail. "I thought it was only hard going up hills," she said. "I never thought about going down them."

"Stop worrying." He looked over at Olivia. "Thanks to you bein' such a spoiled little girl, we got better beds right here with us than what they gonna give you in any hotel. We got everything. A whole life in a wagon. No clouds in the sky neither."

When they were outside the city limits he stopped to fill a lantern with whale oil and hung it on the hook of the wagon post, ready to light. Now she became acutely aware of how alone they were together. Apart from the rustlings of small animals, the only sound was the soft clop of hooves on hard-packed dirt. They saw no one on the side of the road and no other wagons passed them. Neither of them spoke for a long while.

As long as rays of daylight still slanted through the

branches, Olivia could admire the beech, maple, basswood, oak, and hickory trees. Uncle Scruggs was right about that too. The woods towered to the sky and they *were* so green it hurt to look at them. The ground was thick with ferns, berries, and wild grapevines. But since the sun had set, all she saw out there was dark and darker dark. When Mourning stopped again to light the lantern Olivia felt even more isolated, the two of them trapped in a tiny circle of light.

Mourning cleared his throat and made an effort to fill the silence. "They say the land 'round here be real good," he said. "Black and rich. It be mostly clay bottom, so you gotta ditch it to drain the water off. They say you gotta look for a sandy spot, if you be wantin' to build, cause that clay ain't much to be livin' over in wet weather."

Olivia could think of nothing to say. Her whole body ached and all she wanted was to sleep.

"That what the man in the feed store say." He rambled on, sounding as ill-at-ease to be alone together as she felt. "Land be rich as a barnyard, level as a floor, and no stones to clear away. The more you farm it, the more the clay be gettin' worked up into the soil and the better wheat it raise. So I guess my main job gonna be cutting trees. Corn ain't gonna ear in the shade."

"How can you see where we're going?" She peered nervously ahead of them.

"I ain't tryin' to get at look at them monsters over there, hidin' behind all them trees," he teased. "All I gotta worry about is where these animals gonna put their foot down next. I got plenty a light for that. You gotta stop worryin' five steps ahead, Livia. All we gotta do is stay on this road till we get to the turn to this Fae's Landing place. I figure that take us four, five hours. That where we gonna set us down to sleep. Come morning, there be light to see the trail and they ain't gonna be no more bogeymen out there. We gonna find our way all right."

"Sleep on the trail? We can't just lie down on the ground."

"Say who? Course we can."

"What if there are snakes?"

"They don't bother us, we don't bother them. You wanna be 'fraid in the dark, they plenty a things scarier than a poor old snake. 'Sides, what you think you gonna sleep on tomorrow night at your uncle's place? Ain't gonna be no one waitin' to turn down no bed for you."

She sighed in concession. Of course he was right. She turned in her seat to check that the loaded Hawken rifle and her possibles bag were still there, right behind her. They rode in silence for a while longer and then, bored, Olivia asked if she couldn't drive for a while.

"What for? I ain't tired."

"I've got to learn sometime, so it might as well be now. In all the known world, there can't be a flatter road than this one. It doesn't look to me like there's a hill in the whole entire state of Michigan."

"This wagon be almost brand new. I gotta break it in."

"That's a tub of eyewash, Mourning Free."

"What you know 'bout wagons? You ever work at the livery? Spoke a wheel? Set an axle?"

"You just don't want me to drive, do you? Ever. You think this is *your* wagon."

"Someone come round that bend on a wild horse, you ain't gonna know what to do."

"Oh, sorry, I forgot about all the wild horses we've been passing every five minutes."

Olivia let the argument dissipate into the dark, not having been all that eager to drive. In low places they bounced over logs that someone had placed across the road. In some spots the logs lay lengthwise and Olivia worried the wagon wheels would get stuck between them, but Dixby and Dougan kept plodding right along.

They had been riding in silence for a long while when she reluctantly said, "Mourning, you've got to

110

stop for me." She had been holding it in for longer than seemed possible.

He said a gentle "Whoa" and sat ramrod, looking straight ahead. She wasn't about to venture into those dark woods to lift her skirt and so walked about fifty paces back down the road, past the last bend they had rounded. She had foreseen this necessity and was wearing no drawers. All she had to do was plant her feet wide apart and lift her skirts above her knees. The stream of urine hitting the ground made the loudest noise she had ever heard and her cheeks grew hot with embarrassment. *You'd better get used to this too*, she scolded.

When she retraced her steps around the bend Mourning was having a conversation with Dixby and Dougan, while they took turns drinking from a bucket. Olivia climbed back onto the wagon and Mourning joined her. After he settled himself he handed her the reins.

"These animals been trained real good. All you gotta do is talk to them," he said.

They drove on in silence and nearly missed the wooden sign in the dark. Mourning shouted "Whoa" and climbed down to read it by the lantern light. An arrow was carved into it, beside the words "Fae's Landing 3 Miles."

"Oh that's grand, we're almost there," Olivia said.

"We best stop here, lay them mattresses down in that clearing. We never gonna find old Lorenzo's cabin in the dark." He took hold of the team's harness and led them off the road.

"But it's only three miles."

"To the town, not your farm. To your farm we gotta follow a trail, not a road. And 'ccordin' to your map we gotta cross some water. I ain't doin' that in the dark."

He unyoked and hobbled the oxen and gave them feed and more water. Olivia untied the ropes Mourning had wound over their belongings and began moving things around in the bed of the wagon.

"What you doin'?" Mourning asked.

"Making it so I can lay my mattress up here, on top of all this stuff," she said. "I can't sleep down there on the ground. It's too dark. Too many things creeping around. Don't worry, I'll put it back like it was."

"Pioneer lady." He shook his head, but at least he was smiling indulgently, not smirking.

He disappeared between the trees and came back carrying an armload of dry kindling. "This ..." He raised it a bit higher, "gonna be your job from now on," he said amiably and tossed it to the ground. Olivia used their new hoe to clear a patch of dirt in the middle of the road, arranged the kindling, and struck one of their precious matches.

Mourning watched her and said, "Once we settled, we ain't gonna use up our lucifers like that. I show you how to find some good punk wood and use a flint."

She nodded and stood up. "I'll go look for some thicker branches," she said, but hesitated at the tree line.

Mourning strode over to her and touched her elbow. "You go pick some a that lemon grass I seen growing back there by the sign, make us some tea. I get the wood. Them bogeymen in there be ascared of colored boys. Can't see us in the dark. Gonna think I be a ghost." He made a low wooooing sound as he went into the woods.

Olivia smiled after him and retrieved their bag of food from the wagon. By the time Mourning returned with the wood she had broken some green branches from a tree and peeled enough bark away to make a clean fork to toast bread on.

"Cheese, jerky, or jam?" she asked.

"That blackberry jam sit good with me."

"Would you care for some sugar in your tea, Sir?" she asked. "We happen to have a fresh loaf, and I'd be happy to nip some off for you."

The food and tea tasted delicious and she was pleased to find herself comfortable with Mourning, no need to talk all the time. He had lowered himself to the ground and rested his back against one of the wagon wheels. Olivia perched on an overturned bucket. She kept her eyes on the ground as she ate, feeling him study her face in the firelight. She didn't mind, but would have loved to know what he was thinking. She hoped it was something like: "This white girl ain't so bad to be with." She stood, brushed the crumbs from her hands, and announced that she was ready to go to sleep. She climbed into the back of the wagon and stretched out on her lopsided mattress.

"I hear Michigan snakes win all the wagon climbin' contests." Mourning made slithering motions with his hands.

"Hush."

"They weave their way through them spokes, slither right up the side. Lookin' for something soft to curl up on."

"Be quiet, Mourning. Are you going to put the fire out?"

"Nah," he said as he tossed his mattress to the ground next to the wagon. "Ain't no wind and you been smart, puttin' it smack in the middle of the road so we ain't gonna start no forest fire."

She lay in the dark and cursed herself for not having gone to answer nature's call before climbing up there. She dreaded the thought of putting her feet over the side of the wagon to get down in the dark. When Olivia was a little girl Avis had tormented her with tales of the scaly old man who lived under her bed and, every night when the lantern was extinguished, slithered out from between the floorboards. "You watch out when you get in bed, Olivia," Avis would say. "He'll grab you by the ankle, pull you under there with him." Even now that she was grown-up, she had to resist the impulse to take a running leap to her bed.

She peeked over the side of the wagon and saw Mourning sprawled on his mattress, already dead to the world. She leaned farther out and squinted at him, feeling like a thief for stealing his privacy, but unable to resist the opportunity to study his face, shiny in the moonlight. He looked so peaceful.

"Hullo neighbors," a man's voice called out.

Startled and heart thumping, Olivia almost fell over the side of the wagon as she scrambled for the Hawken. Clutching it, she peered into the dark.

"Hullo," the voice said again.

She could see the outline of a man, standing in the middle of the road, about twenty paces away. He had both hands raised shoulder-high, one of them holding a rifle by its butt, with the barrel pointing at the ground.

Chapter Thirteen

"Hullo," Olivia answered. She glanced at Mourning, expecting him to spark back to life, but he emitted a soft snore.

"My name's Jeremy Kincaid. I live not far from here. I'm going to come a little closer," he said.

He took a few steps and she could see that he was tall and thin and wore baggy gray pants. A few more steps showed him to be unshaven and scruffy, with a floppy hat shoved back on the crown of his head.

He halted and she said, "I'm Olivia. Olivia Killion. Pleasure to meet you. If you live near here, I guess we're going to be neighbors."

"Oh? Where are you headed?" Jeremy asked.

"A farm west of Fae's Landing. It used to belong to my uncle, but it's been abandoned for quite a few years."

"The Scruggs place?"

"Yes." She brightened. "Did you know my Uncle Lorenzo?"

"No, he's from way before my time, but I know the cabin. Trappers and hunters use it to grab a kip. Leave it right manky, sorry to tell you. It's about seven-eight miles from my place. So it does look like we will be neighbors."

The cloud that had been veiling the moon drifted away and silvery light washed over Jeremy Kincaid's features. Though somewhat pale and not particularly striking, it was a pleasant enough face, nicely proportioned. He had what Olivia thought of as a snooty-type nose, long and flaring at the end into a soft wide V, the nostrils forming a pair of butterfly wings. Bits of what she thought could only be plant matter clung to his hat and shoulders, as if he had been rolling in the undergrowth. Olivia smiled and set her rifle down, resisting the impulse to smooth her hair.

"Does your husband plan to farm?" he asked.

"Oh, I'm not married. But I've got a hired man who's going to farm my land for me."

She pulled on her work shoes, slid over the mattress to the ladder on the side of the wagon, and climbed down. "That's him right there." She nodded at Mourning's sleeping figure.

"Mourning," she said, bending down toward him. He emitted a grumpy noise and rolled over, away from her voice. She lightly nudged his foot with hers. "Mourning, don't you want to get up and meet our new neighbor?"

"Do you think it will be easier to rouse him if you tell him it's morning?" Jeremy asked as he rested his rifle against the wagon and removed the water skin and possibles bag he wore strapped to his back.

It took her a moment to understand the question. "Oh, no, that's his name. Mourning."

"And does he have siblings named Afternoon and Night?"

"It's m-o-u – like grieving. It's a long story." She nudged Mourning's foot again.

"Perhaps we'd best leave him to his kip," Jeremy said.

"Oh, I'm sure he'd be sorry not to make your acquaintance."

"What?" Mourning stirred and blinked himself awake.

"I apologize for disturbing you, but I wanted you to meet our new neighbor," Olivia said.

Mourning got to his feet and shook himself.

"Mourning Free this is Jeremy ... Kincaid was it?"

Jeremy nodded and offered his hand to Mourning. Olivia was happy to note that he did so more naturally than most white men took the hand of a colored.

"Nice to meet you, Mr. Kincaid."

"Pleasure is mine. It will be good to have someone living in the old Scruggs place."

"Jeremy lives close by," Olivia said. "He can tell us how to get there."

"That be a help." Mourning stretched and lit the lantern. "I'm a get the fire stirred up. Heat us a pot a coffee."

"Sounds good to me," Jeremy said as he walked past the wagon to inspect the hobbled oxen. "Looks like a good strong team you've got."

"Indeed," Mourning said. He turned over a bucket and nodded at it. "You can set yourself on that."

Jeremy stooped to pick up a long stick, then sat on the bucket and scratched lines in the dirt. Olivia watched him, feeling blessed by their good luck: the uneventful trip on the steamer, the ease with which Mourning had found the wagon and team, and now this new friend miraculously appearing to help them find their way. Their meeting in the woods was providential. A sign. This was right. This was what she was supposed to do. People were allowed to change their fate; they were even rewarded for doing so. Jeremy felt like a gift.

"You're here," Jeremy pronounced, tapping the stick on the ground. Olivia and Mourning stepped to either side of him to study the little map he had drawn. "Turn the way the sign points and go about two-three miles until you come to a river. Fae's Landing is on the other side of it. You need to go into town for anything?"

"Nah," Mourning replied. "Miz Killion here know how to shop like nobody else. Thanks to her, we got ever thing anyone ever thought a wantin' right there in that wagon. Farming don't work out, she can open herself a general store. Directions the only thing we need, and if you be givin' us them, we can go straight to Miz Killion's land."

Olivia's eyes darted to Mourning on the second "Miz Killion," but she detected no rancor in his voice. He was doing as they had agreed – playing the part of hired man.

Jeremy gave them detailed directions for reaching the cabin. "That's the easiest way to get there with a wagon," he said, "even though it means crossing water twice."

Olivia took a few steps to where she could study Jeremy's features in the firelight, but couldn't guess how old he was. She did notice the glints of orange-red in his hair and how straight and white his teeth were.

"You be a trapper?" Mourning asked. The fire had come back to life and Mourning found the coffee pot and filled it with water.

"No."

"Farmer?"

"No, never have liked digging in the dirt." Jeremy rose and motioned with his hand. "Never mind the coffee. I should leave you to your night's sleep." He put his hat back on and reached for his water skin. "I'll stop by in a few days time, see how you're settling in. You have other neighbors a few miles southeast of you – Filmore and Iola Stubblefield. Good, church-going folk. Farmers. I'm sure they'll be glad to help you out in whatever way they can."

"Any colored folk 'round here?" Mourning asked.

117

Jeremy shook his head. "Quite a few in Detroit. More across the river in Windsor. But there aren't any colored families in Fae's Landing. Aren't all that many white ones. It's not much of a town." He slipped the straps of the water pouch and possibles bag over his shoulders and picked up his rifle.

"Why is it called Fae's Landing?" Olivia asked, knowing it was a stupid thing to ask in the middle of the night, but reluctant to let him go.

Jeremy set the butt of his rifle on the ground and leaned on it. "It's named for a little baby called Fae. Her mamma birthed her right there on the raft they use to ferry folks 'cross the river. Then a few months later Baby Fae died of the pox and the town they were building – where that raft is tied up – got named after her." He picked up his rifle. "You have a good night. Mind yourself."

"We'll be glad to have you come visit," Olivia said.

"I'll do that."

"We'll be looking to rent out the oxen, if you're interested."

"Got no use for them, but I appreciate the offer." He took a few more steps, turned to wave a hand, and disappeared into the dark.

Mourning waited a moment before letting out a loud snort. "All you hadda do was aks, Livia, I'da tied him to the wagon wheel for you," he said.

She felt her face turn red. "I suppose I'm not allowed to be friendly. Or try to find out anything about this place we're going to."

"You want I should call him back so you can aks what the Sunday sermon been about last week? You forgot to ask him that."

"You can be a trying person, Mourning Free. A most trying person. Anyway, you were the one who started asking questions," she said as she scrambled back onto her mattress. "Good night."

118

Chapter Fourteen

"That gotta be Fae's Landing over there on the other side," Mourning said the next day when the road brought them to a narrow, swiftly flowing river. "And that be poor little Fae's raft." He pointed at the rack of decaying wooden slats that bobbed in the water.

A mill stood on the opposite bank, but there was no buzz of saws or smell of freshly cut lumber. Olivia stood up and craned her neck, looking for someone to call out to. "The whole place looks deserted," she said, sitting back down.

"Maybe they all late risers. Or maybe they havin' a town meeting or somethin'."

"Hmm." She kept straining to look behind her as Mourning drove on.

The road followed the river and soon narrowed into a grassy trail that was just wide enough to accommodate the wagon. They couldn't always see the water through the trees, but they could hear it. Not far downriver the woods thinned and they glimpsed an equally silent gristmill.

"You'd think there'd be somebody about," she said, ducking a branch.

"That fellow said it ain't much of a town."

"Even so."

Soon they were facing the river and a large clearing, with open space and gently sloping banks on both sides of the water. Here the river was twice as wide, but looked shallow enough to cross.

"This must be the place he was talking about," Olivia said. "I think I see a trail over there." She squinted into the sun, scrutinizing the buffalo grass waving on the other side.

"We best get out of the wagon," Mourning said. "It be easy enough for the team goin' down, but gettin' up that other side ... We maybe gotta take some things out and carry 'em over. But first we give it a try."

They climbed down and removed their shoes and stockings. Olivia tossed hers into the back of the wagon, but Mourning shook his head and told her to put her stockings in her pocket and tie her shoelaces to something. She was glad that while Mourning was still asleep she had changed out of her heavy traveling clothes and petticoats, into a plain green work dress with a green and white striped apron over it. She hitched up her skirts and stepped in.

"Uncle Scruggs wasn't kidding about this water being ice cold."

Mourning waded in a few steps, leading the oxen by the yoke and making no attempt to keep his pant legs dry. The team willingly followed him and he shouted to Olivia, "You grab the wagon and hold on. River can fool you. Watch out for holes."

She obeyed. The swift current sparkled over slippery stones and she would have fallen on her backside had she not been holding on tight.

"We gotta wait up," Mourning said, raising a hand. "They thirsty."

The oxen were straining to lower their heads and Mourning freed them, allowing them to drink. Then he put them back in harness and gave Dixby a friendly slap on the rear as he yelled, "Hyahhhhh!" Olivia's arm jerked forward and she struggled to keep up with the wagon as the team charged into the water, which was soon almost waist-deep. The smooth bottom turned to squishy mud studded with sharp rocks that scraped and stubbed her feet.

"Whoa, whoa, now." When they'd made it up the other bank Mourning pulled the team short and stroked their heads. "You boys done one fine job. Guess you earned your breakfast."

Olivia had heard a splash and – once she regained her balance – turned to look behind them. The washtub had escaped Mourning's web of ropes and fallen off the wagon. Luckily the current had lodged it between some large rocks slightly downriver and Olivia slogged back into the water to retrieve it before it was carried it off. Without the wagon to hold on to, she took tiny steps and held her arms out for balance. The tub had a wooden handle at either end and as she reached out to grab one of them, she lost her balance. She didn't fall, however. Mourning had plunged in behind her and was there to steady her. As they waded back to shore she was overcome with gratitude for this small kindness.

She was also disturbed by her reaction. *I'm so pathetic,* she thought. *Other people must do things like that for each other all the time, without giving it a thought. That's what it's like to have a friend. Not silly schoolgirls giggling and being nasty to the girls they don't let into their snotty little group, or housewives gossiping about other women. Those aren't friends. A friend looks out for you. Holds out a hand, without being asked. Poor Mourning picked a great person to be friends with. I always feel sorry for myself because I never had a friend, but I've never been one either. I don't think I know how.*

Mourning tossed the tub back onto the wagon and, after tending to Dougan and Dixby, they sat on flat white stones with their feet in the river, wiggling their toes. Everything about the day was beautiful – the warm sun, the rush of the cool water, the breeze in the treetops. Olivia shook her wet skirt in the sun and watched the sun glint off the water.

"Listen to all the birds! I love Michigan already."

Mourning had his eyes closed, face tilted toward the sun. "I got nothing to complain about," he murmured.

After a while Olivia stood and went behind the wagon to put her stockings back on.

"Here's the trail, right here." She pointed to wisps of waist-high buffalo grass that didn't conceal the deep ruts in the ground beneath them. "Just like Uncle

Scruggs and Mr. Kincaid said."

She expected Mourning to be eager to be on their way, but he remained motionless, eyes closed. She sat back down next to him.

After a while he said softly. "I don't remember ever havin' no moment like this one before," he said. "Not ever. Feelin' like the master of myself. Doin' what I think needs doin' when I feel like doin' it."

Olivia briefly put her hand on his shoulder and squeezed lightly. Then she turned her own face up to the sun and waited quietly. She was in no hurry to plunge back into those woods. Her arms ached from batting insects and branches away from her face. Soon Mourning pulled himself to a sitting position.

"We best be on our way," he said.

They followed the trail through the woods until they came to a shallow stream. Two deer stood in the water, drinking, but snorted and shot off between the trees, flags up. Mourning drove the wagon straight across, no getting off this time. The trail then followed the water downstream, to the point where it fed back into the river, right before a sharp bend.

"Like the man said, there it be." Mourning shielded his eyes to look up the gentle slope on their right.

"Oh," was all Olivia could say, sweet contentment abandoning her.

She had tried to heed Tobey's dire predictions and not expect too much, but nothing in her experience had prepared her for anything as squat, ugly, and depressing as her Uncle Scruggs' cabin. This was Lydia Ann's cozy little homestead? Uncle Scruggs' Garden of Eden? She'd seen drawings of slaves' quarters that looked more inviting than this. She dismally surveyed the scene. The cabin perched atop a low hill. A path of crosswise logs led up to it, but everything was overgrown with prickly, waist-high weeds.

Olivia looked back toward the water. Around the bend, where the river grew deeper, four spindly logs rested over it. That must be all that remained of Uncle Scruggs' famous springhouse. Fields fanned out behind the left side of the cabin. Seven or eight acres had obviously once been cleared, but were now overgrown with thick brush and dotted with new growth trees and old stumps. Around the back and on the other side, the woods encroached. There weren't more than twenty paces to the tree line.

Olivia reluctantly let her eyes go back to the cabin, which was exactly as Tobey had warned her it would be. Uncle Scruggs had cut down logs, notched them, stacked them on top of one another, and filled the wide gaps between them with a clay-like substance, most of which had crumbled away. The walls at either end rose in a triangular shape and a heavy log rested between them, but that center beam was all that remained of the roof. There was an opening in the front wall, slightly off-center to the right, but someone had apparently walked off with the door; nothing but rusty hinges remained. Not only were there no lace curtains at the windows, there were no window openings at all.

"There's no roof," Olivia noted dully.

"That ain't no problem. Roof be easy. Lucky for us that center beam still up there. You got a good center beam, all you gotta do is rest your roof poles on it, tie 'em good and tight, and cover 'em with bark shingles. Bet I can cut them poles and get 'em up 'fore dark tonight. You can help me with piecin' the bark. That gonna take some time cause it gotta dry first, but I bet we gonna have a roof over us 'fore the next rain."

The oxen snorted and pulled them closer. Another roofless log structure, which she assumed was the barn, stood to the right of and slightly behind the cabin. The rickety and well-weathered outhouse in back of it was the only structure built of planed lumber.

Olivia looked sideways at Mourning, expecting him to be furious with her for talking him into coming to this dreadful place, but she saw only enthusiasm on his face. He jumped down and all but bounced through the weeds. She remained in the wagon, not yet prepared to claim the dingy little hovel as her new home. Mourning ducked down to go through the doorway, and she heard him stomping around inside.

"For sure he put a whole lot a work into the floor," he said when his head reappeared in the doorway. "So smooth you could dance on it. Ain't you comin' in to see? Right fine cellar too. Can't hardly see the trapdoor. Need a new ladder and there's something making a stink down there, but that ain't nothin' to fix. Got a real stone fireplace and chimney, real fine workmanship. And there be a great big old table. What you waitin' for, Livia?"

"I had no idea it would be this bad," she apologized as she wearily climbed down and followed him inside. "He always talked about the cozy little cabin he built and how much his wife loved it."

"It ain't bad," Mourning said. "Ain't bad at all. What you been spectin', anyway? Your uncle been a smart man. Invested his time in the things what matter. Lot easier to put up new walls than dig a cellar you don't got. Easier to fix the roof than the floor. This place be just fine. We gonna get a roof on first thing, 'fore it start rainin' down on us."

He paced around, grinning. Olivia felt like sobbing, but did her best to hide it.

"I seen plenty of black ash back there by the trail," he said. "Even seen some lyin' on the ground, dry enough I can peel the bark off today. We stitch that bark together, it keep the wet off us fine. Won't take too long, do up both the house and the barn. While I be choppin', you can fix the chinking, keep all them Michigan snakes out." He puckered his mouth in his ghost face and wiggled his fingers. "I show you how to find the right kind a clay and mix it up. Then I show you how to stitch the bark. We got canvas we can hang over the door for now, but we gotta go to that saw mill in town and order us a real door. It won't be no good, it don't fit 'zactly right, and I ain't got tools for that. But the lintel and jambs be fine." He pounded a fist against one of the jambs.

She dumbly followed him back out to the yard and behind the cabin. From there she could see that most of the back wall of the barn was missing.

"Oh."

"What now?" Mourning asked.

"The barn . . . that whole wall is gone."

"Don't matter none. Make it easy for me to extend it out, fix up a threshing floor. All I gotta do is find trees to cut what got a good crotch to lay poles over. Won't even need a real roof. Buckwheat straw over them poles do good 'nuff. Keep the sun off."

He turned to look up at the treetops. "I guess the wind be comin' from that way." He pointed back toward the river. "So we put the woodpile back here. That be your number two job – gather kindling and split firewood. For now just go in the woods and pick up whatever you find on the ground. I gonna finish with the roof 'fore I start cuttin' trees to burn. But then I gonna fix you up a nice chopping block, learn you how to split wood. Gotta put a roof over that wood pile too, keep it dry. They a long, cold winter comin' and we gonna need lots a wood, so you gotta start lickety-split, do some every day."

He strode to the wagon, hoisted the barrel down, and rolled it next to the door. "That be your number *one* job." He pointed at it. "Keep that full a clean water. You do that and the wood, help me work the team when I gotta pull stumps, and keep my belly full, we do just fine."

She shuddered at the prospect of all the physical labor he was describing and his mention of food added to her distress. How was she supposed to prepare a meal? But his optimism was contagious and she began to see the possibilities. *All beginnings are hard*, she reminded herself.

One thing for sure, she had made herself totally dependent on Mourning. Not just to inherit the land. To survive. She wouldn't last a day out here on her own. Wouldn't make it back to Detroit, if anything on the wagon broke. She didn't even know how to hitch up the team. She began making a mental list of all the things she needed to learn in order not to feel totally helpless.

Apparently Mourning was not expecting any breakfast. While she stood there biting her bottom lip, he unyoked the team and led them into the barn where he put out buckets of feed. Then he took a long drink of water from one of the skins and said, "Team be needing water." He nodded at the river and then at the barn. "They be a trough in there you can fill, don't gotta let them drink out of our buckets any more."

He rummaged in the back of the wagon and then loped off, ax and saw over his shoulder. Watching him walk away, Olivia felt like crying, but shook it off. Good Lord, Killion, what a big baby you are. If Aunt Lydia Ann could do this, so can you.

What should she do first? Mourning would need the wagon to haul logs, so she should unload it. But he would also be hungry, so she should get a fire going and hang a pot of rice and beans over it. Maybe mix up dough to rise for a loaf of bread. But she'd need water to do that. And for the animals. One must always take care of the animals first. She grumbled out loud – "Can't cook until I've got wood and water and can't get water until I cut a path to the river through this blasted mess of weeds."

She took a bucket in each hand and headed toward the river, cursing the thorny weeds that tore at her skirts and scratched her ankles. She knelt on a flat rock to splash cold water over her face before filling the buckets. When she stood to pick them up, she emitted a loud "Oh." How could water be so heavy? Then she slipped on the wet clay around the rock, slightly twisting her ankle, but quickly regained her footing.

"All right Killion, let's be optimistic," she spoke aloud. "What would merry old Mourning say? 'Look how lucky that was, you breaking your leg there. Now you know where to get clay for chinking the logs.'"

Partway up the gentle hill she set her burden down to rest for a moment and stared at her hands. They were already red with a maze of tiny scratches. She took a deep breath and continued, making it to the barn without spilling a drop. She brushed the dust and debris out of the dry trough and poured both buckets in. "There you go, boys." She patted the tops of their heads and they nodded agreeably.

Shoulders aching, she made a second trip, this time setting the buckets by the door. She picked up one of them to pour the water into the barrel, but paused. The inside of the barrel was filthy. Dried leaves and cobwebs clung to its sides. What if there were mouse droppings in there? She sighed and knew she would have to use some of the precious "uphill" water to clean it. She lifted a bucket into the barrel, tipped it, and ran it around the inside walls to rinse them. Then she tied a clean rag around the handle of the broom and swished it around before turning the barrel on its side and rolling it over to where the weeds were the thickest, so that she could tip it upside down without the rim touching the dirt. Satisfied that they would survive drinking from it, she rolled it back to its place by the door, found the dipper in the wagon, and proudly hung it over the edge.

Then she reached for the second bucket of water, but frowned at the leaves and other unidentified debris floating on its surface. No, this wouldn't do. She should strain the water through a clean rag, but didn't have one large enough to cover the mouth of the barrel. She looked around, frustrated and impatient.

"Blast it, you start to do one thing, but you can't do it until you've done some other danged thing, and then you can't do *it* ..."

Finally she went to the wagon, rummaged for the clothes she had changed out of that morning, and freed one of the petticoats from the bundle. "At last you're finally good for something," she said to the annoying undergarment as she spread it over the top of the barrel and tied a rope around it, to hold it in place while she poured the water through it.

When she loosened the rope to peek proudly at the clean water, her smile faded. The bottom of the barrel barely looked wet. Filling it to a level they would be able to reach with the dipper was going to require more trips to the river than she could bear to contemplate.

"One thing at a time," she said "One at a time. Don't think about *all* the things you have to do. Just about the next one."

Chapter Fifteen

The crack of the axe rang out and Olivia smiled. Mourning was not far away. Everything would be all right. She paused to listen to the steady blows and when they stopped she imagined him taking off his hat and wiping his brow on the sleeve of his shirt. If he still had his shirt on.

She carried two more buckets of water and then stood gazing at the river, trying to shake the dull ache from her arms and imagining how it would feel to stand naked in its rushing water. Boys in Five Rocks were always talking about swimming in their birthday suits. Why didn't girls get to do any of the fun things?

She sighed and made two more trips up and down the hill with the buckets and then looked around the filthy cabin. She should wipe down the surfaces, but there was no point cleaning the floor until after the roof was on. In the far corner, behind the table, was a large wooden box that she hadn't noticed before. She dragged the table away from it and happily realized it was a bed. It stood waist high and had no ladder, but she managed to boost herself onto it. She wouldn't have to sleep on the floor! Further inspection revealed that there was no footboard, creating a large storage space under the bed. How clever Uncle Scruggs had been. Her wicker baskets would fit nicely down there.

Aunt Lydia Ann's kitchen consisted of a wide shelf mounted to the left of the door. Mourning was right; this place wasn't so bad. She turned to admire the stone chimney and fireplace. The iron crane creaked loudly as she swung it over the hearth. Then she frowned; that chimney hadn't been cleaned for sixteen years. If she lit a fire she was likely to burn the whole place down. At home, every few months, Tobey put on his "sweep clothes," stepped into their chimney, climbed up a ladder, brushed away the soot, and spread a fresh layer of clay. How was she supposed to do that in a new dress?

She fetched the broom and stuck its long handle up the chimney, banging it against the sides. No bird nests fell down – only some dry leaves and black dust. She crossed her arms and scowled again. Then she went to the wagon, found a burlap bag, and held it up. If she cut holes for her head and arms it would come to her knees. Now all she needed was a knife. Good luck finding that. She climbed into the wagon and began unloading, setting things that were to go into the barn on one side and things to go in the cabin on the other. Finally she came across the kitchen utensils.

She went inside, removed her apron and dress, and slipped the burlap bag over her muslin chemise. Then she took the shovel down to the river, scooped up a blade of the black clay, and carried it back to the hearth. Standing on a wooden crate, she methodically spread clay over the inside of the chimney, making several trips back to the river for more of the black mud. When she was finished she had to use some of the precious uphill water to get her hands clean enough to touch anything. Then she found a clean chemise and towel and ran barefoot through the weeds to the river. She could still hear the ring of Mourning's axe and so dared to pull the burlap off and slip into the cold water in her flimsy undergarment. She lay back, willing the current to wash the grime from her hair.

After a few minutes she thought, *if the boys can do it why can't I*, and pulled the soiled chemise over her head, tossing it onto the bank. The water felt wonderful on her naked body, but she found herself unable to relax and enjoy it. What if Jeremy Kincaid came to call? When she realized that she no longer heard Mourning's axe, she scrambled out of the water and struggled into the clean chemise. Holding the towel around her, she fled back to the cabin.

Dressed again, she swept out the hearth and cabin and went into the woods to gather kindling. She laid and lit a fire, then went to the wagon for rice and beans. Where on earth were the pots and sacks of food supplies? If she wanted to find anything, she'd have to finish unloading the entire mess.

"One thing at a time," she said with a sigh, "one thing at a time." It was so hot. How could the heat be this bad in the middle of May? She grabbed up a pot, filled it with water, put it on the crane to heat, and returned to the wagon for the sacks of food. Mourning was right, why had she bought so much stuff?

She found the rice and beans, but the sacks were too heavy for her to budge. She held the corners of her apron in one hand and scooped rice into it with the other. She managed to descend from the wagon without spilling, shook the rice into the pot, and added more water to cover it. She grimaced at the paucity of the meal. But there was no time to soak and cook beans. Anyway they still had bread, cheese, and jam left from Detroit. At least the rice would be hot.

She had resumed unloading the wagon when

Mourning appeared on the trail, his long legs gliding through the weeds. He had tied the sleeves of his shirt around his waist and his bare chest glistened in the sunlight. She raised her hand in greeting, but he paid her no mind, heading straight for the water barrel.

"There's drinking water in the skins and in that bucket by the barrel," she called out.

He removed the wooden stopper from one of the skins and held it up to let a stream of water pour over his head. She had to bite back a desperate protest: "There's a whole river full of downhill water right there. Why are you pouring out all my uphill water?" But she said nothing. When she approached him, he shook his head and grinned.

"What?" she asked uneasily.

He said nothing, but started laughing.

"What's so blasted funny? You can stop thinking I haven't been doing anything all day. It may not look like I got much done, but I had to clean and clay the chimney –"

"Look like you been clayin' somethin' all right and usin' your face and hair to do it. You best not be findin' your mirror today." He reached out and extracted a strand of slimy plant matter from her hair.

She wiped her hands over her cheeks and they came away black. "Oh Lord. How I must look."

"Little color in your face do you good." He was still shaking his head and grinning when he turned to stick his head into the cabin. "See you got a fire lit. I carry them sacks of food inside for you."

Olivia added a few spoonfuls of salt to the rice before going to the river to clean up. She was squatting on her heels, splashing water on herself, when she looked up and saw a graceful white swan drifting toward her. The lovely creature seemed to be fascinated by Olivia and turned its head as it floated past. Olivia stared until it was out of sight. What a beautiful sign. Another good omen.

She rose and filled the buckets she had brought. When she started back up the hill she saw Mourning, still shirtless, making smooth strokes with the scythe, clearing the weeds in the front yard. She stopped and stared. Those Italian sculptors would have loved his body. Slim, but every muscle and tendon defined. For a moment she tried to imagine him white.

Then she sighed and set her mind back on all the tasks she had yet to perform that day. She strained the water into the barrel and went inside to check on the rice, slice bread, and put the cheese and jam on a plate. When she looked out the door, Mourning was lying on a sheet of canvas he had spread in the little clearing he had made, hands behind his head and still shirtless. She walked over to him with the plate of cold food.

"The rice will be done in a while," she said, setting the plate next to him on the canvas.

"Look at you," Mourning said, shielding his eyes with one hand as he grinned up at her. "Ain't here but a few hours and already got a meal cookin'."

"Some meal. It's just plain rice," she said, but took a great deal of pleasure in his praise. She was smiling when she turned to check the bubbling pot again.

"That sun feel good," he said, rising up on his elbows when she returned with a plate of rice for each of them. "After we done eatin' we gotta finish emptyin' the wagon, so I can go get the trees what I cut. I found some logs too. Faces nice and smooth, like they been cut with a two-man saw. Big 'nuff around to make nice chairs."

He held the edge of the plate to his mouth and used his knife to scrape the rice in. "Mmm," he said. "You gonna win first prize in the rice-cooking contest."

"I'm sorry I was so . . . you know . . . when we arrived," she said. "But I'm feeling better now. I'll get used to things here. I can see that it's not so bad."

"Ain't bad at all. It be real good, Livia. Look how wide and deep that river be. It ain't gonna dry up in the summer. You got your cabin up on a nice slope, so you ain't gonna get flooded and not too much snow gonna pile up on you. But it ain't so steep you think you gonna die walkin' up it. Them things more important than havin' to put a roof on or not havin' no window. Come winter you gonna be glad you ain't got one, lettin' in all that cold."

"I hadn't thought of that."

In truth, she hadn't given any thought to winter. Now that she did, her spirits drooped. With a roof on it, that cabin was going to be dark and stuffy, even on days when the weather was fair enough to leave the door open. The roof poles would be barely two feet above her head in the middle of the room; near the front and back walls she wouldn't even be able to stand. She'd bang her head trying to sit up in that bed. She couldn't imagine being cooped up in there for months, snow piled against the door, no sunlight, only candles and lanterns burning up the little bit of air. But she forced her voice to remain cheerful.

She went back inside to refill their plates and set the coffee pot on the edge of the fire to boil. After they'd had a cup, they finished unloading the wagon together.

"There's a bed in there, built like a platform," she said. "Could you help me slide my wicker baskets under it?"

"Sure."

"And set my mattress on top of it?"

He raised his hand in salute, easily slid the mattress onto her bed, and then said, "Once I be done with the roof, it be easy for me to build you a frame over that bed. You can spread sheets over it and around the sides, like curtains. Goody's wife done like that so she don't gotta worry about the dust what come blowing through the roof getting' on her bed."

Olivia smiled and nodded. He finished moving her things and then hauled the tools, seed, and grain into the barn and spread a sheet of canvas over them. His own mattress he tossed outside, leaning it against the front wall of the cabin.

"Didn't you call her 'Mamma'?" Olivia asked.

"What?"

"Before. You said something about Goody's wife. But she raised you from a baby. Didn't you call her 'Mamma'?"

"Nah. I call her Alice. Like I call Goody, 'Goody.' But if I'd a said 'Alice' you warn't gonna know who I's talking about." He harnessed Dixby and Dougan to the wagon and headed back toward the woods. "These animals gonna need more water," he called over his shoulder.

"Okay, I'll get more."

When he had disappeared she allowed herself the luxury of stretching out on the sheet of canvas for a few minutes. Pressing her back against the hard ground helped to relieve the ache, and the sun felt wonderful. Soothing. When she heard the steady blows of the axe begin again she felt guilty and forced herself up.

She hauled eight more buckets of water, using four to fill the trough. That should do them for today. Now what? More food. She arranged the dishes and utensils on the kitchen shelf and poured some beans in a pot to soak. Then she kneaded water, flour, salt, and some of her yeast culture into dough for a loaf of bread and left it to rise with a plate turned over it, in lieu of a clean cloth.

Next she picked up the scythe and cut more weeds, clearing an area for a fire pit and a path to the river. How had Mourning made this look so easy? Then she got the shovel and dug the pit. She knew she should gather large rocks to set around it, but was too exhausted and there was too much else left to do. That would have to wait for another day. For now she had to gather more firewood, before it was dark. There was no shortage of dry wood on the ground and soon the pit was filled with kindling, with a tepee of thicker branches rising over it. She'd also heaped piles of kindling and branches behind the cabin, enough to last for a few days. She'd have to get Mourning to build something like a spit over the fire pit, so she could cook outside.

She lifted her arms over her head and stretched. Lord, wasn't that enough for the first day? But she couldn't lay down to rest while Mourning was out there swinging his axe. She hauled more water and then gathered their dirty traveling clothes and her chemise into the washtub and carried it down to the river. She was on her way back up the hill for laundry soap and a bucket to use to fill the tub when the woods grew silent. Hallelujah. Please God, let him have declared the work day over.

She had never done laundry and stared at the tub for a few minutes. She knew boiling water was supposed to be involved, but not today. For today "cleaner than they were before" was going to have to do.

Suddenly faint-headed, she knelt on one of the flat rocks and bent over to stick her head in the river. Then she sat back on her heels and asked herself how she was feeling. Was she glad they had come? Homesick? Optimistic? Excited? Scared? She wasn't aware of any strong emotion. Only two things occupied her mind: how much she wanted to lie down and what she wouldn't give for a plate of Mabel's fried chicken.

She sighed and began dipping the hard bar of laundry soap into the river and scrubbing it against a white rock. The suds that finally appeared burned her scratches and broken blisters and brought tears to her eyes. She held each garment in the river, letting the current flow through it, before scrubbing it with the soap and plunging it into the tub. Then she left everything to soak and trudged back up the hill to pick out two trees to tie a clothesline between.

A few minutes later Mourning drove up the hill.

Long, thin, naked-looking tree trunks rested across the back of the wagon, sticking out on both sides. She had finished tying her line, but hadn't the strength to nod or smile in his direction, let alone raise a hand to wave.

Chapter Sixteen

"You gonna help me unload, Miz Pioneer Lady?" Mourning asked. "I get the trees, you get the bark. Spread it out to dry over there on that grass. Get all them books a yours, anything heavy enough to flatten 'em out."

He climbed down, removed his hat, and studied the sky. "They be clouds startin' to stir up over there, but I don't think we gonna get rain tonight."

He pulled one of the thin tree trunks from the wagon, strode over to lean it against the cabin, and then stood watching Olivia gather up some of the pieces of bark. Shaking his head, he went to the barn and came back carrying another floppy felt hat, which he plopped on Olivia's head.

"You can't work in the sun without no hat. Make yourself sick. And black as a nigger."

They worked in silence, until he emitted a loud "Arggh" as he hoisted down one of five fat stumps, each about two feet long, with flat tops and bottoms. "These be our chairs." He patted it. "But make sure you watch out for splinters." He grinned and wiggled his behind.

He turned the log on its side and rolled it into the cabin, then did the same with the second one. The next two he placed outside, on opposite sides of the fire pit. He chopped at the earth with his hatchet and worked the "chairs" into the ground until they no longer wobbled.

Then he rolled the last and largest of the logs off the back of the wagon and let it thud to the ground. "This be your chopping block," he said, as he rolled it to the far side of the cabin. He stood it on end and hacked the blade of the axe into it. "I give you your first lesson tomorrow."

"I can't wait."

After they finished unloading, Olivia stepped into the cabin to feed the fire and then dragged herself down to the river to scrub, rinse, and wring out the laundry. Mourning – who had been studying the roof while pacing back and forth, counting and muttering about run and rise – saw her struggling with the tub of wet clothes and hurried down to take one of the handles and help her carry it up to the clothesline.

"You know you spose to use hot water," he said.

"Yes, I know. I know. But I can't –"

"All right. All right. I just be saying. No need to get riled."

Both of them were grimy, sweaty, and exhausted. Mourning sat on one of the stumps, watching Olivia hang the clothes on the line. When she finished, she sat on the stump opposite him.

"Do you want me to make coffee?" she asked.

"You best sit a bit. Catch your breath." He closed his eyes again. Then he opened them and gave her a warm smile. "You know, Livia, you been right. I gotta say. This be a good place. We gonna be all right here, like you said."

"I hope so."

"Farmers always got problems. Rains too much. Don't rain enough. Too much sun or not enough. One bad storm can wipe you out. Bugs and birds eat you out. Market go down. Seed go up. Always be things that can go wrong. But this here be real good land. Plenty a wood and water. Lot more of it clear than I 'spected."

"I'm glad you don't feel like strangling me."

"Nah. I real glad I come with you. We be ready to put in some corn by the last of the month. Then wheat and some hay. We gotta clear them fields up and there be plenty of sweat in it, but like you said, we got us a

137

good start. A real good start. You can get some vegetables in pretty quick. Fine place for your plot right over there." He nodded toward the right side of the cabin. "Almost flat and plenty a sun. We start keeping the team there at night. Let them lay pies on that soil for a few days and then you turn it over. Plant you some cabbage and peas and onions and turnips and carrots. We be eatin' fine by the end a summer. Just look at you – all set up your first day out, cookin' over your own fireplace, hangin' clothes on your own line, like you been doin' it all your life."

Vegetable garden. She wanted to groan. She hadn't thought of that. What she said was, "You don't have to sound so surprised. I told you I could."

"Long as you know you spose to boil the laundry," he teased and she smiled.

Every inch of her body ached to the bone and her hands were covered with brown streaks of blood. Perhaps worst of all was the way she smelled. She hadn't known it was possible for a girl to smell that bad.

"Ain't so many white women what ain't dirt poor gonna do what you done today. You all right, Livia."

She felt her face flush and realized she was more comfortable with him acting ornery. She was used to that.

"Well, I never had any doubt that *you'd* be all right." She got up. "I'm going to put the bread in. I've been heating the lid like you said."

"Oooh." He grinned. "Your first loaf of kettle bread. Now that be a hard test to pass."

While they were shopping in Detroit, Mourning had reminded her that they wouldn't have a stove and bought a funny shaped pot with a concave lid, over a foot long and about half as high.

Olivia went into the cabin, where the lid to the bake kettle was heating in the edge of the fire. She punched the bread dough down and did as Mourning had told her to: put it in the kettle, set the kettle in some coals

138

on the hearth, put the concave lid on, and filled the lid with coals. Then she went back outside.

"Mourning," she said, her eyes on the ground, "I'd be real appreciative if you could find someplace else to be, while I clean myself up in the river. I want to have a real bath, with soap."

He thought for a moment. "Okay. I stay in with the team. But first come in there with me." He strode into the barn.

She followed him, wondering, *Now what? He wants to show me how to muck it out in case I get bored?*

He began running his hands over the logs in the corner that faced the cabin and the river.

"Just want you to check. See that they ain't no holes in the chinking. No way I can see out," he said. "Check for yourself."

"For heavens sake, I believe you," she said, flushing to the roots of her hair, horrified by the image of him peeking through a hole at her, a possibility that never would have occurred to her.

"No, you gotta see. We both gonna be bathin' in that river till it turn cold and you gotta be comfortable doin' it. You ain't gonna be, you don't check for yourself."

Olivia obeyed while he rummaged through his toolbox.

"Okay, I checked."

He held up a harmonica, slapped it against his palm, and blew into it. "I'm a sit right here with my back in this corner and play. Long as you can hear me playin', you know where I at, and you gonna feel comfortable. I can't move nowhere without you hearin' it. So go get all shiny." He grinned and made a shooing motion with his hand. "And you sure need it, Miz Pioneer Lady. Grizzly bears down south in Canada been trackin' your scent all day."

She made a face and he began playing a halting version of "Amazing Grace." She hurried into the cabin for her soap, a clean work dress, and a towel. The

139

strains of Mourning's music followed her down to the river, where she sat on the white rock and prepared to get naked for the second time that day. She grinned, remembering how modest she had always been. Even when undressing alone in her own room, with the door on the latch, she used to have her nightdress bunched up around her neck, ready to pull down, before she slipped her chemise off. *One day out here*, she thought, *and I can hardly keep my clothes on.*

When she was as clean as one can get in river water and had finished dressing, she shouted to Mourning, "You can come out."

He approached as she was hanging her towel on the line. "Your turn now?" she asked.

"Yeah, my turn." He held out his hand for the soap. "'Less you wanna watch, I give you a holler when I be done." He grinned and Olivia burned red again.

He is a good man, she thought, but this time she didn't mean good of character. He was indeed that, but now she meant good to be with. For the first time the question "Why couldn't he be white?" worked its way consciously into her mind.

Olivia went to check on the bread. The crust looked nice and brown, but when she turned it out of the kettle and tried to slice it, the middle was all dough. There was nothing but a plate of crusts for their supper. Now she would have to prepare something else. The beans wouldn't do for today; they hadn't been soaking nearly long enough to cook them. She only kept herself from crying by repeating, *Just one more thing today. Just one more.*

She fed the fire, shoveled a pile of bright embers onto the hearth, and set the long-handled frying pan in them. Then she quickly mixed up flour, water, and salt for flapjacks, adding two thinly sliced apples to the batter. When Mourning returned from cleaning up, she greeted him with a plate of thick flapjacks, surrounded by pieces of bread crust smeared with blackberry jam.

"Sorry about the bread," she said. "I failed the test."

"Take a while to get the hang of it," he said as he took his plate. "And tonight I gonna eat anything you give me. My stomach been hollerin' for me to put somethin' in it."

They went out to the stump chairs and sat in the dusk, eating hungrily. Olivia balanced her plate on her knees and cut ladylike pieces. Mourning found a good use for his fork – he stabbed it into the center of a flapjack and held it up so he could chomp around the edge. Olivia was tempted to do the same, but remembered reading in Godey's Lady's Book that it was the responsibility of the gentler sex to bring civilization to the frontier. She continued her struggle for proper table manners, but her only reward was a jam stain on her clean dress. When they were nearly finished she once again broached the subject of her mother.

"Mourning, we're going to be here together for a long time and I'm not going to stop asking, so you might as well tell me and get it over with. What you did you mean about my father finding my mother?"

He concentrated on his food, as if he hadn't heard her. After he swallowed his last bite, he set the plate down, raised his eyes to meet her gaze, and shook his head.

"I shudna said nothin'. I thought you knew. That you hadda know."

"Knew what?"

"About how your mamma died."

"How did she die?"

"What they tell you?"

She shook her head. "You tell me what happened. Everything you know. Everything."

"All right." He took another deep breath and said it quickly. "Your daddy come home and found her in the storeroom by your kitchen, only it ain't been no storeroom then. Used to be the pantry."

"Found her what? Lying there sick? Did she fall

down and hurt herself?"

He stared steadily into Olivia's eyes and said, "She been hangin' by her neck. She throwed a rope over the beam and stood on a footstool to put it 'round her neck. Then she stepped aside. That stool been still standin' there next to her. Your daddy come home and found her like that. He stayed real still, just staring. Seem like a long time 'fore he took her down."

Olivia stared at the ground. She was sure no one had ever said these words to her, but even so, they didn't feel new. Had she heard whispers and folded them away, forced herself to forget them?

"How do you know this?" she finally asked.

"I been with him. Been workin' at the store and he aksed me to carry a sack a flour home for him. I come in the back door behind him. I knowed something wrong. Don't know how, cause he ain't said no word, ain't made no noise at all. But I gone to see what wrong and seen him standin' there starin' at her."

"I was almost six when she died," Olivia said softly. "So you would have been eight or nine?"

"Sound right."

"So maybe you didn't understand. You could have been confused, not really understood what happened."

"No." He shook his head. "I ain't been in no confusion. I know what I seen. I seen him step up on that stool and hold her, so he could slip the noose off. He aksed me to help him carry her to the parlor and lay her down. Then he been on his knees on the floor, touchin' her face and cryin'. Cryin' and shoutin'. 'Why? Why? Why you wanna leave us so bad?' Every few minutes he stop cryin' and start hollerin'. 'How could you do this? How dare you? Coulda been Olivia what found you. What kind a mother are you?' Then he started cursin' God. Never gone to church no more after that day." He paused.

Olivia said nothing and he continued.

"I remember thinkin', the way that stool still

142

standin' there . . . she done it real calm like. Made up her mind about what she gonna do and then got up on that stool and done it."

He stopped again. After another long silence Olivia said, "You mean she could have changed her mind. All she had to do was put her foot back on the stool. She hadn't kicked it away."

He nodded and looked away.

She spoke softly, more to herself than him. "You'd think anyone, being choked, desperate for air . . . even then she didn't change her mind. So she hated her life that much."

Mourning spoke again. "I think that what hurt your daddy the most."

Olivia spoke with an edge of bitterness. "It *should* have been me. I was usually the first one home." She lowered her eyes, wondering why she wasn't crying. Why she didn't feel anything. Nothing but empty. "Do my brothers know?" she asked.

He shrugged. "I always been thinkin' so – but maybe that just like I been thinkin' you gotta know."

"How could my father keep something like that a secret?"

"I be the only one what seen her up there, 'sides your daddy. After a while he 'member I there, put his hands on my shoulders and say, 'Boy, you already forgot what you seen here. My wife been a sickly woman, died in her bed.' I promised him I ain't gonna tell no one, 'cept for the Doc and it been your father what sent me to get him. He needed someone to help him carry her up to bed. I warn't strong enough. But Doc Gaylin ain't gonna tell no one, if your father say not to. Course people, they always whisperin'. The church ladies come, want to get the body ready, but your father say he ain't believin' in that, he havin' a closed casket. But they whisperin', always aksin' me, but I ain't never told no one nothin'."

Olivia felt too exhausted to go on thinking about it

and stood up. "I think I'll turn in. Thank you for telling me, Mourning. And for not trying to, you know, make it sound not as bad as it was. I appreciate you telling me the truth."

He nodded. "I remember the way I always been aksin' folks 'bout my mamma and daddy. Wanna know the truth, even if it be hard."

She spread a sheet and comforter over her mattress, let down the canvas flap Mourning had nailed to the door, undressed, and pulled a clean white nightdress over her head for the first time since leaving home. She frowned, trying to think of something to use for a pillow, but was too tired to worry about that. Before lying down she sat on the edge of the bed, rubbing her feet together to brush the dirt off and thinking what a great bed it was. Solid wood clear to the floor – no old man to reach out and grab her ankle. *Of all things*, she scolded herself. *Mourning tells you your mother hung herself and all you can think about is Avis's old man under the bed?*

But her mind refused to focus on this new image of her mother. She sank back onto the bed. The mattress felt wonderful, as if she were floating on a cloud, and she put her arms over her head and stretched. She could hear Mourning outside and guessed he must have swept out the wagon and made his bed in it. For a moment she was conscious of the two of them, alone in the woods, in the dark, nothing but that canvas flap between them. But she was too exhausted to give much thought to Mourning's sinewy muscles.

An enormous white moon hung low in the sky, three bright stars at its side, all in the haze of a pale halo. *Wordsworth should be here to write a poem about this sky,* she thought. The night air grew chilly and damp and she huddled under her quilted blue comforter as sleep crept over her, heavy, dark, and silent.

Chapter Seventeen

"Ain't you never gonna wake up?" Mourning called through the canvas flap the next morning, stomping his feet and clapping his hands. "I got work to do."

Olivia sat up and put her feet over the side of the bed. Beads of dew glistened on the comforter and cold clung to the air.

"I thought I gonna give you a wood splittin' lesson first thing."

"Hold your horses and stop hollering." She slipped into her dress and shoes and went outside, running her fingers through her hair and yawning. "It's early." She looked up at the gray sky. "And cold." She went back in for her woolen shawl.

"Good reason to get movin' 'round," he called after her.

Her cuts and blisters looked and felt worse and when she came back out she showed him her hands.

"They bad all right. 'Fore you light the fire, get some a that soot from the chimney 'n rub it in the ones what bleedin'. Ain't nothing else for 'em." He held his own hands out for inspection. "See mine? Like leather. But you gonna suffer for a few days. Best get some rags to wrap 'round 'em."

That was apparently all the sympathy she was going to get and she went in to prepare herself for the day. When she returned, Mourning showed her a large harp-shaped tool with a jagged blade.

"This here be your buck saw." He walked away, motioning with his head for her to follow him to a dead tree lying at the edge of the woods. He braced one foot on it and held the saw, blade down. "You get over there and latch on to the other handle. We gonna take off a nice log. That get the chill off you."

She took hold of her end of the saw and tried her

145

best to help him, wincing in pain.

"No, not like that. You ain't spose to *push* it," he said. "All you can do to a buck saw is *pull*. First *I* pull, then *you* pull. That why it got two handles. While I be pullin', you don't do nothing but hold it steady."

After a few more false starts they got a rhythm going. Despite her pain, which the wet rags she had wrapped around her hands only seemed to exacerbate, she helped him saw off three logs.

"That's enough for now," she said and stood up straight. "My skin isn't leather yet."

"Okay." He picked up one of the logs and carried it to her chopping block. "Now we go on to splittin'. You can use one of these, if it suit you." He picked up a sharp-edged triangular wedge of iron and held it out for her inspection. "You gotta find the right place in the grain." He pressed the sharp edge into the wood and used the butt end of his axe to pound it in. "And then ..." he picked up a five-pound hammer, "you give it a good old bang."

Olivia admired his grace as he raised the hammer over his shoulder and brought it down with a loud ring of metal on metal. The two halves of the log fell to the ground. He put one of the halves on the block and offered the wedge and axe to Olivia. "Now you."

She managed to pound the wedge into the log and then raised the sledge hammer over her head and brought it down with all her might. She grazed the wedge and sent the log flying.

"You tryin' to break my foot or cut it off?" Mourning yelped.

On her sixth try the wood split into two uneven pieces.

"Okay, that one way. Now have a go with a splitting maul." He offered her a tool that looked like a wedge-shaped hammer.

"No, thanks. We'll leave that for the next lesson." She shook her hands and winced.

146

"Well, okay. You done good for a first try," Mourning said. "Real good."

"I'm going to mix up griddle cakes and make coffee."

"You know, 'fore too long one of us gonna have to shoot something or catch something out a that river. Or we gotta go into town and buy some eggs. We gotta eat something what gonna stick to our inners. Your uncle ever take you fishing?"

"No."

"Don't neither of us got time to sit holding a pole, but I show you how to run a trotline. All you gotta do is pull it in every day, see what you find on them hooks."

"All right. And I'm not a bad shot. Maybe later this afternoon I'll go find a good blind and sit for a while," she said over her shoulder as she headed back to the cabin.

Nothing appealed to her more than the idea of resting quietly – and guilt-free – in the woods, while she waited for a deer to wander by. Of course, if she got one, she could guess who was going to be expected to process and preserve the meat. And she had no idea how to do either.

She unwound the rags, shook her head at the bloody mess, and rubbed her hands with chimney soot before wrapping them back up and lighting the fire. All she felt like doing was soaking in a hot tub, but Mourning had been right about one thing. She wasn't cold any more.

"Come inside, eat at the table," she called through the doorway and then looked up at the sky. Some "inside" their roofless little cabin offered.

Mourning came in and sat on one of the stump chairs. Ignoring his knife and fork, he spread a griddlecake with jam, rolled it up, and picked it up to eat with his fingers. Then he did the same with another.

"You ready for me to show you how to stitch that bark together for the roof?"

She looked at her breakfast, most of which was still

on her plate. "Yes, Massa."

"You want a roof over your head?" He shrugged and rose. "This weather ain't gonna hold forever. Miracle we ain't been soaked yet. It gonna rain sometime soon. I figure we can get most of the cabin roof on 'fore it does. We do the front first. That where the wind be comin' from. If we both sleep with our backs against the front wall, we shouldn't be getting' no rain on us."

"You're fooling me," she said.

He raised his chin. "You 'spect me to sleep out in the rain?"

"Mourning, I can't sleep inside the same cabin with you."

"Why not? Your head gonna start where my feet end. We be farther apart in here than we been on that boat."

"That was different. There were all those people around. And no one knew us. But this is our home. What would people say?"

"What would people say?" he mimicked her, pitching his voice high. "What the hell people?" He stood up and spun around, hands out to both sides, palms up. "Who gonna tell anyone, the raccoons?"

"I'm sure you can figure out some place to sleep besides the cabin."

"Sure, I can go crawl inside one a them hollow trees."

"You could sleep under the wagon. Stand it in the corner of the barn closest to where the wind's coming from. Then hang some canvas over the sides, like a tent, to keep the wet out. That would be drier than the cabin with only half a roof on it."

His stared at her, his face stone.

"Don't you be looking at me like that, Mourning Free. You know you've slept in worse places."

His face remained blank.

"Anyway," she continued, "you're the one ought to be worried about what folks might do if they found a

148

colored man sleeping in a cabin together with a white girl." She thought she saw the line of his jaw relent before he turned toward the door.

"Wait, don't go," she said, gulping down a hasty bite. "I do want you to show me how to do the bark. Just let me finish eating. You haven't even had any coffee."

"Best make it fast. Lot to do today." His voice sounded normal as he wrapped a rag around the handle of the tin coffee pot and poured himself a cup.

When they went outside, Mourning walked to where the pieces of bark were spread on the buffalo grass.

"This bark gonna be laid 'cross the roof in rows," he said. "So first you gotta find all the pieces what be the same length. Don't matter how wide they be, just how long. If they a real funny shape, you can fix 'em like this." He took out his pocketknife and picked up an uneven piece of bark to demonstrate. He turned it over, scored a straight line along the top edge, and carefully bent it to break off the jagged edge. "Just don't be thinkin' like a girl, that they all got to be perfect. They all gonna lap over the other, so don't matter none if they ain't nice and straight."

She nodded and he reached into his pocket for a roll of cloth. Inside it was a thick needle with a wide eye. He handed it to her.

"They's a roll of string over there on the stump. You cut off a bunch a pieces, 'bout eight inches long, thread one of them through that needle. Then you put two pieces a bark together, with the long edges overlappin' by 'bout two inches. Nuff so you got where to use that needle to poke holes through both pieces." He demonstrated, holding two pieces of bark together. "You gonna make two holes near the top corner and tie off the string, then two more near the bottom corner. When you got a row wide as the cabin, I be layin' it over the roof poles, nail it in place. Then the next one on top of it."

"That's the whole roof? That will keep the rain out?"

"You ever see a tree carryin' an umbrella? May be some water gonna drip in, but it keep us mostly dry."

Olivia sat down and began working. Her fingertips were soon covered with painful red dots and she rose to rummage through her wicker baskets in search of a thimble.

When she came back out Mourning was harnessing Dougan and Dixby. "You doin' fine. I'm a go for more trees," he said.

After he disappeared she poured herself a cup of coffee and sat on one of the stumps. She allowed her thoughts to wander to her mother, but they didn't remain there long. She found herself more interested in water – how much she had used washing up and how many times she would have to go up and down the hill, today, tomorrow, and every day after that. Anyway, what was there to think about her mother? Nola June had been determined to die and dead she was. She hadn't given a whit about the people she was leaving behind, so why should Olivia waste energy fretting about her?

She worked on the bark, hauled water, gathered wood, and made a few feeble attempts at splitting logs. Then she put both the beans and a pot of potatoes on to boil. Suddenly aware of how deep her hunger was, she decided that she did indeed need to go hunting today. The woods between the river and stream must be home to a lot of animals. It was too early in the day for many deer to be moving, but she would go pick a good spot and return later. She slung the Hawken and possibles bag over her shoulder, waded across the stream, left the trail, and carefully picked her way through the brush. She lifted her skirt, but it was already covered with brambles. Thorns scratched at her ankles and sharp twigs threatened to poke her eye out. She sighed, wishing she'd taken the high-top work boots she'd seen at Killion's General. She left broken branches dangling to mark her trail, remembering that she hadn't even told Mourning where she was going. How stupid of her. Finally she came upon a small grassy clearing. She licked and raised a finger to check the wind and scrutinized the woods around the edge. There it was – the perfect tree – with an enormous trunk and low-hanging branches, a ready-made blind. She walked over and squatted behind it. Yes, it was a good place. She walked to the opposite edge of the clearing and pulled at the leafy branches of a young tree, breaking a few off and tossing them in a heap. Surely any self-respecting deer would venture two steps out of the woods to browse on those nice tops. Already tasting roast venison, she hurried back home. By the time she got there, Mourning had returned with another load of roof poles.

"Where you been at?" he asked.

"Finding a blind to hunt from. I'm starving. But if I get anything, you're going to have to gut and skin it. I've never done that."

He nodded, and she watched him wield a curved, double-handled draw knife as he stripped the bark from a thin trunk.

He makes everything look so easy, she thought. *And he never whines. Not like me.*

"So why ain't you watchin' out for a deer 'stead a standin' here watchin' me?" he asked.

"It's too early. They'll still be bedded down," she said.

She dished up two plates of potatoes and beans and they sat outside, wolfing the food down. Then she hauled water to replenish the barrel. On every trip down to the river she passed the clothes she had hung on the line yesterday, but was in no hurry to take them down. There was something comforting – homey – about the sound of them flapping in the breeze. Then she sewed together two more strings of bark, while Mourning built a ladder that he stood against the wall of the cabin.

"Maybe I will go settle down, before the deer get up for their dinner," she said. "And maybe I'll start looking for a bee tree. I brought some old honey comb."

"You know how to find one?"

"It's easy. My Mammo Killion taught me. She had to have her honey wine. You burn a piece of honey comb and pretty soon a bee comes buzzing around. Before you know it, there's a whole swarm of them. Then you wait for them to leave and watch which direction they go. They circle round and round till they're high enough and then make a straight line back to their tree. You follow that line as well as you can and then burn some more comb. You keep doing that until eventually the bees start leaving in the opposite direction. Then you just walk back real slow and you'll find the tree."

Mourning's bottom lip covered the top one as he nodded his head in approval. "Then how you gonna get the honey out a that tree, with all them bees buzzing around?"

"That's no thing." She grinned. "I'll call you to chop it down. You know, my clothes are too bright for hunting. You think I can borrow one of your shirts, wear it over my dress?"

Now he grinned. "Like to hear what Lady Grody gonna say about that."

"It's not 'Lady Grody.' The journal is published by a Mr. Godey. *For* ladies." Then she saw from his grin that his mistake had been intentional and grinned back. "Where are your clothes?" she asked.

"Where they gonna be at? Out in the barn where us critters live."

She glanced at him, but was glad to see only amusement on his face. She went to the barn, picked his gray shirt off a nail, and pulled it on over her dress. Then she went to the cabin for the Hawken and her possibles bag and took a wine-colored leather volume from one of the wicker baskets. It was the last thing she had bought in Detroit – a journal. She hadn't yet written a word in it, but now she would have time. She intended to keep track of everything. The work they did, what they ate, even their arguments. She checked the stopper on her pot of ink, wrapped it tightly in a rag, and slipped it and the long narrow case that held her quill into the pocket of her apron. She waved good-bye to Mourning, who was up on his ladder mumbling, and called out, "I'll be on the other side of the stream."

She easily retraced her trail and settled down with her back against the tree. She measured powder, loaded the Hawken, and practiced taking aim before propping the cocked rifle next to her.

Finally she opened the journal, lifting it to her face and breathing in its wonderful scent. The cover was bumpy leather, just like her Bible, but wine-colored instead of black. *This was how Gulliver must have been born*, she thought. *And Chingachgook. A man had put black ink to white paper and created a world of words.* She knew she would never make that kind of magic, but at least she could pass on her memories. At first she wrote as quickly as the quill allowed, trying to get down every clever word Mourning had said, every sound she had heard, every smell and breeze. Then her hand slowed, as she tried to describe her feelings. She tried to write as if no other soul would ever read her words.

She was lost in thought, the end of her quill tickling her nose, when she glanced up and saw them. A doe and two long-legged spotted fawns stood not five yards from her, the doe broadside, presenting a perfect target. Holding her breath, Olivia slowly set her quill in its case, closed the book, and lifted the rifle. She had the doe in her sights and her finger pressed hard on the trigger when one of the fawns perked its head up and turned enormous innocent eyes in her direction. It cocked its head and blinked, and Olivia lowered the gun. Not this one. How could she leave those little fawns alone and helpless in the woods? She watched them lower their heads to eat and then walk slowly away.

An hour later she was sitting with the Hawken between her knees, wondering if Mourning would be angry when she told him why they were having griddle cakes for supper again, when a buck stepped into the clearing. Olivia slowly lifted the rifle to her shoulder and took her shot. The deer disappeared into the woods, but Olivia knew it had been a kill shot and she wouldn't have to track it far.

She loaded the rifle again, left her journal and possibles bag beneath the tree and strode to where the buck had been standing. The blood trail was easy to follow. Plunging eagerly into the woods, she had to force herself to take the time to mark her trail. She soon came upon the buck, its visible eye looking like glass. Finding it already dead was a great relief; there was no need for her to stick a knife into its throat to put it out of its misery.

She looked behind her; Dougan or Dixby would have no trouble making it most of the way in. Mourning and she would only have to drag the dead weight of the deer a few dozen yards. She paused to listen. Mourning must have heard the shot, but she didn't hear anyone coming. She stopped to retrieve her journal and possibles bag and briskly headed toward home.

When she reached the bottom of their hill she could see that Mourning had made good progress with the roof. He had nailed the poles in place and the bottom two rows of bark lay neatly across them. But the ladder was empty and there was no sign of him. She called his name and then stopped short. Two figures emerged from around the barn and waved to her. Jeremy Kincaid. That had to be him with Mourning. When she hurried closer she saw that their new neighbor had indeed come to call.

Chapter Eighteen

"You're looking grand, Miss Killion." Jeremy removed his hat and bobbed his head.

"Good to see you," she mumbled. Then, in a stronger voice, she announced, "I got a deer."

Mourning raised both arms over his head and wiggled his backside. "Hallelujah. Hallelujah. I heard that shot and I been prayin'. I 'bout forgot how meat taste." He glanced up at the sky. "We better get trackin', 'fore it get too dark to follow a trail."

"There's no tracking to do. It was a good shot. Nice-sized buck." Olivia did her best to sound matter-of-fact and not boastful. "Bring one of the team and I'll lead you to it. We won't have to drag it far."

"Well, let's go," Jeremy said. "I'm glad to lend a hand with the gutting and dressing."

Olivia caught the look of relief that flashed over Mourning's face. *He must be afraid of having to do a lot of things*, she thought. *Just like me. Only difference is, he's better at hiding it.*

"Take me a minute to fix Dixby up with a single harness," Mourning called over his shoulder as he started for the barn. "They still coffee in the pot."

Olivia looked at Jeremy, but he silently declined the offer, holding up his hand, palm out and shaking his head. She went into the cabin to put the journal and possibles bag away, pulled Mourning's shirt off, and combed her hair. Then she joined Jeremy, staring down at the river.

"This is a pretty location," he said. "I've always enjoyed the sound of the river from here, the way you can barely hear the rapids."

Olivia smiled and listened to the soft rush of the water.

"You seem to be getting nicely settled in," Jeremy

said.

Mr. Kincaid had cleaned himself up to come calling – he was shaven and wore a dark blue shirt of good linen.

"Can't complain. It's nice to have a visitor, that's for sure." She paused before she nodded at his chest and said, "Shame to get that nice shirt all bloody."

He shrugged. "So, now do I get to hear the long story of how your friend came by the name of Mourning Free?" Jeremy tilted his head toward the barn.

Olivia smiled. "It isn't really so long. His parents were slaves in Virginia and ran north. His mother was with child, with him, but she walked all the way to Five Rocks – that's the town in Pennsylvania that we come from – and the anti-slavery people took them in. His father chose Free as their new family name."

"Fitting choice, I suppose."

"Bit too fitting. The abolitionists tried to talk them out of it – said it was a dead giveaway that they were fugitive slaves. But they were set on it. Then Mourning's father caught the influenza and died. That was just a few weeks before his wife died birthing."

She paused for a moment.

"The colored midwife they'd brought over from the next town picked up the poor little baby ..." Olivia paused and clasped her hands over her heart, looking up at the sky, "held him to her breast and paced about moaning, 'Oh, this mourning child, this poor, poor mourning child.' She said it over and over again and it stuck. Everyone started calling him 'that poor mourning child,' and Mourning was what got written in the church registry."

Jeremy grinned. Olivia feared she may have gone too far; her audience could have taken her to be making light of one of the saddest stories she'd ever heard. And what about Mourning – how would he feel about her telling this story for the entertainment of a stranger? She felt her face flush with shame.

"So he was born an orphan," Jeremy said.

"Yes."

"Who raised him up?"

She wished she could change the subject, but heard herself go on talking. "A colored family took him in for a while, but he always pretty much took care of himself. He worked everywhere in town and whoever he was working for gave him a place to sleep and fed him. He used to help in my father's store – did everything but wait on customers. My father didn't think that even Five Rocks, packed with Quakers though it may be, was quite prepared for a negro store clerk discussing corset sizes with white ladies."

"No, one would assume not. So the two of you grew up together?"

"I couldn't say that, but I've known Mourning all my life. I was the one who taught him how to read and write," she said.

"Come on," Mourning called, emerging from the barn with a rope in his hand and Dixby at his side. "Let's go get supper."

"Take an axe and your knives," Jeremy called back and Mourning went to fetch them. "And something to put the heart and liver in," Jeremy added.

"I'll get a pan," Olivia said.

When she came back out of the cabin Jeremy was bare-chested, hanging his pretty blue shirt on the wagon post. Mourning was quite a way ahead and Olivia hurried along beside Jeremy, remembering a novel in which the young women were constantly stumbling, providing the young men with an opportunity to grasp their elbows. But what if she pretended too well and fell flat on her face? Worse, what if Jeremy had no interest in holding onto her elbow?

"By the way," Jeremy said, "I brought you and Mr. Free a little housewarming gift. I left it on your table. It's a bag of coffee beans. I buy them at a shop in

157

Detroit that gets them all the way from Brazil. Best coffee you'll ever taste."

"Well thank you, Mr. Kincaid. That was most kind of you. We'll enjoy it. We do like our coffee, though neither of us is very good at making it." The moment she spoke, a scowl hovered over her face. She didn't like the way "we" and "us" had sounded – as if she and Mourning were a couple.

"Would you object to calling me Jeremy?"

"No, of course not," she said.

With that, her manners were all used up. Having seldom spoken to anyone she hadn't known all her life, she had no idea what she was supposed to say now. Should she tell him to call her Olivia? Everyone in Five Rocks did, but that was because they still thought of her as a child. Perhaps he was supposed to ask her permission. This was one count Mabel Mears had been right on – Olivia could have used an older woman to teach her these things. Then her stubborn streak took over. What did she care what a bunch of fuddy-duddies thought? Civilization on the Michigan frontier would survive her lack of proper etiquette just fine. As long as you were kind to other people, wasn't that the most civilized thing?

"And Olivia is fine with me," she said. "Truth be told, you're the first person who's ever called me Miss Killion, except for Mourning – and he only does when he thinks I'm acting snooty. And Mourning might faint on the spot if anyone called him Mr. Free."

They were catching up to Mourning and she wondered if he could hear what they were saying.

"Well, then Mourning it will be. He seems a right good skin. Doing a grand job on the roof."

"Oh Mourning is the handiest fellow you'll ever find. He can do anything." If Mourning could hear them, she hoped lavish praise would help compensate for her having spoken about his private business. Then she changed the subject. "How long have you been out

158

here?"

Jeremy thought for a moment. "Going on eight years. Came out in '34."

"How does your family like life in Michigan?"

"I don't have any family here."

She waited for him to embellish or ask her a question, but he remained silent.

"So where are you from?" she asked as they caught up with Mourning.

"Maine."

"Maine? Oh my, then you must have seen the Atlantic Ocean!"

"Certainly have and it is a sight. But if there's one thing not lacking in Michigan, it's large bodies of water. Lake Huron is just as pretty and doesn't burn your eyes the way saltwater does. Lake St. Clair is lovely too and they've finished putting in a road all the way to Mt. Clemens."

"If you don't farm," she asked, "What do you do? Hunt or trap or something?"

"No, nothing like that. I do spend a lot of time in the woods."

She again waited for him to embellish, wanting to know "Doing what?" but he did not seem inclined to volunteer information about himself

"We haven't been into town yet," she said. "We'll have to go soon, get some milk, eggs, and butter."

"Well, I warned you, it isn't much of a town," he said.

They caught up with Mourning and Olivia took the lead. It wasn't long before Olivia said to Mourning, "You'd better leave Dixby here, where it's easy for him to turn around," and continued toward the dead buck. In her haste, she let her dress catch on a branch and stopped to extricate herself, examining the tear in the fabric and muttering about stupid women's dresses.

"So why are you wearing one?" Jeremy asked.

"What else would I wear?"

"I know women who have a seamstress run up trousers for them. At least for when they're working. Or riding."

Olivia was barely able to hide her shock and did not respond.

"There it is," she said, pointing at her buck, but feeling less excited than she had a moment ago. What women?

Olivia left them to their bloody task and spent the walk home pondering what Jeremy had said. Women who wore trousers? Who ever heard of such a thing? The guidebooks made no mention of it. Maybe he'd been fooling with her. And then the truly troubling question kept repeating itself – what women? If he had no family, he couldn't have been referring to sisters or cousins. And what were those women doing that they needed to wear trousers?

Olivia had begun to see herself as special – resourceful and adventurous. Now that feeling abandoned her. She was nothing but a boring girl who obeyed the rules and whined a lot. She imagined one of those trouser-clad women strolling through the woods with Jeremy and riding bareback with him to Lake Huron, to swim in her birthday suit.

When she reached the cabin she washed her hands and face, lit two lanterns, and searched for her mirror. It was the first time since leaving home that she had bothered to look at her reflection and she was pleasantly surprised. She couldn't see that the past few days had made her look as worn down as she felt. It was a good thing she'd done as Mourning said and started wearing her straw bonnet when she was out in the sun. She brushed her hair, rubbed some powder over her teeth, and rinsed her mouth. Some of the women in Five Rocks dusted their faces with flour and then wetted red crepe paper and rubbed their cheeks with it to make them rosy. Olivia stared in the mirror and wondered if that might make her look any better.

Finally she made a face at herself and stood up. Those women looked ridiculous. Besides, she didn't have any red crepe paper. Enough wasting time on nonsense. She looked like she looked. If he didn't like it, too bad.

She decided to celebrate their first real meal – and first dinner guest – by eating inside. Maybe sitting at a properly set table would remind Mourning that some people actually used utensils to move food from plate to mouth and didn't regard their fork as a giant toothpick. She wished they had some honey wine with which to toast Uncle Scruggs and Aunt Lydia Ann.

A small pouch lay on the table. She opened it and breathed in the heavenly aroma of Jeremy's coffee beans, before setting them on the counter next to the coffee grinder. She would serve it to them later, outside, together with one of the jars of sweet peaches she had bought in Detroit and kept hidden from Mourning. They could at least clink their tin cups together in honor of Uncle Scruggs.

She decided to get out the only tablecloth she had brought from home. Aunt Lydia Ann had cross-stitched it in a red and green design – probably for this very table – and it seemed fitting to use it tonight. Mourning was sure to later make some sarcastic remark about her putting on airs for Jeremy and the tablecloth would be one more thing to carry down that hill and launder, but she didn't care. This was a special occasion. She also picked some wildflowers, arranged them in a tall tin mug, and set it in the center of the table. Then she laid and lit a fire in the pit, already imagining the sizzle of fat and smell of roasting meat. A loud snort from the barn startled her and she went to investigate. The biggest, reddest horse she had ever seen stood there, tethered on a long rope.

"Well, hullo." Olivia stroked its neck. "You must belong to Mr. Kincaid. What's your name? You wait right here, I'll go get you a treat."

She returned with a withered apple cut into

quarters. While the horse ate from her hand she spoke to it in a soothing voice. "There, what a good boy you are."

She had always loved horses. When some men in Five Rocks had banged on the front door to tell Seborn they were going to shoot the horse that had killed her Uncle Scruggs, Olivia had run to Ferguson's Livery in her nightdress and stood in front of the horse, arms outstretched like a cross.

"What do you want to shoot him for?" she said, in tears. "He didn't do it on purpose. It wasn't his fault Uncle Scruggs was bending down behind him. If Mr. Sorenson hadn't fired his stupid pistol, this poor horse wouldn't have gotten spooked and kicked." She had prevailed by sobbing. "Uncle Scruggs would never have wanted you to murder him."

"Are you making friends with old Dougan over there?" she asked the big red horse. "Well, I see they've given you feed and water, so I'd better get back to getting your daddy something to put into his belly." She took a step back and noticed its perfectly matched white stockings. "Lord, what a beautiful animal you are. See you later."

She turned to leave, but was guilt-stricken for neglecting poor Dougan. She walked over to stroke his head. "Yes, you're a good boy too. It's not your fault you're not pretty like him, is it? Couldn't beat him in a race either. But you do your job and I want you to know we appreciate it." She scratched behind his ears.

Then she set to peeling potatoes and cutting them into thick wedges to fry up with salt and pepper. Once they were on the plate, she'd sprinkle them with vinegar, the way Mabel did. She imagined the three of them sitting outside after their meal. Olivia's teacher once told her that her cheekbones, and the shadows beneath them, were her most striking feature, so she'd look good in the firelight, wouldn't she? She turned to pick up the mirror again, but stopped, hating this way of thinking, as if the only thing that mattered about a girl was the way she looked.

Instead she pried the cork out of the jar of peaches and poked a sharp knife into the half-inch layer of paraffin. Why hadn't she bought any glass bowls? All they had were tin plates and cups. But when she dipped a spoon into the jar and cut off a bite of peach, she knew it wouldn't matter if she served them on a shovel. Those sweet peaches were delicious and it required some effort on her part not to gobble them all down.

There was still no sign of Mourning and Jeremy, so she decided she might as well use the time for herself. She gathered her journal, pencil, and eraser and walked partway down the hill to sit among the tall weeds. Biting her bottom lip, she stared for a long moment before starting to sketch the cabin. She vaguely remembered watching her mother paint her watercolors, but Olivia had never put her own hand to drawing. She wished she had one of the new, softer erasers Avis had read about, that made it easier to rub out your mistakes. She was still working on the picture when she saw Mourning and Jeremy approaching. Both shirtless, they were walking on either side of Dixby, with the gutted buck slung over his back.

Olivia rose and waved, then hurried inside to tuck her journal under the mattress. Back outside, she set the frying pans – one for the meat and one for the potatoes – at the edge of the fire. She walked down to meet them and took the pan holding the heart and liver from Mourning. Both men had smears of dried blood on their stomach, arms, and chest. On Mourning it was barely discernable. On Jeremy the contrast with his pale skin made him look even whiter, like a bed sheet. With his shirt off, his narrow shoulders and the deep depression where his neck met his breastbone reminded her of a plucked chicken, but she scolded herself for that observation. *The way a man looks shouldn't count for so much either. God gave us our faces and bodies and all we can do is live with them. Pretty people didn't do anything to deserve looking like that. Why should we think more of them for it?* While she cut up and fried the heart and liver, she studied her hands and arms. What had made white folks so sure their pale, fishy skin was better? Why hadn't they thought, gosh, look at these lucky people, they have such lovely dark skin? But she knew the answer. People always think whatever they have is just perfect. Whatever they do, the fact that they did it makes it the right thing to do. Once they choose a religion, that makes it God's holy word.

Mourning and Jeremy were down past the barn, staring up at a tall tree from which a sturdy bough jutted, fifteen to twenty feet off the ground. *Yes,* Olivia thought, *that would be a good place to hang the buck. Far from the cabin and high enough so that not even a bear could get at it.* For a moment she imagined a pack of frustrated wolves or coyotes, leaping up at the carcass time after time and then giving up and going to look for easier pickings – like her or Mourning. They *had* to get doors on the cabin and barn. But there was no point in thinking about that now. Now she was going to have a delicious dinner and enjoy the company of her good friend and the man who – perhaps – had come to call on her.

Chapter Nineteen

Olivia walked toward the two men, carrying a plate of fried liver and heart. Too hungry to resist, she popped a few pieces into her mouth on the way. With her fingers. Now she knew for sure she couldn't be counted on to preserve gentility on the frontier.

Mourning threw a length of rope over the tree branch. Jeremy tied one end around the hind legs of the carcass, while Mourning fastened the other to

Dixby's harness and led him away, hoisting the deer into the air.

"You plan on eating some of this critter tonight?" Jeremy asked.

"Indeed we do." Mourning nodded.

"Then lower it down a bit and I'll cut out the back straps. They're good eating – right tender."

Olivia came up next to them and held out the plate. The meat disappeared in what seemed seconds. Mourning and Jeremy returned to their bloody job and soon joined her around the fire. They put some of the meat they had cut into one of the frying pans and rigged up a spit for the rest.

Jeremy studied the sky. "Normally I'd say leave the carcass hanging to dry for a few days, but it looks like bad weather coming. You'd best smoke it tonight." He looked at Mourning's blank face and continued. "Just finish skinning it, cut the meat into smaller pieces, and hang them over a slow burning fire. You got to watch the wind and keep the meat in the smoke. And the fire not too hot. Four-five hours ought to do it."

"I thought we spose to pickle it," Mourning said.

"You could do that."

While the men went to clean themselves up in the river, Olivia finished frying up the meat and potatoes.

Mourning returned before Jeremy and bent down close to her, whispering. "What he been sayin' back there – 'bout my skin?"

"Your skin?" Olivia asked, puzzled.

"When we been walkin' before, two a you behind me, I heard him say something 'bout my skin bein' good."

Olivia frowned for a moment and then realized what he was referring to and grinned. "No. What he said was that you 'seem like a right good skin.' It's an expression the Irish use – means a good person. My Mammo Killion used to say that about people."

"He sure talk funny sometimes," Mourning said.

Olivia considered this. "He must have Irish grandparents, like me. Doesn't have an Irish accent, but once in a while one of those sayings creeps in."

"He sound like a skin what don't know who he be."

"Well you know, people pick up the way their own folks talk. Don't even realize that other people might not understand some of the expressions they use. You know . . ." She hesitated. "I've always wanted to ask you about the way you talk."

"What wrong with the way I be talkin'?"

"Nothing. Nothing's wrong with it. Not at all. It's just different from the way everyone else in Five Rocks speaks."

She paused, but Mourning said nothing.

"You're the only colored person I know, but I'm guessing other colored folks talk like you. Is that right?"

"Spose so."

"But you grew up listening to white people all day, so I would think you might talk more like us."

"You forgettin' I been livin' with them Carters."

"Well, yes, but even then you worked for white folks. Spent most of your day with white folks. And you ran away from the Carters when you were what, nine?"

"I be talkin' like colored folks cause I be colored folks. Not like Mr. Jeremy Kincaid what can't decide if he Irish or American. I know what I be."

She wondered what had aroused this hint of animosity and glanced over her shoulder to make sure Jeremy was still out of earshot. "Did he do something to make you angry?" she asked. "I thought you two were getting along just grand."

Mourning followed her glance down to where Jeremy was still crouched on the white boulder, splashing his upper body with water. "I ain't meanin' to say nothing bad 'bout him. He be a right good skin hisself, helpin' me with that buck, teachin' me what I gotta do. Ain't bad company neither. But I can tell you one thing – that there be a man what got a whole mess

166

a habits from livin' on his own and likin' it. He ain't gonna change one thing in his life to 'ccommodate no one else." He paused and looked directly into her eyes. "What I sayin' is – that ain't no man what gonna marry you."

Olivia's jaw dropped. "Marry me! What an idea. Honestly, Mourning."

Jeremy had started up the hill and Mourning spoke quickly, under his breath. "I know you been thinkin' on it. I seen the way you be lookin' at him and I tellin' you – that man there ain't gonna be takin' on no wife."

Jeremy's approach saved Olivia from having to respond. She wondered if her face looked as red as it felt and busied herself turning the pieces of meat.

"That felt good," Jeremy said, still shirtless and dripping.

Too distracted to think to offer him a towel, Olivia mumbled, "I introduced myself to your horse. Beautiful animal. What's his name?"

"Ernest."

"Ernest?" She laughed. "Not what I would have expected."

She waited a moment for him to say something else. He didn't. She rose and went inside to grind the coffee beans, wondering what had made Mourning talk like that. Had Jeremy said something about her? Did he dislike her? But he was the one who came calling; if nothing else, he must want to be friends. She sighed and fretted and finally went back out with the coffee pot, setting it near the fire, ready to brew. The three of them sat watching the meat and potatoes fry.

"What are we going to do with all that meat?" Olivia looked back toward the tree where the deer hung. "Maybe we should take some of it into town to sell."

Mourning looked at her as if she were unbalanced. "Let someone else enjoy the fresh venison what our expert hunter lady got? You gone loony?"

"Well, it's not going to stay fresh forever. How much

do you think we can eat in a week or two?"

"Don't you worry. I got a Michigan-size appetite. Feel like I could eat the whole thing. Anyway, you gonna pickle it," Mourning said.

"I don't know how to do that."

"Must tell you in them guide books," Mourning said. "I think all you gotta do is boil up a big pot a water and throw in a mess a sugar and salt and a handful a saltpeter. Once it be good and boilin' you take it off the fire, skim the foam off, and let it cool 'fore you set your meat swimmin' in there. You just gotta remember to put a big old rock on top a the meat, hold it down under the water."

"That's about right. It is quite simple," Jeremy agreed.

"And if I don't do it right, will we know if the meat's gone off?"

"No worry on that account," Jeremy said. "If you make a *hames* of it, you'll smell it. So will people in the next county."

"Well, I guess all I can do is try," she said. She poked at the meat sizzling in the skillet, declared it done, and pulled both frying pans out of the fire. "I set the table inside," she said. "Like a real dinner."

"It's quite nice out here, I thought," Jeremy said. "Air's a little chilly, but we've got the fire. Can make all the mess we want."

"You set yourself down, Livia." Mourning nodded in agreement. "I go get them plates. Tonight I's waiting on you, hunter lady."

Mourning dished the food out and neither he nor Jeremy waited for it to cool. Olivia watched them dig in, eating with their fingers and licking them. Those adventurous women in trousers probably had no use for knives and forks. Olivia hesitantly put her utensils aside and gnawed at the fried venison as enthusiastically as her companions.

After they had eaten more than their fill Olivia

carried over a bucket and they poured dippers of water over their hands and splashed their greasy mouths and chins. Tired, Olivia did not offer to hunt up a towel and neither of the men asked for one – they wiped their mouths on their hands and their hands on their trousers. Olivia raised her arm, intending to use her sleeve, but couldn't. Her dress may be torn and filthy, but she couldn't bring herself to use it as a rag. She wiped her hand across her mouth a few more times.

She set the coffee pot in the fire and served the peaches, which they happily slurped. When she poured the coffee they obliged and shouted a loud, "Hear, hear," in honor of Uncle Scruggs, but the conversation quickly turned to a discussion of how much bark the roof would take. Then Mourning raised his chin and pointed it over Olivia's shoulder.

"You want Dougan and Dixby to spend the night standin' there?" he asked.

She looked at him blankly.

"Your vegetable garden – you want it next to the cabin there, like I said?"

"Oh. Sure." She had not given it a moment's thought. "Do you have a vegetable garden?" she asked Jeremy.

"No."

She managed to find other questions to ask Jeremy, but the result was the same – a simple yes or no.

"Well." Jeremy stood up. "Time I was going. Let you tend to that meat."

"We appreciate all your help." Olivia started to get to her feet, but Jeremy waved her down, saying, "Don't bother yourself. I can find my way to Ernest."

While Jeremy was in the barn saddling his horse Olivia stared into the fire, willing Mourning to keep his big mouth shut.

"Delicious dinner," Jeremy said as he mounted. "We'll be by, Ernest and I." He raised a hand to his hat and said, "After," in farewell.

"You're always welcome," she called to his back, despising herself for the pleading tone of her voice.

"Guess you ain't never heard a hard to get," Mourning muttered as Jeremy disappeared into the dark.

Olivia did not respond.

"That talk about makin' a *hames* – that 'nother one a them Irish things?" Mourning asked as he rose.

"I guess so. I never heard that one before, but it must be." She turned away to clear up the dishes and then scooped up some ashes from the edge of the fire for scouring the frying pans.

"I gotta get to diggin' a garbage pit," Mourning said, more to himself than to her. "Now that we lucky 'nuff we got garbage." He rose and stretched. "You get some water boilin' while I finish butcherin' that animal."

Olivia built up the fire, filled the two biggest pots with water, and wandered about with a lantern searching for rocks large enough to hold the meat under the brine. Neither she nor Mourning was inclined to conversation. When they had finally finished with the meat, Olivia said good night, left her dress in a heap on the floor, pulled her nightdress on, and collapsed onto her bed. She lay looking up at the dark clouds and feeling vaguely angry with Jeremy, though she could find no justification for this emotion. He had behaved like the perfect neighbor – seen that they needed help and stayed to offer his. Had even brought them a gift. So why did she feel so insulted?

He must have a lady friend. So why couldn't he just say so? Nothing would be easier than tossing her into the conversation. "Me and my girl don't plan to farm." "My girl really loves riding Ernest." Then it would be different. Olivia would know. She wouldn't be left thinking that she must be so ugly, boring, or stupid that he wouldn't give her a second look, not even out here, in the middle of nowhere.

Lord in heaven, how many girls were there for him

to choose from? If she were the last one on earth, would he still pay her no mind? Why? What did he think was wrong with her? He'd never heard of Crazy Nola June or Old Man Killion whoring with Jettie Place.

The air had turned cold. Shoot, why was she losing sleep over some stupid man with a chest like a chicken? There was hardly anything left of the night and they had so much to do tomorrow. Mourning said they *had* to get the rest of the roof on. She snuggled under the comforter and fell into a restless sleep.

A loud clap of thunder awakened her, just as a light sprinkle turned into a downpour. She was soaked before she got out of bed. She grabbed the wet bedding and tried to wad it up on the narrow kitchen counter, which was under the finished part of the roof, but her quilt fell to the floor. She picked it up and even in the dark could see the muddy streaks. How would she ever get it clean? It wouldn't even fit into the wash tub.

Where was Mourning? Had he taken the wagon into the barn? The rain let up a little and she peeked out the door, but could see nothing. "Mourning!" she shouted. "I'm an idiot. Come in here if you want."

She searched for their precious lucifer matches and found them on the counter under an overturned pot, miraculously still dry. There did not seem to be any leaks in Mourning's roof. She dragged one of the stumps over and sat on it, shivering, her back pressed against the logs of the front wall. When the rain lightened to a drizzle she crouched by the bed to check that her things weren't standing in a puddle, but the water seemed to be draining toward the door. Had Uncle Scruggs been that clever? Purposely built the floor with just the slightest incline? She checked the lanterns, punk wood, and food stuffs; Mourning had wrapped them all and set them on the counter against the wall, where they would be protected from the rain. Then she found her wooden clogs and ventured outside.

She nearly slid on the wet ground, but caught her balance. *Wouldn't that be wonderful,* she thought, *to be not only chilled and wet, but covered with mud and with no dry wood for a fire?* She took small, careful steps to check on the woodpile. The sheet of canvas was in place and the back wall of the cabin seemed to be offering sufficient protection.

Then she went toward the barn, where she saw that Mourning had followed her suggestion and wedged the wagon into the front corner. She stepped closer and studied his cozy nest – he had prepared a thick bed of twigs, placed his mattress over them, wheeled the wagon in place, and draped sheets of canvas over its sides. Still, he was on the ground and who knew how much more rain would fall. She stood silently for a moment, listening. He must be asleep.

She turned to leave, then stopped and said in a hesitant whisper. "I came to say I'm sorry. If you're getting wet, please come to the cabin. The part under the roof is dry, except for the floor."

The edge of the canvas flapped. "I be fine in here. Nice and cozy."

She moved closer and saw the raft of evenly placed roof poles, as wide as the wagon, that his mattress rested upon. The water would have to stand five or six inches deep for him to get wet.

"You knew it was going to rain, didn't you?"

"Been sayin' so."

"I mean tonight. You knew it was going to rain tonight."

"Thought it might."

"You could have told me, warned me to get ready for it," she said softly.

"Guess I coulda."

Another downpour began and she turned to scurry back to the cabin, but the canvas flap opened wide and Mourning's voice commanded. "Come on, get in here, 'fore you be catchin' it."

172

She hesitated, but the sheet of rain presented a convincing argument. She wiggled in, her head to his feet, hugging the cloak that she had pulled on, and struggling to keep it and her muslin nightgown pulled down past her knees. He squeezed to the far side, leaving space between them.

"I'll just wait here a few minutes, until it lets up again," she said.

"Ain't no place for you to lie down in there," he said. "You think you gonna sleep standin' up by the wall? Here." He was using a sheet of canvas for a blanket and shook it out to cover both of them. "Just pretend I be a lump of clay and get some sleep."

Olivia's head shook slightly as she imagined the look on Mabel Mears' face, if she could see them now. Well, what did that cow think she would have done? Olivia stayed put. Mourning snored steadily and her mind was blank as she felt herself dragged down into sleep.

Chapter Twenty

A few hours later a full bladder woke Olivia. She'd forgotten where she was and tried to sit up, banging her head against the axle and yelping, but this elicited only a whistling snore from Mourning. Mortified, she carefully rolled onto her elbows and extracted herself from beneath the wagon. It was no longer raining, but the air felt wet, more a mist than a drizzle. The sky was still dark, but she knew she was done sleeping. After she hobbled to the outhouse on her clogs and splashed water over her hands and face, she lit the lantern on the kitchen counter and surveyed her soggy home.

Oh Lord, the mattress. She'd been so busy bundling up her bedding, she hadn't given a thought to her lovely new mattress. It was soaked. Dispirited, she slumped down onto one of the stump chairs, elbows on her knees. The long day of drudgery had not yet begun and already she was drained of energy. And where was she supposed to sleep tonight? Making do in an emergency as she had last night was one thing; the idea of tucking in with Mourning again was quite impossible.

For a moment she wondered if there might be any rooms to let in that dismal-looking town. That had, after all, been her original plan – before she knew what it felt like to haul water and chop wood all day. Walk an hour, two hours, alone in the twilight? Then back in the morning, worn out before she'd even started her chores? No thank you.

Tears began to run down her cheeks, though she knew there was nothing to cry about. Had the cabin burned down? Indians attacked them? Mourning fallen ill? No, nothing bad had happened. So what's wrong, little girl, why are you crying? Olivia imagined a kindly gentleman bending down to comfort her. She cringed when she heard her whiny response. It rained last night. Sob, sob, boo-hoo. A short, sharp laugh escaped her, but the tears continued to flow. Her shoulders shook until her body ached even more. Finally she rose and wiped the backs of her hands across her eyes. *Stop feeling sorry for yourself and get on with it. Just get on with it.*

She managed to salvage some dry wood from the bottom of the pile and got a fire going in the fireplace. Then she dragged one of the wicker baskets from under the bed and was relieved to find that her clothes were only damp. She pulled out a work dress, laid it near the fire, and glared at it. Who said she had to wear that stupid thing?

"You got any coffee cookin'?" Mourning's voice startled her from the other side of the flap.

"Oh. Good morning." She pulled the canvas aside. "I'll get some on now. There's a fire going in here. Come in." She reached for the coffee pot.

He did, but then squinted at her and turned away, obviously uncomfortable. She looked down at her chest

174

and was horrified. Even in the dim light she could see the wet patches of her chemise clinging to the hard little knobs of her nipples. She pulled her cloak around her and flushed red.

"I didn't think. I just got up and my clothes are all wet," she stammered.

"Any a them peaches left?"

"No. Are your clothes dry?"

"Surely are."

"I was thinking, could I maybe borrow a pair of your trousers? Just for today?"

"Sure could. But, my, my, my, Lady Grody gonna have a conniption fit."

"When Lady Grody comes out here and starts hunting deer, hauling water, and splitting firewood, she can tell me what to wear."

"I go get you a pair. Shirt to go with 'em too."

The trousers were wide in the waist by a good five inches and the circles worn into the fabric by Mourning's knees hung mid-calf on Olivia. She folded the bottoms of the pant legs into thick cuffs and ran a piece of twine through the belt loops. Then she rolled up the sleeves of the flannel shirt. She felt wonderfully unencumbered and her mood changed. Grinning, she did a little dance around the cabin floor and then kicked each leg as high as she could. It was a whole new world of possibilities. *I could climb over a fence*, she thought. *Or up a tree. Ride bareback.* She spun around.

"I heard 'bout women on the trail goin' over them Great Plains wearin' men's clothes." Mourning's voice came from the other side of the wall.

"I hope you don't mind me borrowing them," she said sheepishly, as she stepped outside and did a little pirouette.

He lifted his right hand to his shoulder, slowly rolled it out, and bent at the waist, as if welcoming a queen into a room. "Nah, I don't mind. Don't want you ruinin' all them 'spensive dresses and thinkin' you gotta buy more," he said and turned away

They worked all morning in a spitting drizzle. By mid-afternoon the sky was clear and Olivia asked Mourning to help her carry her mattress out to dry.

"Ain't no chance it gonna be dry for tonight," Mourning said as they leaned it against the wall of the cabin.

He took up the scythe and cut an enormous pile of buffalo grass laced with weeds. "You get the thorns out a that mess and pile it on your bed. I get you a sheet of canvas to throw over it. Ain't no mattress, but it be better than bare wood."

Olivia smiled in thanks and they both went about their chores. When they stopped for a lunch of venison and beans, Mourning looked up and studied the sky.

"Don't look like they's more rain comin'," he said. "Course that don't mean nothing. One a them men on the boat said Michigan weather be hard to read on 'ccount of the wind blowin' in crazy directions off all them lakes." He stopped to swallow and then asked, "How 'bout tomorrow morning we go into that Fae's Landing, see 'bout gettin' a door made."

"Oh yes." Olivia's smile was wide.

She hummed as she gathered up the sodden clothing and bedclothes. This time she lit a fire down by the river, boiled water, and gave the laundry a proper soaking. She tied up more lines and rinsed out the sheets first.

Later she walked past the bedclothes, enjoying the sound of them flapping in the wind. The scent of sun on freshly laundered linen brought her to a stop, stone still. That smell. That sound. The warmth of the sun on her skin. She was a little girl – maybe five or six – sitting in the grass under the clothes line, watching her mother slip wooden pegs into the pocket of her stiff white apron before shaking out a white sheet and folding it into the laundry basket. Olivia squeezed her eyes shut and lifted her chin. Her mother's face. She had to see her mother's face. Hanging up the wash while her little girl played at her feet. But Olivia could not see beyond her mother's bare feet and the folds of her long brown skirt.

"I been thinkin', maybe we both have us a bath tonight." Mourning's voice brought her back to the present. "Nice hot water. Take the chill off."

"That sounds good," she said. "Are we going to go into town even if it's raining?"

He frowned at the sky. "Dunno. Guess you can have your say 'bout that. I ain't gonna sit inside tomorrow, no matter if it be rainin' or not. Make no difference to me if I be workin' in the rain or drivin' in the rain."

"So we'll go. Even if it's raining," she said and went on with her chores.

Late in the afternoon she called to Mourning that if he wanted a bath, he'd best come get it.

"Sure is dark in here now that you've got the roof on," she said and ignored his sarcastic offer to take it off.

She lifted four buckets of steaming water from the hearth, brought in two of cold, and said, "You go first," as she set the washtub near the fireplace. Before she left him to his privacy, she set a large pot of water to heat on the crane and their only other tin bucket on the hearth, to get started heating for her own bath.

She sat by the fire pit, watching the stars come out and listening to him splash. When he emerged, fragrant with soap and shiny as tar, she noted that he had put his dirty clothes back on.

"You don't have to keep wearing the same clothes forever, Mourning. I'll wash them," she said as she handed him a cup of coffee.

"Don't matter none. They just be gettin' dirty all over again."

"Do you have enough clothes?" she asked. "I mean, if I keep –"

"You mean with you wearin' my pants just for

today?" He finished the question with a grin.

"Well, they are awfully comfortable. I wouldn't mind borrowing them every day. Maybe we could get you some new ones in town tomorrow. Or even some that would fit me better."

"Yeah, we can see 'bout that."

"We've got a special dessert," she said. "I picked some berries today. I don't know what kind they are, but I ate some this morning and I haven't died yet."

"Sound good to me."

"Come help me empty that tub so I can get cleaned up."

At first she sat in the tub hugging her knees, but then sank down, arms and legs dangling over the sides. Her mind blank, she watched the flickering shadows the lantern made on the wall. Coyotes howled in the distance and the strains of Mourning's harmonica joined in. She wished someone would build a fire under her, so she could lie there forever, but the chill eventually drove her out. She put Mourning's clothes back on and joined him in the coolness of the early evening. Mourning had lit a fire in the pit and she put together a simple supper of venison, bread, and the berries.

"Maybe we should buy another barrel tomorrow," she said. "We could set it on the wagon and drive down to the river, so I could fill it up down there, instead of carrying all those buckets."

Mourning thought for a moment. "Could try, I guess. But the mouth a that barrel gonna be awful high, standin' up there. You gonna have to climb up on the wagon, pour the water in, and get back down. Same thing when you get up there."

"Oh..."

"But that be good thinking. And a barrel don't cost much. You could try and see which be easier." Mourning shrugged.

"So we're finally going to see the town," she said as

178

she finished the last of her berries. "Maybe we'll get to know some people. We could drive over and introduce ourselves to those neighbors too – those Stubblefields Jeremy told us about."

"Time for that." He sniffed his nose. "You ain't gonna be goin' over there, borrow no cup of flour."

"They're farmers. He could give you a lot of helpful advice."

"Time for that."

"They might be interested in renting the team. And even if not, it would be nice to have some folks to talk to."

"Folks ain't always a big treat. We don't gotta be goin' 'round showin' ourselves off. Here we be – one sweet young white girl and one big scary black man, livin' on a piece a land what ain't got but one cabin on it. Anyway, I ain't never noticed you been such a big talker back in Five Rocks."

She bristled. "I had friends."

"Must a been the invisible kind." He tossed a piece of wood into the fire.

"What would you know about me and any friends I may or may not have had?"

"Nothing, I guess." His tone had grown gentler

After a long silence broken only by the crackling fire, Olivia asked, "How come you came back to Five Rocks?"

"What you mean?"

"You know – the Carters. Why didn't you stay with them? Were they mean to you?"

He poked at the fire with a stick and shrugged. "Guess it been plenty crowded in that house. They had a passel of kids of they own."

"What are you smiling about?" she asked.

"Just rememberin'. Old Goody got so many kids, he hadda build a loft for them to sleep in. Cut out a hole in the floor, right over the stove, so we gonna get some heat up there. They had the most ugliest cat you ever

179

seen and that bag a fur been wanting to sleep up in the loft with us. It finally learned how to climb up the ladder and we thinkin' it so smart. But then when it wanna get down, it jump through that hole, right straight down onto the hot stove. You never heard such screeching."

Olivia smiled with him and they sat through another long silence before she asked, "Do you believe in God?"

"Spose so."

"Do you ever get mad at Him? I mean, for taking your parents away from you, and for letting there be slavery, and for all the other terrible things in the world?"

"Ain't never thought on it much."

"I know what the ministers say," she said. "That God didn't make slavery. God only made Man, and Man made slavery."

"Indeed."

"But why did God have to make people capable of doing such awful things?"

"That what you be spendin' your time worryin' on?" He rose to feed a log to the fire.

"Not so much any more. When I was little I used to wonder a lot about things like that. You know, why people have to go through all they do, when they're just going to die in the end anyway. You might as well up and die now – save yourself all the trouble in between."

"Folks seem to like bein' alive. Know I do."

"But don't you ever wonder why God made the world?"

He shrugged. "Guess I been luckier than you. I spent my life busy wondering if I'm a have a place to sleep tonight. So when you stop worryin' on all that stuff?"

"One day I heard someone talking. Remember that raggedy old peddler that used to come through Five Rocks? The one with the cart with those big red wheels? One day there were two men out in the street, having a big argument about whose religion was right, the Catholics or the Presbyterians. That peddler came along and shut them both up. He said no one is right. That it's impossible for a person to be right. He said that if God does exist, there's one thing for sure about Him – He never meant for human beings to know the answers to those questions. If they did, then they wouldn't be people. They'd be God. He said it's just like your eyes can't see everything, and your ears can't hear everything, so your brain can't understand those things. So it's no use wondering."

"Bet you give him what for."

"No. I liked what he said. Thinking about that stuff had been making me crazy. But it still doesn't seem right to me, all the bad things that go on, and God just sitting up there watching."

"Damn." Mourning slapped his neck. "You see that one? Big as a hummingbird. Took a bite right out a me. Shoot." He slapped himself again. "God sure coulda done without creatin' these goldarn Pontiacer flies. They gonna get worse, the hotter it get. Then in the summer they say ox flies gonna come out. Folks say they can eat right into the hide of a cow. They like to land on the brisket, right where poor Dixby and Dougan ain't gonna be able to chase 'em away. We gonna have to start rubbing 'em with turpentine and grease."

They sat in silence after that, listening to the night sounds, until Olivia felt the darkness like a weight and went to bed.

Chapter Twenty-One

The next morning Olivia eagerly threw off the comforter. They were going to do something different! She made a tangle of the clothes in her baskets, searching for the soft green Sunday dress that she kept rolled up in a petticoat. The smooth wooden floor was cool against her feet as she stepped into three petticoats. She was dressed and slipping her feet into her Roman sandals when three loud handclaps sounded outside the canvas flap – Mourning's way of telling her that he was impatient to begin the day.

Olivia stuck her uncombed head through the doorway. "You're wearing your work clothes?"

"We ain't goin' to no church on a Wednesday."

She paused, realizing she'd had no idea what day of the week it was. One day blurred into another. "I suppose I'll look silly in this dress," she said, running her hands over its skirt. "I didn't think it was Sunday. I just thought we'll be meeting folks, and I want, you know, to make a good impression."

Mourning's blank face expressed a total lack of interest in her attire and she raised her chin. "Well, I'm going to keep it on. I might as well enjoy looking like a human being for one day."

"Never know, might run into that Jeremy fellow." Mourning raised and lowered his eyebrows.

She ignored him. "Maybe there'll be someplace nice to eat."

"You gonna spend good money on food? We got all the venison we can eat right here."

"Well, maybe we can have a glass of nice cool lemonade."

When she was ready to leave and came into the yard wearing her velvet bonnet, Mourning made a show of dusting off the seat cushion and bowing deeply before he stepped aside for her to climb up onto the wagon.

"Okay, Mourning Free, off we go. Our first trip into the great town of Fae's Landing. Let's take that longer way Jeremy told you about, where we don't have to cross any water."

"Yes, Miz Olivia," Mourning replied, but there was no rancor in his voice and they chatted amiably all the way.

He had removed his shoes as soon as he got up on the wagon, like the guide books said, to save the leather. It made her remember him as a child, going barefooted all summer. Her heart tightened in her chest and she wished that she, or someone, could have looked out for him better.

They entered Fae's Landing on a wide, rutted trail that passed the general store and ran toward the river. "Well I can't say as I've ever seen such a sorry and worn-out looking place," Olivia murmured. "This Podunk town makes Five Rocks look good." She bit her upper lip and shook her head.

"It got a store," Mourning said. "That what we come for."

"Pier Street." She read the battered sign out loud.

Mourning followed it down to the edge of the water. The "pier" revealed itself as a few lengths of straggly rope staked to a flat stretch of riverbank where folks tied up their rafts and canoes. From there a narrow, bumpy dirt road cut north toward the "bridge" Jeremy had told them about – six logs, laid side by side over the river.

"Lord, I'm glad we didn't come up on that thing at night and try to drive over it," Olivia said. "Wouldn't much like to have to go under it, either. Look how low it sits. People on rafts must have to lay down flat and pray they don't get knocked clean into the water."

Mourning declined to comment. He turned the wagon around and drove slowly up and down the two nameless dirt roads that ran perpendicular to Pier Street. They were lined with sagging, weather-beaten, lopsided homes. The houses were all built of sawed lumber, but every part of them that could peel off, fall off, break, or rot away had. There were torn, dirty signs in the front windows of quite a few of them – Fresh Bread, Fresh Fish, Clean Room to Let, Good Food, Corn Whiskey 30¢.

"They don't exactly stir up a desire to rush right in,

do they?" She sighed. "Not one of them looks to have anything fresh, good, or clean to offer."

The town looked deserted. The only human being they saw was an unshaven man sitting in a rocker on the front porch of the house that offered whiskey for sale. He touched a finger to the brim of his hat as they drove past and Olivia nodded back.

"We might as well go back down by the river and get our business with the saw mill done," she said and Mourning silently turned the wagon around again.

A water-powered gristmill sat on the riverbank. The bottom half of it was built of crumbling stone and the top half of weather-beaten wood. Not far from it was a makeshift tannery – a lean-to and some skins hanging on poles. Neither seemed to be working that day. Mourning drove toward the saw mill, which also sat on the water, a little farther south. Its big wheel slap-slapped the river and a small yellow dog came racing around the side of the mill to bark at them.

"I don't hear any saws," she said. "Nothing's buzzing around here but these green monsters." She batted away a shiny horsefly.

"Ain't much business goin' on today," Mourning agreed. He pulled lightly on the reins and eased himself to the ground. She climbed down and followed him, leaving a wide berth around the yapping dog.

"Don't you even think about snapping at us." She shook her finger at the mangy animal.

Mourning pushed the door open and peered into the dim light. "Hullo."

There was a man inside, lying flat on his back on a worktable, feet dangling over the end. Olivia might have taken him for dead, but at the sound of Mourning's voice he sat straight up. He squinted for a moment, then blew his nose into his hand and wiped it on his backside as he got off the table.

"Hullo to you." His white beard was long and stringy and he wore only a floppy gray hat, long-sleeved

184

long johns, and scruffy boots.

"This be a workin' mill?" Mourning skipped introductions. He often avoided having to decide whether or not to offer his hand to a white man, and Olivia was sure that was one hand he had no interest in shaking.

"Sure is. Right busy one. But ever body's gone today. Some kind of goings on over in Anthony. Picnic or some such. Left me here to keep an eye out. You come back tomorrow, you'll see."

"You work here?"

"Don't come here for fun."

"Can I order a door from you?"

"Surely can."

Mourning drew a piece of paper out of his pocket. He had made a drawing of the door he wanted for the cabin, showing the measurements. A pencil stub lay on the table and he picked it up and wrote "Dor fer Skrugs Kabin" under the picture.

"Ain't never seen no nigger what could write." The man sidled over to peer closely at the paper and Olivia guessed he was probably illiterate himself. There was no hostility in his voice, only amazement, as if Mourning had sprouted a second head. Mourning handed the man the paper and he pressed it to his scrawny chest and patted it several times. He promised to give it to the owner of the mill first thing in the morning.

"You tell him I be back soon to settle on a price."

"Surely will. I surely will do that."

"You got a barrel to sell us?" Mourning asked.

"Nah. Might try over at the livery, if they's anyone there." The man had lost interest in them and was busy scratching himself.

Mourning turned to leave, but paused in the doorway to ask, "You know anyone might be wantin' to hire a yoke of oxen?"

"Can't say I do. But I'll let folks know you're

offerin'."

Their next stop was the livery, where they bought a barrel from the fattest man Olivia had ever seen. He was foul smelling and no more friendly than the man at the saw mill, but at least he was fully clothed. Mourning asked him the same question about the oxen and received the same reply.

"Well, I guess that's it for our big day in town," Olivia said when they went back outside. "Lucky I dressed for the occasion."

"You spectin' a welcome committee gonna invite us to Sunday potluck?" Mourning asked, unperturbed by their lack of social success.

"I certainly did expect to see some normal looking folks. Someone who might bother to ask who we are and where we've come from." She climbed up into the wagon and looked around. "This surely is the right place for the likes of us. No need to make up some story about my poor dead husband for the folks in this town. We could probably live out at the farm for twenty years without anyone taking notice."

"He say they all gone to a picnic. Next time we come, folks'll be home."

"I don't think I'd feel like knocking on any of those decrepit front doors, even if folks *were* at home."

She thought she was going to cry, but took a few deep breaths and held it in. Mourning drove back the way they had come.

"At least we can stop at the General Store," Olivia said, though she had lost her enthusiasm. It looked no better than the other buildings – weather-beaten wood and one filthy window. "I think it's open. I saw something move in there."

"You go 'head," Mourning said and stopped the wagon for her to climb down.

A musky smell greeted Olivia when she pushed the door open. A young woman stood behind the counter. She might have once been pretty, before she was

186

marked by the pox. If not for the scars, she would have reminded Olivia of a younger, clean-scrubbed Jettie Place.

"Hullo, I'm new in the area and wanted to get acquainted. Olivia Killion." She offered a hand. "I'm out at the Scruggs cabin. Lorenzo was my uncle."

"Norma Gay Meyers." The woman returned the smile and warmly took Olivia's hand in hers. "Your uncle left here before I ever got to meet him, but I know the place. Nice that it won't be standing empty no more. Always glad to see new faces. Mrs. Stubblefield ..." Miss Meyers turned to a woman in the back of the store. She had been fingering bolts of cloth, but now took a step forward and made no effort to hide her head to toe scrutiny of Olivia.

"Olivia Killion, please make the acquaintance of Iola Stubblefield," Norma Gay said brightly, pronouncing the woman's given name "Eye-o-la."

The face staring at Olivia was plain looking, the kind of woman whose age is hard to tell. Olivia guessed mid-thirties to early forties and almost sighed her disappointment. She'd been hoping her neighbor would be young and cheerful, with a passel of sweet-looking children trailing behind her.

No matter where she was, Mrs. Stubblefield would immediately be recognized as a farmer's wife. Thin, colorless, dressed in brown calico, wispy hair pulled back in a bun. She had a pointy chin that she held slightly upwards and deep lines ran along the sides of her face and between her eyebrows. She studied Olivia with pursed lips, but the smile that finally broke across her face seemed genuinely friendly.

"Mrs. Stubblefield and her husband have a place about eight miles southeast of you," Norma Gay offered.

"Well, praise the Lord, nice to meet you." Iola Stubblefield pumped Olivia's arm. "Can't tell you how good it will be to have neighbors. You need any help settling in, anything at all, all you got to do is holler. My Filmore can grow anything. Strong as an ox and not quite as dumb. And I'm the closest thing there is to a doctor for miles."

Well, here is living proof that women make lives for themselves out here, Olivia thought. But she gazed at Iola's leathery face with concern. *Is that how I will look in a few years? Will my eyes be as steely and cold as hers?* There was something unsettling about those eyes, but Olivia chose to pay attention only to Iola's smile and the words of welcome that passed her lips.

"Have you trained as a nurse?" Olivia asked.

"Nah, none of that book learning. I had the best training there is – doing. I've birthed more babies than anyone calls himself a doctor. My grandma taught me everything a body can know about medicines and you'd be surprised how much more I've learned from the savages. They may be godless heathens, but they have their own ways with the plants growing around here."

"And your husband farms?"

She nodded proudly. "This year he's putting in five acres of buckwheat, five of corn, and two of potatoes."

"Do you have a team of oxen?"

"No, not yet. Filmore does all his own pushing and pulling. Like I said, he's big as an ox himself. And twice as stubborn. Takes on a hired man to help him, come planting and harvest time."

"Do you think he'd be interested in hiring the use of a team? Ours is good and strong. It wouldn't have to be for cash. Could be for eggs, milk, and butter or in exchange for work."

"Well, I think he would. You tell your husband to come over and exchange words with him."

"There's just me. I don't have a husband." Olivia held her breath as she watched for Mrs. Stubblefield's reaction.

"Lordie me, what's a child like you doing out here on her own?"

"My uncle left the land to me. I thought I'd have a go at it. If I don't, I'll lose my claim. I've got a good hired man to work it for me."

"I never have heard of such a thing. Not never in my whole life. Why you're hardly grown. How in heaven's name did your family let you go off like that?"

"We want to keep the land in the family." Olivia took a step back, eager to end the conversation. "Well, it's been a pleasure meeting you, Mrs. Stubblefield," she said in the warmest voice she could muster, forcing her face into a sweet smile. She returned to Miss Meyers and asked for a dozen eggs, a tin of milk, and a slab of butter. She also selected a simple rag rug from the pile on the counter and asked for a calendar. She paid quickly and prepared to flee, before her new neighbor could ask any more questions.

"Please stop by to visit any time." Olivia gave her hand to Mrs. Stubblefield again. "It'll be a lot less lonely knowing we've got neighbors, even if you are so far away. You too, Miss Meyers." Olivia turned back to the store clerk. "I'd appreciate the company. Gets lonely out there."

"Don't I know what you mean," Miss Meyers said. "Gets just as lonely here in town. You take care."

Olivia left the store and climbed up onto the wagon seat, next to her hired man.

"What you be needin' a rug for?" Mourning asked as she tossed it into the back.

"To hide the door to the cellar."

Mourning emitted a loud snort and shook his head. "You been told all the trappers 'round here been usin' that cabin for years. Ain't no one for miles don't know that cellar be there."

"Just drive," Olivia said, looking straight ahead.

Mrs. Stubblefield emerged from the store as they drove off. Olivia glanced back in time to catch a glimpse of Iola's chin hitting the road, when she got a look at Olivia's hired man.

Chapter Twenty-Two

Over the next month they settled into a routine. With Olivia's help, Mourning got a good start on putting a roof on the barn and spent the rest of his time chopping down new growth trees and uprooting stumps.

As Olivia began to feel more at home, she gave names to areas of their property. "The farm" was the two acres closest to the cabin that Uncle Scruggs had once cleared and that Mourning intended to plant first. In the center of the farm, on a small rise, stood a tall old oak tree, whose low branches jutted in all directions. Olivia called it the climbing tree and asked Mourning not to cut it down. That was where her children were going to build a tree house and hang swings. Behind the cabin were the little woods. The big woods spread out beyond the farm. In those big woods Olivia discovered a large clearing, which she guessed to be eighty rods wide. She assumed a whirlwind had taken all the trees down and so called it her windfall. It was there she went to sit on the fallen logs and write and sketch in her journal.

Not that she had much leisure for that. She spent her days keeping the barrel full of water, laundering their clothes, baking bread, and a stirring a boiling pot over the fire. She also put in her garden, became proficient at splitting the logs Mourning and she cut, and helped Mourning in the field. He showed her how to use the scythe to gather the brush around a pile of stumps that needed burning and left her to light and contain the fire.

She had quickly grown used to wearing Mourning's trousers and shirt. When he went back to town for their door he returned with two pairs of boy's trousers and two flannel shirts for her. He also bought the mirror she'd been wanting – so she could try sketching her new "Michigan self" – and a pie safe someone had been selling cheap. The tin panels in its doors were battered, but it would do for storing the flour bin, dishes, and the pies he hoped Olivia would soon be baking.

Rain never stopped them from working, except for the day the wind started howling and the trees cracked loudly. When the first branches blew past, they both ran for the cabin and slammed the door behind them. They took turns standing at the peek hole to watch the trees bowing in prayer and snapping back up, angrily shaking their tops. That storm lasted the day and most of the night. Olivia passed it writing and sketching in her journal, shivering when the lightning and thunder seemed to make the sides of the cabin shudder.

"The wind is so much stronger in Michigan," she said, casting a frightened eye at the roof. "Do you think that's because everything is so flat?"

Mourning shrugged, sucked his front teeth, and got to his feet. "I got to go check on the team again."

"You were just out there," Olivia said. "What's the point of you getting soaked every half hour? I'm sure they're fine."

He ignored her and had to use both hands to pull the door shut behind him.

"You're going to blow the fire out doing that," Olivia called after him, though she wouldn't have minded if he did. She didn't think having the cook fire was worth the way it ate up all the air in the oppressive little cabin. She would have preferred being able to breathe, even if it meant cold food.

The fire did seem about to go out when Mourning returned from the half-roofed barn carrying his mattress. He struggled to get it through the doorway and wordlessly lay it on the floor, as far from Olivia as possible. For the rest of the day he sat on it, playing his harmonica, whittling, or just staring at the wall. Olivia felt him watching her when he thought she wasn't looking, but he did not seem inclined to talk. He answered any questions she asked, but did not initiate conversation. Finally, she put out the lantern and said, "Good night," to which he grunted in response. After lying awake for what seemed like hours, Olivia lifted her head to see if Mourning had fallen asleep. The embers in the fireplace were still glowing and she could see him staring at her, his face a sheet of stone. She turned to face the wall, wondering if she had done something to make him angry. But the next day, when they emerged from their prison into the sunlight, he assumed his usual manner.

Mourning drove into town once a week for eggs and milk, but Olivia chose not to accompany him. It was too depressing. Besides, she thought it best that they be seen together as little as possible. And, most of all, she didn't want to be gone if Jeremy came to call. Olivia had been keeping careful count of the days on her new calendar, and too many of them were passing with no sign of the sorely missed Mr. Kincaid. One morning they did, however, have visitors. She and Mourning were out in the farm together, struggling with an enormous tree stump, when a voice called out.

"Hey there, neighbors."

A dark-haired, bearded giant stood at the side of the cabin waving his hat. A woman stood at his side, holding a basket covered with a white cloth. She barely reached his shoulder. Olivia walked toward them, mortified that she had been caught wearing trousers. She was soon close enough to recognize the woman.

"Mrs. Stubblefield, hullo, how are you? It's so nice to see you again," Olivia said, remembering something she had heard her mother (or perhaps it had been Tobey quoting their mother?) say more than once: "Good manners are for when there's not a thing else in the world you can think of to say."

"And you must be Mr. Stubblefield. I'm Olivia Killion. It's a pleasure to make your acquaintance." He shyly shook the hand Olivia offered.

"None of that Mr. and Mrs. nonsense," Iola said, making no effort to take her eyes off Olivia's trousers. "We're going to be just like family, so we're plain old Iola and Filmore to you." The friendly words did not resonate in Iola's voice. She spoke in the tone of a mother biting back what she felt was well-deserved criticism.

Olivia smiled and nodded. "You must be thirsty after your long walk," she said, trying to keep her voice light and cheerful, as if unaware of the woman's glowering disapproval. "The water barrel is right over here. Please, make yourselves at home. We don't have any chairs yet, but those stumps aren't so bad. I'll be right out, soon as I get out of these work clothes. It's just so dangerous, trying to burn off a field wearing a wide skirt. I learned that the hard way yesterday – set my dress right on fire," she lied.

She escaped into the cabin, closed the door, and released a long sigh. Then she hurriedly tore off her shirt and trousers, pulled a dress over her head, and ran a comb through her hair. When she came back out the Stubblefields were standing as she had left them.

"This is for you." Iola reached down to pick up the basket that she had set in the grass and handed it to Olivia.

Olivia lifted the cloth to find four eggs, a jar of jam, and a slab of butter. "Oh my, that is so kind of you. Thank you so much. We certainly will enjoy it. Let me put it inside, out of the sun."

"That's what neighbors do for each other. We all know how hard it is starting out. Times we had nothing to eat but lumps of flour boiled in milk. Or in plain old water." Iola followed Olivia toward the door and peeked in.

"Come in," Olivia said and showed them to the inside stump chairs.

Filmore had to bend at the waist to pass through the

door and the top of his head brushed the roof poles when he stood straight. It was dark and stuffy inside the cabin and far more pleasant out in the yard, but Olivia thought it more hospitable to invite them in. Iola seemed just as curious about the little cabin as the women back in Five Rocks had been about the Killion home.

"Where has Mourning gotten to?" Olivia wondered aloud. She stepped outside and saw that he was still working in the field.

"Mourning, come meet our neighbors," she called, hands cupped around her mouth.

He hesitated for a moment and then drove his axe into one of the stumps and walked slowly toward the cabin.

"Iola and Filmore Stubblefield, I'd like you to meet my hired hand, Mourning. Mourning Free."

"Pleasure," Mourning mumbled, hat in hand.

"Surely, surely." Iola nodded.

"Nice piece of land you've got to work," Filmore said.

"Yes sir, it is," Mourning said. "I best be gettin' back to workin' it. Nice meetin' you folks."

"Your boy put this roof on?" Filmore asked.

"Yes. Yes, he did, And he's almost finished putting one on the barn. That's where he stays. Out in the barn."

"Fine job. Hard to get good help. How'd you come by him?"

"I ... uh ... asked around in Detroit," Olivia lied badly. "Soon as I got off the boat."

"And you picked up a colored boy and took him along with you? A complete stranger?" Iola raised her eyebrows to her scalp.

"Well, he's not really a stranger. He ... uh ... used to live in my hometown. And some folks back home told me about him before I left, said he was in Detroit and he was a good worker and completely trustworthy. So I

194

went looking for him. Lucky for me, he happened to be in need of a job."

"Right lucky." Iola studied her fingernails with a frown. "Where is your hometown?" She raised her eyes and trained a piercing stare on Olivia.

A sudden chill passed over Olivia and she suddenly felt afraid of letting this woman know anything about them, especially where they were from. Mourning was right, there were plenty of white folks you had to watch out for.

Olivia ignored Iola's question and said, "Let me slice some bread for us to have with that butter."

That day was the first time she had managed to get her bread baked clear through. They had gotten used to eating crusty rings, with the damp yeasty center cut out of each slice, but she could have won a prize for today's loaf and was eager to show it off to her guests. She set out plates and knives, sliced the bread, and put Iola's butter on a plate and a spoon in the jar of jam.

"You got a crate for setting your butter and milk in the river?" Iola asked. Her tone was suddenly neutral, no longer dripping with censure.

"I sure do." Olivia nodded amiably. "I have to thank you again. It was so generous of you to bring this. Especially when you had to carry it all that way."

"Neighbors are meant for doing kindnesses to one another. That's what Jesus teaches us," Iola said.

"I've met another one of our neighbors," Olivia said. "Jeremy Kincaid. I suppose you must know him."

Iola nodded. "That one's a strange bird. But I guess he's all right. Keeps his own counsel."

"How long of a walk is it to your place?" Olivia asked. She put on a pot of coffee and then joined them at the table, spreading a thick layer of butter on a slice of bread.

"'Bout two hours. Could take more. Depends who you're walking with."

Olivia bit into the bread and exclaimed, "Oh, Mrs. . .

. I mean, Iola, this butter is absolutely delicious!" Then Olivia turned to Filmore and made a lame attempt at conversation with him. "So when will you start planting your buckwheat?"

He had been sitting with his head lowered and eyes on his plate, seeming to hide behind his thick, curly black beard. Olivia had no doubt that he would much rather have been out in his fields. Making chit-chat seemed to be an ordeal for him, especially with a strange neighbor lady who wore men's pants and lived with a colored boy. But he looked up at her and valiantly rose to the occasion.

"Don't know that I will plant any. Didn't come to much last year. Wild turkeys trampled it down, ate most of the grain. Had to go out every day and shoot one of 'em."

"That's too bad. At least you must have had a lot of good turkey dinners."

"Yes, missy, that we did." Apparently out of words, he hunkered back down over his plate.

After a short silence Iola seemed unable to contain herself any longer and gave Olivia a long stern stare. "Look, child, I don't mean to be minding your p's and q's, but it ain't right, you and that nigra, alone here like this. You probably think it ain't my place to say, but I feel a Christian duty to speak my mind when I see a body leading herself into sin and peril. It ain't Christian and you ain't safe." She nodded pointedly in the direction of the field.

"Oh, Mourning is –"

"People are so naïve." Iola batted a hand as she cut Olivia off. "Especially young folks like you. Put your faith in anyone. Don't know the things can happen in this sorry world. But you'll see. You live a while, you learn. You listen to an older and wiser sister, you save yourself a world of trouble and sorrow. One thing I can tell you is you can't trust these nigras. Their instincts are primitive. No self-control at all. Why it says so right

196

in the Bible –"

"There's no danger in Mourning." Olivia broke in, her voice firm.

Iola did not respond; she simply stared.

Olivia was surprised by how little she cared for this woman's opinion, considering the way she had fretted about what people out in Michigan were going to think and say. Now the only emotion she felt was anger. She hadn't come all this way, hauled water and chopped wood, and generally broken her back, in order to live her life trying to please an old hag like her. Iola was just going to have to accept Olivia on her own terms or not at all.

But Olivia took a deep breath and calmed herself, hoping to maintain an amicable relationship with this annoying neighbor. So far Iola seemed to be all there was, other than Norma Gay at the store. And Iola was far from alone in holding that opinion of colored men. If you refused to talk to anyone who was prejudiced against them, you'd soon have no one to talk to at all.

"He's making a big thick crossbar for the door, if you think that will make me any safer," Olivia said. Then she smiled and rose to pour coffee.

"Well, it might that, but it still ain't *right*."

"No coffee for me," Filmore said, obviously uncomfortable with the turn the conversation had taken. "Think I'll go take a look at that team of yours." He rose. "Could use some power in front of that plow. Ground's gotten so rooty, you practically got to chop the seed into it with an ax. I'll be outside, Iola," he said, pronouncing his wife's name "Yoo-la," rather than "Eye-o-la," as Norma Gay had. "But take your time. I'll go lend the nigger boy a hand."

Once Filmore was gone, Iola hunkered down, as if she and Olivia were old friends who had only been waiting for a stranger to leave the room. "Now, child, tell me how you came to be out here all on your own."

"There isn't much to tell," Olivia said. "I inherited

this piece of land and decided to come see what I could make of it."

"But dear, you'll never find a suitable husband around these parts. Oh there's plenty of unmarried men all right, but none you'd want in your parlor, let alone marching down the aisle with you."

"I'm not in any hurry to get married."

"You don't want to wait too long. Best to be having your children while you're young."

"I'm not in any hurry for that either."

"Shame on you! Shame! Why you never want to say such a thing! Children are what we all pray to Jesus for. Filmore and I haven't been blessed yet, but I've known from the minute I married him why the good Lord put me on earth. To bear seed. Why, what else makes a woman a woman? God made you capable of creating life. That's a privilege *and* a duty. Every Christian child you bring into this world is a blessing. The most wonderful blessing!"

Olivia's response had been intentionally contrary. She was anxious to have children, many children, but she resented Iola's intrusiveness and being told that her only goal in life should be finding a husband. She knew there was no small truth in what folks said: "Choose a husband, choose a life." Marry a farmer, you might get hauled off to Michigan. Marry a storekeeper and you'd have a whole different life. Don't marry at all, you're a pathetic old maid. Sometimes it seemed to Olivia that the only way a woman could walk around in the world and just be herself was to marry someone and then have him die on her.

"Yes, I know, of course you're right. Children are a great blessing." Olivia tried to make peace with her neighbor and then changed the subject. "Thank you again for the eggs. I forgot what they taste like. Tell me, is it hard to keep chickens?"

"Lord, no. There ain't nothing easier. Ain't what to do but toss grain out in the yard and pick up the eggs.

Twist the head off one and throw it in a pot for your Sunday dinner." Iola leaned back and took a sip of her coffee.

"Don't you have to build them a coop or something?" Olivia asked, relieved that Iola's tone was once again neighborly.

See, Olivia thought, *if you make the effort to get along with people, they're all right.*

"Well of course you got to put a roof over them in the winter, but they ain't about to run off into the woods. Not as long as you keep feeding them. Folks out here don't bother fencing in any of their barnyard animals. Let the cows graze free and call them in at night. I'll tell you a trick." She leaned forward. "Once it gets hot and the mosquitoes are out strong, you keep a smudge pot burning right close by the house. 'Fore long you'll see all your animals standing in a circle around it, never have to go round them up at all. They learn real fast to stay by the smoke, so they don't get bit. Never have to go chasing after them during mosquito season."

"How do you make a smudge pot?"

"Get some wood chips burning real good and throw a handful of dirt on 'em. Or if you got coals, burn a little sugar over 'em. Couple of weeks or so, them mosquitoes will be out something fierce."

"I'm so lucky to have a neighbor like you, who knows how to do everything." Olivia rose to pour them both more coffee and apologized for not having any milk to offer her.

"I'll have to bring you some, next time I come visiting." Iola smiled.

"So you keep a cow?"

"Yes, we do. But that's a lot more work than chickens. You got to milk it every day, morning and night. Then you got all that milk you got to do something with. I can show you how to make butter and cheese you can sell to Norma Gay, but I don't know if a young girl like you wants to take that on. Specially if you're going to be out there working in the field like a plantation hand." She sniffed.

Filmore reappeared in the doorway, but remained silent, just stooping there, looking in.

"There's easier ways to make money," Iola said.

"Like what?"

"Well, if your boy's any kind of shot, you can get between two fifty and five dollars for a deer in Detroit. I seen you got a wagon, so you ain't got no problem getting it there. You ever making a trip like that, we'll be glad to share it with you. Pay our way. Filmore's been chopping cord wood to sell to the railroad."

"They pay money for wood?" Olivia asked.

"Seven shillings a cord, but you got to get it to the depot office in Detroit. But they pay in Michigan state scrip, which is only good for its face to pay your state taxes. You want real money, you got to sell it for six shillings on a dollar. Man can still make two dollars a day chopping wood, but sure is easier to shoot a deer." She took a sip of her coffee and sighed before going on.

"Too bad for us, my Filmore ain't never been much of a hunter. Can't follow a blood trail for his life, not even in snow, bless him. But them niggers are good at it. It's in their African blood. And if your boy sees any coons, their skins go for a dollar apiece. But there ain't no better money than getting a wolf in your sights. Got a bounty on those devils – 25 dollars each. Nobody gives a hoot what shape the pelt's in neither. All they want is proof that the mangy critter is dead. You take the skin to Squire Goodel in Detroit, down by the river."

"Are there a lot of wolves around here?"

"Sometimes I think they eat more of my chickens than we do. Folks say that if they keep laying railroad track and blowing them whistles, time'll come soon we ain't gonna have to worry about no wolves no more. But for now they're still a worry."

"I'm surprised nobody's penned them up for breeding, if they're worth that much."

Iola slapped the table and cackled. "Now, there's a thought. Folks would just about kill anyone tried that. Ain't nothing they hate more than a wolf. You're looking a little peeked, child. That time of the month?"

This question sent Filmore backing out of the cabin again.

"No, I'm just tired," Olivia said. "It's been a long week."

"Aren't they all? But listen child, next time you got the curse coming on you, you drink some of this special tea of mine." She pulled a small packet out of her pocket. "You make yourself three cups a day, you won't have no pains at all."

They sat talking for another half-hour. Iola tried to pry more information out of Olivia, but Olivia politely avoided answering the questions that were too personal. But Iola's nosiness no longer angered Olivia. Wasn't that the way women were? Wasn't that how they made friends? It made Olivia feel grown up to be chatting with another woman. When Iola touched her and called her "dear" and "child," she felt less lonely.

"Yula, we got us a long walk home." Filmore appeared in the doorway again. "That boy of yours seems to know what he's doing all right," he said to Olivia. "I told him I'll be more than glad to have the use of them oxen. Whoever trained 'em made a good job of it. Hope you got what to do with lots of Yula's eggs and butter. And I'll give your boy a day of my sweat, keep us quits. We'll come back for them next week."

"Oh, I'm glad," Olivia said, giving Iola's arm a pat. "That way we'll have all the more reason to visit with one another."

"Praise the Lord. You're going to be just like a little sister to me." Iola gave Olivia a hug. "I told you. We're like family now."

She pulled back and looked Olivia up and down in a manner that was unsettling. But Olivia was willing to ignore these strange quirks. She was glad to have neighbors.

Chapter Twenty-Three

Mourning paused to watch Olivia watering her garden with a tin cup.

"Which a them seeds you been plantin'?" he asked.

"Onions, peas, beans, and turnips." She pointed at the rows. "Now I'm putting in tomatoes, summer squash, greens, and watermelon."

"Watermelon? Don't remember buyin' no seeds for no watermelon."

"Mrs. Stubblefield gave me some before they left. Says you can sell the melons in Detroit for a shilling apiece."

"You like her pretty good?"

"I'd like her more if she weren't as old as a rock, but she seems all right."

Olivia almost mentioned the way their neighbors had spoken about coloreds, but bit those words back. Why make him uncomfortable? She did tell him what Iola had said about selling deer in Detroit.

"Okay. You get out there and shoot three deer, we take 'em to Detroit. We could stay over a night, take that ferry south to Canada."

She smiled, appreciative that he had remembered, and changed the subject. "I think tomorrow I'm going to try chopping down some of those." She pointed at the stand of young trees a few yards from her garden.

He nodded. "Start out with them soft little maples. They ain't gonna break your head, they fall on it. And once you decide you a tree-chopping expert, we can always use more punk wood. Can't never have too much a that."

"We still have lots of matches."

He shook his head. "Don't matter. You always gotta keep some punk wood in your pocket or in that

202

possibles bag you carry 'round, 'long with a flint and a knife. You ever get yourself lost and havin' to spend the night in the woods, fire gonna be your best protection."

"How do you find punk wood?" Olivia asked.

"Cut down an old tree what got black knots near the top. Saw it off above and below them knots, and you most likely gonna find it full a punk. Look all brown and wrinkled like. Feel like you pullin' a wad a cloth out a that tree. One good tree can do you for a year or two, but you gotta keep it dry."

Mourning jealously guarded their lucifer matches. He had wrapped some of them in bark coverings and buried them at the edge of the farm, so that even if both the cabin and barn burned to the ground, they wouldn't be left without the means to start a fire. After a long argument, he also convinced Olivia to let him hide her Hawken rifle in the woods.

"You gotta be plannin' for the worst," he said. "Spose I be out in the farm and you be down by the river when a band of Indians be comin' up on us? What we gonna do? Even if you be near the cabin, rifle ain't gonna do you no good in there. It ain't got no window to shoot from. Ain't gonna take wild Indians five minutes to burn you out a there. Best we be runnin' into the woods, have a rifle waiting on us there."

"There aren't any wild Indians around here."

"Robbers, then."

"If you're so worried about robbers, why don't you keep the rifle with you? I wouldn't mind that. But I'm not about to leave it hanging in some tree, out in the rain, where anyone could walk off with it."

"It be fine. I'm a cover it with bark, and you gonna go out there regular and clean and oil it."

Olivia finally agreed to relinquish her precious Hawken. She kept the shotgun loaded by the door and the pistol hidden down in the cellar.

"She brought us four eggs," Olivia said. "I thought

we'd each have one for breakfast and I'd use the other two to bake a cake. We ought to get a couple of chickens of our own. It'd be nice having eggs."

"Good with me. Next time we see them, I ask Mr. Stubblefield if it suit him to pay us in chickens for usin' the oxen."

"What did you think of them?"

"White folks." He shrugged and turned to go back to work. Then he stopped and added, "Ain't no friends of the colored man."

"How do you know that? Did he say something mean to you?"

"Don't gotta. I can tell."

Later, when they were drinking coffee by the fire, she asked him again about the Stubblefields. He avoided answering.

He doesn't want to talk about it because I'm white, she thought. *That's what I am to him. White. Not his friend.*

She tried another subject. "What was it like? Growing up without a family?"

"Can't tell you nothing 'bout that. I ain't never growed up with no family, so I guess I don't know the difference."

She looked up at the stars coming out and then back at him. "It's amazing when you think of it. Here we lived in the same town all our lives, but we might as well have been on different planets, for all one of us can understand what it would be like to be the other."

He took his time answering. "I figure you can say that 'bout any two peoples. Folks think they understand each other, but they ain't none of 'em do. Ain't nobody knows what it be like to be nobody else." He got to his feet while he was talking. That seemed to be all the conversation he could tolerate.

"Do you think a man and a woman ever understand each other?" She looked up at him.

"They don't gotta understand each other. They gotta

204

need each other."

"What's a man need a woman for, if not understanding? Companionship?"

"Man need a woman plenty and I don't mean just for ... you know. Not ever body be like your daddy, can bring anything he want home from his store, pay that Mrs. Hardaway to keep his house. Look at the way things use to be, 'fore they had ever thing in stores. Man could grow all the wheat in the world, but if his wife ain't been grindin' the flour and bakin' the bread, he warn't eatin'. That the way things still be for folks what ain't got no money."

Olivia smiled. "That isn't what Lady Grody says. She says a woman's job is to create a retreat of peace and quiet for her husband."

"Ain't so quiet if his stomach be howlin'. She best be makin' a racket in the kitchen."

"When I was a little girl I used to daydream about how I would keep house for my husband. Keep his shoes shined and his collars pressed. I even imagined the wood box next to the stove, the way I'd have all the sticks of wood in neat rows, all the same length."

"That be crazy women stuff you gonna do for you, not him. He know a short crooked stick burn as hot as a long straight one." Mourning turned to retreat to the barn, muttering about something he had forgotten to do.

Left alone with her thoughts, Olivia's mind kept running in circles around Jeremy Kincaid. Maybe she should take him a loaf of bread. He'd brought them that tin of coffee, hadn't he? What was wrong with a neighborly gift? But how would she find her way to his cabin, knowing only the general direction? She rose and began throwing dirt on the fire. *He knows exactly where to find me,* she thought, *and hasn't come within a hundred paces. He isn't sitting around hoping to see me coming up the trail. He plain doesn't care one whit about seeing me.*

But what if something's happened to him? What if he stepped in a gopher hole and broke his ankle? Or was on his way to pay me a call when Ernest got spooked and threw him? He could be lying somewhere in the woods right now. Shouldn't good neighbors check in on one another from time to time, make sure everything is all right?

She scolded herself again. *Put out the fire, get ready for bed, and think about something else. Tomorrow is going to be a long day. The Stubblefields are coming to take the oxen and I guess I ought to invite them to stay for dinner.*

"They should be here soon," Olivia said the next day when Mourning walked in from the farm to help her carry a tub of wet wash up to the line. "After I hang these, I'm going to start getting the meal on the table. I'll bang two pots together when it's time to wash your hands."

"You go 'head and eat. I get something later, after they gone."

Olivia wrinkled her forehead. "Why would you say that?"

"I told you 'bout them."

"You can't know what they think about coloreds."

"I know what I know."

"Well even if you're right, who cares? This is my cabin and it's where you break your bread, long as you're working for me. They don't like it, they don't have to accept any more invitations. What do you think I'd do, if you and I went over to their place and they invited me in for something to eat and not you?"

He shrugged.

"Well of course I would decline the invitation. I've always said a person can't fight the whole world, but this isn't the whole world. This is my place. I sure have the say about what goes on in my own home. That's the way things will change – when people start behaving right to the people standing next to them."

The Stubblefields soon arrived. Olivia saw them exchange glances when Mourning took his place on one of the stump chairs, but they settled into conversation quickly enough, as if they sat to table with negroes every day.

"You got to put in some Indian corn, boy," Filmore said. "Not this year. Too late. But come the end of next May. You ain't had good eating till you had Michigan sweet corn. It'll grow most anywhere, but you got to eat it fresh. Course you also gotta put in some other strains what keep better. We just about live on meal. Why Yula here –"

"That's right." Iola broke in. "I make a right tasty mush and I'll have to teach you how to make my ashcake." She turned toward Olivia. "I'll bring you over some of my corn pone and hominy."

"I see you're clearing more trees 'round the cabin," Filmore said. "That's good. Land out here is rich, but it's got too darn much shade." He clapped his hands at a mosquito. "You get your land ditched and a lot of those will disappear. You don't, they'll eat you alive."

"Your meat came out quite tasty," Iola said as she took a bite of venison. "Few more weeks the mushrooms will be out. I'll show you how to find the right kind, make a catsup sauce. It's right delicious with fish and meat. Even on a spud."

"Have you ever seen any Indians?" Olivia asked Filmore.

"None that would bother you. Only heard of one ever killing a white man and that was for chopping down his bee tree. But they can scare the bejeesus out of you –"

"Filmore! I will not have you taking our Lord's name in vain," Iola said.

He flinched and apologized, like a small boy to his mother, then continued. "But it's true. Injun will waltz right into your cabin, real quiet like, without so much as a howdy-do or knock on the door. See, the way they do is, if they put a stick lying on the ground across the entrance to their wigwam, you ain't supposed to go in. So if you ain't got no stick, they feel welcome to sashay right in. Course most of 'em around here don't live in no wigwams. They got houses like us, except a whole mess of families live in the same one together. Still savages, but they farm the same as white folk."

During the meal Mourning kept his eyes on his food and did not speak unless asked a direct question. When Filmore's plate was clean, he pushed back and removed his pipe from his pocket.

"You get on outside with that filthy thing." His wife batted a hand at him.

Mourning followed him. As soon as the men were out the door Iola leaned over and adopted her cozy "girl talk" tone, passing on harmless gossip about people in town that Olivia had never heard of. Olivia did her best to hide her boredom, wearing a strained smile and nodding. Iola seemed to especially enjoy telling her about all the diseases folks were afflicted with and the remedies she could have brewed up for them, if they only had the good sense to ask. Then she began quizzing Olivia again about her time of the month.

"Did that tea I gave you help?"

"Yes, it did. I usually get real uncomfortable right before and on the first day, but this month I hauled water and chopped wood, just like any other day."

"And how long ago was that?"

Olivia didn't want to answer and looked away.

"I'm only asking so I can bring you some more tea. I do it up different, depending on what time of the month a woman gets the curse."

"Well, yesterday, actually."

"You started bleeding yesterday?" This somehow seemed to cause concern to Iola.

"Yes," Olivia said stiffly.

"Well, it's good for me to know." Iola patted Olivia's

arm. "When Filmore brings them oxen back, I'll send some tea with him for next month."

"That's kind of you." Olivia's tone was cold.

Iola turned her gaze on a pair of trousers that hung on the nail Olivia had pounded into the back wall. "You still traipsing around in them? It ain't right, you know." Iola seemed oblivious to Olivia's obvious resentment of her prying. "I don't care if you are all alone, with no one but a colored to see you. It still ain't right. Ain't Christian. Bible says a woman shouldn't wear a man's clothing. And here you are, in togs that belong to a nigger man."

"It's much easier to work in them." Olivia spoke through a forced smile and clenched teeth. "How's your garden doing, Iola?"

Olivia was relieved when they finally walked off with Dixby and Dougan. Maybe having neighbors wasn't so wonderful after all. She'd begun to harbor a creeping misgiving – perhaps coming to Michigan had been a mistake. Not because they couldn't harvest a crop; she knew they could. So far things had gone better than she'd dared hope. The fears that had begun to plague her had nothing to do with money and property.

The night before, while sinking down into sleep, she'd had a vision of herself slowly shriveling up. Uncle Scruggs' fields blossomed and flourished, while she stood in the midst of the plenty they yielded, turning brown and wrinkled. Faceless people stood at a distance, but she said nothing to them. She had forgotten not only her manners, but how to speak at all. She was alone and would be forever.

But how could coming here have been a mistake, when she had no alternate version of herself? *Work the land for a year*, she thought. *You're already here, might as well sell a crop and make some of your money back. Then you'll see. Anyway, you promised Mourning.*

Still, doubts nagged. At eighteen, a year seemed

forever. By twenty folks would be calling her an old maid. She might start looking like Iola. What if she started thinking and talking like her?

After the Stubblefields left, Olivia changed into her work clothes and found Mourning in the barn. The last thing she felt like doing was working.

"I'm going for a walk," she told him.

"A walk?" He looked puzzled. "I thought with the team gone, you gonna help me burn the rest a them stumps."

"Tomorrow. I'll help you first thing in the morning. I promise." She turned toward the trail.

"You keep that shotgun loaded by the door and now you goin' off alone into the woods without it?" Mourning said to her back.

"I'm not going far. I just need a little time to think."

Mourning shook his head and grumbled, loudly enough for her to hear, "Think. She gotta think some more. Ever time that girl say, Mourning, I been thinkin', I know I be in trouble."

Once she was out of his sight she slowed her pace and then stopped to sit in a small clearing, with her back resting against a tree. It was dark and cool under the canopy of the forest and the rustling of small animals was somehow comforting. A woodpecker ra-ta-tapped in the distance. There was so much life in the world. She looked around her and sighed. It was a beautiful country. No wonder Uncle Scruggs had missed Michigan so much. But not even he had wanted to stay here without his Lydia Ann.

What did I think I was I going to do, all alone on a stupid farm? Whatever was wrong with me in Five Rocks is still wrong with me here. It has nothing to do with my mother. Or my father carrying on with Jettie Place. It's me. No man is ever going to want me. At least back in Five Rocks I had Tobey and Mrs. Hardaway and Miss Evans.

210

A mosquito began to annoy her and she rose and walked on farther, too distracted to bother marking her trail. Then she heard breaking branches and froze. That was no small animal. Lord, let it be a deer. She moved silently to the thickest tree and watched from behind it. The steps came closer and she crouched down.

It was Jeremy Kincaid who came into sight.

Chapter Twenty-Four

"Jeremy!" Olivia straightened and stepped from behind the tree. "Hullo, Jeremy! It's Olivia. Over here." She waved, making no effort to hide how happy she was to see him.

"Olivia!" he shouted and waved back. She was relieved that he seemed pleased to see her. "What are you doing out here alone?" he asked.

"Just going for a walk," she said as they crossed the clearing toward one another.

Once the gap had been closed, neither of them seemed to know what to say.

"So how are you?" he asked.

"I've been keeping well. And you?"

"Grand. I'm grand."

"What are you doing? Hunting?" She nodded at the shotgun and water skin slung over his shoulder.

"No, I was just going to check on something." For a moment he stared at her in a vague, unfocused way, as if making up his mind about something.

He's not really looking at me, she thought. *He's trying to figure out how long good manners require that he stand here bored to death talking to me.*

"You might want to come with me," he said.

He had looked away from her, busying himself rolling up his shirtsleeves. She could see the taut muscles running up his forearm and felt an urge to run her finger over them.

"Where?"

"Surprise." He grinned and put a finger to his lips. "Come along."

He turned and she followed, hoping his water skin held enough for two, as she had brought none and was already thirsty. He walked on, never looking back to see if she was still there. The trail was narrow so she had no choice but to trudge along behind him.

Like one of those squaws, she thought, remembering the day she and Mourning had driven over to see the Wyandot Indian village. Olivia had brought her journal and began making a sketch of the long houses.

"Look, here come the tribe," Mourning said.

A long line of people was moving into the clearing, single file. The women were all at the end of the line, carrying everything in the world on their backs. Olivia could see only the hems of their dresses and their feet, as they shuffled along under piles of stuff.

Well, at least I'm not carrying a mountain, she thought, as she watched Jeremy's back and wondered if he intended to ever say another word. They continued in silence for half an hour before coming to the river, at a place where it was too deep to wade across. Flat-topped white rocks formed a zigzag trail across it and Olivia assumed he intended to lead her over them.

Aha. Now he'll have to offer me his hand.

But Jeremy paused under a spreading maple next to a stand of bushes and motioned for her to follow his example and sit down.

As he settled himself, back pressed against the trunk of the tree, he said, "If we both keep very quiet you have a good chance of seeing something special."

"What?" she asked.

"Wait and see." He put his finger to his lips again.

She sat a short distance from him and fidgeted. Finally she moved around so she could rest her back against the opposite side of the trunk.

"You don't have any food with you, do you?" he asked over his shoulder. "In your pockets or anything?"

"No, sorry."

"I'm not asking because I'm hungry."

"Then why are you asking?"

"You'll see."

They sat in silence. The bugs didn't seem to be bothering Jeremy, but they were all over Olivia and she batted her hands at them. She was hot and tired and soon grew restless. What were they waiting for?

Jeremy fiddled in his pocket, twisted around, and motioned for her to lean toward him. At last. Her irritation evaporated. He was shy and had been getting up his courage. Now he would say or do something of a romantic nature. Tell her how pretty she looked, or run his fingertips over her cheek, or lightly brush the hair back off her forehead. She closed her eyes and, finally, he touched her. His greasy finger briefly tapped the tip of her nose.

"Ick! What's that?" Her eyes sprang open and she pushed his hand away. "Ugh! It stinks something awful."

"Hold still." He dabbed her cheeks with more of the disgusting concoction. "Now rub it in. It will keep the flies and mosquitoes off you. Make sure to get some on your wrists and ankles."

"That stuff would keep the devil away from a lost soul," she said, but obeyed and witnessed its immediate effect.

"Maybe now you'll be able to hold still," he said. He leaned back against the tree and they sat through another long silence.

"How long are we going to sit here?" she asked.

He paused before asking, "You don't much care for this new life of yours, do you?"

It sounded like a criticism and she hesitated a moment before answering.

213

"Well ... I do get bored," she said, shifting around so she could see his face. "There's nothing to do but work. Nobody to visit with or anything. No books. No music."

"Nothing to do." He put his head back and looked up. "I never have understood folks who prefer drinking tea in someone's front parlor to this." He held his palms up and let his eyes run over the forest ceiling. "Or think someone sawing on a fiddle makes better music than the sound of this river or the wind in the treetops."

"It's beautiful." She followed his gaze. "Of course, it's beautiful. But after an hour sitting in the same place, you pretty much get the idea."

"Shh..." He tensed and peered at the far bank of the river.

She began to regret not having brought her shotgun. He rose to a squat and took small crab-like steps to move behind the tree, as far into the bushes as he could get. Olivia squeezed herself in beside him. He put his finger to his lips again and pointed toward the river.

On the other side of the river, about fifty yards upstream, a black mamma bear and two cubs lumbered out of the woods. Olivia gasped and Jeremy softly shushed her again, without taking his eyes off the bears as they waddled toward the water. The mother put out a paw to test one of the rocks in the river before carefully stepping onto it. She kept her head down, watching the water, facing Olivia and Jeremy. The two cubs clumsily chased one another and one of them let out a sudden growl. The mother jerked her head up and lost her balance. All four paws flailed and she slid into the river. The current wasn't strong and she easily swam ashore and pulled herself out, slow and deliberate. Olivia imagined her counting to ten, trying not to lose her temper.

The mother bear ignored her cubs, shook herself off, and returned to her perch on the rock. Then one of the cubs tried to join her, snuggling up to her side, but the mamma moved her body in a way that said, "Not now."

The cub wouldn't leave her alone and finally, with a look as exasperated as any human mother Olivia had ever seen, mamma batted a paw at it and sent it sprawling into the river. Olivia gasped again as its head went underwater, but it bobbed back up and the other cub jumped in to join it. They played around in the water, nipping at one another's snouts.

A sudden swoosh of mamma's paw sent a silver streak flying out of the water. She lumbered onto the bank and gobbled the fish down before it had time to stop flopping.

"Doesn't she feed her babies first?" Olivia whispered.

"They haven't been weaned yet. Won't be for another month or two."

"How old do you think they are?"

"Six, seven months. A good guess would be that they were born in January."

Mamma caught more fish and, after finishing her meal, went in for a swim with the cubs. Then they lay on the bank sunning. The babies nestled up against mamma while she groomed them.

"She looks so motherly now," Olivia said softly. "You think she meant to hurt the one she knocked into the water?"

"If she'd meant to hurt him, he'd be dead. A bear can kill a full-grown deer with one swipe. Watch her now," he said.

Mamma tilted her head to one side, as if listening real hard for something. She got up, raised her front paws, and stood on her hind legs to full height, like a person. Then she lifted her nose and sniffed the air.

"She knows there's something out there," Jeremy whispered. "She just doesn't know what we are or where. Keep completely still. I don't think she can make out the shape of us from that distance, but if you move, she'll see it. And if you had any food on you, she'd smell it."

Mamma remained with her nose in the air for a few minutes. Standing like that, she looked thin and graceful. It was hard to believe she was the same clumsy-looking animal. For a moment the bear seemed to be looking straight at them, but she lowered herself to all fours and shambled off into the woods, her twin children behind her. Neither Olivia nor Jeremy spoke until they were well out of sight.

"That was really something," Olivia said. "I've never seen a real live bear before. I had no idea they were so cute."

"You won't think they're cute if you ever get too close to one. I'm surprised they haven't bothered you."

"Mourning found some tracks by the cabin, said they were made by a bear, but we haven't seen it."

"They can smell fish or anything else you fry from miles away. Some folks claim they can smell the apples in your cellar. Mourning did get a door on that cabin, didn't he?"

"Yes. I have a proper leather string on the latch that I take in at night, along with a crossbar to let down, so I'm quite well fortified. So is Mourning. He got one of those doors that rolls on a rail for the barn, where he sleeps. How did you know those bears were going to be here?"

"Didn't really, just hoped they might. I've been watching them for months. They don't turn up here every afternoon, but often enough."

"Is that what you do then, sit in the woods and watch animals?"

"Could say." He took a drink of water from the skin and handed it to her.

"What for?" she asked and then drank and wiped her mouth with the back of her hand.

"I love the woods – watching the plants grow, the trees change. I've been here eight years and haven't been bored for one minute of it. I enjoy watching the animals more than anything else. They have a world of their own, parallel to ours, only more interesting, since they don't hide behind good manners the way people do."

She stood and brushed herself off. "Well, thanks for bringing me along. You're going to have to point me in the direction home."

He squinted at the sun. "It's early enough. My place is only about forty minutes that way." He nodded upriver. "We can make it there, have a cup of coffee, and get you on your way home before dark. 'Bout time you and Mr. Free know where I live, case you're ever in need of anything."

Olivia was too overjoyed to manage anything but a smile and a nod.

Chapter Twenty-Five

Olivia huffed along behind Jeremy until they came to a large flat rock that jutted out into the water. Jeremy stepped onto it and offered his hand to Olivia, and they both stood facing upstream. The river flowed straight as a ruler until the next bend. Tall willows, oaks, and maples lined the banks, skirted in the bright red of sumac. The trees arched over the water, as if trying to join hands, but the river was just that much too wide.

"This is the place that gave the river its name," Jeremy said.

"I've been wondering why it's named after Jesus."

"It isn't. Its name is G-e-e-s-i-s." He spelled the letters out. "The G should be hard. Geesis is Algonquin for sun. If we had time to wait for the sun to set, you'd see it framed perfectly between the trees on either side of the river and leaving a long reflection, right down the middle. Some white man must have written down the name and then when other folks *saw* it instead of *hearing* it, they all mispronounced it."

217

"How do you know things like that?" She bent to pick up a stone and skipped it over the water.

"Mostly from talking to people over at the new university in Ann Arbor. They're thinking about setting up a faculty for the study of Native American culture." Jeremy found a flat stone and tried to do as Olivia had, but it plunked into the river. "You're pretty good at that," he said.

"Mourning taught me. When we were kids. He can make five jumps. Do you have brothers and sisters?" she asked.

"Four sisters – all of them schoolteachers until they married. And one younger brother. He took over the family printing business."

"Do we have time to sit here for a few minutes?" she asked.

"Sure."

Olivia removed her work shoes and socks, rolled up her trouser legs, and dangled her feet in the cool water. "Oh, that feels good. Why didn't *you*? Take over the business. If you're the oldest son, shouldn't it have gone to you?"

"Didn't want it. Never liked being inside." He sat beside her and pulled off his own footwear – soft, comfortable-looking leather boots. Olivia eyed them jealously, thinking he must have gotten them from an Indian. "Anyway, my father wasn't all that keen on having me in the business." Jeremy tried his luck with another stone, managing one half-hearted skip. "He was set on me being the first Kincaid to attend college. Get a piece of paper says I'm smart. I went for a while – took some classes in history and literature."

"That must have been interesting."

"Not really. A bored professor stands at the front of a hot lecture hall, reading texts to bored students. You might as well sit somewhere more comfortable and read them yourself. And having removed us from our parents' care, the college felt obligated to provide adequate supervision. So it felt more like being in prison than being educated."

"Did you have a sweetheart?" Olivia imagined Jeremy in a frock coat, strolling along a riverbank and holding an open book. At his side was a faceless girl, twirling her parasol and listening in rapture as he read Emerson aloud.

"Where was I going to find a sweetheart at a college that accepted only men? But I surely got one when I returned home for the summer. Before I knew what was happening, I was engaged to be married. To a nice girl named Francie Everman."

"Did you love her very much?" she asked softly, prepared to hear a tragic end to this story.

He took his feet out of the water and wiped them on his pant legs as he said, "I didn't love her at all."

"Then why did you want to marry her?" She began drying her own feet.

He leaned back on his elbows, knees bent, face turned up to the sun, eyes closed. "Never told you I did. Like I said, Francie was a nice girl and certain to grow up to be an excellent woman. At my mother's urging, we started keeping company. You can imagine my surprise when I heard that a wedding date had been set. By my mother and hers."

"Surely you must have proposed."

"Not that I recall. Those women were arranging the ceremony before I got around to objecting."

"So why didn't you tell your mother that you didn't want to get married? At least not to Francie?"

He sat forward and shook his head. "I couldn't think of a good enough reason why not. It would have seemed such bad manners. After all, she was a nice girl. Pretty. She was always baking pies and things. There was nothing wrong with her. Nothing I could have told my mother that she would have understood and accepted. Francie was a nice-looking, well-mannered girl, and her family had money. My mother couldn't imagine anything else a man could ask for."

"What else *would* you have asked for?"

He glanced at Olivia, his face seeming to close up. "Not pies and lace tablecloths," he said and pulled his boots on.

Olivia grimaced. Was he thinking about the embroidered tablecloth she had put on the table, when what he'd wanted was to sit outside and eat with his fingers? Good Lord, what if she had shown up at his door bearing a pie? That picture almost made her laugh.

"To be left in peace. Allowed to find my own way. To find someone who is my intellectual equal." He looked up at the sun and said, "We've got to get going," and got to his feet.

Olivia hurriedly tied her shoe laces. She expected Jeremy to offer a hand to help her up, but he didn't. "But you have to tell me what happened. How come you're not married to Francie Everman?"

"I ran off like a dog, a month before the wedding."

"The poor thing!"

He stepped off the rock onto the river bank and turned to give Olivia a tolerant smile, as if she were a small child first learning the ways of the world. "I never did worry my mind much about old Francie. Figured I'd done her a big favor. I was right, too. It wasn't six months before she got herself wed to someone respectable and well-fixed. Bit of a dullard, but I'm sure she's far happier with him than she would have been trying to keep up with me."

"Have you seen your family since then?"

"Yes." He started walking and talked over his shoulder. "About a year after I left. I wanted to set things square with them. You see, when I ran away I helped myself to some of their money. I had inherited a little from my grandmother, but I also walked off with the cash my father was keeping in his top bureau drawer, for my next year's college tuition. It wasn't a large sum, but stealing is stealing. I tried to pay him back, but he refused to take it. I thought he'd be furious, but it turned out he wasn't the least bit angry. He even slipped some more coins into my pocket and said it had all been for the best."

"I guess parents can forgive their children for just about anything."

"Well, yes, I suppose they can, but I think it was more than that. That was the first time I'd ever thought much about *his* life, and I think he might have been more envious than indignant about what I'd done."

"What on earth would he be jealous of?"

"He'd probably spent his own life regretting not having the nerve to run out on my mother, when *her* mother started talking about when would be the best date for them to get married."

Olivia couldn't hide the look of dismay on her face. Mourning was right; Jeremy seemed to consider all women a dreadful fate, to be avoided at all cost.

Well, I can't complain, she thought. *I keep telling myself it would be different if I only knew what he felt and thought. So now I know.*

"We do have to get going." Jeremy started up the trail. "Won't be time for coffee. Just enough to show you where I live."

"Have you had any jobs since you left home?" she asked.

"A few. First one was up in the northern peninsula, looking for copper. But working in a mine is no life for a man. Certainly not for a man like me. Then I worked for a while as a guide for tourists. After that I –"

"Tourists? What tourists?"

"Silly rich people who come out here from New York and pay a lot of money to dress up as Daniel Boone and shoot a buck or a bear. Some of those fools are just as happy to let you shoot it for them, as long as they get to take the antlers or skin home. Most of them don't even want to eat the meat. Most sickening job I ever had, but

221

those touring companies do a steady business. After that, I went to work for a blacksmith. Even clerked in a general store for a while. Then I built my cabin and I've been here ever since. I invested my father's money in a tract of land up north, with plenty of good timber on it. By the time I'm skint, I figure the lumber companies will have moved out this way and be ready to start slaughtering up there. Should show me a good profit. And once I get a little cash together, I'll start giving people mortgages."

"You mean like a bank?"

"Folks out here would rather deal with a face they know than a bank. And there's good money in it. Going rate of interest is 7%. But no one who has any money comes to someone like me in the first place, so most of them can't make their payments. You can foreclose or, if they have it, you can charge them 20% shave money to let it ride. After that they only pay the 7% interest each year, but nothing on the capital. If that goes on for eleven years, you've got all your money back, and they still owe you their farm."

"Doesn't 'foreclose' mean to take their farm away?"

"Yes."

"But that would be awful, to force people out of their home."

"Well, they could always stay on and work it for a percentage. You know, like hired hands. I wouldn't be throwing their children into the snow." He made a sad face. "Their choice."

"Still. I think that would be awful."

"Then business is awful. But if you're going to take someone's money and not pay it back as promised, you've got to accept the consequences."

Olivia could think of no response to that. "Didn't you ever want to be a farmer?" she asked.

"Live at the mercy of the Chicago grain pits? Never. When they get done robbing you, it's the turn of the railroads, elevator companies, and steamship lines.

Farmers work harder and get paid less than anyone in America. They work like fiends all spring, summer, and fall, and hibernate in their holes all winter. And their wives. Lord. Who do you think is filling up all the insane asylums they keep building?" He stopped for a moment to face her. "But don't worry, I don't plan to spend all my time dispossessing local farmers. I also write articles for a journal that the university puts out. A page every month discussing what I learn about the plants and animals around here."

"So *that's* why you sit out in the woods."

"I sit out in the woods because I enjoy doing so." He resumed his brisk pace. "Fortunately for me, other people are willing to pay to read about the experience."

"You write about bears?"

"Bears, wolves, snakes. Last month's article explained why a rabbit being chased will always head for high ground. I don't suppose someone like you has ever wondered about that."

"Never chased enough rabbits to notice that's what they do."

"Well it is. I could never make sense of it. One would think there'd be more places for them to hide down low. Fallen trees, thick underbrush, and such. But when you chase a rabbit, it always heads up. You can't figure out why, unless you watch them long enough. A rabbit can outrun anything going up, but on a downhill slope I or even you could catch one. Reason is, its hind legs are much longer than the front ones. That's what gives it so much force when pushing itself up. But going downhill it gets all tangled up in itself. I've seen them flip right over. You see, no one would know things like that, if men like me, with a feel for the world and the intellect to understand it, didn't sit out in the woods watching. People try to study animals in zoos, but you can't learn anything with them locked in a cage. It won't be long before those professors over in Ann Arbor set up a faculty of the Life Sciences. They're

223

extremely interested in my work."

It occurred to her that she hadn't been showing nearly enough enthusiasm. She began stumbling through her first attempt at gratifying a male ego.

"Well, of course they're interested. Those articles you write are so important." The words felt thick and sticky coming out of her mouth. No wonder she'd had no gentleman callers. She had no idea how to talk to a man. First she insulted him by not showing enough interest in his work, and now she had probably angered him by spewing empty flattery, as if he were a five-year-old showing her one of his drawings.

He surprised her by brightening, stopping to face her again, and saying, "I can give you some of them to read."

"That would be grand," she said and changed the subject. "Before, when you were talking about your land, you said that they'd be ready to start *slaughtering* the trees. That sounds like a funny word to use."

He turned back to the trail. "That's what the loggers call it when they first come in, to cut off the valuable wood. I didn't make up the word, but I do think of it as a slaughter. They move in, strip the land bare, and move on. We need another president like old Andy Jackson, to put a stop to things like that."

"My brother says we should be grateful to the lumber companies for giving jobs to so many people."

"They may provide men with employment, but it's temporary, at slave wages, and under dangerous conditions. Then they take all the money with them and move on to the next mountain."

"But you can't farm with trees all over your land. I would love for someone to come in and slaughter the trees on my land and then pay me for their trouble. And people need the wood. We couldn't build anything if we didn't have the lumber companies providing us with wood."

"And making outrageous fortunes doing it. Look,

I'm not saying they shouldn't make money, but I don't think they are entitled to all of it. The trees are there. The lumber companies did nothing to produce them. They make no capital investment to justify the size of their profits. Some of that money should stay with the people of the state. Those companies use the roads and bridges and water lines the states build, and now all the states are skint, can't even repair the roads they have. Why shouldn't the big loggers put money back in that pot?"

"You did nothing to produce the trees on your land, but you're eager for those loggers to cut them down for whatever profit you can get. I don't imagine you'll be donating any of that money to the public domain." She felt torn between wishing she could keep her big, critical mouth shut and thinking why should she? Wasn't a woman entitled to an opinion? She loved a good argument and seldom chanced on one. "Not that I think you should, but I don't see a big difference between you and the lumber companies."

"Yes, you're right about that. I quite intend to keep every penny. I'm no crusader. But I can see when a thing's wrong, even if I put my own hand in it. People like you miss the point – which is that it ought not to be allowed. The government shouldn't let it happen. The government's supposed to protect the public domain, not help the rich men who own the railroads and logging companies and insurance brokerages get richer."

"I've never thought about it that way before. Most of the time I'm too busy wondering how I could get to be one of those rich people getting richer."

"Dreaming of a house with seventeen bedrooms and a ballroom?"

"At this point I'd settle for a couple of windows in my cabin."

"That's little enough to ask." He turned and smiled at her. "Windows are usually put in before the walls go up, but you can cut them out later. But you'd best wait until you've passed your first winter here before you go cutting any holes in your house. That's the reason your uncle built it that way. You get a five foot drift up against your wall, you worry a lot less about light and air and a lot more about how to keep from freezing to death."

"That's what Mourning says."

Neither of them spoke for a while as she trudged along behind him. Then he stopped at the edge of the clearing in which his log cabin stood.

"Oh Jeremy, it's beautiful." She edged around him, eager for a closer look at his home.

A spacious roofed porch ran across the front. On the far right side, where the porch wrapped around, stood a large stone bake oven and stove top. Pans and cooking utensils hung on the wall next to the front door. A table and two chairs stood in the center of the porch and a string hammock hung between two posts at the far corner.

"What a clever idea – to do all your cooking outside." She moved closer.

"Try to. Weather's got to be really bad before I'll fry up anything inside."

"It's the exact opposite of what my father used to say – people design their homes to hide the kitchen way at the back, so you can't see how they're trying to poison you."

Jeremy's big red horse stood free in the yard, munching on buffalo grass. "Hullo Ernest." Olivia approached him and the animal took a few steps to allow her to stroke its head.

"We don't have time for much hospitality," Jeremy said. "It's later than I thought it would be. Unless . . ." He looked at her again in that unfocused way, as if making up his mind about something. "I could take you home on Ernest, but you'd have to ride behind me. Western. And bareback. I don't suppose you know how."

Olivia thought she saw him regretting the offer the moment it was spoken, but she accepted it anyway. "I love riding bareback. My Uncle Scruggs used to take me all the time, when I was little. He didn't care much about the things people say little girls aren't supposed to do. And I'm dressed for it." She tugged at the sides of both trouser legs and did a little curtsey.

"Well, all right then. You shouldn't be on the trail alone, especially without a weapon. So I guess I'll start a fire and do you for a cup of coffee. Feel free to have a look-see around. Go inside if you want."

She wasted no time, climbed the three steps to the porch, and lifted the latch on the door. The small cabin was simple, but the most perfect home she'd ever seen. She stood in the doorway, nodding her approval. He had stripped the bark from the logs and treated them, so the walls glowed a bright reddish brown. The chinking was all even-colored clay – no rags, moss, or newspapers – neatly done and kept in good repair. A stone fireplace and chimney rose from the back of the cabin. Not far from it stood a double bed, covered by a feather comforter and with three big pillows propped against the headboard. A lantern hung at the side of the bed, at just the right height for reading. Two cheerful rag rugs gave color to the room. Two windows – real glass windows – let in the rays of afternoon light. He had tacked pictures to the wall on either side of one of the windows. One a portrait of George Washington, the other of Andrew Jackson. Next to Andrew Jackson was a framed document under glass. She looked closer and saw that it was the deed to Jeremy's land, signed by none other than Andrew Jackson himself.

"Your home is beautiful." She rejoined him outside. "I see you are a big admirer of Andrew Jackson. Because of New Orleans?"

"No." Jeremy shook his head as he finished laying a fire in the pit in the yard. "I agree with an article I read when he was President – killing two thousand five hundred Englishmen in New Orleans hardly constitutes a proper qualification for the Presidency. And that's absolutely right. But Jackson's more than a general."

"My father used to say it was Adams who can write against Andy who can fight."

"Well, lots of people thought like that, but that just means your father wasn't the only one who was wrong. It was Andy who believes in the rights of man against Adams who believes in the rights of property. Too bad Jackson couldn't run again, but I guess he's too old and sick, even if he had been allowed." Jeremy struck a flint to light the fire.

"How can you call a person who owns slaves a believer in the rights of man?"

Jeremy sat back on his heels. "That is a problem. But he did take six hundred free black men with him to fight in New Orleans. Stood up to a lot of protest about that. That's more than most white men have ever done. He didn't invent slavery and he's always opposed succession from the Union. The good he has done this country far outweighs whatever support he has lent to that unfortunate institution."

"Unfortunate institution!" Olivia remembered the article in the newspaper that had called people like Mourning the unwanted debris of an unfortunate institution. "It's not an unfortunate institution! It's a crime. A sin."

"Yes." He got to his feet. "It surely is. So is the way we treat the Indians. Your farm is on land that was taken from them. Do you plan to give it back?"

She stared at him with pursed lips.

"We all make our way in an imperfect world," Jeremy said.

She sighed. "That's what I always say. You can't change the world. All you can do is look after your little corner of it."

"That's a simplistic way to look at it, though not

228

without merit. Let me go get that coffee."

Olivia was relieved to have the conversation over. What kind of girl wanted to chat about Andrew Jackson and the Battle of New Orleans? One who didn't know how to socialize, that's who. One who especially didn't know how to talk to a man.

She suddenly felt sad. She hadn't spent a single minute being homesick for Five Rocks, but Jeremy's cozy little cabin had aroused a vague longing to have a place on God's earth that she cared about, where she wanted to spend her life. A place that would feel like a real home, with people she loved and wanted to take care of. Where she would belong. And Uncle Scruggs' cabin wasn't going to be it.

Neither was Jeremy's. When she'd first stepped into his cabin she couldn't help but picture herself nestled among the pillows in that welcoming bed, reading Jane Austen while Jeremy sat at the table, hunched over one of his articles. He would glance up at her with soft eyes, smile, and read out a sentence for her approval. But this vision required them to be at ease with one another, and she found it hard to imagine feeling that way with Jeremy. He would probably give her a reading list and quiz her on every book.

In any case, he wasn't interested. She was in his home only because they had met by chance. True, today he had finally been forthcoming about himself, but he hadn't asked a single question about her. He had ignored several opportunities to lay a gentlemanly hand on her. There had been no lingering gazes.

And she was no longer certain she wanted him to look at her that way. Was it supposed to be this exhausting to spend time with a man? Her girlish ideas of love had always included a lot of laughing together. There was much to admire about Jeremy, but where was the fun?

"Cold or not, windows make such a difference," she said, stepping outside.

"Those were a gift to myself. I join a poker game at a tavern in Northville every other Saturday night. Play so badly, I'm the most popular man at the table. Usually allow myself to lose five dollars and quit, but one night I won a big pot. So I bought a hand-tooled saddle for Ernest, a comforter stuffed with goose feathers, and the glass for those windows."

"How did you get it back here without breaking?"

"That was the hard part. Rigged a travois to Ernest and rode real slow. I didn't do the final cut until I got it here. Had to buy a special tool."

"Well, it's a lovely home. You must be proud of it."

He poured ground coffee into the pot, filled it with water, and set it on the fire.

"What's that?" She pointed at a low-roofed structure of rough lumber down by the river. She needed to use his privy and that was the only thing she had seen resembling one, though she couldn't imagine him putting it there, so close to the source of his drinking water.

"Ice house. Come see."

He opened the door of the little room, which was dug deep into the ground and had a thick layer of sawdust between its double-walls. A large puddle filled with sodden straw stood in the middle of it.

"I'll invite you for ice cream next spring. Last of this year's ice melted just a few weeks ago."

"Mmm."

She smiled and once again scanned the area for the outhouse, but there was none to be seen. Need finally triumphed over reticence and she asked him where it was. When he held out both arms and looked around at the woods, she felt herself go red.

"Sorry. Just fooling with you. I do actually have one."

She followed him around the side of the barn, where he picked up what looked like a heap of hide, bark, and poles. "I use this in the winter." He carried it over to the far edge of the clearing, stood it up, fiddled with the poles, and a little wigwam materialized. Then he strode back to the barn and returned with a wooden chair that had a large hole cut in its seat. He lifted a flap of hide and set the chair inside the wigwam.

"There's newspaper and matches inside that pouch hanging on the back of the chair."

"Matches?"

"For burning the paper. Just take care you don't set the woods on fire. You'll figure out the rest."

She bent over, entered the wigwam, and looked in the pouch. Along with scraps of newsprint and matches, it also contained a small digging tool. So that was "the rest" of what she was supposed to figure out. Instead of one big, stinking hole with a permanent structure over it, you buried your business as you went along, like a cat. Once she overcame her initial astonishment, she thought it a brilliant idea.

When she emerged from the wigwam Jeremy was down by the Geesis, pulling on a rope to draw a crate from the river. She joined him, kneeling to wash her hands in the cold water, and he held up a tin from the crate, asking "You take your coffee with milk?"

"Yes, I do. What's that contraption?" Olivia asked, nodding at the tree behind them. A pulley was nailed to it. A rope with a large hook hanging from it ran back up the hill to another pulley, nailed to another tree.

"That's what I have instead of you," he said. "Watch."

He picked up the bucket that stood at the foot of the tree, dipped it into the river, hung it on the hook, and pulled hand over hand on the rope to send the bucket sailing uphill to the other tree. Then he yanked on something that caused it to stay in place and walked up the hill with Olivia traipsing behind him in awe. They came to a table holding an enormous pot with a spigot. Jeremy tipped the bucket to pour its contents into the pot and then opened the spigot to complete his demonstration of the system.

"This is where I do my washing up." He held his hands under the stream of water. "My shaving, too."

"I want one of those!" She was already planning how she would have her second pulley right over the water barrel.

"No problem to fix one up. All you need is enough rope and two pulleys. Those are for washing up the rest of you." He gestured toward the two large leather pouches that lay on the ground a few yards away. "Filled them this morning so they've been in the sun all day, heating up. Water should be nice and warm."

Jeremy picked up a piece of rope that hung over a tree branch, with a hook tied to its end. He attached the hook to a metal ring sewn to one of the pouches.

"Watch this," he said and whistled for Ernest. The horse clomped over, took the other end of the rope in its mouth, and walked away from the tree. It seemed as if Ernest actually looked back over his shoulder to make sure the bag of water was high enough.

"There, stay there, Boy," Jeremy said and Ernest obeyed.

Then Jeremy removed a plug from the bottom of the skin and stood back to hold his hand under the stream of water that spurted out. "It is nice and warm," he said, getting splashed as he returned the plug to close off the flow.

Olivia stared up, again in awe. It was so simple. Why didn't everyone do this? There was a mirror nailed to the tree and nails for hanging up clothes. A block of soap rested on a tiny shelf. There was even a ramp of wooden slats on the ground, to protect bare feet from the mud. He had thought of everything.

"What's that?" She pointed at a small container.

"Special soap the Indians use. They make it from yucca root. Say it's good for your hair."

She wanted one of those too and flushed as she imagined standing naked in the open air under a stream of water, her clean skin tingling. *It would probably be easy for Mourning to rig one up, once he saw the idea,* she thought. *But would I dare use it? Why not? It doesn't have to be out in a clearing like this. Mourning can put ours behind the barn.*

I have to stop being so timid. So conventional. That's why Jeremy hasn't come calling. He knows life with me would be prison. I'm Francie Everman in trousers and I don't even know how to bake a pie.

Chapter Twenty-Six

"Did you think up this wonderful invention up all by yourself?" Olivia asked Jeremy.

"No, saw something like it in a book. There have always been people like me, figuring ways to wash under running water. An Indian helped me fix it up. Those 'savages' use a similar system and laugh at the 'civilized' white men who sit in a tub of their own filth."

He went into the cabin for cups and came back out to the porch, where he set them on the table. There was that sinewy forearm again. His hands were delicate, the nails white and neatly trimmed. He moved gracefully, at ease with himself. How different life would be if Jeremy wanted to share it with her. If he chose to make her feel good about herself. All the drudgery would serve a purpose. They could build something together.

Jeremy went back inside and returned with a bowl filled with lumps of brown sugar.

"Where'd you get the maple sugar?" she asked, struggling to hide the strain in her voice.

"An Indian gave it to me. Kitchi Sucsee." He spoke the name as if he expected her to recognize it.

"Who's that?"

"The Indian who works for the banks."

"An Indian works for the banks?"

"Someone must have told you about him – the one

233

who brings the reserve money down the river." He looked as if he expected her to say, "Oh yes, I know about him," but her face remained blank.

"I don't see how you've managed to live here for more than ten minutes without hearing that story."

She shrugged.

"Well, can I assume that you *do* know that the banks out here print their own wildcat bills?"

"Yes, I've heard of that."

"But the law requires them to keep a reserve of federal money." He paused to sip his coffee. "And a bank examiner comes around every so often to make sure they have enough of it. But these arsewise banks around here hardly ever have *any* real money. What they do is, they pool all their federal money into one kitty of reserve cash to show to the examiner. He always visits the same bank first, so that's where they keep the money. After he finishes counting it at the first bank Kitchi Sucsee – that's Indian for Great Deer – takes the bags of scrip to the next bank down the line. Since he goes by river in his canoe, he gets there before the examiner, who then counts the same money all over again."

"You're fooling me."

"No, it's true. Everyone who lives here knows they do it. That's one of the reasons they all hate the banks. But that's not the story. The story is that one time Kitchi Sucsee got to the first bank a little late and had to hurry – or, if you ask me, he was probably drunk as a sow, the way these bloody Indians are with whiskey – but for whatever reason, he tipped his canoe over. Lucky for him, he managed to fish the bags of money out, but obviously the notes were soaking wet when he got to the next stop. So the bank manager gave that examiner all the whiskey he could tipple, taught him how to dance a horn, and then fed him a five-course meal and pie. Kept him busy long enough for those bills to dry out by the fire."

Olivia laughed along with him, but all she could think about was the ride home, her sitting behind him on that horse. Did she still want to put her arms around him?

"Well, I'd better get Ernest done up."

He slipped the bit into the horse's mouth, smoothed a blanket over its back, and hoisted himself up. Then he turned and offered Olivia his hand.

"I think I need you to go over by one of those stumps," she said.

He wore the expression of a man who is being patient with a lesser being as he clucked for Ernest to take a few steps. Then he grasped Olivia's hand while she put her left foot on the stump and swung her right leg over the horse's back. Settled close behind Jeremy, she breathed in his woodsy scent.

She spent most of the ride home wondering if there was a woman in Northville. It was a long way to go every two weeks just to lose at poker. She held her back painfully rigid and her knees clamped so hard around poor Ernest's flanks, she worried she was going to break his ribs. To her surprise, the urge to put her arms around Jeremy was not hard to resist.

"Are you a Democrat?" she asked, unable to think of anything else to say.

"You can bet I don't vote Whig."

"Not even for Harrison? Son of the Middle West?"

"Not even. Course, there's nothing to say Tyler will be any better. I'll give him one thing – that log cabin bill he wants to pass is all right."

"What's that?"

"Haven't you heard about that either? It would let a settler claim 160 acres of land before it's offered for public sale. Then later, once he's scraped the money together, he can buy it for $1.25 an acre."

"In Michigan too?"

"I guess everywhere. It's a federal law."

"For coloreds too?"

235

"Don't remember it saying anything otherwise."

She quickly figured in her head. This sounded like a far better deal than the one she was offering Mourning. After a long silence she changed the subject, asking Jeremy if he would vote for an abolitionist party.

"I don't believe in one human being owning another, no matter how black his skin is, but no, I wouldn't vote for the abolitionists."

"Why not? How do you think the slaves will ever get freed, if people don't vote for a political party that wants to free them?"

"I vote for a man, not a party. And no one but naïve women like you trusts reformers of any stripe. They get carried away with themselves, do more harm than good. Think their cause justifies whatever they feel like doing."

"What harm could the Abolitionists do?"

"Spoken like a truly naïve woman. Don't tell me you haven't heard what your abolitionists have been spouting lately about 'wage slavery'?"

"No. What's that?"

"They say that the first battle they have to fight now is against the low wages paid to white men. Ending negro chattel slavery would only throw millions of coloreds on the labor market and drive low wages even lower. So the white slaves have to be freed before the black ones. And most of your reformers would just as soon ship your beloved free negroes off to Haiti, which I don't suppose you would approve of."

She bit her bottom lip. All day this man had lectured her in a tone that grew increasingly superior. Now he seemed to have gone out of his way to make her feel condescended to. She was impressed that he knew so many things, but had grown weary of his company. How could she have longed so desperately for this chicken-chested blowhard to touch her?

It was growing dark when they rode up to the cabin. Mourning was still out in the farm, but walked in to meet them.

"Hullo, Mourning," she said.

Mourning nodded to Jeremy and then asked Olivia, "Where you been at? I thought sure a bear or wolf went and et you."

"I ran into Jeremy and he showed me the way to his place."

"Look at you, ridin' bare back, just like an Indian warrior." Mourning held out his hand to help her down.

She scooted back and put an indifferent hand on Jeremy's shoulder while she slipped her leg over Ernest's back and then gripped Mourning's hand and descended with a thump.

"We'd be happy to have you stay for supper." She looked up at Jeremy, hoping he would refuse.

"No. Thanks for the invite, but I've got to be going. Get some kip. Mind yourselves. Good to see you again, Mourning. After." He touched his hat and rode away.

Mourning stood next to Olivia, watching Jeremy disappear into the dark.

"So I guess you had a good time," Mourning said.

Olivia stared at the dark trees for a long pause before she turned to face him and said, "No. No, I didn't. Not at all. He's got a great cabin and you have got to see this pulley system he rigged up for bringing water up from the river. And his shower. It's amazing. He's a clever man and a good neighbor, but you'll be glad to hear he's like you said."

Mourning looked at the ground. "Never said I be glad 'bout that. But least he be your friend. Ain't what you want, but havin' the person you care 'bout as a friend ain't nothin'."

Olivia looked into Mourning's face, appearing startled, as if she had just awoken. As if the clouds had parted and a mystery had been solved. It was a devastating realization.

It's Mourning, she thought. *Mourning is the one I care for. Has been for a long time. Not just as a friend.*

237

He's the one it could be wonderful to share a life with. But with Mourning there is nothing to hope for, no "if only he wanted me." Never. I might as well wish both of us dead as wish for him to express desire for me. Nothing will ever change that. And no other man will ever feel like part of me, the way Mourning does.

She slowly raised her hand to touch Mourning's cheek before she spoke. "You're absolutely right. Having the man I truly care about as a friend is not nothing. I'd say it's quite something." The words hung between them for a moment and then she said, "I'll go start supper. I apologize for running out on you today." She turned away.

"I already put a pot of beans on to boil." He called to her back. "Figured to eat 'em with some a that venison."

"All right. Thank you for doing that."

"You been hidin' more a them peaches, ain't you?"

"Indeed I have," she called over her shoulder. "I'll get a jar."

Later, after they had eaten and were sitting by the fire having their coffee and peaches, she poked at the embers with a stick and said, "I suppose you can see that I'm feeling low, but it's nothing to do with Jeremy. I guess I'm getting lonely out here, with no women to talk to except that Iola –"

"Oh, I forgot to tell you. They come to get the team this afternoon and she say she gonna be coming back to visit you again tomorrow."

"Lord spare me. What on earth for?"

"Ain't said nothin' special. Just that she be comin' to pay you another visit. I thought you gonna be glad, that you wanna be all friendly-like with her."

"Well I do, but sometimes she gives me the collywobbles. There's something about the way she looks at me."

He played his harmonica for a while and she told him Jeremy's stories – about how the river had gotten its name and the banker Indian.

"You know," she said, "he told me something else. You should go over to that Backwoods town and ask the colored farmers there about it."

"'Bout what?"

"He said that President Tyler is trying to make a new law – or maybe he already did – that let's you claim 160 acres and pay for them later. And when you do pay, it's only a dollar twenty-five an acre."

"Colored people too?"

"I asked him that. He couldn't say so for sure, but he didn't remember reading or hearing anything that said they couldn't. But you should go to Backwoods, find out. They might have a colored newspaper or a colored lawyer you could ask."

"I'm a do that. I been wantin' to visit over there any how."

"If it's true, you'd be better off working your own land than staying here –"

"I ain't gonna walk out on you."

She smiled gratefully. "Well, that's good to hear. But you should find out about it. So should I, for that matter. Can I come with you?"

"You think I gonna trust you here, alone with my tools? Course you gotta come."

She lay in bed that night, hating how sorry she was feeling for herself. She should be thanking her lucky stars. How many people had a friend like Mourning?

When Olivia woke the next morning she lay in bed for a while, feeling miserable. She had no desire to move a finger, but her chores awaited and nosy old Mrs. Stubblefield was coming over. Olivia dragged herself out of bed and went to work. Iola turned up after lunch and Olivia took her inside for a cup of tea.

"You're feeling all right, aren't you?" Iola asked, patting Olivia's arm. "Your time hasn't come early, has it? You're looking a bit peeked."

Olivia pulled her arm away and thought, *This old bat is going to make me homesick for the busybodies*

239

in Five Rocks.

"It's always such a shame." Iola reached to squeeze Olivia's arm again. "Every time a woman bleeds, it's a child lost to Jesus."

Olivia's face was blank as she listened to Iola's long lecture, impatient for her nosy neighbor to be gone. But when Mrs. Stubblefield finally took her leave, Olivia went back to feeling lost and alone.

Chapter Twenty-Seven

All the following week Olivia moped. She could feel Mourning's eyes on her, watching. Worrying. She no longer hummed while she worked or begged Mourning to play camp songs in the evening. She went to bed early and rose late, but was always tired.

One morning she woke with a good excuse to lie in. She felt weak and shaky, sticky with sweat, but told herself it was only the unusual weather they'd been having – unbearably hot during the day and cold at night. The dank smell of the cabin, combined with the unpleasant odor of her body, made her feel worse. Faint strains of Mourning's deep voice drifted in:

> The birds without barn
> Or storehouse are fed,
> From them let us learn
> To trust for our bread

Hearing Mourning sing a hymn usually aroused her curiosity about his religious convictions. That morning the only thing on her mind was how she was going to get out of bed. She staggered to the door and saw Mourning behind the plow, heading toward the back section of the farm where he planned to put in winter wheat. Still in her chemise, she braced herself against the outside wall of the cabin before she struggled to the woodpile for kindling and firewood. Once she had a fire going, she collapsed back onto the bed and lay listening to the birds.

Then her stomach cramped and she fled to the outhouse. Afterward she stood by the water barrel, gripping its rim with both hands and garnering the energy to wash up and take a few sips of water. Feeling slightly better, she went in and pulled on her clothes, mixed up dough for bread and left it to rise, and trudged down to the tub by the river, carrying a bucket filled with dirty clothes. She started scrubbing a shirt against the smooth boulder she used, but suddenly doubled over and vomited into the river. Then she crawled a few feet upstream to rinse her mouth and face. The cool water made her shiver and the ache in her bones told her she was good and sick. She turned and dragged herself back up the hill to bed.

Later she forced herself up, first to stoke the fire and then again to put the bread in the kettle to bake. Then she lurched out to the yard, threw up violently, and stooped to paw some loose dirt over the mess. She splashed water from the barrel over her face, blew filth out of her nose, rinsed her mouth, and went back inside, carrying one empty bucket and one filled with water. She sprawled on the bed, the usually tantalizing smell of baking bread causing her stomach to turn. Not many minutes passed before she had to get up and vomit again, and then again. Each time there was less in her stomach and it began to feel as if she were going to spit out internal organs. By the time Mourning came in for something to eat, Olivia was lying on the bed like a rag, soaked in sweat. He stood hesitantly in the doorway.

"Livia? You 'sleep? You all right?"

"I'm sick. There's bread in the bake kettle that should be ready to come out, but I'm sorry, I didn't do anything else."

He came to her bedside and hesitantly put the backs of his fingers to her forehead.

241

"You burnin' all right. I best be gettin' that Mrs. Stubblefield."

"No. No point in that."

"I ain't much on doctoring, but I bet she got some medicine, bring that fever down." He dipped a small towel in the bucket of water, wrung it out, and gently swabbed her face.

"I'll be all right ... as long as I keep drinking." Speaking required a terrible effort, but Mourning looked so scared, she tried to keep her voice steady. "Folks are always all right," she said, "as long as they manage to keep liquid down."

Mourning frowned for a moment, then turned and stooped to pull the bake kettle out of the fire. He had wrapped both hands in rags, but dropped it, cursed, and shook his burnt fingers. Then he folded the rags over double, bent down to remove the lid from the kettle, and shook the loaf out onto the wooden counter.

"I be outside eatin' some apples, till it be cool enough to slice," he said and stepped through the doorway.

Olivia lay in bed, wishing he would disappear for the rest of the day.

"The jam's there on the table," she said when he came back in.

"You want I should fix you something to eat?"

"Lord no."

He set a pot of water on the crane and swung it over the fire, then stood in the doorway eating bread and jam and casting nervous glances her way. When he finished, he made a cup of tea and brought it to her, but she shook her head. He touched her forehead again and said, "I best go get her."

"No. I'd just as soon not have her around. Go on back to work, Mourning. I'll be all right. I can take care of myself." Olivia wanted him far away – fast. She was uncomfortably aware of how awful she smelled and her bowels were churning.

He came back to check on her a few times during the day. The first time Olivia pretended to be asleep, but later he caught her eyes open and asked, "You ain't gonna die on me?"

"I almost wish I was," Olivia said and turned away. She had no tolerance for pain and sickness and derived some illogical satisfaction from thinking how bad Jeremy would feel if she did die. That would show him.

"I once seen Mrs. Monroe fixin' something for a fever," Mourning said. "I 'member what she done – boiled up some milk and poured a glass a wine in it. Kept cooking it till it got all full a lumps. I could go into town, get some milk and wine."

"Go back to work, Mourning. Thank you for worrying about me, but I'd rather be alone. Go plow your fields."

After the steady thuds of his footsteps faded away, Olivia lay in bed feeling worse than just sick. She was tired. Of everything. A swamp of exhaustion had begun sucking her down into it, even before this illness came upon her. She knew she would soon get better, be able to go back to her chores – but what for? Why bother? It had come upon her unexpectedly, this not caring about anything. She could remember how anxious she had been to get to Michigan, claim this property, and make a new life; she just couldn't remember why.

For the next two days, as she lay in bed slowly recovering, she failed to regain any sense of urgency. So she would have her own farm; so what? There was no one to share it with. Mourning would go off to claim land of his own. She would go on hauling water and cutting wood to heat an empty cabin in the middle of nowhere. If she fell into the river and drowned no one would notice – or care if they did.

Not two months had passed since they'd boarded the boat in Erie, but it seemed so long ago. She was no longer Olivia Killion, the storekeeper's daughter, but neither had she turned into someone new. She was

243

nothing but two pairs of limbs that got up every morning to do chores.

The only time her mood briefly improved was when she managed to work up some anger at herself. *What's the matter with you? There used to be things you cared about and wanted to do for yourself, the same way Jeremy does. Are a few weeks of hard work more than you can take? Look out for your own self, your own future. Who needs a man any way? All they want with a woman is someone to boss.*

It didn't work for long. She always ended up admitting that she surely did want a man. Not bossing her around, but giving shape to her life.

A few times each day Mourning came in to gently feed her spoonfuls of tea and Olivia managed to smile at the big black guardian angel hovering over her. He might as well have been the only other human being left on earth. When her fever finally broke, he brought his mattress from the barn, threw it down in front of the cabin, spread a sheet over it, and helped her outside.

"You sit out here in the sun," he said. "Fresh air gonna do you good."

He brought her a pot of tea and a plate of bread and jam. He also tossed down a blanket, towel, clean nightgown, bar of soap, and a washrag. He lugged the washtub over near her and filled it with water he had heated over the fire. Then he hauled Olivia's damp mattress and bedding outside and spread them to air on the buffalo grass.

"I be choppin' trees 'round back, so you can clean yourself up, if you be wantin' to," he said. "I come back in an hour or so, see if you be needin' anything."

"Thank you." She smiled, wanting to tell him how much she appreciated having him there, but not knowing how. "I'll give a whistle when I'm finished."

That tub of clean water was what she needed first. After he'd been out of sight for a few minutes and the

244

steady blows of his axe began, Olivia pulled off her sour nightgown. She first knelt next to the tub, stuck her head in it, and shook her hair out. Then she stood in the water and bathed herself.

Not only her fever had broken; the heat wave was over and the cool air felt wonderful on her worn out body. When she collapsed on the mattress, she imagined the Stubblefields coming up the trail and finding her lying there, naked except for the towel. That thought, however, was funny rather than frightening. What did she care about them? What did she care what anyone thought?

Once she felt completely dry, she pulled the clean nightgown over her head and covered herself with the blanket. Then she put her thumb and forefinger to the sides of her mouth and produced a loud whistle. She curled up and slept, until clouds blocked the sun and the chill in the air woke her. Then she rose, dragged her mattress and bedding back inside, cleaned her mouth with tooth powder, and brushed the tangles out of her hair. She climbed into bed and quickly fell asleep. Next thing she knew, it was growing dark and Mourning was rustling around the cabin, trying to scrape up something to eat without waking her. He saw that her eyes were open and came near the bed, squinting at her in the dim light.

"You feelin' better?"

"Yes." Olivia nodded with a smile. "Much better, thank you." She lightly touched his hand. "I never had anyone take such good care of me."

"You feel like eatin'?"

"Maybe just some toast."

He put a chunk of bread on a stick by the fireplace. The warmth of the cabin felt good and the smell of the toasting bread aroused her appetite. Olivia watched Mourning throw potatoes into the pot for supper and put the kettle on. He handed her a plate with the toasted bread and she ate, still watching him. He pulled a stump chair close to her side and told her what he had managed to get done that day and that Filmore had brought the oxen back, along with some eggs and butter.

"That was a fright you gave me," he said, as their eyes met after a long pause.

He looked ill-at-ease and rose to take the kettle from the fire. When he brought her a cup of tea, he moved the chair aside and rested his left hip on the edge of the mattress. Then he hesitantly put his arm around her shoulders, as if she required help sitting up. Feeling the warmth of him through her thin nightdress, Olivia closed her eyes and flushed red.

I don't need any help to sit up and drink my tea, she thought. *And he knows that I don't. And he knows that I know that he knows.*

She allowed herself to lean against him. He was so warm, so strong, so kind. Why did white people have to be so stupid? He must have cleaned himself up in the river; he smelled so good. Without thinking, she turned toward him and put her arms around his neck. Her breasts, unrestrained under the muslin chemise, pressed against his chest. The tin cup fell from Mourning's hand, splashing tea on the floorboards, and he froze for a moment before returning her embrace. He held her close and she pressed the side of her face to his neck, breathing in the scent of him.

You can't do this, you can't do this, a silent voice screamed from somewhere far away. Olivia ignored it. She was so tired of being alone. She didn't care what people thought. Especially horrid people who said hateful things about a wonderful man like Mourning. *What do they know, ignorant corn-crackers?* Then the voice changed its refrain. *What's the matter with you? His being colored has nothing to do with it. No one but a slut behaves like this with any man, of any color.*

But Olivia couldn't make herself care. She wanted to stay like that, with Mourning's arms around her. It felt warm. Safe. When had anyone else ever cared about her he way he did? Besides, there was no one here to know, to talk. No one. There was only her and Mourning.

Chapter Twenty-Eight

Mourning leaned back to look into Olivia's eyes for a long moment. She returned his stare, unblinking. When he pulled her close she took in a deep breath and clung to him, both arms around him and face pressed against the side of his neck, eyes shut, close to tears. No one had ever held her this way. No touch had been so welcome, comforting and exciting at the same time. Her mind remained shocked by what she was doing, but her heart wanted his body against hers. Her aches and pains had disappeared; something else was flooding through her.

He leaned away from her again and she opened her eyes. His gaze locked on hers as he reached both hands behind his neck and took hold of her wrists. She let him pull them away, releasing her embrace, but after a moment she raised her hands again, placing her palms lightly on either side of his head.

"Yes," she said softly.

"Move over."

She slid down the mattress and farther toward the middle. He rose and shifted his body so he was still sitting, but facing her. He put his hands on her shoulders and continued to look into her eyes. Then he gently touched her face and brushed her hair away. She took in another sharp breath when he placed his hand on her breast and began tracing gentle circles through the cloth. Olivia closed her eyes and lay still. She had never imagined her body capable of producing such sensations and allowed herself to be lost in them.

Then she began to feel as if she were hovering over the bed, watching. *There is Mourning Free down there and, look, that girl is letting him put his hands on her breasts. How can she do that? Isn't she ashamed? No decent girl would let a man do that.* Warmth spread down her body, until the soles of her feet felt as if they were on fire. *Tell him to stop. You must tell him to stop. You know he will, if you just tell him to.*

But she kept silent and let him do as he pleased. When his hand reached under the chemise and touched her down there, her only fear was that he *would* stop. She didn't know what she'd expected the things that men and women do together to be like, but certainly not this. No one ever talked about it feeling good. On the rare occasion that women in Five Rocks could be overheard whispering about the unspeakable, it was as something to be endured.

Olivia let herself drift into pleasure, struggling to push away the sense of shame that kept creeping up. When Mourning tugged at her nightgown she cooperatively lifted her hips, letting him bunch it up under her arms. She turned her head aside, eyes squeezed shut, astonished that she was allowing him to study her naked body in the dim light. Then he placed his warm hands on her belly, ran them down to her thighs, and spread them apart. Had her mother and father done this? Her father and Jettie Place? When the Reverend and Mrs. Dixby came to mind, Olivia almost giggled. Then she stopped thinking at all. Mourning had lightly rested the palm of one hand between her legs and was moving it in a slow circular motion.

"Open your legs wider," he said, his voice hoarse.

Olivia obeyed and peeked at him. For a moment she returned to awareness and was curious. Had he done this before? He must have. He was working on her body with the same look of concentration he wore while whittling a whistle or mending a wagon wheel.

"Try to relax," he said, as he bent her knees and pushed them apart. "You gonna like it better if you do."

He moved away from her for a moment while he

took off his shoes. Then he knelt between her legs. From beneath partly closed lids she contemplated the tent pole pushing his pants out and thought, *so that's where it is, that's how they do it.*

He unbuttoned his trousers and when he leaned over her Olivia went cold with fear. But then he touched her again and she floated off on a cloud of sensation. Her feet were burning and the pleasure she felt between her legs was so sharp it was almost painful. *What is wrong with me? Do any other women feel like this?*

Mourning's face hovered over hers for a long moment, as if giving her a last chance to push him away. Then he put his hand to his mouth and touched her down there again, his fingers slippery with saliva, before he slid his hands under her bottom, raised her up, and plunged into her with one long thrust.

Now there was pain. He pushed in and out, so heavy on her she could hardly breathe, for what seemed forever. Finally he pulled out of her and issued a loud moan. He rolled over with his back to her and lay still for so long that she began to fear he had died.

Then he turned back and looked into her eyes again before kissing her, his tongue exploring her mouth. Olivia put her hands on both sides of his head and gently forced him to lift himself, so she could see his face. For that moment she felt neither shame nor fear. She smiled, pulled him close to her, and kissed him back.

"Open your legs," he said and began touching her again, managing to make her forget the burning pain.

When she woke the next day Olivia was alone in the bed. She listened for him, wondering if he had remained at her side last night or gone to the barn. She wished she could sink back into the oblivion of sleep and forget what they had done, but a dull pain down there made that impossible. Her face flamed red as she relived the details. She felt moist and sticky between her legs and dragged herself out of bed to wash. Lifting her nightgown, she saw that her inner thighs were streaked brownish-red. A smear of dried blood formed a sad-looking heart on the bed, next to another light-colored stain. She tore the sheet off, dipped a corner of it into the water bucket, and used it to clean herself. Then she plunged the sheet into the bucket, splashing the floor.

She crawled back onto the bare mattress, feeling desolate and paralyzed. Eventually she forced herself to dress and go out. Mourning was walking toward her, coming up from the river. His pace slowed when he saw her standing by the water barrel. *Dear Lord, what will he say?* They managed to exchange greetings without actually looking at one another.

"Thirsty?" Olivia held out a dipper of water.

He took the dipper and drank.

"I'm feeling much better now," Olivia said. "I'll be going back to work."

"Good."

"I'll make breakfast," she said, wondering how late it was. The sun had already climbed halfway up the sky.

He nodded and strode to the barn, where she could hear him clanking things around. She lit a fire outside and fried up eggs with strips of venison. While it was sizzling she fretted about her morals – or lack of them. But that worry succumbed to anxiety about what Mourning was thinking. He wouldn't have done those things if he didn't have some kind of good feeling for her, would he?

She didn't expect declarations of undying love. She knew, as he surely did, that they could never do that again. It had been a terrible mistake that could bring nothing but disaster upon them. But why did he seem unable to tolerate the sight of her in daylight? Couldn't he at least smile? Say something nice? Let her know he didn't think she was a filthy slut? She felt like a discarded old boot.

I am a slut. Only a slut does things like that with someone she isn't married too, and not even married women are supposed to like it. What is wrong with me? Now I have lost my only friend.

Another part of her despaired that Mourning wouldn't ever touch her like that again. Kiss her again. Look at her that way. Would anyone? She tried to imagine doing that with Jeremy and couldn't.

Maybe Mourning wasn't disgusted by her. Perhaps this was simply the way men behaved. She remembered being in Mrs. Place's bakery once when she was a little girl, short enough to be invisible to anyone on the other side of the counter. Olivia had overheard Mrs. Place in the back, laughing with some woman who was visiting her. "Don't you go believing that," Mrs. Place had said. "You think Seborn keeps coming around because the lovemaking is so great? Believe me, it ain't. But that don't matter none. You know what's so attractive about women like you and me? They don't got to talk to us much in between times."

Olivia's stomach churned as another sorry fact occurred to her. No white man would have her now. If no one had wanted her before, who would now that she was a fallen woman? Most folks would say a white woman couldn't fall any lower than lying down with a colored. Olivia imagined everyone she'd ever known whispering behind her back. "Olivia Killion? Don't you know? She's that nigger's whore."

She knew those folks were despicable. None of those gossiping, bigoted, hateful people were anywhere near as honest and good and smart as Mourning Free. But she also knew it didn't matter. That was the world she lived in – one in which Mourning was a nigger and she had just become the worst kind of white trash. No, no white man would have her. Not if he knew. Not the fiercest abolitionist and not the most quivering Quaker.

Olivia thought about Mrs. Place and the way she

251

stayed in Five Rocks and ran her business with that tight smile on her face, knowing how everyone talked about her. No one invited Mrs. Place anywhere or sat in the same pew with her on the rare occasions that she ventured into church – and she had been sinning with a white man.

When the food was ready Olivia called Mourning.

He sat on one of the stumps with his plate with nothing to say but, "Sun feel good."

"Yes, it does."

Olivia sat across from him, picking at her food. It took her a while to come to a startling realization – there was no reason anyone need know what they'd done. After all, Mourning wasn't going to be posting any notices. It was a novel thought to Olivia – that a person could do something so utterly unacceptable, yet suffer no consequences. She felt as if it must be stamped across her forehead. One look at her face and anyone would know. But the longer she sat there studying on it, the more it seemed possible for them to simply go on with their lives, as if nothing had happened. Wasn't that what Mourning was trying to do?

She brightened for a moment before real fear seized her. What if her belly swelled up like a watermelon? For the first time she understood why they called it "getting caught" – because if you didn't grow heavy with child, no one would ever know. She put a hand on her stomach and wondered how you could tell, what it felt like to have a baby growing inside you.

She had set her plate down and kept her eyes on the ground, but now raised them to Mourning. "Are you as scared as I am?"

He looked at her, a strange mixture of resentment and apology on his face. "I got a reason to be? No point bein' scared, less you got cause."

"How do I know? I don't know how you can tell." Her hand went back to her stomach. "Can a girl be with child after just one time?" she asked softly.

"Course she can." His face softened. "But it be takin' some time 'fore she can tell."

"How can she tell?"

"Ain't no woman never told you nothing? First thing is the next month when she don't ... you know."

"Oh."

"They be things a girl can do," he said, averting his gaze from her. "Things a doctor can do. Need be, I go to that Backwoods place, try and find you one."

"Well." Her voice grew stronger. "I guess there's no point in worrying about that yet. But we can't ... not ever again."

"I know. And, Livia, I got to know, no matter what, that you ain't gonna be sayin' I forced it on you."

"You think that of me?" She stood up and put her fists on her hips. "That's what you've been looking so angry about? You think I could do that to you?"

"Don't know. Happen to plenty a colored men."

"Well, it won't happen to you. You should know that without me having to say so." She stomped away.

"All right then. Guess I do." He called to her back.

They both set to work and didn't speak again until supper. When it began to grow dark, he lit a fire in the pit and played his harmonica. Olivia joined him and poked a stick in the flames as she hummed along to *Green Sleeves, Yankee Doodle*, some hymns she didn't recognize, and then his favorite, the one he always played last – *Amazing Grace*. The sky was soon black and she looked up at the stars, hugging herself. Maybe everything would be all right. Maybe he would still be her friend. She could get through anything, as long as she wasn't all by herself.

She relaxed enough to grow curious. There were so many things she wanted to ask him. Here she was, what folks call an experienced woman, but she didn't feel that way. She hadn't even seen his mysterious thing. He'd sat there studying every little nook and cranny of her body, but Olivia hadn't gotten a single glimpse of his privates. She almost giggled, imagining herself asking him to be fair – drop his pants and let her poke around.

"Mourning," she said when he stopped playing, "you've done that before, haven't you?"

He shrugged.

"Is it different with different people?"

"People got different faces?"

"Oh."

He rose and threw dirt on the fire, then turned his back to her before he spoke. "I heard there ain't so many men what know how to do the way a woman need. You gotta find you one what does. You ask me, most white women be plain stupid. When they huntin' themselves up a husband, all they aksin' is how much money he got. Then for the rest of they lives they sit around together, drinkin' tea in fancy cups, and wondrin' why ain't none of 'em happy. You gotta find a man what can do right for you. Then you got to do right for him. You 'llowed to move. Don't gotta be lyin' there like no dead cat."

"Oh," Olivia said and fled into the cabin, her cheeks burning.

The next day Iola came up the trail, calling, "Yoo-hoo, Happy Almost Fourth of July," reminding Olivia and Mourning of the upcoming holiday they had completely forgotten.

She was all smiles and good cheer, bearing more eggs and butter, exclaiming how glad she was to see Olivia. She kept patting Olivia's arm and calling her "dear child." That was all the proof Olivia needed – as long as her monthly visitor arrived on time this month, she and Mourning would never be found out. If nosy old Iola didn't sense anything different about her, not a soul on earth would. There was something possessive about the way Iola kept laying her hands on Olivia, but

Olivia didn't pay it much mind.

"I got a great big favor to ask of you," Iola said. "I'd be real grateful if you could see your way to come by our place tomorrow and help me put out fruit to dry for the winter. I'll have it all washed, but the cutting and stoning goes by a whole lot quicker when you got company. We can have us a nice long chat."

Olivia could think of no good excuse for refusing. Anyway, Iola was quick to promise her a sack of dried fruit for her trouble. After Iola left Olivia went out to the farm where Mourning was working. He took off his hat, wiped his brow on his sleeve, and put it back on.

"She asked me to go over there tomorrow, help her cut up fruit to dry. I don't know how I'll stand her all day, but I guess it'd be good for me to learn how to do that. I'll get something cooking for you before I leave."

"You don't gotta worry 'bout that," he said, his voice and eyes soft. "I can feed myself. You gonna be wore out, walking over there and back in this heat." He slapped a mosquito on his neck. "Don't be feelin' like you gotta hurry."

They had become careful of one another, but unfailingly kind. Olivia wished he could find his way back to ornery teasing. She constantly longed to touch him and believed he felt the same. She didn't see how they could go on staying there together. And she didn't see how she could bear not to have him near her.

"Maybe day after tomorrow we should plan on going to Backwoods. Find out about that new law," she said.

"Maybe we should."

The next day Olivia rose before sunrise, baked a loaf of bread, rinsed and hung the laundry she had left soaking overnight, swept out the cabin, and put a pot on to simmer for Mourning's dinner.

She was wearing a pair of his trousers, but sighed, remembering what Tobey had said about trying harder to fit in with society. She pulled a dress over her head, cursing the stupid things women had to wear, filled a skin with water, and tied her summer bonnet under her chin. It was straw with a red ribbon and she peeked in the mirror, liking the way she looked in it. When she was ready to leave Mourning was out in the farm swinging his hoe. She gave a loud whistle and waved good-bye. He took off his hat and waved it back.

She stood looking at him for a long moment, wondering why she felt so sad – as if she were starting on a long journey and might never see him again.

Chapter Twenty-Nine

Olivia gathered her skirts and plunged into the cool woods. The blow of a deer was followed by the crash of hooves, but she caught only a glimpse of its white tail. She had never seen light as beautiful as the morning sun filtering through the canopy and turning the leaves a hundred shades of green. How had that greedy John Jacob Astor dared to call Michigan a useless swamp?

She had never been to the Stubblefields, but – as Iola had promised – the trail was clear and she wasn't worried about getting lost. She was, however, tired out by the time she emerged into their clearing. Iola had obviously been watching for her and rushed out. Filmore stood by the barn and Olivia waved to him. He took off his hat, but then slapped it back on his head and kicked at the dirt, head down. Olivia smiled at his shyness.

"Did you buy a horse?" Olivia asked Iola, nodding at the lovely black creature with white stockings that was tied to the hitching post.

"No, no, Filmore borrowed Beauty, just for today." Iola wiped her hands on her apron and put an arm around Olivia's shoulder. "Come in, child, come in. It's so good of you to offer your help."

"Why is Filmore moving all that stuff outside?"

Olivia asked, staring at the pile of farm implements in front of the barn.

Iola gently nudged Olivia toward their home, as if she were a small child. "Sometimes a person has got to make room for more important things," she said as she led Olivia inside.

Their cabin was no bigger than Olivia's, but had a high roof with a sleeping loft under it, leaving more space on the ground floor. Filmore was a skilled carpenter and spent his winters building furniture. He had made a table and four splint-bottomed chairs, a rocking chair, a wardrobe, a bureau, and two stools. Olivia marveled that someone so big and clumsy looking could do such beautiful work.

"Here, dear, let me take that." Iola relieved Olivia of the water skin and sat her down in the rocking chair. Olivia had expected the cabin to be a shambles of fruit in various stages of preparation, but it was spotlessly clean.

"I thought you'd be ready to start," Olivia said.

"In my kitchen? Nah. Not enough room in here to swing a cat. Everything's ready for us out in the barn. But first you've got to have a nice cup of tea after that long walk."

"Thanks, Iola, but I'd as soon have water." Olivia was glad to hear they'd be working out in the barn. The Stubblefields' cabin didn't have a cellar under it and smelled even worse than Olivia's.

Iola went to the barrel and dipped a cup for her. "There's your water. But I insist you have a cup of tea. It's my newest blend. This one has special strengthening powers and the good Lord knows, out here we need all the strength we can get. I don't want to hear any argument. You had a long walk and you got to learn to take proper care of yourself."

There was a pot brewing and Iola poured out a cup.

"It's bitter." Olivia made a face and pushed it away, wondering if anyone ever managed to say No to Iola.

"Don't you bother about the taste. You know I only mind what's good for you. Here, I'll put a lump of maple sugar in it. That will ease it down."

Iola studied Olivia while she drank and Olivia was reminded of the seagull on the rail of the steamship from Erie. Same tiny eyes, no light in them. Iola didn't seem to be in any hurry to get to work and insisted that Olivia have a second cup of tea, together with a piece of her apple pie.

"So whose horse is that?" Olivia asked.

"Beauty? She belongs to Emery Meyers. Filmore borrows her once in a while when he needs to get around in a hurry."

There was something strange about the way Iola said that, but Olivia couldn't think what it was.

"That must be a harder walk than I thought," Olivia said, feeling dizzy. She put her hand to her forehead and Iola nudged the teacup closer to her.

"Drink it all up," she said. "It'll make things a lot easier on you."

Olivia's brow creased, but she let Iola's strange remark slip by and obediently drained the cup.

"Well, I guess it's time we got to it," Iola said.

Olivia rose and put her hand to her forehead. "I'm feeling so lightheaded. I'm sorry, but I don't know how I'm going to make it out to the barn, let alone help you with your work."

Iola took her elbow. "Don't you worry none. That's just the tea taking its effect. Soon everything will be all over and you'll feel right as rain." She led Olivia outside.

Filmore was nowhere to be seen. Iola gave the barn door a shove and it rattled open on its iron rail. Olivia didn't see any fruit or drying racks. The barn was empty, except for a bed pushed up against one of the walls. Iola guided her to it.

"What's a bed doing out here?" Olivia asked, feeling groggy.

"You're looking a little pale, dear. You best have you a nice lie down."

Iola sat her on the bed, where Olivia soon collapsed and passed out.

Chapter Thirty

When Olivia regained consciousness her first impulse was to curl up on her side and hug her knees. But she couldn't. She was flat on her back, her arms over her head. Her shoulders and neck ached, and something was cutting into her wrists. Grogginess gave way to terror that she was paralyzed or trapped under a fallen tree, and her eyes snapped open. She was under a roof. The surface beneath her was soft. Then she turned her head and saw Iola, sitting on a hard-back chair, haloed in the rays of sunlight that slanted through the open barn door. A cloud of dust motes danced around the black Bible she was holding. Still in a daze, Olivia opened her mouth to speak Iola's name, but some instinct silenced her.

Carefully, not wanting to draw Iola's attention, Olivia moved each limb an inch or two. No, she wasn't paralyzed. She was capable of moving her arms and legs, but they were restrained. She forced her chin to her chest and saw that she was barefoot. Ropes bound her ankles to the foot of the bed. Why on earth would Mrs. Stubblefield tie her to a bed in the barn?

Olivia willed her muscles to relax and her mind to think. She remembered nothing but feeling woozy. Could she have become delirious? Perhaps they'd had to restrain her for her own safety. Or maybe she had some illness that was so contagious she had to be quarantined. No, that didn't make sense. This bed had already been in the barn before she got there. She did remember that. Iola had practically shoved her down onto it. Fruit. They were supposed to be drying fruit, but there hadn't been any. The barn had been empty, except for this bed and a pile of hay. Maybe Iola thought she'd seen the symptoms of an awful disease in Olivia and tricked her into coming over. But Olivia had been feeling fine. No fever. The only thing wrong with her was whatever had been in that God-awful tea. Now she remembered that as well – Iola all but pouring two cups of it down her throat.

Olivia turned her head to look at Iola again, just as the older woman lowered her Bible. Their eyes met and Olivia shuddered. There it was – that flat stare, like a bird. Or a snake. Eyes like dull stones.

"Good. You're awake," Iola said. She rose, closed the Bible, and placed it on the seat of the chair. Then she removed her round spectacles and neatly folded them next to the book. "Slept longer than I expected," she said and came to stand at Olivia's side.

Olivia stared up at her. What had this maniac put in her tea? "Iola," she said, trying to remain calm, to keep hysteria from her voice. "What happened? Why am I tied up like this?"

Filmore stepped into the doorway and stood there chewing the tip of his long beard. Olivia tried to sit up, but could lift her head only a few inches.

"Shh ... be still, dear." Iola put a motherly hand on Olivia's arm. "You won't mind so much, once it's past helping." A second chair stood near the bed and Iola pulled it close. She sat down and began stroking Olivia's forehead. "Best to get it over with quick as possible."

"What are you talking about?" Olivia's voice grew shrill with panic. "You let me go right now."

"Shush." Iola patted her shoulder. Then she turned to her husband and issued a sharp command. "You get on with it."

Filmore hung his head and retreated a step. "Iola..." He gave his wife a pleading look.

"We've had enough words. You know your duty. The

Lord's ways are mysterious, but the signs he's given us are clear enough." Then she spoke more softly and gave him an encouraging nod. "Don't worry, I'll get her ready." She rose from the chair.

"What is the matter with you? Untie me!" Olivia shouted. "Have you gone crazy?"

Iola ignored her. Olivia turned her face toward the roof and let out a long, piercing scream.

Shaking her head as if Olivia had disappointed her, Iola sighed. Then she put one hand on Olivia's shoulder, raised the other high, and brought it down in a resounding slap across the face. The blow reverberated along Olivia's body and she thought she might pass out. When Olivia opened her mouth to scream again, Iola's hand rose threateningly.

"You know there ain't no one going to hear you. All your hollering's gonna do is make this a whole lot harder on all of us than it needs to be." Iola fished a rolled-up sock out of her pocket and held it up. "If you can't keep yourself still, this will. You want me to shove it down your throat, you keep carrying on."

Olivia shut her eyes and sensed Iola moving toward the foot of the bed. "Untie her right ankle," Iola ordered Filmore. Then she spoke to Olivia. "And don't you get any smart ideas about kicking anyone, Little Missy, or I'll see that you're good and sorry."

Iola gripped Olivia's thigh with both hands while her husband untied the rope. "Keep good hold of her ankle. You," she said to Olivia, "you bend your knee. Unless you want me to bend it for you."

A length of lumber had been nailed upright to each side of the bed. Iola held Olivia's leg, knee obediently bent, against one of them while Filmore wound a rope around it. Then he slipped a small noose around her ankle.

"Wait, don't forget this." Iola took a rag from her pocket and handed it to him. He wrapped the cloth around Olivia's ankle before binding it tightly to the

261

wood.

Olivia had realized what they must be intending to do to her and looked from Filmore to Iola in disbelief. She struggled to raise herself up, the ropes burning her skin, but couldn't move. She couldn't breathe.

She began to cry. "Iola, please, why are you doing this to me?"

Iola ignored Olivia's sobs while they finished tying her legs, forced apart. The skirt of Olivia's dress had ridden up and fallen bunched between her legs, so it still covered her.

Iola returned to the head of the bed and put her hand on Olivia's forehead. "You hush that crying," she said. "The first time is the worst, so it's best for us all if we get it over with double quick."

Iola nodded sternly at her husband, who stood motionless at the foot of the bed. Then she grabbed the fabric of Olivia's skirt, yanked it up, and gasped.

"Shame. Shame on you. Traipsing around with no drawers. And calling yourself a Christian woman." Iola pursed her lips and shook her head, staring at Olivia's nakedness.

Olivia shrieked, in shock at being suddenly exposed, unthinkably violated. "You! You're the devil."

She thrashed from side to side, her heart pounding. Her humiliation – Filmore standing there gaping at her – was complete. Then she stopped moving and stared at him. He was biting hard into his bottom lip, his eyes darting from side to side.

He doesn't want to do this, Olivia thought. *It's Iola making him.*

He hesitantly placed a sweaty palm against the bare skin of her calf. When she jerked away in revulsion, he pulled his hand back, as if from a flame.

"What's the matter with you? You can't do this," Olivia shouted. "Let me go. You let me go."

"The pain will pass." Iola stood next to her. "It's nothing. Pay it no mind. No mind at all. But salvation is eternal. There's no use in you fighting it. It's His will. He brought you here to us. You'll see the right of it, come time."

"Iola ..." Filmore took a step back.

"I told you to get on with it." Iola lowered her voice and that was more frightening than shouting would have been. Filmore scraped his way back to the foot of the bed, climbed onto it, and knelt between Olivia's legs.

Weak and dizzy, Olivia couldn't believe this was happening. Then Filmore put his hands on her knees. His touch was sickeningly real and she knew this was no nightmare from which she would awake.

"Get your filthy hands off me!" She jerked her knees from side to side, the little she could.

Filmore shrank back. Iola set her mouth in a hard line and gave Olivia another resounding slap across the face. Everything went black again, this time with exploding bursts of color. Olivia lay still before she began weeping. She wanted to die. Iola had knocked the fight out of her with that second blow.

"I told you, no point making this harder than it already is. I don't want to put that sock in your mouth for you to choke on, but I will," Iola said. She raised her hand and struck Olivia a third time, though not as hard. Then she leaned over, her onion breath an inch from Olivia's face, and put her hands on Olivia's shoulders, all of her weight crushing the young girl to the bed. "You'll do as you're told. You hear me? You'll do as you're told. You're here and that's the way things are. You can make it easy, or you can make it hard. Ain't nothing going to happen to you don't happen to every woman."

"How can you do this?" Olivia whispered. "You're supposed to be a Christian. What would Jesus say?"

Filmore mumbled something and the terrified look Olivia saw pass over his face gave her hope. He at least still seemed to possess a sense of shame. But Iola drew a flask of whiskey from her deep pocket and handed it to her husband.

"Drink that, if you must," she said. "And you." She turned on Olivia. "Shame, shame on you. You're a fine one to call on our Lord Jesus. Prancing about half-naked, living with that nigger boy and wearing his clothes, behaving like a harlot. You're lucky to have found your way to us. It was Jesus led you here, on your path to redemption, to fulfill his will."

Filmore put his head back and took a long swig of whiskey before Iola jerked the flask from his hand. "Just get it done and over with," she said. "Remember, it's God's will you're doing."

Olivia thought she could see him struggling, seeking the courage to defy his wife. But she watched in horror as the last remnants of his humanity drained away. She could see his mind cross over a line. There was no longer any Olivia, that nice young woman he knew, his neighbor. There was no person at all. She had been reduced to a helpless female body, totally at his mercy. He raised his eyebrows and slowly ran his tongue over his bottom lip.

Iola picked up her Bible, sat on the chair at Olivia's side, and began reading aloud – verses about being fruitful and multiplying. Helpless, Olivia tried to will herself to lose consciousness. When Filmore laid his hands on her, she spoke quietly. "You know this is a sin. You know it." He was motionless, staring between her legs.

Iola's voice droned on and Olivia began to feel faint. "Mamma," she mumbled. "I want my mamma."

"Iola, go on outside," Filmore said, his voice slurred.

"We agreed that I would be here." She held the Bible out in front of her, but her eyes were on Olivia. Now they shone with a sickening glint.

"I can't do this with you sittin' here watchin'."

"Of course you can."

He hesitated, but lay down on Olivia and began

rubbing himself against her nakedness. His ratty beard chafed against her neck and then she felt his thick, moist lips rub across her face. She gagged from the stink of him. He grew heavier and heavier, until she couldn't breathe. Then he lifted himself up and got to his knees, pushing her legs apart to stare at her exposed genitals. Leaning back, he took a deep breath. When he reached forward to squeeze one of Olivia's breasts his wife reprimanded him. "There's no call for that." Olivia thought she saw a glimmer of hatred for his wife pass over his face before he looked down and began fumbling with the buttons of his trousers.

"Please, don't, please," she cried, looking in horror at his engorged penis. "Mamma. Mamma. I want my mamma."

The physical pain of him tearing into her body was excruciating, but it was the emotional torment of the violation that made her scream. She willed her mind take her elsewhere, but she was trapped in that barn, writhing beneath his unwashed body. He pushed himself farther in and felt enormous, as if he would rip her apart. The whiskey took its effect and he tilted his head back and howled like a dog, before he began moving with rapid thrusts.

"Stop." Olivia tried to shout, but her voice was a whimper. "Stop. Get off of me. Mamma."

He let out a loud gasp and collapsed on her. She turned her face away from the stench of him and felt close to suffocation before he rose, pulled up his trousers, and staggered to the barn door.

Eyes gleaming, Iola stood and set her Bible down. "See, I told you it would be over before you knew it." She patted Olivia's arm again and then pulled her skirt down between her knees, primly arranging it. "It's what all women have to endure."

Olivia turned her face toward the wall. The world had fallen to pieces and she had shattered along with it. Bewildered and physically destroyed, she desperately wondered what she had done to deserve this.

"I'm going to untie you now," Iola said as she began loosening the ropes around Olivia's knees. "But you remember that Filmore is right outside. There's a barrel of water over there in the corner and a chamber pot under the bed. I'll be back shortly with your dinner."

Chapter Thirty-One

Olivia remained frozen until the barn door rattled closed. Then she sat up and hugged her knees to her chest, rocking back and forth, every muscle painfully contracted. She wanted to tear off her clothes and race to the river. To run until she dropped with exhaustion. To subject her body to exertion so extreme, it would expel the physical memory of everything else that had happened.

She didn't know how long she sat there, one moment imagining clawing Iola's eyes out, the next feeling unworthy of existence. She began scratching at her thighs, raising angry welts. If only she could peel off her skin, discard her body, escape not only this barn, but herself. She could no longer bear to be Olivia Killion. Olivia Killion was filthy. Disgusting. Indecent. Was this her punishment for what she had done with Mourning? For leaving her family? For not going to church? For wearing trousers? Paralyzed by self-loathing, she found no escape into the easy release of tears. She could not free her mind of that horrible image of herself, tied down like an animal, legs spread wide apart.

She rose and stumbled to the water barrel. There was no towel or rag, so she reached under her skirt and stepped out of her cotton petticoat. She bunched up its bottom edge and sloshed water onto it, using her cupped hand in the absence of a dipper. She cleaned between her legs and tossed the filthy, wet undergarment onto the pile of hay. Then she splashed water on her face, rinsed her mouth, and spat several times before taking a long drink. She wanted to kick, scream. To kill Iola and Filmore, tear them to shreds. But she remained motionless, hands on the rim of the barrel.

You have to think, she told herself. *They are going to come back. Maybe they plan to tie you up again.*

The sight of the discarded petticoat, stained with her blood, made her feel like vomiting. She wadded it up and shoved it into the pile hay where she wouldn't have to look at it. Then she studied the barn in the dim light that filtered through the cracks between the boards. It was empty except for the bed, two chairs, the hay, and the water barrel. That was why Filmore had moved everything outside – so there would be nothing sharp or heavy in here, nothing for her to use as a weapon. She rose and paced the length of all four walls, placing her hand on each board, fruitlessly searching for one that was loose or rotten.

The floor was of dirt. Perhaps she could dig under the wall, if only she had some kind of utensil, even a tin cup. Then she remembered the chamber pot Iola had mentioned and got to her knees to retrieve it from under the bed. It was tin, with a thin lip all around the edge, and she could already imagine herself crawling out of her prison. She chose a place to dig behind the hay, where they wouldn't see it the moment they came in, but the dirt floor was packed tight. She barely managed to scratch it. Perhaps if it were wet. She went to the barrel and cupped her hand, splashing water over the side to fill the chamber pot, but quickly lost patience. She had no time for that tedious process, had to get out of there before they came back.

Overcoming her disgust, she plunged the tin pot into the barrel that she was to drink from. She poured water over the scratches she had made and filled the pan again and again, but the earth remained unyielding. She rose and walked the walls again, desperately kicking at the dirt floor, searching for a softer spot. It was no use. She'd never manage to dig her way out of here, even with a shovel. She sank down onto the hay and put her face in her hands, but the hay scratched her calves and ankles, forcing her back to her feet.

Fire, she thought. *This hay is as dry as hay gets. Must be last year's. I'll move a heap of it up against the wall and set it ablaze. Folks in Fae's Landing are sure to notice the smoke. Nothing brings people running like a fire. Mourning will see it too, and Jeremy. They'll both come to help put it out.*

She eagerly reached into her pocket, searching for her flint and punk wood. They were gone. Iola must have taken everything after Olivia passed out. Her disappointment was like another slap in the face and she felt herself dissolving. Then she heard the faint strains of their voices.

"I gotta be getting Beauty back over to Emery's," Filmore was saying.

"First let me give her dinner," Iola said. "Chicken's just about ready. You can go after that, once she's all locked up."

Their steps faded away. Olivia slid the chamber pot back under the bed and ran her bare foot over the floor by the wall, concealing her attempt to burrow a way out. Then she sat on the bed, hands clasped in her lap.

Think, Olivia told herself. *This may be the only chance I'll get, the one time I'll know for sure that Iola is out there alone. I'll hear the horse's hooves, know exactly when Filmore leaves. It will take him at least an hour and a half to ride into Fae's Landing and walk back. There must be a way to get Iola to open the door while he's gone. So when she brings me the food I have to behave ... how? Not like I want to murder her. I have to seem subdued, as if I'm not a threat. Perhaps I can even make her believe I understand why they are doing this. Salvation. God's will.*

Olivia shook her head. *How could Iola believe that? Because she's crazy. Because she believes it. But what does she believe? What does she think they are doing? She must want Filmore to get me pregnant with a child for Jesus, but then what? Does she think they can hold me prisoner for nine months? Then what? Kill me, after she's got her hands on the poor baby?*

Olivia heard someone coming and froze. The door rattled open and Olivia watched silently as Iola came in with a tray and set it next to her on the bed. To Olivia's great shame the smell of the food made her realize how hungry she was. Iola had brought two pieces of fried chicken, a heap of fried potatoes, string beans, a biscuit thick with butter, and a slice of apple pie. *What kind of poison did you put in that, you witch,* Olivia wanted to scream; but she sat stiffly and nodded at the food.

"That smells goods," she said, straining to keep her voice neutral. But she couldn't help saying, "You didn't add any of whatever you put in the tea, did you?"

"That was for your own good," Iola said, shaking her head. "Ease the way. No need for it now. But any time you'd like more of my tea, or even some whiskey, you've only to ask. No shame in requesting a little help when you're doing the Lord's work."

Olivia imagined Iola slowly sinking into a cesspool of diarrhea, the filth filling her mouth and nostrils. Iola had left the door open and Olivia could see the shadow that Filmore cast as Iola rose to leave.

"No," Olivia said and forced herself to continue. "Please. Stay while I eat. I want to try to understand."

Iola pulled up a chair. She put a hand to Olivia's forehead before she sat down. "You're looking a little peeked," she said. "Good meal will do for you. You got to keep your strength up."

"There's only a spoon," Olivia said as she moved the plate aside.

"I know. Did you expect me to bring you a knife?"

Olivia took a few hesitant nibbles before she began to eat hungrily. Iola nodded, smiled, and said, "There's a good girl." Olivia hadn't eaten since yesterday and she certainly did need to keep her strength up. There was no napkin and when Olivia finished she wiped her hands on her skirt.

"I can get you some tea," Iola said. "Just regular tea and sugar."

"No. Not right now." Olivia's voice was low and dull. "But I would like you to tell me why. Why in God's name are you doing this?"

"Why? Because that's exactly what it is. In God's name. Who do you think brought you to us?" Iola leaned forward eagerly. "Do you really believe it was chance that delivered a wanton, Godless girl like you into our hands? If ever a couple was deserving of a child to raise, with a true Christian education, it's me and Filmore. Why, you're not fit to be a mother. You know that. Said right out you don't want to have any children. Shame on you. So Jesus sent you to us, to bear Filmore's child. My child."

"But you can't expect ... What do you think, that I'm just going to agree to have a baby for you?" Olivia strained to keep her voice level, as if this were a normal conversation, two neighbor ladies discussing a mutual interest.

"Well, of course not. We knew it would take you some time to see your way to it. That's why ..." She raised her hands, palms up, and looked around the barn.

"You can't be sure that I'll become with child."

Iola sat back, looking crafty. "Can't I? I know when you last bled. Regular as a clock, you are. This is your time of the month to conceive. And conceive you will."

The realization was awful. Iola must have started planning this the very first time the Stubblefields came over to welcome their new neighbors. All those nosy questions – did Olivia bleed regularly, what time of the

270

month, for how many days – had begun the first time Iola laid eyes on her.

"So you plan on keeping me tied up in your barn for nine months?"

"Oh no, there's no need for that. A week will suffice. Long enough to be certain the seed has been planted."

Olivia had to bite back a cry. A week. Seven days. Seven times to suffer Filmore tearing her apart. The sickening smell of him. The weight of him crushing her. Iola sitting next to her, gloating.

"And then what's to stop me from telling everyone what you've done?"

"Oh, you won't do that. Not once you've had time to think on it. Who exactly are you going to tell? We're your only friends. Oh, I know, you think you're going to run to your nigger boy. Well, you can forget about him. Not that he'd be any help to you, but that's neither here nor there. He's gone. Filmore saw to that. You won't be seeing any more of him."

"What have you done to Mourning?" Olivia cried, rising and clenching her fists to refrain from striking her.

"We haven't done anything to him. You can thank us for that. Not that a soul would pay any notice or care if we had. Nobody's going to miss that pet coon of yours. We haven't done him no harm, but he's gone and I promise you he won't be coming back."

Olivia sat and tightly clutched the sides of the seat of the chair, wishing she could strangle the life out of this evil woman. What had they done to poor Mourning to make him go away? Was she lying? Had they killed him?

"I'll tell folks in town," Olivia said, managing to keep her voice steady. "Not if you let me go today. If you do, I promise not to say anything to anyone. But if you keep me here for a whole week, I'll tell the world."

"Oh you will, will you? Just who do you think is going to believe you? You have no friends there. What fool's going to take the word of a girl like you – what up and left her own Christian family to go live with a nigger – against respectable church-going folk like us? You know what they'll say? Shameless girl got herself in trouble and now she's looking for some poor man to lay the blame on. Think about it, dear. If someone had told you a story like that about me and Filmore last week, would you have believed it? I hardly think so."

She leaned back and smiled. "So there's no good to come of you telling anyone. You'd only be shaming yourself. You can't go back home, either. Not in that condition. No, your only good lies in keeping quiet and letting Filmore's seed come to fruition. Last three or four months, depending on how big you get, you won't go into town. You know as well as I that no one will miss you. You're alone, Olivia. Alone. We're all you have. We're your family and your friends."

"How do you think you're going to explain the sudden appearance of a baby?"

Iola's eyes lit up and she rose to pace. "I'll put pillows under my skirt." She spread her hands across her stomach. "Folks will know the Lord has finally visited me with the joy of a child. And he has, Olivia. You're going to bring me that joy. What higher purpose could you serve? There's no meaning to your life now. We're going to give you that meaning. You'll come to thank us. You don't want to be a mother, so the Lord wants us to use your healthy young womb to bring new life into the world." She stopped at Olivia's side. "I'll do the birthing for you and once it's done, you can go wherever you please. In the meantime Filmore will tend your fields and I'll see to all your needs. You've nothing to worry about. You'll be well cared for. You sure you don't want that cup of tea now?" Iola asked as she picked up the tray and turned to leave.

Chapter Thirty-Two

The door rolled shut and the clank of a chain was followed by the horrible, final click of a lock. Olivia rose and paced, imagining her tormenter's skull being crushed to pieces. Her hatred focused on Iola. Filmore deserved to die, but a bullet between his eyes would do. But Iola. Olivia would happily stick a jagged knife in her eye or douse her in kerosene and strike a match.

What would convince the she-devil to open the door while Filmore was gone? There was no point in whining about being hungry or wanting to bathe. Iola would have to believe that Olivia was in danger, that something posed an immediate threat to her healthy young womb. Did they have poisonous snakes in Michigan? Olivia vaguely remembered someone on the boat talking about Massasauga rattlers, but hadn't he said they lived in swamps? What about deadly spiders? Olivia didn't know. All she could think of was to claim to be bleeding heavily between her legs. But first she had to have a weapon, something she could use to splatter Iola's brain.

She picked up one of the chairs. It was heavy enough. Too heavy. She could barely raise it shoulder-high, let alone swing it around. One of its legs would make a good club. She could hide it in the bed, tucked between the mattress and the frame. But how could she take the chair apart? Perhaps if she bashed it against the side of the bed. No, Iola would be sure to hear that. Olivia put the chair down and sat on it, enraged by her helplessness.

She heard their voices outside. Then the horse clop-clopped away and Olivia looked around in desperation. There must be something. Maybe they had forgotten a piece of rope. She tore the sheet from the mattress and shook it out, then got down on her knees and peered under the bed. Nothing. She looked at the sheet again. She could tear it into strips and braid them together. That would choke the life out of Iola as well as a rope. Better yet, she could use her petticoat. It would be easier to rip to pieces and there would be no bare mattress for Iola to notice when she opened the door.

Olivia retrieved her bloody undergarment from the pile of hay and looked for something to help her start the tear. She remembered a rusty nail she had unsuccessfully tried to pull out of the wall and used it to pierce a hole in the cloth, near the seam. Once she had split the hem the material gave easily, ripping with a sharp, clean sound, all the way up to the waist. She tore six strips, careful to leave the section of the garment that was stained with her blood intact. That's what she would show to Iola when she opened the door a crack. Olivia twisted the strips of cloth together in pairs, braided the three pairs, and knotted both ends. She had her weapon.

Now she needed more gore. Gritting her teeth, she scraped her left forearm across the head of the nail, tearing the skin open. Oblivious to the pain, she let the fresh blood drip over the old on the remains of the petticoat. Then she lay on the bed, facing the door, her knees curled up to her chest, her "rope" hidden under the top edge of the sheet, and the bloody cloth wadded between her legs.

"Iola," she called out softly.

There was no reaction and she shouted four more times, each time more loudly.

"What?" Iola asked through the door. "You should be getting some rest."

"Something's wrong. I'm bleeding ... down there."

"That's perfectly normal. Nothing to fret about."

"No, please, help me. I feel awful and there's so much blood." Olivia tried her best to imitate a dying woman, gasping for breath. "Maybe you have some kind of tea."

"I'm telling you, it ain't nothing to worry about. Every woman bleeds her first time."

"It's not a little. It's gushing all over. I feel like I'm going to die."

There was a long silence before Iola said, "I'll be in with some tea for you when Filmore gets back."

Olivia kept still.

"Olivia?" Iola called out. "I said I would bring you some tea."

Olivia waited a moment before emitting a low moan.

"You're not fooling me, Little Missy. You're perfectly healthy. Not one thing wrong with you."

Olivia moaned once more, barely audibly, but heard Iola walk away. A few minutes later footfalls returned.

"I'm going to open this door," Iola said, "but not until I know you're over on the bed. Let me hear your voice."

"I ... I am ..."

"You stay where you are. You'll be good and sorry if you don't."

The lock and chain clanked again and sun streamed into the barn. Iola stood silhouetted in the strip of light, surrounded by dancing motes, peering at Olivia. She cautiously approached the bed.

"Take that cloth from between your legs and throw it here."

Olivia appeared to attempt to obey, but her limp wrist let the cloth drop next to the bed. Only then did she notice that Iola was holding a pistol, pointed at the floor. Iola moved toward the foot of the bed, but remained at a distance and raised the weapon.

"Open your legs."

"I can't. It hurts too much."

"I said spread your legs. Roll over on your back and let me see you. Pull that skirt up."

With a great show of difficulty, Olivia did as told.

"Ain't no bleeding. Ain't nothing wrong with you at all."

In one movement Olivia was up and off the bed, the braid of fabric clutched in her right hand, hidden behind her back.

"You stay put, right where you are." Iola waved the pistol.

"What are you going to do, Iola? Kill me? Kill your baby?" Olivia took slow steps toward her. "Go ahead. Shoot me. I'd rather be dead than let your stinking, disgusting clodhopper husband near me again."

Olivia took another step forward and Iola took one back.

"I'm walking out of here," Olivia said. "The only way you're going to stop me is to kill me. But you won't do that, will you? What use am I to you dead? For all you know, your husband's foul seed is already growing inside me."

"You don't need your legs to have a baby," Iola said. "You take one more step and I'll make a cripple of you."

Olivia stopped. She heard a rider approaching and from the way Iola turned her head Olivia knew she'd heard it too. How could Filmore be back already? Jeremy. Maybe it was Jeremy.

Olivia lunged at Iola, knocking the pistol out of her hand. Both women fell to the ground, Olivia on top. Olivia put her right knee on Iola's chest, leaned into it with all her weight, and managed to wrap the braided cloth around the older woman's neck. She desperately pulled the ends in opposite directions as the horse's hooves grew closer. If it was Filmore, Olivia had to get to that pistol, fast. Olivia leaned forward, applying more weight. Then she punched Iola in the face as hard as she could.

"How do you like it?" she shouted and pummeled her again and again.

Iola's nose gushed blood. Olivia glanced at the pistol. Could she release her hold on Iola long enough to go for it? Then she saw Filmore, framed in the doorway.

"What ..." He didn't seem to understand what was going on.

Iola came back to life and began shrieking, "Get her. Get her."

Olivia hesitated. The pistol was too far away, she'd never make it. So she tightened the cloth around Iola's neck.

"You come near me, I'll kill her," Olivia said. "I'll strangle her dead right here." She pulled hard. "We're going to get up and walk out of here." It took all of Olivia's strength to drag herself to her feet, bent over and still clutching the ends of the cloth.

Filmore watched dumbly, as Olivia struggled to pull Iola to her feet.

"Get her now you damn fool!" Iola sputtered, as she raised her right knee and brought her work boot down hard on Olivia's bare foot. "Don't just stand there like a stupid ox! Get her!"

Olivia was doubled over, nearly blinded by the pain in her foot, and Filmore had no difficulty overpowering her. One hard shove sent her sprawling to the floor. Iola spun around and raised a foot as if to kick her in the stomach, but stopped herself.

"Get her back on the bed," she ordered her husband, her voice seething with contempt. "You stupe. She near killed me with you standing there watching." Iola rubbed her throat, wiped her still bleeding nose with her apron, and then bent to pick up the pistol and put it in her apron pocket. "Look what she done to me." She put her hands to her disfigured face. "I come in here to help her and that's the thanks I get."

Filmore was standing over Olivia, not touching her.

"Well, what are you waiting for? Get her back on the bed."

Iola picked the braided rope off the floor and added it to her pocket. Filmore grabbed Olivia's upper arm, yanked her to her feet, and shoved her toward the bed.

As they locked the door, Olivia heard Iola ask

Filmore what he was doing back so soon.

"Come for the money I owe him. Forgot to take it."

"So sometimes having a dimwit for a husband can be a blessing in disguise," Iola muttered, her voice fading away.

Olivia put her face in her hands and sobbed until she was beyond exhaustion. Then she lightly probed the top of her foot, wondering if Iola had broken any bones. It was extremely painful, but she could stand and put her weight on it. She curled up on the bed, resigned, knowing there would be no escape. They were going to keep her there for six more days. Six more times to submit to Filmore's assault on her body. Her thoughts lingered on the head of that rusty nail. That was her only way out of here, to tear both wrists across it. It might hurt terribly for a few minutes, but then consciousness would quietly drain away. It would be over. Nothing left to endure. But she knew she wouldn't do that. She had to find out what they'd done to poor Mourning. He might need her help.

She spread her hands over her stomach and prayed she was already pregnant with his child. That would put her in a fix, but at least she would be able to love the tiny new life growing inside her. Wouldn't want to rip the monster child out. Maybe she wasn't being punished for lying down with Mourning – maybe it was just the opposite. God had led Mourning and her to seek the comfort of one another's bodies that night in order to keep her safe. Mourning's child was already nestled securely in her womb, protecting her from Filmore.

Chapter Thirty-Three

Later Iola returned with another meal. Olivia was on a chair, hugging her knees to her chest. She smiled when she saw the left side of Iola's face, swollen and painted shades of blue and yellow. Iola set Olivia's tray on the bed, picked up a large wad of something wrapped in muslin, and held it out to Olivia.

"Put that on your foot. Keep the swelling down."

Olivia ignored her.

"Up to you." Iola shook her head. "But a nice poultice of stewed white beans is the best thing for it."

Olivia declined to take it from her, but raised her face to stare into Iola's. "I want to know what happened to Mourning. If you tell me where he is, I won't give you any more trouble. I promise."

Iola replaced the poultice on the tray and put her hands on her hips. "Oh, I'm not worried about that. You get to feeling like you're dying again, you're just going to have to go ahead and die." Iola brought her face close to Olivia's. "I even brought you a fork to eat your dinner with, I'm that sure of you behaving yourself from now on. Because I've got a promise to make to you." She leaned in closer. "You try to get away again, you raise your hand to either of us, you know what's going to happen to you? One of us will come into this barn alone, but it won't be me. I'll help tie you up, but then I'll leave Filmore with a bottle of whiskey and tell him I have to go into town. He'll have to manage on his own. He'll be free to do whatever he wants. Now I know you're young, don't have any idea of the kinds of disgusting things a man can want to do to a woman. Not to mention what he'll want you to do to him. You sure don't want to find out, but you will, you give my any more trouble. So you enjoy your dinner while you consider on that." She turned and left.

Olivia had no appetite. She laid the poultice over her foot and sipped the tea, but let her food go cold. She picked up the fork and imagined stabbing it into Iola's eye, but set it back down, beaten. When Iola came back for the tray, neither of them spoke. Then Iola noticed the blood where Olivia had cut herself and grabbed her arm.

"Stupid girl," she said and stomped out. When she returned she was carrying a small glass jar and smeared some of its contents over the wound.

Most of that night Olivia lay awake. *Don't think about it,* she told herself. *Don't think about tomorrow. There's no way you can stop it. They'll only hurt you more. All you can do is wait for it to be over. Save your anger and hatred for later, after they let you go. Stay strong. You've got to eat. Get up and walk around. It only lasts a few minutes. Think about other things.* When she finally escaped into sleep, she dreamt of her father's funeral, of jumping down after him into that black pit.

The clank of the barn door woke her in the morning. Her limbs felt heavy, as if she could barely move. When she opened her eyes and remembered where she was, the rage that filled her quickly dissipated into apathy. Iola put her head in and told her to get up and use the chamber pot. They left the barn door open while they stood outside and waited for her to finish. Then they came in and Olivia succumbed to being tied up without a struggle. Filmore, drunk again, enthusiastically climbed up and shoved himself into her. It took longer this time.

After they left, Olivia rolled over and sobbed, weakly beating her fists against the mattress. Five more days. She couldn't survive five more days of this. Not one more day. She didn't want to. She wanted to die. She didn't want to inhabit this body. Finally, she stood, went to the barrel, cleaned herself, and splashed water over her face.

No, she thought, *they are not going to get away with this. They have stolen my life, it will never be the same, but they are not going to get away with it. If I get through this without losing my sanity, I will tell people what they did to me. Someone will believe me.*

When Iola brought her a breakfast of fried eggs, buttered biscuits, and an apple, Olivia kept her voice steady and said, "I want two buckets of warm water, a washrag, some soap, and a towel. And a dipper. And I want a hairbrush. And something else to wear while you launder my dress. And a blanket."

Iola hesitated before she nodded and said, "All right."

Olivia forced herself to eat. Iola soon returned with the things Olivia had requested, including one of Iola's worn housedresses. She set them down and said, "Take off your dress and hand it out the door before we lock it."

"I want you to leave the door open a crack, enough to let some light in. And I want some books."

"You know we aren't going to leave the chain off the door."

"I didn't ask you to. I said open enough to let some light in. Just a strip of light, too narrow for me to get through, but wide enough to read by. And to let some fresh air in here."

"We don't got no books, 'cept for my Bible."

"I do. On my bed at home. Go get them. *The Pioneers* and *The Last of the Mohicans.*"

Iola stood staring at her for a long while. "All right. But it won't be until later. We got a farm to take care of, in between waiting on you."

Filmore tested the lock on different links of the chain until he was satisfied. After Olivia heard him clomp away, she tore her filthy dress from her body and tossed it outside. Then she scrubbed herself. The water tingled on her skin and for a moment she felt almost human.

Left with nothing to do but think, Olivia tried to puzzle out why Filmore had needed a horse on the day they abducted her. It may have had something to do with Mourning, but what? Filmore had been home when Olivia arrived and hadn't gone anywhere since then, except to return Beauty to Emery Meyers. So what had he needed the horse for? Then she remembered. That first day – was it only two days ago? – she'd been unconscious for Lord knows how long. That was when he'd done it – waited until she was safely captive and then gone to do whatever he did to Mourning. Made sure Mourning wouldn't come looking for her. Yes, that was the only explanation. Mourning had been fine that day, working out in the farm. She imagined him hearing a rider approaching, looking up and seeing it was Filmore, taking off his hat and coming to greet him with a smile. Then what?

Iola looked exhausted when she brought Olivia's books with her supper. "I need something for my feet," Olivia said, the only words either of them spoke. "At least a pair of socks."

When Iola came back for the tray and to empty the chamber pot she wordlessly placed some woolen socks on the bed and a pair of house slippers on the floor.

When they came the next morning, Iola said to Filmore, "I don't think we need to bother with the ropes today."

She was right. Olivia lay lifeless while he violated her, though she did whisper in his ear, "You know you'll burn in hell for this."

"It's God's will," he slurred.

"You're sick. Both of you. You'll go to prison."

"No, we won't," he said. "No one will believe you. We go to church and you don't."

It was like talking to a child who wasn't right in the head and she gave up. Iola kept her nose in the Bible, pretending not to hear. When it was over, she brought Olivia another clean dress and laid it on the bed.

Every time they came into the barn he seemed to smell worse. Olivia stopped thinking of him as a human being. He was a wild animal. While he was on her, she turned her face to the wall and counted. Once it took only up to ten; once as high as eighty-four.

"What did you do to Mourning?" she asked every day.

The response was always the same: "What makes you fret so much over that ignorant nigger?"

Every day, after they left, Olivia cleaned up and then sat by the door reading. When she lost control of her thoughts and they threatened to destroy her resolve, she repeated over and over: *They are wild beasts. This will not last forever. I will survive. This is not my fault. I will make them pay.* The thought that helped most to keep her strong was: *Mourning needs my help.*

Filmore began to whisper things in her ear while he was raping her: "You like this, don't you? Not like Iola." Or "Ain't doing God's will fun?" On the seventh day, he rose up off her, leaned back, and howled: "Woman is the gate of the devil – the path of wickedness – the sting of the serpent." Then he half-fell off the bed and staggered out.

After a long pause Iola said, "So, you'll be going home today. I told you it would be over before you knew it."

But she locked the door behind her. When she returned with the usual bucket of warm water she also set Olivia's shoes on the floor next to the chair. Then she drew a pair of her own drawers out of her apron pocket and laid them on the bed.

"I'll not have you leaving here half-naked, like a whore. It's time you learnt to behave like a decent Christian woman. You wash up while I go get your dress and your breakfast. You have to eat well now. Take care of yourself."

Again the door closed behind her. The sound of the lock clicking shut paralyzed Olivia. They were never going to let her go. But she dragged herself off the bed and began cleaning Filmore from her body. Iola soon returned, set a tray of food on the bed, and then held out the dress Olivia had been wearing the day she came.

"Go on, put it on." Iola nodded disapprovingly at Olivia's thin chemise. "Get yourself covered up. Learn

283

some modesty."

Olivia took the dress, but her fingers felt numb and she stared as if she didn't know what to do. Finally she pulled it over her head.

"One of the buttons fell off when I was washing it, but I sewed it back on for you," Iola said as if expecting thanks.

Olivia's head jerked up as a sickeningly familiar smell reached her. Filmore came in, set a water skin and leather bag next to the breakfast tray, and hurried out without looking at Olivia.

"There's some fruit and bread in there for you to take home with you," Iola said, nodding at the bag on the bed while Olivia fumbled with the buttons of her dress and ties of her apron. "Get them drawers on you," she ordered and Olivia obediently stepped into them, shivering with revulsion. "Well, go on now, sit down and eat," Iola said impatiently. "Your eggs are getting cold."

Olivia sat and stared at the plate. Fried eggs dusted with black pepper and two flapjacks generously spread with butter and jam.

"Go on, eat. Then it's time for you to go home," Iola said. "Filmore will come by tomorrow, see what needs doing around your place. He'll bring eggs, butter, and bread. Tomorrow's Friday, so he has to deliver eggs and butter to the store anyway. I'll send some chicken too, if I have the time to fry one up. If not, you still have plenty of venison. You get yourself a good rest. It's been hard on you, I know, and now you've got to look after yourself. The walk home will do you good, but you best lie in bed after that. I'll stop by day after tomorrow, see how you're feeling. Bring you some of my tea."

Olivia recoiled when Iola reached out to pat her arm. On her way out Iola paused in the doorway and turned to say, "You don't got to worry about Filmore bothering you none. That's all behind you. He wouldn't dare. He knows I'll be talking to you."

Iola disappeared from the doorway and Olivia remained motionless, frowning at the food. It took a few minutes for her mind to register the fact that Iola had left the door standing open. As if all Olivia had to do was stand up and walk out of hell. She rose and took a few hesitant steps. It looked like a beautiful day out there.

Go, she told herself. *Get away from them. Fast. Before she comes back. Go. Go. Go.*

But her limbs didn't obey. She walked hesitantly to the door and stopped at the threshold, leaning forward to peek out. A few chickens were scratching in the yard, but she saw neither of the Stubblefields. She turned her head the other way. There was the trail. The way home.

Suddenly alive, she took quick steps to the bed and sat to pull on her shoes, fumbling with the laces. Clumsy in her panic, she sent the tray of food clattering to the floor. She rushed to the door and paused again, looking out at the clearing as if she had never seen it before.

She stumbled toward the trail and into the woods and ran until her lungs felt ready to burst. When she tripped over a branch and fell, loud sobs escaped her. It had rained lightly the night before and she lay on the damp ground for what seemed a long while before sitting up and looking around, still in a daze. Above the treetops was a brilliant blue sky, scattered with cotton clouds. A gentle breeze whispered and songbirds chirped to one another.

But it's a different world, she thought. *For me it will never be the same. For the rest of my life I will dwell in a dark secret place. No one else will ever be able to understand. There's no way for anyone to set me free from it. I'm out of that barn, but I'll always carry a different kind of prison on my back.*

It required a tremendous effort to force herself to her feet. She felt as if the blood had frozen in her veins and began trembling with cold. Something rustled in the underbrush and she shrieked. Someone was coming! Filmore was after her! She hid behind the thick trunk of an elm to watch for him, but the trail remained empty. She began to fear that she would find him waiting for her when she got home. She'd open the door to her little cabin and there he'd be, lying on her bed, leering. Her knees buckled at the thought.

He won't be there, he won't be there, she chanted and forced herself to walk. *Go home. Fast. Filmore won't be there. Not yet. Hurry. Not until tomorrow. Iola said he would come tomorrow.*

A few minutes later she heard breaking branches and stopped again.

Stop being ridiculous, you can't let every raccoon and squirrel terrify you.

But she listened closely. That was not the rustle of small animals. Those were human footsteps crashing through the woods and they weren't far away. She hid behind another tree, shaking. Whoever it was, he was walking fast. But he wasn't coming after Olivia; the sounds were receding in the opposite direction. She stepped back on the trail and rushed toward her cabin.

Where did I leave the shotgun? Where it always is, leaning against the wall behind the door. Please let it be there. Mourning, where are you? What did he do to you? Please be home. Please be safe. I am going to get through this. I have to think. Plan. Keep walking. Get home.

Shame and guilt brought back the dark thoughts and slowed her down. Why had she gone to Iola's? Why hadn't she refused to drink that tea? Why hadn't she fought harder? What had she done to deserve this? What made them think they could treat her that way? Was she what they said, a dirty little whore?

It's not my fault. It's not my fault. It's not my fault. They are evil. They are evil. They are evil. They will be punished. They will be punished. They will be punished.

She soon regretted that she hadn't eaten and hadn't taken the skin of water. She felt faint and the trail stretched endlessly. She wanted desperately to arrive home, to find Mourning standing outside, waving his floppy hat at her. Would she tell him what they'd done to her? How could such a thing be said in words? Would she ever be able to put those sentences together? And if she did, would he believe her? Would anyone?

Feeling dizzy, she stopped under a tree. The long grass around its roots was soft and dry, and she lay down and curled up in it for a few minutes. Her hands clutched her belly. Could a woman feel it? Know? All Olivia felt was torn up. She forced herself to her feet and continued stumbling toward home. When she'd walked this trail a week ago had there been so many branches and roots grabbing at her ankles? Clumsy, she fell several more times before she at last came to the clearing and then the stream. She gratefully threw herself down on its bank and lay in the mud, scooping water into her mouth and over her head, before getting to her feet and continuing around the bend. She let out a cry when the squat little cabin came into sight, but even from a distance it looked deserted. The door was standing open, creaking on its hinges.

Chapter Thirty-Four

Olivia began shouting hysterically. "Mourning! Mourning! Are you here? Where are you?"

She could see the handle of his precious hoe sticking up out in the field. Something had made him leave it; he would never have gone off and abandoned a precious iron tool to the rain. She ran to the barn, shouting his name. The oxen were in there. The trough was full of water and a small pile of hay stood next to it. Dixby and Dougan turned stupid, indifferent eyes

287

toward her.

She went back out to the yard and shouted Mourning's name a few more times, but there was no response. There was no sound at all, other than birds twittering in the trees. She entered the cabin and looked around. Everything seemed to be as she had left it, except there was no shotgun behind the door. Who had taken it, Filmore or Mourning? What about the pistol? What would she do without a weapon? She frantically kicked aside the rug, opened the trapdoor, and scrambled down the ladder.

She hadn't taken the time to light a lantern and the cellar was dark and foul smelling. She heard the scurry of mice and impatiently clapped her hands and yelled "Shoo!" before groping her way to the crate that stood against the far wall.

Relief flooded over her. The pistol was where she'd hidden it, behind the crate. So was her possibles bag. Mourning must have taken it down there. Let Filmore come now. She'd be waiting for him. Then her hand touched something else metallic. She wrapped her fingers around it and lifted. Thank God, it was the muzzle of the shotgun. Olivia pulled it out and cradled it in her lap. The fact that Mourning had hidden these things meant he was all right, didn't it? Filmore couldn't have just ridden up and shot him. She could imagine no scenario in which Filmore would have hidden the shotgun in the cellar. So Mourning must be alive.

Olivia couldn't manage the ladder while carrying both the pistol and shotgun, so she made two trips. Then she took the shotgun outside and sat on a stump chair while she cleaned and oiled it, measured black powder down both barrels, rammed a wad and shot down each, and raised it to her shoulder. She squinted into its sights and imagined Filmore coming up the path, as he was sure to do tomorrow. Nothing would be easier than squeezing off two loads of buckshot. Splat in his face. She aimed at one of the trees and fired one barrel and then the other, taking comfort in the loud explosions. She'd always hated the smell of black powder, but today its scent was sweet. She was safe. She could protect herself. She was never going to be helpless again.

Now she could begin her search for Mourning. With the reloaded shotgun over her shoulder, she spent the rest of the day methodically walking around the cabin, in increasingly wider circles, and periodically calling his name.

"Mourning! Mourning, it's all right. It's me, Olivia. I'm alone. I'm going to be real quiet now. Make any kind of noise that you can. Just move your foot in the leaves. I'll come and find you."

It was dusk before she gave up, hoarse and exhausted. Mourning was gone.

She dragged her feet back to the desolate cabin, where she numbly lit lanterns, removed her clothing, and threw it in a heap on the floor. The scent of Filmore seemed to be oozing out of her pores and she felt as if she might be sick. She wrapped herself in a towel and took the shotgun with her down to the riverbank, where she immersed herself in the cold water, oblivious to the sharp stones on her bare feet. A week ago she had worried about water moccasins slithering past her; now there seemed to be nothing left that could frighten her. She crouched in the deepest part, letting the swift current wash Filmore downstream with the other waste. She splashed gallons of water over her head and then faced upstream and lay back to let the river run through her hair. There she remained until she was nearly frozen and her teeth were chattering so hard they hurt. She climbed out and wrapped the towel around her, then returned to the cabin and slipped naked under the covers, keeping one hand on the gun.

What am I going to do? She answered herself: *Go back to Five Rocks. There's nothing else you can do.*

It was not a solution. What would she do in Five Rocks, in all likelihood pregnant and not knowing what color the baby would be? But she couldn't think about that now. Right now all that mattered was getting away from here. And isn't that where Mourning would have gone? Back to the place he felt safe, where Mr. Carmichael looked out for him and everyone knew him?

While cleansing herself in the river her mind had settled into a decision: she was never going to tell anyone what they'd done to her. Not Mourning, not Tobey, not some sheriff, not anyone. Not ever. She couldn't say it out loud. Saying it out loud would only make it real, harder to forget. No one would believe her anyway. It wouldn't do any good.

All right. I'm going back to Five Rocks and I'm not going to tell anyone what happened. But then what? I can go home for a while, but if I am carrying a child I'll have to go to one of those places for wayward girls. It sounded simple when she spelled it out like that. She clung to the comfort of knowing she still had enough money to live on for a while.

The money! She had forgotten to check if her gold coins were still there. She jumped up, pulled on a shirt and trousers, took a lantern, and scrambled back down to the cellar. She crawled to the far corner and felt for the loose earth, digging frantically with her bare hands, until her fingers touched the burlap she had wrapped around the red velvet bag. She took it back upstairs, poured the coins on the table, and counted them. There should have been $380; there were $300. She counted again and stared at the coins for a long while, thinking. Then she smiled. *If a band of thieves or the Stubblefields had found the bag, they would have taken it all. It could only be Mourning. He had needed some money to get away. That was sure proof he was alive.*

Remembering her emergency money, she lifted the

mattress and ripped open the seam that she had loosely sewn back together. The fifty dollars that she'd kept hidden, even from Mourning, were still there. She stooped to pull one of her wicker baskets from under the bed, retrieved the money belt she had sewn for the trip, poured all the coins into it, and tied it around her waist. She filled a skin with water and set it by the door. Then she tucked the loaded shotgun and pistol and her possibles bag under the covers. No one was going to surprise her in the night, and she was ready to leave in an instant, if she had to.

She picked up the lantern and started out to the barn to check on the oxen. Halfway there she turned back for the shotgun. She wasn't going anywhere without it, ever again. She stroked Dixby's neck and added another bucket of water to the trough. It felt good to do something normal. If only she could get up in the morning and blister her hands splitting firewood. Make Mourning's dinner. Try to catch a fish for supper. Complain about the way the laundry soap burned.

She knew she wouldn't sleep and so stacked kindling and wood in the fire pit and lit them with one of the precious matches. No point in saving them any more; scavengers would soon take whatever she left behind. She waited anxiously for the flames to take the logs, part of her still hoping that Mourning was hiding in the woods and would see or smell the fire and come to see who it was. She went inside, picked the dress she had been wearing and Iola's drawers off the floor, and fed them into the flames. She watched the clothing go up in smoke, her only physical tie to that barn. Then she went to look for something to eat and sat on a stump chair with some jerky and two apples. She kept the gun by her feet and peered at the blackness that surrounded her.

She had stopped asking herself what she had done to deserve this, for she at last believed her answer to that question: *Nothing*. She had also found the frighteningly simple answer to the question, what had made them decide to do it to her? *Because they believed they could.* It was a horrible realization. Was the world filled with people who wouldn't hesitate to do evil, as long as they thought they could get away with it?

That's what religion is supposed to be for, she thought. *It's a brilliant attempt to make us think we can't get away with anything. God is up there watching. But it doesn't seem to work very well. The Stubblefields consider themselves good Christians. They simply convinced themselves they were saving my soul. And plenty of devout Christians own slaves. First they decide they need some slaves, then they come up with the excuses.* Olivia had never given much thought to what it would feel like to be a slave. Now she knew. Like being locked in that barn from the day you're born until the day you die.

She stared in the direction of the Stubblefield cabin, knowing they were over there going about their lives. Laughing. Planning. Having their supper. Filmore greedily licking grease from his fingers. Iola probably couldn't stop yapping about their baby. They were pleased with themselves. Everything had gone as planned. They would sleep well tonight.

Olivia set her face hard. *All right. That goes both ways. You thought it was all right for you to do whatever you did to Mourning and to steal my life away, just because you could? Well, I can do things too. I have more than one weapon and I'm a great shot. I could walk back over there right now and blow your ugly heads off. Bam. First barrel for Filmore. Bam. Right in Iola's face. Who's going to suspect me? Why on earth would I kill the nice neighbors who bring me milk and butter? So that's what I'm going to do. I will go home to Five Rocks. But first I'm going to shoot them dead.*

292

Chapter Thirty-Five

Olivia didn't worry that God, if one existed, would know she had shot the Stubblefields. It was the right thing to do. She was going to hold her gun on them and threaten to shoot them dead, unless they told her what they'd done to Mourning. And after they told her, she was going to shoot them dead anyway. It wouldn't make things right – nothing would ever do that – but at least she would know they no longer breathed the same air she did.

She wistfully surveyed her little homestead, thinking that perhaps once the Stubblefields were gone she could stay there. She could take a boat back to Five Rocks, find Mourning working at the Feed & Grain, and bring him back. If she wasn't pregnant. And if she didn't get arrested for killing Iola and Filmore.

Only then did it occur to her – Mourning is the one most likely to be blamed for that. If a sheriff finds two white people murdered at about the same time that a stranger – a black man – disappears, who's he going to go after? Well, if it comes to that, I'll just have to confess. Then she frowned. If Mourning is arrested in Michigan, there's no way I'll ever hear about it in Five Rocks. No one is going to be writing me letters. No one in Fae's Landing even knows where we came from, except our wonderful neighbors, the Stubblefields. Did I ever mention the name of the town to Jeremy? I don't think so, but even if I did, small chance that he'd been paying any attention.

Jeremy. She was never going to see him again. She paused for a moment, noting how totally indifferent she was to that fact. But she should call on him. Stopping to say good-bye was the natural thing to do and she didn't want him or anyone else to think she had run off in a panic.

She would tell Jeremy that Mourning had left, but when? When was the last time Jeremy had seen him?

Probably three weeks ago. She would say that Mourning had left a few days after that. Left to go where? Back home. Why? They'd decided they weren't cut out for farming, that's all. She was just stopping by to wish Jeremy well. She'd say she'd just come from bidding her farewells to the Stubblefields, providing testimony that they'd still been alive and well weeks after Mourning left.

She picked up a stick and poked at the fire, searching for inconsistencies in her story. A wry smile crossed her face as she thought, *Jeremy not believing what I'm going to tell him about when Mourning left isn't the problem. Jeremy not hearing a word I say is more like it. I'll have to think of a way to say it that will grab his attention. If the Law comes asking about Mourning, Jeremy has to remember that he left Fae's Landing weeks before the murders.*

I can think about that later, she thought. *What I have to do now is pack up and get out of here before the sun comes up. Way before Filmore gets here. Then I have to figure out how I'm going to take him and his she-devil wife by surprise.*

It wouldn't be easy, the way their cabin stood in that large clearing. The front of it was a good forty paces from the woods and plowed fields spread out from the other three sides. They were sure to see her coming with her shotgun. She could be on the trail before sun-up tomorrow, lying in wait for Filmore, but if she shot him close to their place, Iola would hear it and come running with that pistol of hers. And if he was found near Olivia's cabin, folks would be even more likely to put it on Mourning. She'd have to drag the body off the trail and bury it. She sighed and stirred the fire. It was all too complicated. She wanted to shoot them and walk away. The last thing she wanted to do was touch Filmore's stinking carcass.

If only she knew of some time they'd be gone and arrive home together, then she wouldn't have to sneak up on them. She could be waiting for them inside their cabin. They'd open the door and find her sitting in Iola's rocker, both barrels trained on them. The shotgun would bring one of them down; she'd have the pistol to finish off the other. Then Olivia's eyes opened wide, and she sat up straight. Didn't they pride themselves on being steady churchgoers? That meant their cabin must stand empty for a few hours every Sunday morning. Anyone could walk in.

What day of the week was it? Olivia had no idea. What day had it been the morning she'd walked into their trap? She couldn't remember. Wait, hadn't Iola said something about today being Friday? No, tomorrow. Tomorrow was Friday, Filmore's day to take eggs and butter to the store. So Sunday was the day after tomorrow. She could wait that long. Not in the cabin. Not with Filmore supposed to come tomorrow.

I'll spend what is left of this night and the next camped in the woods. Some time tomorrow I'll go say my goodbyes to Jeremy. I'll ask him what day it is, just to be sure. And then maybe Jeremy will remember that I left for Detroit on Saturday, a whole day before they were killed on Sunday. Except who's going to know what day they were killed? It might be weeks before anyone finds them. How on earth will they know it happened on Sunday morning? Because they'll be wearing their church clothes, that's how. And they'll have been seen in church, alive, the day after Jeremy will say I left for Detroit. Weeks after he'll say Mourning left the area.

She picked up the lantern and walked through the cabin and barn, making a mental list of what she would take with her to Detroit. She set aside those things that she needed to keep handy, in order to survive a day and a half in the woods. There wasn't much food in the cabin. She mixed up bread dough and left it to rise, before setting a pot of rice at the edge of the fire. There was strawberry jam, the pickled venison, some dried-out apples, and two more jars of peaches. *We should be grateful for our bodily needs,* she thought. *Seeing to them is sometimes all that keeps us from losing our minds.*

Then she noticed the pile of clothing lying on the bed. She walked over and picked up a few items, fingering the cloth. Who had put this here? Then she remembered. That morning, before she'd left for the Stubblefields, she'd hung up laundry. This brown work dress had been on the line. Filmore must have taken them down when he'd come over to feed and water the oxen. She shuddered and was enraged at the thought of him touching her things.

Should she pack up Mourning's things and take them back to Five Rocks? What if he came back to the cabin looking for them? He'd just have to manage without. She had to take them away. If he'd left three weeks ago, why would his things still be here? Should she leave a note for him on the table? No. If he had left before she did, there was no logic in her leaving a note. Maybe she could leave a note for him down in the cellar; no one else was likely to find it there. No, she couldn't take the chance.

Then she remembered the Hawken rifle, hidden it that tree. That was where they were supposed to meet in an emergency, and this was a bigger emergency than either of them had ever imagined. She would leave the rifle in the tree, but put a note for Mourning in it. She looked for a scrap of paper, but had to tear a page out of her journal. What could she say? It had to be something no one else would understand. In the end she wrote only "Gone to 5R." She carefully rolled it up and put it in her pocket with another scrap of paper.

It took her a while to find the tree in the dark. She cleared a space on the ground to set the lantern, hoisted herself onto the lowest branch, and began climbing like Mourning had. When the Hawken was at eye level, she steadied her right foot on a thick branch and hugged the trunk with her knees while she rolled up the note and slipped it into the barrel of the rifle. Then she crumpled up the other scrap of paper and shoved it in, like a stopper. Her message should be safe in there, even from the rain.

Back at the cabin, she looked at her wicker baskets, doubtful that she could manage to hoist them onto the wagon alone. She emptied their contents into piles on the bed and lifted the empty baskets into the bed of the wagon. Then she made endless trips back and forth to repack them. When she went into the barn to look for a piece of rope, she tripped over Mourning's toolbox. She intended to take the shovel, rake, and plow – and the hoe that was still out in the farm – to Detroit to sell, but what would she do with Mourning's collection of hand tools?

She stood and stared at the box for a long time, unable to decide. Selling it and its contents in Detroit made the most sense, but she knew how proud Mourning was of those tools. He'd been accumulating them since he was nine years old. What if he came back looking for them? Penniless in Michigan, he would need those tools, which he referred to as his Most Precious Belongings. But if she just left them sitting there they would be stolen in no time. She decided to hide them. She opened the box and smiled sadly at how clean and neatly arranged everything was. Then she removed one item – Mourning's compass. She might need it.

A small haystack stood in the back corner of the barn. She cleared part of it aside and dug a hole just deep enough to hold the box. She wrapped it in canvas, lowered it into the ground, smoothed the dirt over it, and covered it with hay. She returned to the cabin and wrote a second note – "Your MPBs are deep in D&D's house under their food" – and hurried back to the rifle tree. She retrieved her first note and rolled the second up with it, before reinserting the paper stopper in the barrel.

Then she resumed packing the wagon, trying to create a level surface on which she would be able to lay her mattress. As she gathered up miscellaneous utensils and wares, she began to understand why they had gotten everything so cheaply in Detroit. The seller must have been someone like her – too worn out and despairing to care about a few dollars more or less. Just looking at the big sacks of feed and seed in the barn made her want to sit down and cry. There were some empty sacks, so she could have done as she had with the baskets – put an empty sack in the wagon and fill it up bucket by bucket – but she shook her head and turned away. She needed her strength for things more important than trying to salvage a few dollars. She would take only enough feed to get her to Detroit; the raccoons were welcome to the rest.

More wearing than the physical exertion was the fatigue of being alone, a tiny figure under an ink-black sky, huddling in a halo of lantern light, no one to talk to, no one to care what happened to her, no one to pour her a cup of coffee. With each hour that passed her conviction grew. There was no choice. She had to go back to Five Rocks. Let the biddies cluck their tongues. She craved familiar faces. Tobey. Mrs. Hardaway. She even missed Avis and Mabel Mears. Mr. Carmichael's long white features. Maybe something as simple as a smile would help her feel human again.

She punched down the bread dough, put it in the bake kettle, and set it at the edge of the fire. After she burned her tongue eating some rice straight out of the pot, she put the lid back on, and stuck the pot in the back of the wagon, the spoon still inside. Then she went to the river to wash again. After she combed her hair and tied it back, she stared at her dim reflection in the broken piece of mirror that still hung on the wall. It seemed impossible, but a face that looked just like Olivia Killion stared back at her. How could she look the same?

She hitched up the team and hung the lantern on the wagon post, the way Mourning had done on their way out. Then she pulled the bake kettle out of the fire, doused the flames, filled all the skins with water, and took a last look at the pathetic little hovel she was abandoning. She left the door standing open – her silent protest at being forced to leave – climbed onto the wagon, and said "Giddap." Before she had gone a hundred paces she reined the team in, jumped down, and ran back to the cabin to pull the door shut and put the latch on. It had been her home, after all.

About three miles down the road she saw an opening into the woods. It was big enough for her to take the wagon off the road and be completely hidden among the trees. Would Filmore come looking for her tomorrow when he discovered her gone? Good thing he wasn't a hunter. What was it Iola had said? He couldn't follow a blood trail in the snow.

She unyoked the oxen and gave them feed and water. She was too tired to bother hobbling them and patted each of their noses, asking them to please not run off and leave her. Then she lifted the lid off the pot and mechanically ladled a few spoonfuls of cold rice into her mouth. Exhausted, she climbed onto her lumpy mattress – still in her clothes and work shoes – put the lantern out, and fell into dreamless sleep, hugging the shotgun.

Chapter Thirty-Six

Olivia woke early in the morning, damp with dew. There was no blissful moment in which she greeted the new day with no recollection of where she was and why. She knew the instant her eyes blinked open. Feeling weak, hollow, and alone, she climbed down from the mattress and moved away from the wagon to empty her bladder. After splashing water on her hands and face, she stood still, listening to the woods.

All she could think about was her room at home – the quilt Mrs. Hardaway and her friends had made, the way the late afternoon sun slanted through the windows, the stack of books on her nightstand. Then her stomach growled, prompting her to lift the lid of the bake kettle. Too stiff and tired to bother looking for a knife, she took the spoon from the pot of rice and jabbed it into the burnt crust, carving out large chunks of the soft inside. She smeared them with strawberry jam and went to sit on a fallen log, near the oxen. Dixby stamped a foot and pressed his nose against her back.

"I know, I know. I'm supposed to feed you first." Olivia made a circle with her shoulder to nudge him away. "But you weren't up all night packing, were you?" She turned to look into his placid eyes. "But I will say, you were both very good boys, not escaping into the night."

She licked her fingers and wiped them on her pants before she rose, stretched, and bent to touch her toes while she counted to ten. Then she tended to the oxen, patting their backs and saying, "Happy now?"

The sun was barely peeking over the horizon; it was much too early to go to Jeremy's. What should she do while she was waiting? She considered creeping back to the woods outside her cabin and watching for Filmore. Did they really expect her to be sitting there, waiting for him? How stupid could they be? If she lay in wait for him, she'd know whether he'd come carrying a weapon and what he did after he discovered her gone. But what did it matter? Besides, she didn't want to have to look at him. I only need to see that hateful creature one last time, through my sights, right before I pull the trigger.

Anyway, she knew exactly what he was going to do – run from the cabin to the barn and back and then stand in the yard chewing his disgusting, smelly beard and scratching his head, looking like the imbecile he was.

There was only one thing a man like him could do – run home to tell his wife.

Olivia longed for a cup of coffee, but didn't dare light a fire. She climbed back onto her mattress and watched the sky, thinking about what she was going to do the next morning. Finally she deemed it late enough to comb her hair, put on a dress, and go bid farewell to Mr. Kincaid. It felt wonderful to get her aching feet out of her work boots.

Jeremy must have heard the wagon coming. He opened the door and came onto the porch and down the steps to greet her. Unshaven, he wore buckskin pants, a plain brown linsey-woolsey shirt, and moccasins.

"Well, hullo neighbor." He took hold of the team's harness. "This is a nice surprise."

"Hullo Jeremy." Olivia wound the reins around the post and climbed down. "I've come to say good-bye – I'm on my way to Detroit and then back home."

"Back home? What happened? No bad news I hope."

"No, nothing like that. Mourning and I just decided that farming isn't quite what we expected. And Fae's Landing ..."

"Not a nice little town with lace curtains in the windows."

"Something like that."

"Where is the good Mr. Free?" Jeremy asked as he led the oxen toward his barn, looking behind him as if expecting Mourning to leap out of the back of the wagon.

"He left a while ago. Let's see, it must be two, no, three weeks –"

"Left? You mean you've been all alone over there for three weeks?" He stopped walking.

"Now you sound like Iola. I just came from their place. Went to say my good-byes to them, and she went on and on –"

301

"Well, she's right. I don't know what Mourning was thinking, leaving you on your own. He should have waited until you were ready to leave too." Jeremy left the team at the trough and pulled the barn door shut.

"Oh, I insisted he go. There's a logging camp near home and they always do their hiring in the summer. Besides, I wanted some time on my own, to think about what I'm going to do now."

She followed him onto the porch. Sheets of paper filled with cramped writing covered the table.

"I just finished a new article." He nodded at the pages. "You're welcome to read it while I get us some coffee. I was just about to make some."

He disappeared into the cabin and she idly gathered up the papers and began to read. She glanced up when he came back out, bare-chested and with a towel draped around his neck. He set the coffee pot on the stove top and raised the straight razor he held in his other hand.

"You'll have to excuse my bad manners," he said. "Need to spruce myself up for the day."

He went to the table by the tree, lathered his face, and began shaving, his mouth stretched into a tight O. She would have been inclined to sit and watch, but he glanced back at her so often that she felt obliged to continue reading. After struggling through all ten pages, she straightened them into a neat stack and then looked up to see him standing at the foot of the steps, waiting.

"So what did you think?"

"Interesting," she said. She studied him for a moment. When he told her the things he knew about animals it was interesting, but he had a special talent for dragging one tiny bit of information out into the ten most tedious pages she'd ever read. "You do discover a lot of fascinating things. But does this journal you write for insist that it be so . . . so..."

"So what?"

"So ... I don't know, formal." She wanted to say so long and eyes-falling-out boring. Since she was never going to see him again, she did allow herself to ask what she knew to be a tactless question. "Does everybody over there at the university have to write like that, like they're trying to make it hard to understand?"

"You understood it, didn't you?" His body had grown visibly tense.

She had gone too far. She didn't need him hating her. "Yes, of course. And your article is quite fascinating. I just meant that it's so much more ... vivid when you talk about it."

He seemed mollified. "Oh, I plan to give lectures too. Eventually. You hungry? I'm just going down to check my lines, see if there're any fish."

"Can I help?" The mention of food made Olivia realize how hungry she was. Any resentment she felt for him faded away. He was quite a nice neighbor.

"You could get a fire going. I'm such a duffer. Didn't notice I was setting the coffee pot on a stone cold stove. There's kindling and wood out back."

Grateful to have a task to perform, Olivia brought wood and lit the stove. Then she went inside to look for a rag to wipe the table and noticed the calendar on the wall by the door, with the days marked off.

"Is that calendar in there right?" she called to Jeremy from the porch. "Is today Friday?"

He looked up from the fish he was gutting on a flat rock by the river and thought for a moment before shaking his head.

"No. Must be Saturday. I always cross yesterday off when I get up in the morning, but I didn't do that today, seeing as I got unexpected company and all. You go ahead and mark it off for me, will you? And there's some bread in there somewhere, you feel like slicing it."

She sighed with relief that it actually was Saturday and found a knife next to the cutting board. She heard Jeremy come up from the river and set a pan of oil on the stove, and soon the smell of frying fish made her feel faint with hunger. She was arranging jagged slices of bread on a tin plate, her back to the door, when a hand grasped her shoulder and her mind went black. She shrieked and blindly spun around, her clenched fist hitting the side of Jeremy's head.

"Jesus!" he shouted and jumped back, hand to his ear. "What the ...?"

Olivia blinked, disoriented. He staggered outside and fell into a chair on the porch. "Christ, Olivia, what was that?" he shouted.

"Oh Jeremy, I'm so sorry." She followed him outside and knelt at his side. "I didn't mean to hit you. I'm so sorry. Let me see." She moved toward him, but he leaned angrily away.

He rose and brushed past her, strode down to the river, and stuck his head into the cold water. Olivia watched from the porch, mortified. She was not, however, too mortified to notice that those delicious fish were starting to burn and removed the pan from the hot stovetop. Jeremy got to his feet, leaned over to shake the water from his hair, and returned to where she was waiting, her eyes on the ground in humble apology.

"I can't tell you how sorry I am," she said. "It's just ... I was so startled ... I didn't hear you come in. It's ... it's ..." She paused, working out a plausible lie to tell him. "Last year I was in my father's store one day, sweeping the storeroom, when a man, a stranger, came up behind me. He grabbed me and began touching me ..."

"Where was your father?"

"He'd gone out on the sidewalk, trying to get someone to move his wagon away from the front of the store."

"What'd they do to the man?"

"Nothing. I never told anyone. The whole thing only lasted a few seconds. He'd rushed out and ridden off by the time my father came back in. He wasn't from our town. I'd never seen him before. I was too embarrassed to tell my father or anyone else. I felt like I'd done something wrong. Ever since ... since that man ... I've been real jumpy about anyone coming up behind me."

"Yeah, I would say so." He managed to smile at her. "I'm lucky you didn't have that knife in your hand. I guess those fish are ready." He glanced at the pan.

Jeremy moved the fish to two plates while Olivia put the bread and tin cups of water on the table. Jeremy added a bowl of cold boiled potatoes and they sat down to eat in silence. When their plates held only heaps of bones, Jeremy got up to pour coffee.

"I left some sacks of feed and seed in my barn," she said. "Lots of other things too. You're more than welcome to anything you find there that you have a use for. Or anything you can sell."

"You don't want to be giving everything away. What if you decide to come back?"

"I don't think that's likely. At least not soon. In any case, it will all go to ruination before I ever get back here. Trappers will clean it out in a lick. I'd rather you have it. So please, take whatever you want."

"What will happen to your place?"

"I don't know." She shrugged. "It will still belong to me. Of course, to folks around here I suppose it will still be the old Scruggs place. Soon enough no one will remember that Mourning and I were ever here."

He shook his head. "More like a lot of stories about you and your mysterious disappearance will get told around campfires."

"There's nothing mysterious about a person giving up and going back home."

"But people like stories, don't they? They'll have you off robbing banks or running the Underground Railroad. Maybe turn you into a light-skinned run-away who was passing."

"Well, you'll just have to set them straight. It's been

ages since I robbed a bank. Let me clear up," Olivia said as she rose and took the dirty plates to the table by the tree.

Jeremy went down to the river and sent a bucket of water flying up the hill on the hook. Olivia smiled as she tipped it to fill a washtub of suds, and Jeremy sent another one, for the rinse water. While she was busy washing and drying the dishes, Jeremy went into the cabin. He came out with a double sheet of newsprint and sat on the porch reading

This must be a little of what being married feels like, she thought. *Except that hopefully the man and the woman actually like each other.*

"Listen to this – here's one of the things that're wrong with this country." Jeremy rattled the paper and began reading aloud. "Not a road can be opened, not a bridge can be built, not a canal can be dug, but a charter of exclusive privileges must be granted for the purpose ... The bargaining and trucking away of chartered privileges is the whole business of our lawmakers ... A man should not be shut out of a certain enterprise because he possesses too little capital to be chartered by the State..." He put the paper down and looked over at her. "That's William Leggett talking, but it might as well be Andy Jackson himself."

Jeremy's voice droned on for a long while. *Whoever he ends up marrying better like the sound of it*, Olivia thought. The next time he paused, he looked up to find Olivia standing in front of him. She noticed for the first time how close together his eyes were. How had she once thought him handsome?

"I'd better get on the road. There's so much I have to do in Detroit," she said, while he pushed his chair back and got to his feet. "Thanks for the breakfast. It was good having you for a neighbor."

"Well, I'm truly sorry to see you go. I was hoping to get to know you better." He looked into her eyes and she thought she actually saw some regret in his. "I'll look in on your place from time to time. Try to see that the trappers don't tear up the floorboards. Where would I send a letter, if there's anything to tell you?"

"That's kind of you. Killion's General, Five Rocks, Pennsylvania." She moved toward the barn to harness the team.

"Let me do that for you," Jeremy said.

He took his time, glancing at her often. When they were standing by the wagon he said, "I wish there was something could change your mind." He offered his hand and did not release hers. "It's been grand having someone to talk to."

"For me too," she said.

She pulled her hand away and climbed onto the wagon seat, anger rising in her. She drove off without so much as a glance back at him. Once she was out of earshot, she threw her head back in a bitter laugh. God did have a sense of humor. Then she convulsed in sobs, arms folded over her knees, forehead resting on them. When she quieted, she couldn't find the energy to sit up and retrieve the reins, let alone commit murder and drive to Detroit. All she wanted to do was die. She began scratching her arms, hating her body.

It was all Jeremy's fault. If the stupe had shown the tiniest speck of interest in her, before she was all packed up and come to say good-bye forever, none of it would have happened. If the Stubblefields thought she had a beau, they would never have dared. And she wouldn't have thrown herself into poor Mourning's arms. She wouldn't have to wonder whose child might be growing inside her. Mourning would be safe and sound at home, complaining that she warn't never gonna learn how to bake. She wouldn't have to go shoot two people dead.

She finally calmed herself and wiped the tears away. She knew it was ridiculous to blame poor Jeremy, but she didn't care. *Stupid Jeremy.* She repeated it over and over as she picked up the reins and drove. *Stupid,*

stupid Jeremy. A few miles up the road she turned onto a trail that she was fairly certain was the one that would take her into the woods near the Stubblefield cabin.

Chapter Thirty-Seven

The trail began to narrow and Olivia whoa-ed the team to a halt at a place where the wagon could still turn around. Anxious to find her way to the Stubblefield cabin and back before dark, she quickly saw to the oxen and changed into trousers, a loose-fitting shirt, and her work shoes. She took her mother's gold watch from the money belt and slipped it into her pocket, together with Mourning's compass. She made careful note of the time, needing to know exactly how long it took to walk there. Then she slung the shotgun, a skin of water, and the possibles bag over her shoulder and tucked the pistol into her waistband.

"You two behave yourselves," she called over her shoulder to the oxen. When she realized she was going to have to sell Dougan and Dixby in Detroit the thought made her sad. She shook her head and said aloud, "Well don't that say something about me. My only friends in the world are a couple of cows."

The woods enveloped her and she felt even more alone. She was too tense to appreciate her favorite kind of weather – cool, crisp air and lacy wisps of clouds in the sky. She walked at a steady pace, head down, grimly set on her goal.

When she stopped to rest and quench her thirst doubts began to pick at her brain. She tried considering the possibility that Iola was right. Maybe she was being stupid and the only logical thing was to stay here until the baby was born. Then next year she could go back to Five Rocks and claim the land that Filmore would have been working for free. No. No. No. How could she even think of such a thing? Nothing – not being a social outcast, not prison, not being dead – *nothing* could be worse than staying here with the Stubblefields looking after her. And how could she even think of letting them get their filthy hands on an innocent little baby? She would, however, have loved to see the look on their faces if "their" baby turned out to be black.

What you have to do, she told herself, *is concentrate on getting through tomorrow morning. That's all there is right now. Everything else has to wait on that. Once it's over and done with, you'll get yourself to Detroit and onto a boat. Then you'll have plenty of time to lie around blubbering and worrying about the rest of your life. For now, you have to be strong. If you're going to walk up on them holding a loaded shotgun, you sure and well better be prepared to pull the trigger.*

After she began moving again, a horrible thought struck her. What if they brought someone home with them, for Sunday dinner? Olivia imagined herself blasting at the door as it swung open and then saying "Oops!" when Emery Meyers fell dead at her feet. What else could go wrong? What if she'd just shot them and then some fool dropped by for a visit? She gave her head a short violent shake. There was no point in fretting. She was going to do what she was going to do and just had to pray that nothing like that happened. Anyway, Iola hadn't been afraid to hold Olivia prisoner in the barn without gagging her. That must mean that they got about one visitor a decade.

Concentrate on relevant details, she told herself. *Should I bury the bodies? No, that would take too long – and I would have to touch them. If I don't bury the bodies, the wolves will have at them. Or bears. People will think it was a bear that killed them. Yes, sure,* she shook her head, disgusted with her muddled thinking. *They're definitely going to think it was a bear that emptied two barrels into them.* Could the Law tell they'd been shot, if only bones were left? Olivia had no idea.

It took her close to an hour to reach the edge of their clearing. She arrived out of breath, tired, and more than a little surprised that she had actually found the way. Hidden well behind the tree line, she stared at the barn. Such an innocent-looking building. Memories slithered from the dark corners of her mind and she felt queasy, recalling foul breath, whiskey, and sour sweat. Her knees grew shaky and she bent over, nauseated, but did not vomit. She straightened up and steadied herself against a tree. When her head cleared she frowned at the pile of farm implements still outside. She would have expected them to dismantle the bed and put everything back the moment she'd run up the trail. Were they that sure she wouldn't tell anyone? They felt safe to leave all the evidence sitting there?

How long have I been standing here? she wondered and looked at the watch. Almost twenty minutes. *Why is it so quiet?*

No smoke curled from the chimney and the only movement was that of the brown and white hens pecking in the yard. What if they'd gone away? Hadn't Iola once mentioned a friend somewhere near Pontiac? No, that was ridiculous. They were busy conspiring, not paying social calls. There was only one place they could be – out searching for Olivia. Right this minute they were probably in her cabin, peeking out the door for a sign of her. She pictured herself drumming her fingers on the table in their cabin, while they paced anxiously around hers.

She watched for another half hour before turning to go back. It was unsettling, not knowing where they were, but she felt certain they would return home to sleep in their own bed. They had to get ready for church in the morning. And Olivia had to get to their cabin early enough to watch them leave.

She walked rapidly back to the wagon and had a short conversation with Dougan and Dixby. When her empty stomach complained, she ate a few spoons of jam and chewed on an apple. Then she prepared for her second night alone in the woods, again sleeping in her clothes and shoes. She had no nocturnal visitors, human or otherwise, and managed to sleep, waking well before the sun was up. She stared up at the black sky, her mind blank.

Suddenly the pinched face of Mrs. Brewster, the self-proclaimed moral compass of Five Rocks, filled Olivia's mind. It's all a test, she said from under her nest of tight white curls and sky blue poke bonnet. To pass it, you must find forgiveness in your heart.

Olivia dismissed that notion with a blink. She most definitely could *not* find forgiveness. Wouldn't even try. She didn't want their evil brains alive, remembering what they'd done to her. She'd rather spend eternity down in hell with people who thought like her, than up in a heaven with a raft of fools willing to grant pardon to the likes of Iola and Filmore Stubblefield.

She climbed down from the mattress. While she retied her work shoes, she wondered if she would panic, lack the courage to squeeze the trigger. *You'll know soon enough*, she told herself. She cleaned and reloaded the shotgun and pistol, then stood and took deep breaths, one hand on Dixby's back.

"You know what I think?" she asked the disinterested cow, who continued chomping on the long strands of buffalo grass protruding from either side of his mouth. "I think it *is* a test – but I'll fail it if I *don't* go through with this."

She scraped the last dried-out spoonfuls of rice from the pot, swallowing without tasting. Then she freed the oxen. She hated to risk them wandering off, but hated more the image of them dying a slow agonizing death, tied to a tree, if she didn't come back. When the horizon began to weep a thin line of pink she gathered her weapons and water and set off. For the first time she noticed the whooshing sound Mourning's old gray trousers made as they flapped around her legs. They'll hear me coming a mile away, she fretted.

When she arrived at the clearing she stationed herself behind the same tree she had the day before, both hands on the shotgun, watching the silent cabin. Lazy, nearly horizontal, rays of sunlight filtered through the trees, and the air was still cool. Everything looked the same. No one stirring, no smoke coming from the chimney, pathetic-looking brown and white hens scrabbling about the dusty yard. Olivia squatted on her heels, took a long drink of water, and waited. Why was there no smoke? Iola always bragged about her Sunday dinner bread – how she set her bake kettle just exactly so on the edge of the hearth, so that by the time they got home from church they had a perfect loaf, still warm, but not one bit burnt. What if they weren't coming home for dinner?

Suddenly the front door opened, just a tiny bit, and Olivia pulled back behind the tree. No one came out. Then a strong wind rose up and the door swung into the cabin with a loud bang. No one pushed it shut. No one was home.

Olivia watched for another ten minutes but knew Iola could not be inside. She would never have left the door standing open like that, for dust and leaves to blow in. But neither would Iola have left home without pulling the door shut tight and putting the latch on. So where was she? Perhaps they'd left for church early and then robbers or Indians had been in the place. What if the robbers were still there? No, Olivia had been watching for too long.

Before she dared step out in the open, Olivia circled around through the woods behind the barn. From there no one in either the cabin or barn could see her. She set down the skin of water, bent low, clutched her weapons, and scurried to the back wall of the barn. If Filmore was anywhere, it would be inside the barn. And if she was going to encounter them separately, Filmore had better be the first to go. She edged her way around the far side of the barn, still hearing nothing.

Go on, get inside and out of sight fast, she said to herself. *No one's in there now, but they could come up the trail any minute.*

Still bending low, she took the last steps to the door and looked around warily, thinking she heard a swarm of bees. Then she put her hand out and pushed, cringing at the horribly familiar sound of that door rattling on its rail. After another moment's hesitation, she took a deep breath and stepped inside.

It smelled like a skunk having a breakfast of rotten eggs and the buzzing grew louder. The light was dim, but straight ahead Olivia could see Filmore sprawled near the back wall. A cloud of horseflies swarmed around him, evil glints of green reflecting off their wings. Her first thought was that he must have gotten drunk and been sick on himself or soiled his drawers. She raised the shotgun and took hesitant steps forward, until she was close enough to see that half of his face was missing and the top of his head was a bloody stump. The hay he lay upon was a mass of congealed blood. Had it been an accident? Had something fallen on him? Could a single blow do that much damage, or had someone in a rage beaten him repeatedly?

A rough-edged piece of lumber lay a few feet from him, its surface dark with what she assumed was blood. She kicked at it, thinking it must be one of the boards Iola and Filmore had tied her to. She turned toward where the bed had stood. It had been disassembled into pieces of lumber that lay in a pile. He must have been taking it apart when whoever killed him came in.

Only then did she notice Iola, on the floor next to the pile of wood. She lay flat on her back, limbs splayed, staring wide-eyed at the ceiling. Flies buzzed around her, but there was no gory mess. Olivia knew she must be dead, but with no visible injury felt compelled to nudge Iola's ankle with the toe of her boot. Not until she bent closer did she see the thin trickle of blood forming a line out of the side of Iola's mouth and the long white maggots crawling out of her nostrils. Olivia gasped, straightened up, and backed away a few steps. While she stood there staring, a brown and white barn sparrow alighted on Iola's nose and began pecking, piercing her open eye with its beak. Olivia doubled over and vomited.

She remained bent over, hands on her knees, until the nausea passed. Then she went to the water barrel to clean out her nose and mouth. She rolled the door farther open and set a chair outside, far from the smell. She had to think. They must have already been dead when she was here yesterday. Who could have done this? Mourning was first to come to mind, but why would he? He had been gone for a week. Why on earth would he come back on just the day they let her go? Maybe it was robbers? Or someone else they had done some awful thing to. Maybe she wasn't the first girl they'd tied up in their barn. There might be droves of people who wanted them dead.

She rose, went back inside, and stood over Filmore, studying the floor around him. Then she paced back and forth across the barn. There was nothing. No scraps of paper or cloth. Nothing but Filmore's rifle, which lay near Iola. Whoever had battered the Stubblefields to death had done so without leaving anything of his own behind. And had not been much of a thief or he wouldn't have left the rifle. Olivia bent to pick it up. She stared at Iola for a long while, wishing her the worst hell had to offer, not a drop of forgiveness or pity in her heart. She raised the rifle and took aim at Iola's head. After a long moment she lowered it and spat into the odious face. It wasn't enough that she and her husband were dead. They were supposed to have died knowing who killed them.

Olivia went back outside to sit on the chair, both her shotgun and Filmore's rifle resting across her knees.

314

Last night she had fantasized about burning the whole place down, watching flames devour that barn, but nothing would bring folks running quicker than a fire. Besides, with no ball or buck shot in them, it would be best to let the bodies lie as they were. The wolves would pick them clean. She was surprised they hadn't done so yet, but then remembered that the barn door had been closed.

No one would ever know for sure what had happened, but she didn't think the Law would be in any rush to search for a human killer if they could blame the deaths on wild animals and be done with it. And they would, unless they found that bloody piece of lumber. She went back into the barn, picked up the incriminating weapon, and carried it into the woods. Then she stood in the yard, wondering what folks would make of that pile of lumber in the barn and all the farm implements piled outside. She wished she could eavesdrop at the trappers' camp fires and hear the yarns they would spin, never coming within a million miles of the truth.

The wind came up again and the cabin door banged, causing Olivia to jump. She left the rifle on the chair, took cautious steps, and nudged the door open with the barrel of the shotgun. As far as she could see, everything was in place. She stepped inside, leaned the shotgun against the fireplace, and sank into Iola's rocking chair, exhausted and glad to be out of the sun. The wagon seemed so far away. Detroit might as well have been on another continent. She knew she should get out of there, but was depleted of energy. She felt like climbing the ladder to the loft and curling up in their bed. No one was going to come and what if they did? She could say she'd come to say good-bye and found them like that. It had been such a shock, she had to lie down.

She remained rocking in the creaky chair for a long while. Then she rose and idly walked about the cabin.

315

There was a silver watch on the mantle piece. She hesitated for only a moment before slipping it into her pocket. Then she went to the cookie jar where Iola kept her egg and butter money and took the three dollars she found. When she climbed up to the loft and overturned their mattress, she found a hidden treasure – close to fifty dollars in gold coin. She added it to the money bag and straightened the bed.

A large soup pot was overturned on the kitchen table. Olivia lifted it and discovered a plate of Iola's fried chicken. She bent down and sniffed. She knew it must have been there since at least yesterday, but it smelled all right. Her stomach demanded food and she sat at the table, no plate or utensils, and gnawed on a drumstick. She quickly devoured all three pieces, tossed the bones outside, and licked her fingers. Then she rose and foraged for more food, for the trip to Detroit. Better her than the raccoons. Beneath another overturned pot she found an uncut apple pie. She took the wicker basket that stood next to the hearth, set the pie in it, and tossed in a few apples, some tired-looking cucumbers, and some jerky. Then she retrieved her skin of water from the woods behind the barn and Filmore's rifle from the chair in the yard.

As she strode back toward the cabin for the basket of food, she heard the milk cow and her calf. Poor things. They must have been shut up in the cow shed all this time. On her way to let them out she also noticed how miserable the chickens looked, pecking at the bare yard. A barrel of chicken feed stood by the door to the shed. Olivia lifted the lid, tossed them a few handfuls of grain, and let the lid fall back in place. Then she frowned. Who knew how long it would be before anyone happened this way. Next Friday, when Iola didn't show up at the store with her butter and eggs, would anyone bother to come check on them? If not, it could be weeks. Months. She set down everything she was carrying and pulled with both hands to tip the barrel on its side, letting the grain and seed spill onto the ground.

Then she entered the shed. The cow was fine – still had plenty of feed and a trough half full of water – and her calf was closed in the stall with her. Olivia considered leaving the door to the shed open so they would be able to get out, but decided against it. She'd only be letting the wolves in for a steak dinner. She hauled water from the Stubblefields' well until the trough overflowed and then filled every bucket she found with water and set them in a row by the inside wall of the shed. A pile of hay stood in the corner and Olivia opened the door to the stall so the cow would be able to get at it.

"Sorry to leave you like this." She stroked the cow's nose. "But someone's sure to come find you. Lucky you've got your baby with you, so you don't have to worry about not being milked."

That reminded her of the crate Iola kept in the stream that ran behind the farm. She walked down to the bank, yanked the rope to draw it out of the water, and added the two bottles of milk and slab of butter to her basket. Then, laden with her provisions and weapons, she strode toward the woods, now anxious to be hidden among the trees.

She had gone some way up the trail before it occurred to her – she couldn't walk off with every penny. A bear wouldn't have pocketed Iola's egg money. If everything of value was gone, that could make the Law think a human had robbed and killed them. She stood among the trees for a moment, reluctant to go back, but then sighed and set her burdens down. She half-ran back to the cabin, carrying only one of the guns, and returned the three dollars to the cookie jar.

Then she marched out, finally turning her back on the Stubblefield place for the last time. But she felt no relief. None of the comfort she had expected. She felt hollow and incapable of confronting the rest of her life.

She walked as fast as she could. The basket of food was heavy and awkward to carry, and she kept switching it from one hand to the other. Her body ached and she thought she might be getting ill. She did not think about Iola and Filmore. She forced one foot in front of the other and thought about a hot bath, a cup of coffee, and a soft mattress. After a while she stopped and sat on the ground to drink one of the bottles of milk, which seemed to help settle her stomach. When she reached into the basket for the second bottle, she noticed that the butter was already beginning to melt and tossed the greasy mess aside.

After finishing the milk she paused to listen to the woods. They seemed too quiet – nothing but the buzz of a fly or bee. *Remember the sounds,* she thought. *Remember the gentle slopes of this forest. The trees that reach up to the sky. The carpet of ferns, the wild raspberries, strawberries, and grapes. This may be the last you'll ever see of the Michigan woods. Uncle Scruggs' paradise.* She sighed as she got to her feet and pitched the empty bottles into the woods, far from the trail.

Dixby and Dougan were waiting patiently, but Olivia had nothing to say to them. Annoyed by the flies, she removed the pie from the basket, set it on the wagon seat, and turned a bucket over it. Then she splashed water over her face and took a long drink. Feeling limp and used up, she dragged herself up onto the mattress, curled up into a tight ball, and quickly escaped into sleep.

When she woke a few hours later it was still light. She sat up and looked around, blinking as if she had no idea where she was. Then she lay back down and cried until she was worn out.

Chapter Thirty-Eight

When Olivia's sobs subsided she stretched out on her back, hands behind her head, and stared up at the blue sky. Before long the force of her new habit drew her hands to her stomach. Was she? Was it Mourning's?

"Ain't no use worryin'." She sat up and spoke aloud, mimicking Mourning's deep voice. "You gonna know when you gonna know. And feelin' sorry for yourself ain't gonna get you no closer to Detroit City."

It won't be so hard, she consoled herself about the trip ahead. *It's only a four hour drive to Detroit. Four hours is nothing. Why would a wheel decide to fall off today? Once I find my way back to the road, all I have to do is stay on it. There's no way I can get lost. I'll be there before dark, if I ever get myself moving. I'll take a room in one of those nice hotels, pay for it with Iola's money. She can treat me to a bath and my supper too. Tomorrow morning I'll sell the wagon and team and all this junk. I already know how to get on a steamboat. Once I'm stuck on that tub for three days I'll have nothing but time to stew about the rest. All I need to worry about today is today.*

Hungry again, she took the overturned bucket off the pie and attacked it with the rice-encrusted spoon, eating straight out of the tin pan. She let the crumbs fall where they may and noisily spat out the few apple seeds she encountered.

"So this is how men acquire such terrible table manners," she said to Dixby and Dougan. "I guess it would be pretty easy to get used to acting like a pig, on the trail all alone. Or with other people who are just as piggy."

She ate without tasting, until her stomach began to ache. Then she looked down, amazed to discover she had devoured more than half the pie. She heaved what remained of it, pan and all, into the woods. Then she wiped her mouth on her sleeve, her hands on her trousers, and released the first uninhibited belch of her life.

While she harnessed the team she again felt frightened of traveling back to the city alone. She made sure all three weapons were loaded, put the shotgun on the seat beside her, tucked the pistol into the waistband of her pants, and placed Filmore's rifle behind her in the bed of the wagon. She fretted a bit about robbers and strange men, but mostly was terrified of Iola and Filmore. She kept imagining them leaping out of the woods onto the road in front of her.

The trip was uneventful. The only distractions were a mob of wild turkeys waddling down the side of the road and a deer crossing in front of her. But the lack of diversion was not to her benefit. Flashes of the past week began to torment her. The stench that permeated these memories was so real that she more than once turned around to make sure Filmore wasn't crouching behind her. She tried to keep up a steady stream of conversation with Dougan and Dixby.

She knew she was approaching Detroit when she saw farmers putting up a fence and then had to circumvent three men laying down new logs in the road. They removed their hats and offered greetings; she nodded politely and kept one hand on the shotgun. Then there it was. Civilization. Buildings. People. Too late, she realized she should have stopped to change out of Mourning's trousers, but didn't really care. So she wouldn't stay at one of the fancy places. The United States Hotel was good enough. She surprised herself by actually finding her way to the livery where Mourning had bought the team and wagon.

"I would like to leave my wagon here," she said to the owner, a short bald man with an enormous mustache, "and ask you to look for a buyer for the team and wagon and everything in it. Except for those." She pointed to the two wicker baskets.

"Bad time to be selling things." He rubbed his chin. "I'm not sure I can get you –"

"I have great faith that you'll get a fair price for it all," she said crisply. "Is there someone who can take those two baskets and the water skins over to the United States Hotel?"

"Yes, ma'am."

"I'll need them as soon as possible."

"Yes, ma'am."

"They are to be delivered to Miss Olivia Killion."

"Yes, miss."

She carried the pistol, shotgun, rifle, and possibles bag with her and started up the street, avoiding eye contact with the respectable women she passed, knowing she must look as if she were off to war. But she didn't attract as much attention as she might have, thanks to the other bizarre sights on the street that day – a group of wild-haired white men in Indian garb, trappers in outlandish fur hats and pelts, and long-haired Jesuits in flowing brown robes.

Relieved to see the red, white, and blue flag over the entrance to the hotel, she marched in and asked for a room. The clerk did not bat an eye at her apparel. After he handed her the key she said, "My things will be delivered shortly. Please send them up when they arrive and then I'll be wanting a hot bath. In the meantime, I would greatly appreciate a cup of coffee. Hot. Very hot."

The clerk nodded amiably at each request and she climbed the stairs to her room. It was simply furnished – single bed, dresser, small table, and two chairs – but appeared to be clean. She hated to sit on the blue and red flowered bedspread in her filthy clothes, but couldn't resist sinking down onto the soft mattress. She hadn't been lying there long when a quick rap on the door brought her back to her feet. The clerk and another man carried her baskets in and a boy of ten or

321

twelve handed her a tin cup of coffee covered with a china saucer.

"Just one moment, miss," the clerk said and went out, leaving the door open. He soon returned with a large tin bathtub, a towel and washcloth, and a bar of soap in a tin holder. "When would you like us to bring the water to fill it?" he asked.

"Now. I mean, as quickly as you can. Please."

When they closed the door behind them she picked up the coffee and took a sip. It was delicious, but hot. Very hot. She set it back down and removed the things she needed for her bath from the baskets. Then she moved one of the chairs to the window and drank her coffee while watching the bustle in the street below. When she finished she unlaced her shoes and took a deep breath before gingerly working her feet free. It was not as bad as she'd feared, after so many hours in them. She straightened her legs and wiggled her toes. Peeling her socks away was another matter; they had clotted into her bloody blisters and she ripped one and then the other off, almost crying with pain.

The clerk soon returned with two rough-looking men. They brought with them five buckets of steaming hot water and one of cold. The buckets were large, almost twice the size of those Olivia had carried up their hill, and she rose to grip one of the handles, checking to see if she could lift it.

"You want we should pour the water in for you, miss?" the clerk offered.

"Yes, that would be kind of you. But please leave one bucket of hot water aside."

They did so and she was finally alone. Standing naked on the rag rug and using the remaining pail of hot water, she scrubbed herself with the washcloth, removing the worst layer of grime. Then she stepped into the tub, squatted in its blessed warmth, and gripped the sides as she slowly sank down. The tub was small – she had to sit with her knees folded against her chest – but the hot water was soothing, especially to her battered and bloody feet. A tin cup hung from the side of the tub and she poured cup after cup over her head. When the water cooled she dried herself quickly, slipped under the bedcovers, stretched, and then curled up. *All night. I get to sleep on this amazing bed all night. Everything smells so clean. I smell clean.*

She was still naked under the covers when there was a rap on the door and a man's voice asked if he could remove the tub. She jumped up, pulled Mourning's shirt and trousers back on, and opened the door. One of the rough-looking men came in and dipped a bucket into the tub. He pitched the water out the window without bothering to check if anyone was on the sidewalk below and went back to fill the bucket again.

"Wait. What if there's someone standing down there?" Olivia went to the window.

"Then the fool better move his arse."

She backed away. When he was gone she returned to the paradise of that bed. *There's no reason I have to leave tomorrow*, she thought. *The longer I stay, the better the chance of getting a good price for the team and wagon. Why not linger here in heaven, where people who know nothing about me bring me anything I ask for, and Iola pays for it?*

And so she did. The next morning Olivia put on the dress that looked the cleanest, sent the rest of her clothing out to be laundered, and went in search of a dress shop. She paused in front of one on Fort Street called "*Chez Mademoiselle Lafleur.*" A white card in the window advertised original designs all the way from Paris, France, as well as a rack of "ready-mades" just in from New York.

A tiny bell jangled when Olivia entered, causing the woman behind the counter to look up from the book she was reading. Olivia found it difficult not to stare at her. The tight curls that framed her face were bright blonde and her large brown eyes were fringed by thick lashes. The light olive tone of her skin glowed next to the gold and green brocade of her dress. She radiated warmth, emphasized by the shiny brown-red she had painted her lips.

"Hullo," Olivia said.

"*Bonjour, Ma chérie*. How nice to have you visit my shop." The woman came from behind the counter and offered her hand, speaking in what Olivia assumed to be a French accent. "I am Mademoiselle Lafleur. But you must call me Michelle."

Olivia had guessed her to be in her thirties, but now saw that she had the figure of a younger woman. She was obviously proud of that figure; the bodice of her dress was low-cut, displaying the ample cleavage her corset showed off. Olivia wondered if it was customary for shop owners to introduce themselves. Seborn certainly never had; he'd just looked up and waited for them to tell him what they wanted. Of course, he'd already known everyone who came into his store.

"Olivia Killion," she said and shyly slipped her hand into Michelle's.

"What a lovely name. But, *Mon Dieu*, look at your hands! What have you done to them?"

"I've been working on a farm." Olivia pulled her hand away, embarrassed.

This woman even smelled elegant and Olivia felt like a graceless clodhopper. She had grown proud of her blisters and scratches – badges awarded for a hard day's work – but next to soft, stylish Michelle, she felt coarse.

"Here in Detroit?" Michelle tipped her head to the side and smiled at Olivia, obviously curious about her.

"No. About 35-40 miles west of here. I'm just passing through on my way back East." Olivia kept her eyes on the floor.

"You must be tired from your journey. You look a bit peeked. Pardon my asking, but I can recommend a good place to eat if you're hungry."

"Thank you, but I've eaten." She didn't know why, but the woman's kindness made her feel like crying. "Could I see your ready-to-wears?"

Michelle showed her to the rack and Olivia looked through it, pausing at a gingham dress in two shades of blue, with white trim at the neck and sleeves.

"Yes," Michelle said, "that one looks about your size. I'm sure it will look lovely on you. I have a room in the back where you can try it on."

Olivia nodded and continued looking at the other dresses, wishing Michelle would go away.

"Please excuse me. I will be back in just a moment." Michelle seemed to have read Olivia's mind and walked out, setting the bell on the door ringing.

Olivia looked around, wondering if a clerk she hadn't noticed was minding the shop, but Michelle seemed to have left her alone. A few minutes later the jingling bell announced her return.

Michelle set a brown bottle on the counter and reclaimed her seat on the stool. "Let me know if I can help you with anything." Her attention returned to the book while Olivia continued pulling dresses from the rack. She picked up the blue gingham and was looking to see how much of a hem it had, when a hand touched her shoulder. She did not punch Michelle in the face as she had Jeremy, but flinched and pulled away, almost tipping the rack over.

"I'm sorry ... I didn't mean ... are you all right?" Michelle bent to look into Olivia's face.

"No, no, it's I who must apologize." Olivia's face was red. "I ... I ..." She didn't feel like repeating the lie she'd told Jeremy. "I don't know what's wrong with me. I'm sorry. I'll be going."

"Please, no, don't be silly. There's no reason for you to leave." Michelle reached out, as if to place her hand on Olivia's arm, then pulled it back.

Through the fog of her humiliation, Olivia noticed that Michelle's French accent had evaporated.

325

"Sit down and rest for a while if you'd like. That blue dress would be lovely on you. It'd be a shame for you not to try it on."

Olivia stood staring at the dress and said nothing.

"Better yet, first let me fix your hair for you."

Olivia's hand went to her head and she felt her face flush again. It must have been weeks since her hair had a proper washing.

"Forgive me for saying so," Michelle said as she drew closer, "but your hair . . . It's a shame. A lovely girl like you. Why don't you let me give you a good shampoo? I do that for many of my customers. I have a special basin in the back. I originally meant this place to be a ladies' hair salon."

"Do you have yucca soap?" Olivia couldn't help asking.

"Something much better. And I'll see what I can do with those nails." Michelle gently took Olivia by the arm and led her toward the back of the shop. "But before we make your hair all clean and shiny . . ." she lowered her voice and leaned over, whispering in Olivia's ear, "I have something even better for you. Something that will make you feel brand new, more than a silly dress. You should let my girl Sarah May give you a good body rub. She's just next door and could come right over, if you want."

Olivia looked at her blankly, having no idea what she was talking about.

"She hardly charges anything. Your hair, nails, the body rub, everything, together with the dress, would only come to four bits."

Feeling as if she were entering a foreign country, Olivia allowed herself to be led into a windowless room containing only a waist-high bed. Michelle handed her what looked like a chemise.

"Just hang your clothes on those hooks there." Michelle nodded at the wall. "And put this on."

Olivia took the chemise and held it up. "It's open

down the front," she said, a scowl coming over her features. "It doesn't even have any buttons."

"Actually, it's open down the back. How else can she rub your back?"

"I'm sorry, but I have to be going." Olivia let the garment fall to the bed and turned to leave. *Is this woman crazy?*

"Wait. Please." Michelle came after her. "I'm sorry if I said something that upset you. Please, don't go."

Olivia turned to face her.

"I'm sorry." Michelle went on. "You're so young. I should have explained, should have guessed it might frighten you, a complete stranger telling you to take off your clothes, here in a store." She took a step forward and put her hand lightly on Olivia's arm. "I'll just wash your hair if that's all you want, but there's nothing for you to be frightened of. I promise. No one but Sarah May will come in and there's a bolt on the door, so if you want, you can lock it from the inside."

Olivia didn't move or speak.

"You really should try it. I promise you'll be glad you did. You look so ... so worn out. Like a big, bad wolf could blow you right over, with just one huff. Wouldn't need a single puff."

Olivia couldn't help smiling.

"Sara May does a wonderful job. You wouldn't believe it looking at her, she's so tiny and all. But that girl has hands on her like a vise. And she knows how to use them. I let her work on me every week."

Olivia continued to stare at the floor and Michelle lowered her head, trying to peek into Olivia's face. "You look so sad and exhausted. I think it's just what you need."

Olivia was amazed to find herself submitting to this woman and allowing herself to be led away.

"Just hang your dress up and put that thing on," Michelle said, smiling as she picked a towel from a shelf. "Lie on your stomach. If you're shy about Sarah

327

May seeing your drawers, you can cover your behind with this." She tossed the towel onto the bed. "I'll go get her. Just give a holler when you're ready for her to come in."

Olivia still felt uneasy, but was too intrigued not to obey. She bolted the door before she undressed, hung her dress, apron, and chemise on the hooks, and removed her moneybag and slipped it under the mattress. She waited until she heard Michelle return before unbolting the door.

"All right, I'm ready," she called out, once she was settled on the bed.

She craned her neck to see a thin young woman about her age come in and slide the bolt shut again.

"Hullo, Miss Killion, I'm Sarah May."

"Hullo."

"I'm gonna use oil," Sarah May said, setting a large brown bottle on the shelf, "but don't worry none, I'll towel it off before you get dressed. And I'll get oil in your hair when I massage your scalp, but Mademoiselle is gonna give you a nice shampoo, so don't worry you none about that neither. You just relax."

It was unsettling for Olivia to feel a stranger's touch, but she did not recoil when Sarah May began working on her neck and shoulders. Olivia could feel her skin greedily sucking up the oil and was indeed amazed by the strength of the girl's hands. Olivia's surrender was soon complete and Sarah May pummeled the knots out of her aching body. When the girl stepped away from the bed Olivia thought she had finished and was about to ask if she could pay her double to do the whole thing over again.

But Sara May spoke first. "I'm gonna turn to face the door now, so you can get rolled over onto your back. Here's another towel to cover yourself up top."

When Olivia said she was ready Sarah May turned around and made a show of carefully arranging the two towels Olivia had draped over her chest and hips. Then she moved to the head of the bed to slowly massage Olivia's face, scalp, neck, and shoulders. She worked on both arms and hands, giving each finger a little tug. Olivia's legs, feet, and toes received similar treatment, with Sarah May artfully avoiding the blisters.

Then she was finished and used another towel to absorb the excess oil. "I'll go get you a robe for while you're getting your hair washed."

"That was wonderful," Olivia said. "I can't thank you enough."

Sarah May smiled and turned to leave.

"Wait," Olivia said, "Can you hand me my apron from over there?"

The girl did so and Olivia rose up on one elbow to fish a nickel from the pocket and hold it out to Sarah May.

"Oh no," Sarah May said. "Miss Michelle pays me. I ain't allowed to take no tips. I'll be back in a lick with the robe."

Olivia put on the fluffy pink robe and peeked out to find Michelle waiting in the tiny corridor.

"See? All shiny and new. I could tell you's a gal what'll know how to appreciate it." Michelle smiled and began walking. "Come, back here."

In another tiny room was a wooden chair with a back that sloped toward a basin. Olivia settled into it and Michelle dipped cups of water from a large bucket to pour over her hair.

"Are there shops like this in all cities?" Olivia asked while Michelle gently massaged something that smelled of flowers into her hair.

"Couldn't say. Certainly hope so. Every woman needs some pampering from time to time."

"You are very kind," Olivia said.

Michelle rinsed Olivia's hair, motioned for her to sit up, and wrapped a towel around her head. Then she nodded at another wooden chair in front of a long, narrow looking-glass. Olivia sat and Michelle stood behind her. Their eyes met in the mirror.

"I don't know how to thank you," Olivia said. "I really was quite worn out. I feel so much better now."

Michelle smiled and began brushing Olivia's hair, just like her mother used to. That memory brought tears and Olivia swiped a finger under her eye, hoping Michelle hadn't noticed.

"There, there," Michelle said, leaning down to give Olivia's shoulders a hug. "Listen, Hon, I don't know who done what to hurt you so bad, but whatever it was, the world is gonna go on spinning, for you too. I promise you that. Don't stop for no one's sorrows." She pulled a chair next to Olivia's and made her voice cheerful as she said, "Let's take care of them hands while your hair is drying." She tsk-tsked when she began trimming the jagged nails.

Michelle hummed as she finished the manicure and then twisted Olivia's still-damp hair into an elaborate arrangement. Olivia was grateful for not being required to carry on a conversation.

"See how beautiful you are?" Michelle leaned down and squeezed Olivia's shoulders again, watching her in the mirror. "I think you're ready to face the world now. I'll go get that dress for you."

Olivia dressed slowly, wondering what she should do next. When she went out to the shop and handed the four bits to Michelle, Michelle slipped the money into her pocket and then took Olivia's hand.

"Listen," she said softly. "I can see whatever happened to you was bad, but you're going to be all right. You're a strong girl. You have wonderful eyes. I don't mean just pretty. I mean the eyes of a good human being. One who deserves good things."

Olivia might have thrown herself into Michelle's embrace, but didn't. She felt incapable of responding and stood speechless. All she could manage was an ineffectual thank you for everything.

"Don't go yet." Michelle smiled. She picked up a

straw hat trimmed with red flowers, green leaves, and a blue ribbon and plunked it on Olivia's head.

"A present from me," she said. "To go with your new dress."

Olivia managed a smile. Noticing some shelves at the back of the shop, she asked, "Do you sell men's things?"

"Sure do."

"I'd like a pair of trousers and a shirt, please."

"How big is the fellow?"

"They're for me. I might want to go for a ride tomorrow and I prefer not to wear a dress."

Michelle's face broke into a wide smile. "Aren't you full of surprises? Sure I can fix you up. Probably need boys' sizes, but I got them."

Olivia didn't want to bother trying the clothes on and just held them up. Then she noticed a stack of men's caps on a shelf. She removed the straw bonnet and tried a beige flat cap. "I'll take this too." She carried it and the trousers and shirt to the counter.

Michelle wrapped them in newsprint, with Olivia's old dress, and Olivia paid the difference.

"You've been so kind to me. I really don't know how to thank you."

Michelle smiled. "Just take care of yourself. Time will come, some other woman's gonna need you to be kind to her."

Out on the street Olivia was once again anonymous, but no longer took comfort in it. How quickly she had grown accustomed to Michelle's warmth. How wintry the world felt without it. Like stepping away from a campfire, into endless cold and dark.

She walked aimlessly for a long while. Her feet hurt terribly, but she didn't feel like going back to the hotel. Then a shop selling beaded moccasins caught her eye and she went in to try on a pair. They were soft and gentle to her throbbing feet.

"I'll take them," she said to the clerk, nodding at her

feet. "And I'm going to keep them on. You can wrap my shoes up." He raised an eyebrow, but wordlessly took her money and handed her the package.

Out on the street she was drawn toward the river, where she stood watching the boats. There were not as many as on the day she'd arrived with Mourning on the *Windsong*, but it was still an impressive show. She craned her neck, searching in vain for one of the French Voyageurs. Every other type of craft bobbed in the water and the shouts of the stevedores working on Merchants' Wharf reached her ears. She wondered if they felt lucky to be living in this young, exciting city.

She seated herself on a large rock near the water and considered making Detroit her home. Why not? Her farm wasn't far way. She could let it to a tenant farmer and use the money to start some kind of business. Plenty of women had their own businesses, didn't they? Look at Michelle. She remembered her first glimpse of the city as they'd rounded the last bend in the river, the sunlight glinting off tin roofs. The feeling that this was where she was supposed to be. But that feeling was gone. She would never belong anywhere. Anyway, what did she know about running a business?

She rose and began walking again. Before long she saw an older woman seated on a bench in a park and sat down next to her.

"Hullo," Olivia said. "I was wondering if you might know if there are any teaching positions available here in Detroit."

"Humph. Don't no woman in her right mind want to be no school teacher in this town." The woman waved the question away in obvious disgust. "My daughter was one. Lost her job last year when they closed the public schools."

"There are no schools in a big city like Detroit?" Olivia asked.

"Oh there's schools all right, you got the money to

fork over for 'em. They're trying to get some kind of tax passed, but for now the great guns are saying they only got enough to open the public schools for four months – and that's only if the pigeon teachers agree to work for $6 a month."

"Oh." Olivia thanked her and rose. Nothing in life was simple. She was back where she had begun. A woman incapable of supporting herself.

She turned and walked to the livery, looking forward to greeting Dixby and Dougan, but they were gone. The owner of the livery proudly informed her that he had sold them just an hour ago, and for a good price – $35. The sadness that tugged at her made her feel ridiculous – how pathetic was a person who missed a pair of cows? The man counted out the money and said he also had a buyer for the wagon and the rest of her possessions. A Dutch man. He would be by later to see if she'd agreed to his price. Olivia nodded, barely listening to him explain why she should accept the offer.

"That will be fine," she said. "I'll come back tomorrow to settle up." At the door she turned back. "Do you think you could save me the trip by letting me have the money now?" she asked. The price was low enough that she was not surprised when he readily agreed.

So that was that. There was nothing else for her to do here. No reason to stay in a city where she had not a single friend. Olivia was grateful to Michelle for the warmth and generosity she had shown. They had eased some of the pain. But they had also made her feel like an object of pity. Was her neediness so obvious? On her way back to the hotel she concentrated on trying to look like a normal person, but it was so hard to smile.

Chapter Thirty-Nine

Olivia stood on Merchant's Wharf, clutching a first-class ticket and watching a stevedore with a large trunk and both of her wicker baskets stacked on his back make his way over the gang plank onto the *S.S. Walk-in-the-Water*. Her stomach felt as if she had swallowed an angry porcupine. "Later" was here and now she had only the two or three days the trip would take to decide what she was going to tell her family. She closed her eyes. Everything will be all right. Mourning will be back in Five Rocks. He said there are things a girl in trouble can do. He'll find out what. He'll tell me where I have to go.

The sun was setting when she straggled aboard to begin her journey home. She had booked the cheapest private cabin they had to offer and a broad-backed porter in a black uniform led her down a steep flight – more like a ladder than stairs – and turned the key in the lock for her. The only furnishings were a straight-back chair and a narrow wooden bed that looked like a long crate with a mattress on top. A raggedy curtain was tacked to its side, and the porter lifted it, revealing that the bed was actually a wooden shelf with her baskets stowed beneath it. The sheet that covered the straw mattress was coarse, but looked clean. In place of a pillow, a folded woolen blanket lay at the head. There was a small shelf on the wall and a kerosene lantern hung next to it.

The bareness of the cabin suited her. She required nothing more than four walls and a deadbolt to shut out the world. Feeling as if she could sleep all the way to Erie, she lay down and stretched out. It didn't take long, however, for the walls to seem to close in on her rather than offer protection. When she heard the engine snort and growl to life she rose and climbed up to the deck. Passengers crowded the rail and Olivia squeezed in among them.

She soon regretted having left her cave. Everyone around her was talking and laughing, making her feel even more alone. She clutched the rail and held back tears, reminding herself how much she had to be grateful for – food in her stomach, money in her pocket, and a home to go back to. For the time being anyway. Until they realized she had a baby in her belly. Would they toss her out into the snow? She had heard of such things. Perhaps she could make up a lie. Say she had gotten married in Michigan and her husband had died of the fever, just like Aunt Lydia Ann. But what if they believed her and then the baby turned out to be colored? She tried to imagine the look on Mabel's face and might have laughed, if the prospect hadn't been so devastating. She descended the stairs to her cabin and once again counted the days. She should get her monthly visitor today or tomorrow, but felt none of the familiar cramping.

She lay down, remembering her father lecturing them about how to make a decision. "Make a list of your choices and the best and worst possible outcome of each." Her first decision had to be made soon, if she didn't get her monthly visitor by the time they reached Erie. What were the possibilities? Don't go home – go straight to a home for wayward girls. Go home, don't tell them anything, and find out how to get rid of the baby. Go home and tell them about her poor dead husband. Go home, break down in tears, and tell them she had been raped. Or that some young man had promised to marry her and then disappeared.

She tried to consider the outcome of each, if the baby was white and if the baby was black. Most of her options were nothing but disastrous if the baby turned out to be colored. Why had she lied about a husband or beau, or not mentioned that her rapist was black? What black man was she trying to protect? And if she said she

335

had been raped by a black man, a stranger to her, and then the baby was white? It was all too complicated. The first choice – go straight to a home for wayward girls – was the one that made most sense, but the one she could least bear the thought of. She was tired of being alone. The steady drone and thump of the engine, together with the rocking of the boat, eventually lulled her to sleep, though she stirred often during the night.

The next morning she woke to the sound of a downpour and stayed in bed, nibbling at the loaf of bread she had brought. When the rain subsided into a light patter, she rushed up to use the latrine and then bought a cup of the gritty coffee. The sun came out later in the morning and she strolled through the puddles on deck, but did not converse with any of the other passengers.

The dining room offered tasteless fare – a bowl of greasy soup, a slab of fatty meat, fried potatoes, dried out chocolate cake, and more of the bitter coffee. The passengers shared long mess tables and Olivia chose a place next to a family with small children, knowing they would be too busy to make more than a brief attempt at polite conversation with her. Olivia smiled and nodded and rose as soon as she'd finished.

She made her way to the back of the boat, to the deck over the engine, and stood watching the coloreds huddled there. They sat on their baggage and spoke in soft tones. One of the mothers noticed Olivia staring at them and pulled her little girl closer. Others also began casting suspicious glances her way, lowering their eyes to avoid Olivia's timid smile. She sighed, shook her head, and turned away.

Back in the white section she stood at the rail and thought what it must have been like for Mourning, growing up the only black-skinned person in town. She bent to rest her forehead on her knuckles and allowed thoughts of him to fill her mind – working under the hot sun with his shirt off, sweat trickling down his

336

shiny back; balanced on a roof beam, calling down to her to toss him a sack of nails; humming while he lit the fire, his voice as smooth as coffee with cream. For a brief moment she even allowed herself to remember his hands on her body, but the magic of that memory had been almost entirely eradicated, buried beneath the sludge of a different type of physical contact.

When the boat docked in Erie she marched to the stagecoach office.

"Just in time," the man behind the caged window said. "Got one leaving in about twenty minutes. It'll be going through Five Rocks before dark."

"Is that the only one?"

"Only passenger coach with regular stops."

"What else is there?"

"All else we got is a delivery wagon going to Reuben's Bend, passes through Five Rocks. But it ain't leaving for three-four hours. Won't get you there till after ten at night. 'Sides, it ain't no passenger coach. Sometimes a body might sit in the back, with all the sacks of feed and whatnot, but it ain't no place for a lady."

"Has anyone else asked to ride in it today?"

"No, but –"

"Then I'd like a ticket for that, please."

"I told you, miss, it ain't a regular coach. That ride will shake you so you don't remember which way's up. And everything'll be closed that time of night. He'd have to let you off in the street, all alone."

"No one meets it in Five Rocks?"

"No, like I told you, it normally don't stop at all, just passes through."

"Is there room for me and my things?"

"Well, yes, but –"

"Then it will be perfectly all right. As long as the driver will help me on and off with my things, I'll be fine."

He stared at her for a long moment. "All right, you say so, lady. You be back here, right out there on that sidewalk," he said, jabbing his finger at the door, "at a quarter to six. You might gotta wait an hour. Like I been tryin' to tell you, it ain't a coach with a regular schedule. Leaves when it's ready. Gets here when it gets here." He paused, apparently waiting for her to change her mind. Then he sighed and scribbled something on a piece of paper. "I ain't gonna charge ya nothin'. You give this to the driver." He handed her the paper. "Name's Sully. He's a great big fella with a wild bush of rusty hair. Wears one a them buckskin jackets with long fringes. Slow as they come, but ain't no one got a better nature. You don't gotta worry nothin' about him. He'll see you standin' there and stop. You tell him Jonas said it was all right."

Olivia told Jonas she would arrange to have her belongings delivered to the stagecoach office and he promised to move them out to the sidewalk before he closed for the day at half past five. She returned to the boat and looked through her wicker baskets for the hateful poke bonnet she'd bought in Detroit and her black hooded cloak. She didn't want anyone in Five Rocks recognizing her before she'd had time to talk with her family.

The ride wasn't as bad as she'd expected. It was too bumpy to try to nap, so she'd spent it sitting up front next to Sully, mostly trying to teach him his multiplication tables. When they approached Five Rocks, Olivia reached for the hood of her cloak and pulled it over her poke bonnet, casting her face so deep in shadows she wouldn't have been able to recognize herself.

Sully reined in the horses outside Ferguson's Livery, across from the Episcopalian church. The moon was bright enough for her to read the big sign that declared, "Fear not if you have sinned and repented – A step backward often precedes a great leap forward." *Tell that to Mabel Mears*, she thought.

The street was empty. She climbed down and whispered to Sully, "Could you please shove my baskets into those bushes over there behind that sign, but be real quiet about it? No one knows I'm coming. It's a big surprise for my family." His face lit up and he gladly obliged. She had a time convincing him that she would be perfectly safe walking home alone, but he finally drove off. Olivia turned onto Main Street, but in the opposite direction of her brother's home.

Three long days on that boat and she still had no idea what she was going to do. She felt sick to her stomach, dreading facing her family. She would have to knock on the front door like a stranger. Tobey might not even live there any more. Mabel and Avis were most likely married by now. Good luck waking Avis. Mabel would be the one getting out of bed and tromping down the stairs, not knowing whether to be annoyed or alarmed. Now Olivia understood the real charm of a big city. They had hotels.

She found herself walking toward The Circle, where the road curved around on itself, forming the *cul de sac* on which Jettie Place's house and bakery shop stood. She told herself she just needed a short walk to clear her head, but knew that wasn't true. It wasn't by chance that she'd chosen this path for her walk, past the home of her father's mistress, the one person in Five Rocks who might not judge her.

A light was burning in one of the downstairs windows. Olivia thought Mrs. Place's home should have been sad and lonely-looking, the only house down there, all by itself. Its light gray paint was peeling off and dead leaves blew across its saggy front porch, but that glowing window somehow managed to look cheerful and inviting. Olivia had been standing in the road for a long while, trying to imagine herself climbing up those steps and knocking on the front door, when

339

Mrs. Place opened it and called out.

"Angel! Angel! Come here, kitty, kitty, kitty." Mrs. Place paced the length of the porch, clutching her flannel robe. Then she looked up and noticed the hooded figure.

"Oh hullo there. You ain't seen a little white kitten?"

"No, ma'am, I haven't." Olivia raised a hand to swipe the hood from her head and then untied and removed the poke bonnet.

"Olivia Killion?" Mrs. Place squinted at her. "Is that you?" She descended the first step and Olivia saw that her feet were in slippers made of rags, similar to the ones Mrs. Hardaway wore.

"Yes, ma'am." Olivia took a few hesitant steps toward the infamous "fancy lady."

"Why, indeed it is. I ain't heard nothing about you being back in town. Wondered what become of you. All kinds of stories been going around. How long you been back?"

Olivia was grateful for the casual tone of the woman's voice, as if it were the most natural thing in the world to find Seborn Killion's daughter lurking outside her house.

"I just got here," Olivia said. "A delivery wagon let me off by Ferguson's Livery."

Mrs. Place frowned through a long silence, one eyebrow raised. "I see. So you ain't been to see your family yet?"

"No, ma'am. I felt like taking a little walk first."

"I see." Mrs. Place studied Olivia for another moment. "Well, you sure look to me like someone what could use a hot drink. And I'm getting right chilled out here. Can't believe the nights are this cool in July. Strangest weather we been having. Can I invite you in?"

Olivia's stuttered response was unintelligible.

Mrs. Place descended the last two steps and walked over to take Olivia by the arm. "Come along now. You don't gotta worry. Ain't nobody coulda recognized you with that blanket you had draped over your head. No one's gonna know you been keeping company with 'that woman.'"

She led Olivia toward the house. "Oh look, there's my little Angel, right there under the steps." She stooped to scoop up a fluffy white kitten. "Ain't you the sweetest thing?" She held the kitten up and rubbed its nose to her own. "And so smart. You're gonna be the best mouser I ever had." She held the kitten to her chest with one hand, opened the front door with the other, and reverted to her adult speaking voice.

"Found this poor little thing out by the barn. Throw your wrap on that rack there. Make yourself to home here in the parlor while I put the kettle on. Get acquainted with Angel." She handed the kitten to Olivia and disappeared through an arched doorway that led to the back of the house.

Olivia kept her cloak on and perched on the seat of one of the ladder-back chairs. She nervously petted Angel and wondered how she had dared come here. And why? What did she think she was going to say to this woman? Well, at least she could count on Mrs. Place's discretion. If there was anyone in Five Rocks a person could trust to keep a secret, it was Mrs. Jettie Place. No one in town spoke to her, so who was she going to tell?

"Why don't you come back here to the kitchen?" Mrs. Place called. "Might as well have us a little bite to eat."

Olivia put Angel down, hung her cloak on the rack, and walked toward Mrs. Place's voice. The kitchen was large and square, with a heavy wooden table in its center. It was the kind of table you would expect a large noisy family to gather around, not two lonely women. A lantern in the middle of it cast a pleasant glow and the fire in the cook stove had taken the chill off the room. There was a pot of beef soup next to the coffeepot. It smelled wonderful.

341

"That soup is still warm and won't take but a minute to get nice and hot. Meantime, warm yourself up with this." She set a cup of coffee in front of Olivia and took the chair next to her. "I see you been earning your daily bread." She nodded at Olivia's hands.

"I was farming. Out in Michigan."

What did you need to tell her that for? Olivia scolded herself. But she was too exhausted to concoct a lie.

"Yes. Your brother Tobey said something like that. Warn't speaking to me, of course. I heard him telling Mrs. Burton that might be where you was at. Said he was thinking of going out there himself, try and bring you back, but I wouldn't suppose he did, did he? Not out of lack of concern, mind you, but, we all know how that brother of yours is. Sweet soul, but not exactly ... So, you come home for a visit?"

"No. Not a visit. I mean ... I don't know."

Mrs. Place rose, ladled out a bowl of soup, and sliced some bread. "Don't be shy." She shoved it closer to Olivia. "Go ahead and eat. If you don't, the cats will."

Olivia did, hungrily, amazed at the way Mrs. Place managed to keep the air between them filled with idle chatter about Angel. For someone with no social life that Olivia knew of, she sure was good at chitchatting. When Olivia finished, Mrs. Place cleared the bowl away, sat back down, and placed her hand over Olivia's.

"Honey, you can tell me, or you can not tell me. But if you came here 'cause you got something to say, or something to ask, you'd best spit it out."

Olivia opened her mouth, but no words formed in her brain.

"I gotta guess you're in some kind of trouble. And there's only one kind a trouble I can imagine a girl like you choosing a woman like me to tell about. Is that the kind of trouble you're in?"

Chapter Forty

Olivia answered Mrs. Place's question in a tiny voice. "I don't know."

"Well, at least you're consistent." Mrs. Place smiled. "You don't seem to know much of anything."

Olivia took no offense; she knew the teasing was intended to lighten the mood rather than be hurtful. Still, she seemed unable to reply.

Mrs. Place waited a long moment before asking, "When'd you last get the curse?"

"My monthly visitor should have come two days ago. Maybe three," Olivia said, looking away.

"Oh, Honey, three days ain't nothing to fret about." Mrs. Place leaned back. "Sometimes it can be weeks late for no good reason. No good reason at all. Tell you one thing – worrying about not getting it is the best way to make sure you don't. You been to see a doctor?"

"No."

"Just as well. Takes time for them to tell. So you left the might-be-a-father out there in Michigan?"

Olivia opened her mouth to say, "I don't know," but switched to "Yes."

"You didn't think he'd do right by you?" Mrs. Place asked.

"It wasn't anything like that," Olivia whispered.

Mrs. Place waited a long moment before asking, "You feeling inclined to tell me what it *was* like?"

"It wasn't a romance. It was ... you see we had these neighbors ..."

"We?"

"Me and Mourning. You know, Mourning Free?"

"Well, sure I know him. I live in Five Rocks, don't I? Heard he found himself some relatives, went to stay with 'em. You don't look much like no long-lost cousin of his."

Olivia shook her head. "He made that up. Truth is, I talked him into going to Michigan with me, as a hired

343

hand to work the farm I inherited from my Uncle Scruggs. But we wanted to keep that a secret."

"You don't mean that you . . . with Mourning Free . . ." Mrs. Place's eyes opened wide.

"No," Olivia exclaimed. "No, not Mourning. Mourning would never do anything like that. It wasn't him. But, see, that's the reason we didn't want to tell anyone he was going with me, so they wouldn't get the wrong idea, like you just did."

"So there warn't nothing between the two of you?"

"No. No. No." Olivia shook her head. "Of course not. He stayed on the farm and I took a room in the little town nearby. But there was this couple, lived on the next farm ..." Olivia stopped and stared at her hostess.

Mrs. Place had so easily plucked her from the street and was now sitting patiently, occasionally offering the comfort of a nod or the stroke of a warm hand, behaving exactly the way Olivia imagined a mother or older sister would. Olivia's resolution never, ever to tell anyone what the Stubblefields had done to her crumbled. She couldn't hold it inside any longer. Once she began speaking, her slow trickle of words became a flood she couldn't stop. She was soon pouring out all the horrible details she had sworn to lock away. At first Mrs. Place's interjections were murmured softly; as Olivia's story progressed her voice gained the volume of outrage.

"You poor dear, my Lord, oh sweet Jesus, those monsters, absolute monsters, so wicked, and a child like you ..."

Olivia did not tell Mrs. Place about her one night with Mourning. Neither did she tell her about planning to kill the Stubblefields, finding them already dead, and suspecting that Mourning may have been responsible for that.

She had begun her story dry-eyed, but quickly dissolved into shaking shoulders and sobs. Mrs. Place fetched a handkerchief and a glass of water and pulled her chair closer, rubbing Olivia's back with one hand. When Olivia looked up, she found in Mrs. Place's eyes the one thing she most needed to see – belief. The woman didn't doubt a single word Olivia had told her.

"Poor child," Mrs. Place said at last, leaning forward and gathering Olivia into her embrace. "Poor, poor child. How long did those devils keep you there like that?" She sat back and looked into Olivia's face.

"A whole week. He came in every day for a whole week. Sometimes twice. Drunk most of the time."

"And now you're afeared you got this monster's child inside you." Mrs. Place shook her head.

Olivia nodded and wiped her eyes.

"And you ran back here to feel safe, but can't bring yourself to tell your family."

Olivia nodded again.

"Well," Mrs. Place said, "you maybe don't got nothing to tell them. No point in saying a word before you know. That's one cart you want to keep way back behind the horse." She took both of Olivia's hands as she locked eyes with her. "There's one thing you don't understand – that you got to keep this secret to yourself. Truth is, you shudna told me."

"I didn't mean to. I don't know why I came here, but it wasn't because I was planning to tell you," Olivia said. "I swore to myself I'd never tell anyone. But you're being so nice. It just came out. There's no one else I could tell something like that to."

"What got you thinking you could tell me?"

"I don't know." Olivia shrugged, miserable. "I just thought I could."

"Well, you warn't wrong. I won't be giving you away. But you took a big chance and you shudna. A woman can't trust no one with a secret like that, no matter how big a hole it's burning in her. Most especially not another woman. That's something you got to learn. For all you know, I could be right glad to have something to lord over Seborn Killion's snotty daughter, up on her

345

high horse, thinking she's better than me. I could rush out tomorrow, tell it all over town."

"I don't think I'm better –"

"I know." Mrs. Place squeezed her hands. "I know you don't. You were real sweet to me. I'm just saying, you didn't *know* that warn't the way I felt. You don't know one stitch about me, but you came straight in here, trusting me with a secret that could ruin your life. And believe me it could, even though it warn't none of your fault. That's the sorry truth. So you best not be telling anyone else. I mean anyone. Including that brother of yours. I know you think the world of him, but he wouldn't be the least bit of comfort to you and you never know what harm he might do. Oh, he wouldn't mean to, but weak people with good intentions can be the worst." She released Olivia's hands and placed her palms on both sides of Olivia's face. "Now you listen to me good. Day might come you have some special close friend and you feel you want to tell her. But you can't. Not a word of it. And when you meet some nice young fellow wants to marry you, you might feel obliged to bare your heart. Don't you so much as think about it. I don't care how much he swears nothing could ever make him stop loving you, or how much you trust him, or how much you hate keeping a secret from him. Not a single word. You got to keep this inside you for the rest of your life."

"I know..."

"Do you? You shudna told me, but you already done that, and you can't take it back. Just don't go telling anyone else. Not ever. You understand me? Never."

Olivia nodded.

"It's the type of thing will always make people surprise you for the worst. You think they'd understand, feel nothing but sorry for you, seeing as it was forced on you. There's no way they can blame you. That's what you'd think. But that ain't what happens. You can count on them to find a way."

"I won't tell anyone else."

"Anyone see you get off that stage?"

"It wasn't a stage. It was a delivery wagon. I was the only passenger."

"And no one saw you get off it? No one else knows you're here?"

"No." Olivia picked up the handkerchief and blew her nose.

"Well, I think we could both use a night to sleep on this. You can spend it here. No point in making any hasty decisions. You get a good rest and we can talk at noon tomorrow, when I come in for my dinner. After that, you go home if you want. No reason your folks wouldn't believe you just got off some other delivery wagon. But first we'll think it through together, see what's best. Where'd you leave your cases?"

"In the bushes behind that big sign in front of the Episcopal Church."

"All right, I'll wait till it gets a bit later and go get them."

Olivia shook her head. "There are two wicker baskets. Big ones. You won't be able to carry them."

"I got a wagon I use to bring sacks of flour and sugar from your brother's store."

Olivia started. It was strange to hear it called "your brother's store" instead of "your father's store."

"I'll come with you."

"Well I suppose that'd be all right. You put that monk get-up back on, no one will ever guess it's you. And anyone asks, I got a long-lost cousin come to stay with me." Mrs. Place pushed her chair back and stood up. "Let's say we go out to the parlor, talk about something else for a while. Come on, Angel."

The kitten followed her like a dog. Mrs. Place sank into a stuffed wing back chair. A basket of needlework stood on the floor next to it and she tossed the kitten a ball of bright red yarn. Olivia took the uncomfortable ladder back chair and watched Angel tangle herself up in the yarn.

"You don't much favor your mother." Mrs. Place glanced over at her.

"No. No one ever said I did."

"You can thank the good Lord you don't look much like your father neither. And even more for not giving you his personality, cantankerous old goat that he was."

"Did you hate him?" Olivia asked timidly.

"Hate him? Course not. I guess I loved him in my own pitiful way. But it warn't nothing like what a young girl like you thinks of when she thinks of love. I seen too much and gotten too hard for that. But I cared for him and I loved having someone to care for, even that little. And I think he might a cared for me in his own stingy way. It just didn't come natural to him. Either that or he used it all up on your mother." She shook her head and then smiled. "I think he maybe worked at keeping himself mean, so I wouldn't have any expectations of him making me Mrs. Killion number two. Well, he didn't need to worry none on that account. Never thought he would. Don't know if I woulda wanted him to. There *are* advantages to an arrangement like the one we had. When they're your husband, they never go home."

Olivia stared at the toes of her shoes, hands in her lap. Her hostess seemed oblivious to her embarrassment. Mrs. Place yawned and glanced up at the clock on the wall. "I think maybe it's late enough for us to go get your things."

Olivia rose for her cloak and then followed Mrs. Place out to the barn where she kept the wagon. It was larger than a child's toy, but rode low to the ground like one. They walked to the church in silence, without a lantern, Mrs. Place dragging the wagon behind her. The town looked deserted and they saw no one outside, but the clatter of the wagon's wheels sounded deafening to Olivia.

"Don't worry," Mrs. Place said. "There's sure to be

348

one of them women God put in charge of the town looking out their window, but they'll think you're one of my outcast friends come to visit. Just don't take that cloak home with you when you go."

The baskets were where Olivia had left them. The two women balanced them on the wagon, one on top of the other, and Olivia held them steady as they walked back. Mrs. Place helped Olivia get them up the porch steps, one at a time, and inside the front door.

"You're on your own getting whatever you need upstairs," Mrs. Place said, out of breath. "With my knees, I'm doing well to drag myself up them steps. Just leave everything here for now. Take out whatever you need for tonight and I'll show you up to the extra room. You can worry about the rest later, if you decide to stay here for a while."

Olivia's eyes opened wider at this round-about invitation, but she said nothing. While Olivia searched for her nightgown and hairbrush, Mrs. Place lit another lantern. She carried both it and the one that was still burning by the window as she led Olivia up the stairs to the guest room.

It was small and done up simply – a nightstand between two single beds covered with patchwork quilts. A chest of drawers stood against the opposite wall, next to the window. All the furniture was of the same dark wood. If not for the peeling wallpaper – a pleasant blue and white floral pattern – it looked the way Olivia would have imagined a room in a nunnery, not one in the home of a woman of ill repute. Mrs. Place set one lantern on the chest of drawers and went out carrying the other. She soon thumped back up the stairs and knocked on Olivia's door to hand her a pitcher of water and a towel. When she turned to leave, Olivia's voice stopped her.

"Mrs. Place?"

"Yes?"

Olivia hadn't intended to ask so soon, but couldn't

wait. "I was just wondering, do you happen to know when Mourning Free got back to town?"

"Didn't know that he did. Ain't heard or seen nothing of him since he left."

Chapter Forty-One

The next morning Olivia lay in bed, staring at a rusty watermark in the shape of Lake Erie that stained the wallpaper above the window. She put off facing the day for a while by trying to place Buffalo, Erie, Cleveland, Toledo, and Detroit on it. The room was half-dark. The yellowing blind on the tall narrow window was down, but sunlight leaked around its edges and through the hole in the middle of it. Olivia finally rose and peeked through that hole, assuring herself that the window looked out over the empty fields before yanking on the pull string. The blind flew up with a loud snap and Olivia froze, listening, but the house remained silent.

She tiptoed to the door and pulled it open a crack, hearing only the ticking of a clock. She had used the chamber pot during the night and pulled it out again, knowing she dare not visit the outhouse in daylight. Then she poured water from the pitcher into the basin and washed, wishing she had some tooth powder. There was nothing else for her to do but gaze out the window, her mind blank. A few clouds drifted across the sky, but the sun was bright. If only she could walk down to the river and Mourning would miraculously come sloshing up the bank.

Restless, she put on her dress and opened the door. Mrs. Place had set a pair of fluffy pink house slippers in the hallway and Olivia slipped into them. The ticking was coming from a shelf in the hallway and Olivia started. The clock on that shelf used to sit on the desk in her father's study. She stared at it for a moment, wondering if she minded, but felt nothing. It was just a thing, a timepiece. It was only a few minutes after nine o'clock, so she knew she had time to herself. Mrs. Place would be in her bakery all morning, until she closed for an hour at noon.

Olivia tiptoed down the stairs, which creaked loudly in the empty house. Mrs. Place had left the curtains in the parlor tightly shut and Olivia peeked around the edge of one of them. A pair of women in identical brown poke bonnets came to the bakery and quickly left, but neither of them glanced at the house. She watched for a while longer, hoping to catch a glimpse of Tobey coming for an apple pie, then pulled back from the window and studied the parlor furnishings.

She half-expected to see more things that had once belonged to her father, but nothing else looked familiar. Two flowery wingback chairs with matching footstools were arranged with a small round end table next to each. On the wall opposite, to the left of the arched doorway that led to the kitchen, a china cabinet displayed silver goblets, fussy pink and white plates, and china figurines of women of various nationalities in exotic dress. Next to the cabinet, two ladder-back chairs and a rocker with a bright red cushion and matching footrest completed a ring around the circular rug that covered the center of the floor. Olivia didn't share Mrs. Place's taste in furnishings, but that rug was the only thing in the house that Olivia considered hideous. It was blotted with enormous red and pink flowers, with leaves in two shades of sickly green. The background was somewhere between yellow and dirty white.

Olivia sank into the rocker and stared at the wing back chairs, trying to imagine Mrs. Place and her father passing an evening together. Mrs. Place was easy. She'd be knitting or embroidering, passing on the gossip she'd overheard in her shop that week, getting up to serve him coffee and a slice of her peach pie. That had always been his favorite. And the taciturn Seborn Killion? Did he talk about his children? About his wife's sickness and death? Complain about the customers in the store? Olivia tried to imagine him playing with a kitten, but couldn't. Neither could she imagine him sustaining a conversation.

A tiny pair of scissors and some spools of thread lay on the table next to the chair Mrs. Place had occupied last night. Olivia guessed she must spend most every evening in that chair, doing some kind of needlework. There was no evidence of it in the house, however. Olivia hadn't seen any samplers or embroidered cushions. It made her sad to think of Mrs. Place sitting in that chair all alone, night after night, decade after decade, nothing to look forward to but Old Seborn's visits. That being the highlight of anyone's week was a truly dismal thought.

Olivia's mind returned to the present. What was she going to do? There was still no sign of her monthly visitor. What had Mrs. Place meant when she said, "If you decide to stay here?" Had that really been an invitation for Olivia to hide-out in Mrs. Place's house until she knew for sure, one way or the other? It was a comforting idea. If she wasn't with child, she could simply go home the day after her bleeding started. And if she was? Well, perhaps Mrs. Place would let her stay for a few weeks, put off going to one of those homes for a while. Then, when it was all over, she could come back to Five Rocks and pretend to have been out in Michigan the whole time. No one would ever know the difference.

Delicious aromas began to emanate from the kitchen and drew Olivia through the arched doorway. Embers glowed in the stove and Olivia lifted the lid of the cast iron pot on top of it. A meal of chicken and potatoes coated with honey was slowly cooking. On the table were a pot of coffee waiting to be heated, a still-warm loaf of bread, and a jar of thick strawberry jam.

Olivia helped herself to breakfast and then washed her plate and cup and wiped up the crumbs.

With Mrs. Place safely out in the shop, Olivia felt free to nose round, starting with the kitchen. There was something depressing about how clean and orderly everything was. The walls were painted a bright yellow and decorated with pictures cut out of a ladies' journal: the head of a bored-looking woman with an elaborate hairstyle, a couple in evening dress holding glasses of wine at what seemed to be the rail of a steamer, and three orange kittens playing with a ball of blue yarn. Yellow and white checked curtains covered the window over the washing up basin. Olivia went to the basin and worked the arm of the rusty iron pump for a glass of water.

The strong smell and taste of minerals in the well water – so different from the cold, clear Michigan stream – brought her back home. Her father hadn't gotten a kitchen pump until she was ten or eleven. Before that, they'd had to go out to the yard to pump water. Olivia remembered the joy of having a lark with Tobey in the hot summer sun, the strong smell of iron in the air as they splashed one another.

She opened the back door and peeked out. A gravel path, sheltered by a makeshift wooden structure, led from the back porch of the house to the hinged door that had been cut into the narrow sidewall of the barn. Olivia knew that Mrs. Place did all the baking in the roomy back of the barn. The small front area had been walled off and converted into her shop, with a small porch and roofed entrance that jutted out toward the road. The shop even had glass windows and a fitted door.

Olivia went back upstairs where she found only a room filled with what looked like discarded furniture, a linen closet, the room in which she had slept, and Mrs. Place's spacious bedroom. Olivia entered it shamelessly, listening for the sound of the back door. A lumpy-looking double bed with a brass bedstead stood against the far wall. The pink cover thrown over it matched the throw rug on the floor. Olivia reached under the cover and felt the sheets. Plain white muslin, like the ones on her bed. She had expected perfumed silk. She wondered if anyone had shared that bed with Mrs. Place since Seborn died. Perhaps every older man in town had seen himself as a likely candidate to replace him and droves of them had come calling. Mrs. Place wasn't what you'd call pretty, but her body was still slim, unlike most of the women her age. Olivia thought there must also be something appealing about her wide-open eyes and quick smile.

The door to Mrs. Place's wardrobe boasted an inlaid mirror, surrounded by fat little cherubs carved into the wood. Most of the clothing looked vaguely familiar, except for a long boa of white feathers and a shiny red dress with puffy sleeves and a plunging neckline. Olivia took the red dress out and held it against her body, closing the door of the wardrobe so she could admire herself in the mirror. She tried to guess when a younger version of Mrs. Place might have last worn such a dress. Had she lived some other mysterious life, before being trapped in the dull routine of the bakery in Five Rocks? It would have to have been a long time ago. For as long as Olivia could remember herself, Mrs. Place had been behind the counter in her shop, every day except Sunday. And there had never been any sign of a Mr. Place, dead or alive.

As Olivia continued to snoop through the room and reflect on the life lived by its occupant, she began to understand why Mrs. Place had so readily offered her hospitality. How lonely she must be. Olivia returned the dress to the wardrobe and closed it with a sigh. The only other furniture in the room was a large dressing table. Cosmetics and the tools for applying them were scattered on its glass top. Her arsenal, Olivia thought. Weapons to fight off more than encroaching age. She must have known how the church ladies talked about "all that paint" she wore, but she sat there every morning and defiantly applied her mask. Poor Mrs. Place.

Looked at another way, however, Mrs. Place's life was anything but pitiable. She had her own business. She didn't depend on anyone. Olivia wondered how much of the feminine disapproval heaped on her was rooted in plain old envy.

She gave up ruminating over Mrs. Place's life and returned to her bed to worry about her own. Whether she returned home now or first had to go away and birth a baby, then what? Stay in Five Rocks and wait for some young man to come calling? Smelly Billy Adams perhaps? Marry him and join Avis and Mabel for Sunday dinner every week? She realized what had made Jeremy so attractive. A life shared with him might offer love and friendship, as well as some material amenities, without the usual constraints of respectability. Jeremy wouldn't have objected to her wearing trousers, riding bareback, or having her own money.

That's why people go west, she thought. *To get away from all the silly rules. They're willing to trade comfort and safety for freedom.* She remembered Jeremy asking, "Why do they bother making all those rules? Good people don't need them, and the bad ones aren't going to follow them anyway."

At a few minutes past noon, when the back door predictably opened and slammed, Olivia was downstairs sitting in the rocker. The pump handle creaked a few times and then Mrs. Place came into the parlor holding a glass of water.

"Sleep well?" she asked.

"Yes. Thank you," Olivia replied.

Mrs. Place settled herself in her wing chair. Olivia nodded at the other one and asked if it would all right if she sat there.

355

"Well, of course. What a question. You make yourself to home wherever you want. I hope you got some breakfast."

"Yes. Thank you."

Mrs. Place leaned back and stretched.

"Is this where my father used to sit?" Olivia asked, after moving to the softer chair.

"Yes. Yes, it is. He bought the pair of them. Brought 'em back from one of his buying trips, a very long time ago." She reached down to the basket on the floor and picked up some knitting. "We'll have our dinner right quick," she said. "That chicken's been done for a while, but I like to sit on something soft for a few minutes, after a morning behind that counter."

"Did he ever make you laugh?" Olivia asked.

"Beg your pardon?"

"My father – did he ever make you laugh?"

"Well, I don't recall him telling jokes, if that's what you're asking."

"No, that's not what I mean. I mean . . . I've never been in love, but when I try to imagine what it must be like, there's always a lot of laughing. I picture a man and woman lying together in a field of daisies, talking forever and finding the same things about the world funny. That kind of laughing."

Mrs. Place dropped the knitting into her lap and looked over at Olivia with a wistful smile.

"And my father ... Well, I just can't imagine him . . . Of course, none of us knew him very well. He didn't exactly wear our ears off. Never said much at all, except for telling us to do our chores and homework, and keep our marks in school up, and not give the teacher any guff. Sometimes at Sunday dinner he'd read things out of the newspaper, but he never really talked to us. I've always wondered if he talked to our mother. I can't begin to think how they ended up married. Or how he got to be your ... friend."

Mrs. Place wore an uncertain smile. "You asking?"

356

Olivia nodded.

"Sure you want to know?"

Olivia nodded.

"You're in the middle of all these terrible problems of your own and that's what you got on your mind?"

Olivia nodded again, thinking her terrible problems weren't going anywhere, but she might never get another chance to ask the "fancy lady" about her father.

"You sure you aren't going to pull out a little pearl-handled pistol and shoot me?"

Olivia smiled, shook her head, and raised her right hand to draw an X over her heart.

"Well, all right then, I can understand you wanting to know. But let's go in the kitchen." Mrs. Place leaned forward to struggle out of the chair. "We can talk while we eat. I saved a peach pie for our desert."

Mrs. Place sliced a plate of tomatoes and cucumbers and, after they each had a chicken leg on their plates, began talking.

Chapter Forty-Two

"Well, tell you the truth, it was me what got your father coming over here," Mrs. Place began. "I guess you could say I set my bonnet for him, but I don't mean that I planned for it to happen. Not in the beginning, anyway. He was in Carlton, on one of them buying trips of his, and I was there having myself a vacation." She stopped to chew, swallow, and take a drink of water. "I used to do that when I was younger. Had to get out of here once in a while. I was in one of the hotels, having myself a drink, and there he was. I was already seated in the dining room when he came down for his supper. I guess my face looked familiar, but I'm pretty sure he hadn't worked out exactly who I was. If he had, he wouldn't never have offered me his company." She paused again to eat.

Olivia delved into her own childhood recollections. Carlton. She vaguely remembered her father and Avis talking about a place called Carlton where he used to go for merchandise, but didn't any more because it was far enough away that he'd had to stay overnight. Olivia only remembered him going to Hillsong or Erie. He'd be up before sunrise and come back late the same night. Once, a few years ago, he'd taken Avis with him to Philadelphia and stayed over two nights. But Carlton . . .

"He'd already sat down before he noticed the glass of whiskey in front of me," Mrs. Place continued. "Once he did, he got this puzzled look on his face, trying to figure out who this strange, liquor-guzzling woman was. He never came into the bakery, you know. It was always you children came for the bread and pies." She swallowed another bite of her meal and wiped her mouth with her napkin. "Course, he'd seen me in his own store often enough, especially after he started selling my pies. I could see it slowly dawning on him. I was that woman none of the ladies invited into their parlors. He started fidgeting and looking over his shoulder, but he was too much of a gentleman to get up and leave. We got to talking and after a while he relaxed and ordered a whiskey for himself. We had our supper together and then another whiskey. I don't remember what we found to talk about and I couldn't say how much laughing went on, but he made himself pleasant and I was more than glad for the company. He wasn't a handsome man, your father ..." Her eyes glazed over. "But he had a certain stuffy charm about him. And he always tried to do what he thought was the right thing. That's something to admire in a man." She looked into Olivia's face.

"I don't remember him ever going to Carlton," Olivia said, careful to keep her voice neutral. "So you meeting up with him there – that must have been a long time ago. When my mother was still alive." She

358

didn't know what she felt. Numb. She had grown up knowing about Mrs. Place, but had never considered the possibility that it had begun before her mother's death. A poor widower finding some consolation with an unmarried woman was one thing, but a married man sneaking off and lying to his wife?

Mrs. Place looked up and studied Olivia. "Honey, Seborn adored your mamma, like no man ever loved a woman. Never did care for me anything like that. Not the least little bit. But when a man's married to a woman who's not right in . . . I mean has problems like your mamma –"

"My mother was not crazy!" Olivia pushed her chair back and grasped the edge of the table.

"I didn't say crazy," Mrs. Place said softly. She tried to put her hand over Olivia's, but was batted away. "I never said crazy. But she was . . ." She paused. "Olivia, I know you were just a little thing, but surely you remember something of how she was. All those days she refused to come out of her bedroom, kept the curtains drawn."

"So what if she felt poorly sometimes? She was just fine in the head. She played the piano, and painted pictures, and wore the most beautiful dresses. She was way prettier than you. Just because she was delicate and took cold easily, that's no excuse for you –"

"No, you're right, I'm sorry." Mrs. Place stared at her plate. "I owe you an apology, Olivia. I don't know what I was thinking, saying something like that to you."

"My mother was not crazy." Olivia glared at Mrs. Place. *Who does she think she is? A slut like her, daring to say things like that about my mother, pretending to be my friend. No wonder no one in town speaks to her. Why did I come here? Why did I tell her anything?*

"No, she warn't crazy," Mrs. Place said. "She was a lovely lady. Very special. Very talented. But delicate, like you said." She hurriedly finished her meal and rose to put her dishes in the basin while Olivia sat in silence,

359

her untouched plate in front of her. "I have to get back to the bakery. I can see I've upset you. I suppose you feel like stomping out of here and I can't blame you if that's what you want to do. You shouldn't though. What with me prattling on like the old fool that I am, we haven't discussed your situation at all. Don't make it worse than it has to be, just cause you're riled with me. We'll talk it over after I close up this afternoon. Don't do something you might regret. And you got to eat. Whatever's coming, you need your strength to face it."

After the door closed behind Mrs. Place, Olivia sat at the table for a long while. Then she shoveled the cold food into her mouth, rose to do the washing up, and could think of nothing else to do. She returned to the rocking chair in the parlor, her expression blank. Mrs. Place must know about her mother hanging herself. Of course, he would have told her. That's why she thought Nola June was crazy. Olivia did remember tiptoeing past her mother's closed door. Mrs. Hardaway leaving trays out in the hall that remained untouched. The housekeeper and her father whispering in the kitchen. Now that she thought of it, she could hardly remember a Sunday dinner with both her parents at the table.

Although she had no appetite, she went back to the kitchen and cut herself a generous slab of the peach pie. She stood holding her plate over the basin while she put one forkful after another into her mouth. Before she had swallowed the last bite, she cut a second piece and took it to the parlor with her. She quickly ate it and returned for a third. She felt sick to her stomach, but finished it all, even the crust. Two hours later, when the back door opened, Olivia was once again in the parlor, rocking in the chair.

"Good," Mrs. Place said when she came into the room. "I'm awful glad you're still here."

Olivia waited for Mrs. Place to settle into her chair before asking, "Is it true about my mother, that she hung herself?"

"Why on earth would you be asking –"

"I'll forgive you anything, except lying to me about that," Olivia said, her voice low and steady. Then she leaned forward. "Tell me. Please."

A long silence stretched out before Mrs. Place answered. "Yes. Your poor mother took her own life."

"In the pantry of our kitchen?"

"Yes."

Olivia had not doubted what Mourning told her. She just had to hear it again. She asked, "Where was I?"

"There was no school that day. The teacher was sick or some such and it was Mrs. Hardaway's afternoon off. You three children had gone out to play in the snow, thank the Lord. Your father found her when he came home for his dinner. It was him took her down. All by himself. He sat next to her crying for a long while. Then he carried her up to her bed before he went to get Doc Gaylin. Locked the house up, so you children wouldn't be able to get in before he was back."

"So our mother didn't care a whit about us," Olivia said, feeling as if she might vomit all the gluey pie she had eaten. "That one of us could have come in and found her. And what about her husband? Why didn't she think about how awful it would be for him? She didn't care about any of us."

"Honey, when your mamma got in one of her states she didn't think at all – not about anything. Something just warn't right with her. Never was. I know you don't want to hear it, but that's the truth. One day she'd be strolling down to the river with her easel and watercolors, happy as a lark, prettiest smile on her face you ever saw. The next she'd crawl into bed and refuse to get up for days. Sometimes weeks. Wouldn't eat a thing. Doc Gaylin said she warn't sick. Not in her body. Some folks are like that, poor souls, and ain't a thing can be done for them. You just try to remember the way she was on her good days. She was so charming then. So full of energy. Wasn't a sweeter woman in the whole world. Seemed to love everyone."

"Do my brothers know?"

"I don't know. Your father asked Doc Gaylin to keep it quiet, say it was the influenza what took her. Warshed the body himself and had a closed casket, but there was always talk."

"I never knew. Not until Mourning Free told me, while we were out in Michigan. My father didn't go home alone that day. Mourning was with him, carrying something from the store for him. Mourning watched him take her down and helped him carry her upstairs."

"Seborn never told me that," Mrs. Place said softly. "I guess he had his reasons. Might have just forgot. You know how it is with Mourning Free – he's around all the time, but the way he keeps his peace, it's easy to forget he's there."

Neither of the women spoke for a long while.

Then Olivia asked, "How could you do that? With a married man? A man with a wife who wasn't well?"

Mrs. Place studied her hands and then looked Olivia straight in the face. "I know you won't want to believe it, but there ain't no doubt in my mind – Nola June knew and was just as glad. You remember, don't you, that your parents had separate bedrooms? She'd lost her interest in that part of marriage. Ever since that little brother of yours, the one who died, what was it they called him? Jason Lee, I believe. Well, after he was taken from her, she never welcomed Seborn between her sheets again. It was so hard on your father. Losing his son and then as good as losing his wife. You were still a tiny thing when he made that trip to Carlton. After that he started going out for his card-playing nights. Before he left he'd go in and sit on the edge of Nola June's bed, ask her if she didn't want him to stay home. She'd say, 'Why no Seborn, you go. I want you to go. You mustn't be trapped here with me all the time.'"

Olivia and Mrs. Place sat in the quiet room, listening to the rocking chair creak.

"But that don't mean I'm wrong about him always trying to do the right thing," Mrs. Place said. "He never thought of keeping company with me as a sin. If he had, he wouldn't a done it. He wouldn't a done anything to hurt your mother. He made sure his sweet Nola June had everything she wanted and needed and didn't think the few hours a week he spent with me had anything to do with the rest of his life. And they didn't, Olivia. They really didn't. You can't rob a person of something they don't want." Mrs. Place stopped for a moment, her eyes on Olivia.

"I'll tell you one thing, your mamma never crossed the street when she saw me coming, the way them other women do. She always gave me a smile and said hullo, sort of shy and embarrassed. I'll tell you what I thought. I thought she knew her husband had a difficult life and, having a kind heart like she did, she was grateful he managed to find a little comfort with me. Helped her feel like less of a burden. Not that I thought she spelt it out like that ... them are the kinds of things a person don't put into words. Not even in their own head. We just feel them deep inside. Now, I don't expect you to believe that . . ."

Olivia blinked. "Actually, I think I do. I'm not angry with you, if that's what you think." Her gaze returned to the floor and her voice trailed off. The faintest thread of memory had begun weaving itself into her thoughts. She heard a woman's voice. Was it her mother's? Who else could it belong to? The voice was saying to Avis, "No need to go telling anyone about your father's Saturday night poker games. That's not anyone's business but ours."

"He did his best." Mrs. Place sighed and leaned forward. "Look, I'm sorry I opened my big mouth and now you got all this on your mind, when what you oughta be thinking about is your own situation."

Olivia looked away and shrugged.

"The last thing you want is my opinion, but I'm

giving it to you anyway. You'd best stay here with me till you get the curse. Then that very day you can prance home with a peaceful mind. And if you don't get it, well, your family never has to know about that. I can take you to one of those places, say you're my niece."

She paused and waited for a response, but Olivia went on staring at her toes.

"Or, if you wanted," Mrs. Place continued, "you could just stay on here. Time come, I'll take you to some town where they got a good doctor or midwife. We can stay in a hotel while we wait for the baby to come. Have us a little vacation. I know being here all that long time would be hard on you, what with having to stay inside all that time, but I could keep you busy. Put you to work. I'd get you up before the roosters, so you could come out to the barn, help me with the baking till folks start stirring. You'd be earning your keep and I'd be more than glad of the extra pair of hands. And the company. Sundays I could get a buggy and we could have ourselves a nice ride, long as you keep that monk costume over your head till we're out of town."

Olivia blinked, feeling as if she might cry. "That's awfully kind of you."

"Ain't nothing kind about it. Told you, I'd be more than glad of the help and having a body around to talk to. I wouldn't turn away a stranger in the fix you're in, and what with you being Seborn's daughter and all . . . You know, it's me what never thanked you properly for the kindness you showed me that day. Guess it's true. Everything does come back at you, you wait long enough."

Mrs. Place leaned back in her chair and reached for her knitting needles and then spoke softly. "I can't imagine how beside himself your father would be, if he knew all what's happened to his little girl. But I think he'd be glad that you felt like you could come to me. That you warn't all alone."

Chapter Forty-Three

Without formally accepting Mrs. Place's invitation Olivia simply carried her things upstairs and stayed on. Each morning Mrs. Place rapped on her door while the sky was still black and Olivia came down to join her in the kitchen for a cup of coffee. They maintained a polite distance – no more personal questions – and it took only a few days for the two women to settle into a routine. Olivia was first out the door. She shrouded herself in her cloak and ran out to the barn where she kindled the fires in the four big bake ovens. Then the two women worked side-by-side. Olivia mixed up bread and cookie dough, while Mrs. Place cut lard into flour and salt for her famous pie crust. One morning Olivia hauled the heavy cast iron frying pan out to the barn.

"What do you want that old thing for?" Mrs. Place asked.

"Can I use some of those?" Olivia nodded at the bushel of apples under the counter.

"Sure." Mrs. Place shrugged. "I got plenty."

"Then I'm going to fry up a batch of Michigan apple fritters. It was the devil-woman who taught me how to make them, but they're good anyway. So sweet you think your eyes are going to fall out, but everyone loves them."

When Mrs. Place came in for dinner that day she told Olivia that the shop hadn't been open for two hours before her fritters were sold out.

"If you want," Olivia said, her voice carefully nonchalant, "you could put up a sign saying you'll have them every Thursday."

"That would be good. Real good."

And that was how Olivia told Mrs. Place that she would be staying and how Mrs. Place responded that she was most welcome.

Olivia enjoyed working in the back of the barn. In the early morning the heat of the ovens felt good, not oppressive as it became later in the day. It always smelled homey and delicious, even after Mrs. Place was done with the day's baking. That was when the townswomen started bringing their meats to roast and puddings to bake. For the few pennies Jettie Place charged, they preferred to let her keep a fire stoked, especially when the days were so hot.

Most days Olivia went back to the house before the shop opened, but sometimes she stayed, lurking in the back room, freezing like a statue whenever the bell announced the arrival of a customer. She always wore her soft moccasins, so she could silently creep over to her chair to sit, often with dough-covered hands held out to her sides, as she eavesdropped on what the customers had to say.

No one ever made any mention of Mourning Free. Olivia also listened for Tobey, half eager to hear his voice, half just as glad he didn't come in. It would have felt awful to be hiding from him on the other side of a wall. When everyone had gone and the store was empty again, Mrs. Place would rap her knuckles on the wall three times, letting Olivia know she was free to go back to peeling apples or spooning gobs of dough onto cookie sheets.

Other days Olivia stayed in the house, reading and napping between frenzies of cleaning. A few times she got careless and opened the back door to shake out a rug or scrape mud from a shoe, but she never saw anyone in the field. Mrs. Place brought her a few books from the reading room and Olivia spent the evenings with her nose in them or being taught how to knit. After their initial burst of too much candor for comfort, the two women remained careful of one another. Their conversation was spare, consisting mostly of Mrs. Place repeating what she had heard in the shop. Olivia choked back the questions she still longed to ask about her parents.

Life in prison was boring, but boredom seemed to

be what Olivia needed. Memories still tormented her, but she gradually began to relax and sleep through the night. Without being intrusive, Mrs. Place managed to make her feel mothered. Taken care of. She lived in a warm, orderly home with a kind woman. Perhaps living through enough uneventful days would make her feel human again. She read and knitted the evenings away, taking comfort from the tedium.

When three weeks had gone by with no appearance of her monthly visitor, Olivia sighed. "I guess I'd better start knitting booties."

"Still too soon to say for sure," Mrs. Place replied. "But, yes, it does look that way. Don't you worry, we'll work out what to do."

Olivia was sure. That night she lay in bed, palms pressed to her stomach. She felt no revulsion and considered that a sure sign that Mourning was the father. There was still no news of him, though Olivia often begged Mrs. Place to inquire about him.

"I don't got to ask. I woulda heard. Ain't no way Mourning Free is back in town without my customers yapping about needing him to do one thing or another."

"Please, Mrs. Place. Maybe he's outside of town, working on someone's farm. Please, just ask in the Livery and the Feed and Grain. They would know."

"All right. All right. But only if you stop calling me Mrs. Place. Jettie will do."

The idea of calling an older woman by her given name appalled Olivia. Who had ever heard of such a thing? Olivia didn't even know what Mrs. Hardaway's Christian name was. Or Miss Evans'. But she nodded her acknowledgement of the request and again begged Mrs. Place to ask about Mourning.

But no one had heard a thing about him since he'd left.

Mrs. Place continued to behave as if Olivia's presence in her home were the most natural thing in the world and Olivia accepted her benefactress for what she appeared to be – a kind-hearted, lonely woman, with affection in her heart for the daughter of the man she had tried to love.

One rainy day after closing up shop Mrs. Place told Olivia that she needed some things from Killion's General and would be back shortly. This was not unusual; Mrs. Place went to the store at least once a week. But when two hours had gone by and she hadn't returned, Olivia started pacing and peeking out the front window every few minutes. By the time another hour passed she had begun imagining awful things – Mrs. Place slipping in the mud and being trampled by horses, keeling over in the street as she clutched her heart, being shot by bank robbers, bitten by a poisonous spider, or attacked by a pack of wolves.

Olivia was ashamed to realize that most of her worrying was on her own behalf. Imagine the troop of church ladies that would lay siege to the house, in search of a dress in which to bury poor Mrs. Place. Once "that woman" was dead, they would surely welcome her into their congregation. Imagine them discovering that Killion girl cowering in a corner. "Tsk tsk, What did I always tell you about her? Shame, shame, there the little slut was, in the family way, living with that harlot. Well, no wonder. Birds of a feather. Old Man Killion must be spinning in his grave, but what could he expect, the example he set. And him with his poor sick wife."

Olivia realized how totally dependent on Jettie she was and began to harbor second thoughts about her decision to stay. But those dissipated the moment she heard familiar footsteps on the back porch. Mrs. Place nudged the door open with her hip, hidden behind a tall stack of books.

"I know, I know, I had you worried. You don't got to waste your breath saying it." She huffed and puffed.

She set her burden down on the kitchen table,

steadied the top of the pile to keep it from toppling over, and shook the raindrops from her coat before hanging it on the hook by the door.

"But you're gonna forgive me, once you know the reason." She nodded at the books. "I'd just about finished settling up with your brother when those two Wainwright sisters come in, brimming over with the good news that Old Mrs. Steadman died last night." She turned to hang up her bonnet and grab a rag to wipe the floor. "Not that her dying is good news, Lordy me, no, I didn't mean that, even though she was a nasty old toad, may she rest in peace. The good news is that she had a roomful of books and left all of them to the town, to start a real lending library. Those Wainwright sisters are volunteering the use of that storage shed out behind their place and they'll be the librarians. But they were telling your brother Avis how they needed someone to catalog the books. So who do you think butted right in and said she'd be glad to do it?" She beamed with pride, watching Olivia pick the first book off the top of the pile.

"Well, you can imagine the look those old crows gave me. Don't think I know how to read a book, let alone catalog one. They swung their pointy chins around to stare at me, right on cue with each other. You'd think they'd been practicing. And you know the way they squeeze those bushy eyebrows of theirs all together." Mrs. Place wrinkled her face in an excellent imitation of them and Olivia giggled.

"Those two old birds come into my shop 'bout every day, but I never said a word to them except, what can I get you ladies today? So it might as well have been the broom what piped up and offered to organize their library for them, that's how surprised they were. But I kept on; I don't tell too many stretchers, but once I get started on one I'm pretty good at it. I said that in my younger days I'd worked at one of the biggest libraries in New York City, so I know just about everything there

369

is to know about cataloging books. Said I'd be more than happy to take care of it for them. Course I couldn't possibly do the work anywhere but right here at home. So from now on they're going to bring a new stack of books to the shop every Monday morning and I'll give those books back to them the next week, with their catalog cards all written up." She finally paused for air and to give Olivia an uncertain look. "You're gonna figure out how to do that, ain't you? Your daddy always said he hardly knew what you looked like, the way you always had your nose in a book."

Olivia stared at Jettie, feeling the same way she had that day in the river, when Mourning saved her from falling. She wasn't used to anyone doing anything for her without being asked and had no other experience of another person anticipating what she might want or need.

"Yes, of course, I can figure that out." Olivia couldn't think how to thank her and feared she might cry. All she could do was repeat, "Of course I can do that." Then she added, "This was so kind of you, Mrs. Place."

"Ain't you never going to stop calling me that? You better, you don't want me to start calling you Miss Killion." Looking pleased, but slightly embarrassed, Jettie made herself busy, moving things about the kitchen. "Well, I guess that will work out then. I figured you'd want them. Never was much for books myself, but you – even when you were a little thing you always seemed to be carrying one around. So there's your first batch." She patted the stack of books. "Good thing the rain let up. They hardly got wet at all. There's about three hundred more where those came from. A few stacks of journals too. You can do as much or as little as you please. You get tired of it, I'll just tell them I don't got as much time as what I thought."

"I won't get tired of it." Olivia used her skirt to wipe the damp, reddish-brown volume she had picked off the top of the stack. Its musty smell reminded her of walls of books and ladders on wheels.

"Ralph Waldo Emerson," Olivia read the name of the author. "I've heard of him."

She set it aside. Next on the pile was a well-worn pamphlet of a play called *The Indian Princess.* "Oh look, this is the one about Pocahontas," Olivia said.

"Poke a what?"

"Pocahontas. You know, the Indian lady who helped the Pilgrims."

"I know. I know. I was having you on. Even an ignoramus like me's heard of Pocahontas."

"Miss Evans taught us about this play. Said it was interesting. I think I'll start with it." Olivia set it aside and moved some other volumes off the pile.

Mrs. Place smiled and tied her patchwork apron on, turning away to start putting the supper Olivia had prepared on the table.

"Look, here's Charles Dickens. I bet you'd like him, Mrs. ... Jettie."

"Book written by a man? Bet he kills off all the women in it."

"Why would you say that?"

"Same reason most a them fairy tales are about orphans. Children in 'em might have a kindly grandmother putting food on the table, but no parents. They love to daydream about not having anyone bossing them around from sun up to sun down. Same as a man daydreams about no women nagging him. No responsibility."

"Well, I haven't read all of Mr. Dickens' books, but I don't believe he does away with all his female characters. You really should try one. I'm sure you'd like it."

"I'm more sure to like some food in my stomach. Go ahead and clear them books off the table for now."

"Fenimore Cooper." Olivia held up another one. "He's wonderful. I've read this one. I bet you'd like it too. Next time they come, ask if they have *The*

Leatherstocking Tales. I haven't read it yet. Oh, look at the way this binding is falling apart." She held up a volume of Keats. "Tell them to get you some glue and binding tape. If there's going to be a library, the books need to be kept in good repair. And ask them what the library is to be called, so I can properly label them, Property of the Five Rocks Public Reading Library, something like that." She had begun moving the books to the parlor and spoke in installments, as she moved between the two rooms. "And I'll need paper, so I can make little pockets to paste into them."

"What for?"

"To hold the card. For keeping track of who borrowed the book and when they're supposed to bring it back. I'll need some regular paper for the envelopes and thick paper for the cards."

"Guess those old cows are going to have to start believing Jettie Place worked in a library. That oughta rattle 'em good."

"How is Avis?" Olivia asked later when they sat down to eat.

"He's Avis." Mrs. Place shrugged. "Like I told you, him and Lady Mabel have been living in your father's house since they got married a few months back."

"You call her that, too?" Olivia raised her eyebrows. "I thought I made up that name for her."

"Everyone in four counties calls her that. They still have Mrs. Hardaway keeping the house for them cause Mabel's always busy in the store. Like I'm sure you can guess, she gets after Avis pretty good. And you'd really hate the way she hovers over your Tobias. He takes something out of a box and puts it on a shelf, she comes along right behind him and moves it over an inch. It'd be funny, if it didn't make you want to strangle her."

"How is Tobey, other than having to put up with her?"

"Appears to be just fine. She doesn't seem to rile him. No matter what she says or how often she repeats it, he just nods his head and shuffles away. But like I told you, he took himself a room over at Mrs. Monroe's, so at least he's got his evenings to himself. Does take all his meals with them, though."

"That's no surprise. If there's one thing I'll give Mabel, it's being a great cook. Is he still keeping company with Emma O'Keefe?"

"Far's I know. I see them walking down toward the river every once in a while. Must be where they go to do their canoodling."

Olivia felt a pang of loneliness. It would be so nice to see him and that wobbly smile of his. But what could she tell him? Nothing. Not about Mourning and not about the Stubblefields. She remembered what Mrs. Place had said about weak people with good intentions. That was Tobey.

"You never talk about your family." Olivia changed the subject.

"Don't have much of one. Father ran off when I was a little thing. He could come begging at my door, I wouldn't know who he was. I got two older sisters, but it's been a good, oh, I'd say ten years since I seen either a them. I do got a cousin I'm in touch with, Susan, comes to visit me once a year or so."

"That must be nice for you. But what about your mother?"

Jettie studied her plate for a moment, then looked up, smiling and shaking her head. "She warn't much of a mother. Was my sisters what raised me."

"Why? Was she sick?"

"Yes. Bad case of bottle-itis. Maybe she was nice when she was sober, but I couldn't say. I don't know how, but she did manage to hold a job, cooking at one of the hotels."

"Where did you live?"

"Up in Erie. Had a little shack on the water. I'll tell you one thing, owner of that hotel found her real entertaining. Said the customers loved her. He woulda let her tend bar, if he warn't afraid of her drinking him stick dry. See, she had a friendly streak. Loved to talk with anyone what would listen. Her opinions about life on this planet kept everyone laughing. And once she got started drinking, she'd set into philosophizing and using a lot of them sayings, only she'd get them all mixed up. 'Well, you can't teach a sleeping dog to lie,' she'd say. Or, 'You can beat a dead horse, but you can't make it drink.' My favorite was, 'Spare the rod and spoil the victor.'"

Olivia grinned and asked, "How long has it been since you've seen her?"

"Since she fell off a boat and drowned. Day after my fifteenth birthday."

"Oh."

They finished that meal in silence.

Chapter Forty-Four

Olivia spent the next day in the company of Pocahontas.

"That must be some story," Jettie said that evening, when Olivia barely looked up from the pamphlet to say a word.

"The play's okay. But trying to decide what you think about the comments Mrs. Steadman wrote in the margins is what's interesting. She says all kinds of stuff about what really happened to Pocahontas. Want to hear?"

"Sure. Everyone always said you'd grow up to be a teacher and here's me having a private lesson."

"So the Pilgrims were going to starve their first winter until Pocahontas showed up with a raft of food, right? Miss Evans taught us that she did that in secret, against the wishes of her father, the Chief. But Mrs. Steadman says that wasn't true. Her father was the one who sent her, only he didn't want anyone to know that.

He couldn't figure out what to make of the Pilgrims any more than the Pilgrims knew what to make of the Indians. So he sent just enough food to keep them alive, and he sent it with his daughter, so she could spy on them."

"Smart Chief."

"But Mrs. Steadman says that when the Pilgrims kidnapped Pocahontas, it wasn't like Miss Evans taught us, so they could get the Chief to do what they wanted. She says back then a lot of white folks held to a notion about converting the Indians to Christianity and marrying them. They thought that was the way to have peace between them. America would be colonized by whites and Indians all mixed up together."

"Like to see that happen 'round here," Jettie said. "First the Protestants gotta kidnap a slew of Catholics and marry them. See if *they* can get along together, 'fore they start hobnobbing with the Mohicans."

"Pocahontas was supposed to be the first example, so they got her married to one of the men who kidnapped her. He took her back to Europe to show her off, show folks back there how the Americans were Christianizing the wild Red Man and spreading the word of God. But a few years later poor Pocahontas got murdered and then some whites massacred a whole lot of Indians and after that the idea of marrying them and making peace that way sort of petered out."

"Yes, well, I can see where slaughtering the families of the brides and grooms could put a damper on wedding plans."

"But look at what it means. It means that back then there were a lot of white folks who didn't think a man and a woman couldn't be together unless their skin was the same color. They thought children who had one white parent and one Indian parent were going to be the new Americans, not mongrels. And those people were the Pilgrims. The people who started our country. Who came here because they believed in freedom."

Jettie looked up from her needlework and studied Olivia over her spectacles. "Old Mrs. Steadman sure got your dander up."

"A bunch of stupid, selfish men ruined everything. Taking all the land from the Indians and then kidnapping African people and making them slaves. Out in Detroit I was always hearing about the things white people learned from the Indians, about medicines and hunting and trapping and farming. We'd have a much better country if congress had passed a Greedy White Men Removal Act instead of an Indian Removal Act."

Jettie shook her head and smiled. "Probably so. I think I'm about ready to turn in."

Olivia idly picked up one of the newspapers Jettie had brought home and her eyes opened wide. Congress had passed the law Jeremy had told her about, the General Pre-Emption Law. Squatters could purchase 160 acres of land, at a dollar twenty-five an acre, and not pay for it until later. Mourning could have had his own place right now, if she hadn't meddled in his life.

The following evening Jettie set her needlework aside and made a show of studying the calendar.

"It's September 5th. Far as I recall, you've been here forty-six days. And you must a spent at least three days on the boat and what ... two days in Michigan after they let you go? And the week that they ..." She raised her eyes to look at Olivia. "I'd say that, all together, it's time you saw a midwife."

Olivia sat quietly, hands folded in her lap.

"I ain't saying you got to think it's for sure. It could be from the shock of all what happened out there," Jettie said. "Women can stop bleeding for a lot longer and for a lot less reason than what you been through. But if you are carrying a child, a midwife or doctor ought to be able to tell by now. And you need to know early on, case you want to do something about it."

376

Olivia nodded in numb agreement.

"It might have to be a doctor," Jettie said. "I don't know no midwives 'round here what don't know every soul and devil in Five Rocks. Ain't one a them I'd trust not to flap her jaws about Old Man Killion's girl."

So a few days later Jettie hung a "Closed" sign on the door of the bakery and rented a buggy. Olivia cowered inside her cloak and they drove two and a half hours to Weaverton. There Jettie inquired in the general store and was referred to Doctor Murdock, who saw patients at an office in his home. Jettie had given Olivia a ring to put on her finger, telling her to turn it around, so the stone wouldn't show. She told Olivia to call herself Mrs. Springer.

The door was opened by an older man with sloping shoulders, a round pot belly, and thin wisps of hair. Wearing a sour expression, Doctor Murdock silently led them back to his office and told Olivia to get up on the table behind a screen. He examined her quickly, while Olivia all but bit through her bottom lip.

"You can get down now," he said and went to the basin to wash his hands, before seating himself behind his desk.

Olivia rearranged herself and came around the screen to seat herself on the rickety chair next to Jettie's.

"Well, congratulations, Mrs. Springer. You are definitely going to have a baby. I'd guess the happy occasion will be in another seven and a half, eight months."

Jettie reached over and squeezed Olivia's hand, which remained limp in her lap.

From the way the doctor was looking at her and the distaste with which he had pronounced "Mrs. Springer" Olivia was sure he knew she was a girl who'd gotten herself in trouble. He recited vague advice about getting enough rest and not moving heavy furniture and seemed relieved when the two women quickly rose to leave. Neither of them spoke as they climbed into the buggy. Jettie drove out of town and then pulled to the side of the road. Olivia stared silently ahead.

"You best do your crying and cursing," Jettie said. "Get it out of you now."

"I just want to go home," Olivia said. "I mean to your house. I just want to go home."

"Straight back to prison? No, that ain't what we're gonna do. Not on a day like today. Buggy's paid for till evening. You'll have enough days shut up in that house. We're gonna have us a nice drive and find some sinfully expensive place to stop for lunch. Let someone wait on us for a change. Then we'll take us a long walk in the sunshine. Do you good."

"I don't feel like it, Jettie."

"I know you don't. That's why you're gonna do it." Jettie turned and took both of Olivia's hands in hers. "Look, once you get over feeling sorry for yourself – which I know you got every right to be doing – you got to figure out how to go on living. I think a nice walk in the sun would be a good start. That's how I do my best thinking. Way out here you don't even have to wear that damned shroud."

Olivia started crying and Jettie put her arms around her. "There, there. At least now you know."

"What am I going to do, Jettie?"

"What do you want to do?"

"Want? There's nothing for me to want to do." Olivia sat up straight and blew her nose into the handkerchief Jettie handed her.

"In this life there's always a price to pay for whatever you do. You got to lay out all your choices and pick the one that looks the least bad to you."

"That's what my father always used to say."

"You can have the baby in one of them places and give it away." Jettie raised one hand and started bending back its fingers with the other. "You can –"

"Not now. Please." Olivia had no patience for this

378

conversation. Without knowing that Mourning might be the father, Jettie had no advice to give.

"If I were younger, I'd ask you to let me raise it. But then I'm not younger." Jettie sounded sad.

Olivia raised her eyes, realizing that to someone like Jettie this predicament might not seem so awful.

"Would you really have had a baby? All by yourself?"

"Well, anyone would prefer having a husband. Even a useless one would at least keep you respectable. Certainly is easier on a child. But of course I would have wanted a baby. Why wouldn't I? Imagine how different my life would be, if I had a child to care for. Might even be some grandbabies by now."

"But the way people would talk about you ..."

"What they gonna say what's worse than what they already do? That's the thing about respectability – you can only lose it once. When it's gone, it's gone. Long as you don't kill no one, ain't much more they can do to you. Anyway, I coulda gone off somewhere. Out to Michigan. Claimed to be a grieving widow. Who would have known the difference?"

She handed Olivia another clean handkerchief, seeming to have an endless supply of them in her pocket. Jetty gazed out at the fields surrounding them and then looked back at Olivia.

"I tell you, Olivia, if you decide to have that baby and give it away, I just might ask you to give it to me. You might think it wouldn't be fair to the baby, me being old and alone and in my social situation, but I've got money put away. I'd hire someone to help in the bakery, so I could take proper care of it. And when I'm gone, well, there's the business. That child would never want for anything, that's one thing I can promise you."

Olivia burst into sobs. At that moment she was incapable of caring what would be good or bad for the baby. She felt like shouting, "What about me? None of those choices are any good for *me*."

Chapter Forty-Five

They rode aimlessly through the countryside. When they entered the next town Jettie nodded at a long storefront with a sign that said "Eating House."

"Guess we best stop."

"If you want," Olivia said. "I'm not hungry."

"You just haven't gotten around to noticing that you are. Pregnant women are always hungry. Look, there's a livery right up the street."

Olivia silently got out of the buggy and followed Jettie back towards the restaurant.

"I can't force you to eat," Jettie said, "but I ain't driving home with my belly howling like a banshee."

"You can beat a dead horse, but you can't make it drink," Olivia mumbled for no reason.

Their eyes met and both women gave a half-hearted laugh.

"See, I knew you was stronger than you been making out to be," Jettie said, putting an arm around Olivia's shoulder. "You're gonna be all right. You'll see. You ain't the type to fall apart. It ain't in your nature."

Suddenly calm – and hungry – Olivia followed her inside. They were seated at a table by the window and ordered the special: all the fried fish you can eat and a baked potato. Jettie also ordered beer for both of them.

When the waiter was gone, Olivia leaned forward and asked, "What would I have to do, to get rid of it?"

"Don't rightly know. Drink something I think."

"Like poison, you mean?"

"If it's gonna kill the seed growing inside you, it ain't medicine. But it's done every day. I ain't saying there ain't no danger in it, but it's not like there ain't no danger in birthing a baby."

"How do you get the poison?"

"Go to a doctor and ask for it."

"Just like that? I always thought they aren't allowed. I mean, you never hear anyone talk about it. Like it's a big secret."

"You gonna advertise in the newspaper if you do it? Most everyone wantin' it done are girls like you, in trouble. Even if they're married, doing it for their own health reasons, or cause they got no money, or cause they just don't want another child, who wants the whole world to know they done that? And ain't no doctor wants a reputation for bein' an abortion doctor, cause then tongues start flapping about any woman seen going into his office. So no woman will go near him, even if she all she needs is a check-up, and his practice disappears."

"So you just go to any doctor?"

"Go to one and ask. He says no, go to another one. Some got religious convictions against it. And ain't many will do it after quickening."

"What's that?"

"When you can feel the baby move. After you're three or four months gone."

The waiter approached with their plates and a very large platter of very small fried fish.

"So I'd have to do it right away," Olivia said when he was gone.

"The sooner, the better. Is that what you want to do?"

"I don't know," Olivia said as she picked up a piece of fish in her fingers and took a bite. "Mm, it's good. Got a great crisp on it, but watch out for bones."

"I see you learned some Michigan table manners."

"Manners are an easy habit to break," Olivia grinned. Now that she was over the shock, she felt a kind of relief. At least she knew what she had to deal with. And that she could count on Jettie to help her through it.

The platter was soon empty and while they waited for the waiter to bring more fish, Olivia asked, "What do *you* think? Do you think it's wrong?"

"What I think is the last thing on earth that

matters." Jettie folded her napkin. "Ain't no one got a right to give you advice about this."

"But I want to know what you think. Is it a sin?"

"No. I think a woman's got the right. She's the one gonna spend the rest of her days worrying after that child. And it's hard enough being a child in this world when you got a mother what wanted you."

Olivia stared at a knot in the wooden tabletop, trying to convince herself that a child like the one inside her was better off not being born. But she couldn't hold with that. *People don't give up their own lives,* she thought, *no matter how bad they are. They hang on, hoping for better, even when they know darn well there's not much chance of better coming to call. Look at Mourning, born without any parents. Do I think it would be better if he'd never come into the world?*

"The quickening," Olivia said, leaning forward again, "is that when the baby starts to be alive?"

"Lord, Olivia. You're asking *me* to define the essence of life? There ain't no doctor or priest what can do that. All I know is, the law allows it and I think that's all you got to know." She stopped speaking while the waiter set down another platter of fish. "You got to do whatever your heart tells you to do. I think that's God's way of speaking to us. If it feels right, it is right. God don't give everyone the same answer. What's right for some other girl ain't right for you. Why don't you try deciding to get rid of it and walk around for a few days with that decision in your heart, see how it sits?"

They didn't talk much on the way home. By the time they arrived, Olivia knew. She didn't need to walk around for a few days. She wasn't going to drink any poison. She was going to have the baby.

November was gray, the trees bare. The last leaves blew in circles, close to the ground. Snow was still a month away, but the ground was hard and cold and the wind strong enough to keep folks inside. It was a time of year Olivia had always found oppressive.

One Monday the pile of library books Jettie brought home included some issues of *Godey's Lady's Book*. Olivia could tell they were Mabel's, by the way so many of the pages were dog-eared. She glanced through the articles. Yes, those were topics Mabel would want to return to. She smiled, feeling something close to affection for her sister-in-law.

There were also two issues of *Life in America* and one of a journal she had never heard of, called *Nature*. She flipped it open to the Table of Contents and there it was, "The Wildlife of Michigan" by Mr. Jeremy Kincaid. The article was longer than his usual single page, providing a survey of all the mammals and reptiles that were native to the state. Olivia started reading in the middle, where he wrote about bears.

There was a drawing of a bear standing on its hind legs, its head cocked to one side, as if it couldn't quite make out what someone was saying. It looked just like the mamma bear they had seen by the river. Olivia wondered who had drawn it for him. She closed her eyes, remembering that day, the caress of the sun on her face, her feet in the cold rushing water. That day she'd thought the most important thing in the world was the possibility of Jeremy's skin brushing against hers. That the worst thing that could happen to a girl was to not be loved by a man she thought she wanted. It was a story about somebody else.

Cooped up together with nothing but a gray sky to look out at, Jettie and Olivia began to snip at one other. Jettie seemed to grow fussier by the day, had to have things done just her way. Olivia dreaded the early evenings, when she had to put her book down and sit through a tedious description of each customer who'd come in that day. Though she eagerly awaited the rare scraps of gossip about "those Killions" that Jettie picked up in the shop, Olivia felt like shouting in protest at the rest of it. *What do I care if Mrs. Brewster paid you with a Quarter Eagle gold piece? Don't you know how boring it is to listen to you telling me how many times Mrs. Monroe came back to check on her stupid pudding? And if you don't shut up about the way Mr. Lindstrom's teeth click, I'm going to scream.*

But somehow their bickering made Olivia feel even more at home. Mrs. Place could go to her room and slam the door without Olivia fretting that she was going to be asked to leave. They had molded themselves into a family of sorts, each taken for granted by the other. It was not a relationship that either would end because of an argument. And Olivia's annoyance always passed quickly. Her feelings for Jettie were stronger than mere gratitude.

Jettie began knitting and sewing for the baby.

"Just for the beginning." She peered at Olivia over her glasses. "For the first month. Till you've had time to decide what you're gonna do. No point looking farther ahead than that. You can't make no decision about giving your baby away till you've held it in your arms. Looked into them bright little eyes and fallen in mad love. Or looked into them and not been able to see nothing but the monster what raped you."

Olivia couldn't imagine either scenario. The baby wasn't real to her. It was a concept and a problem, but not a person. She didn't feel like talking about it and changed the subject. "Does Mrs. Hardaway ever come into the shop?"

"No."

"What about Lady Mabel?"

"Are you fooling? That woman was born too busy to do her own errands. And now she's hired a young boy in the store. Sends him with her order, both for Killion's General and for home."

"What about Tobey?"

"No. That sweetheart of his, that Emma O'Keefe,

does come once in a while for one of my pies, but a mouse has more conversation in it than that girl does."

"What about when you go to Killion's General to do your shopping?"

"You know ain't none a them chat with me. All I can tell you is that both your brothers look to be in perfectly good health."

Two weeks before Christmas a blanket of snow covered the town. Jettie dragged a scraggly little tree into the parlor, fitted it into a wooden stand, and wrapped a green velvet skirt around it. Then she got a box of shiny red and orange glass bulbs out of the attic and gave Olivia the makings to tie red bows on pine cones, string acorns, and cut out paper decorations. The pathetic tree leaned to one side, but that didn't matter. Neither of them was alone. During the week before Christmas Jettie made a nightly ritual of pouring two cups of hot chocolate or eggnog and asking Olivia to sing a few carols. On Christmas Eve she poured herself a large glass of whiskey and Olivia couldn't help wondering if she usually spent Christmas drunk. In past years had she decorated a tree for herself? Or perhaps gone to spend the holiday with the cousin she'd spoken of?

The next morning Jettie sliced one of her special holiday coffee cakes and after they finished their coffee they exchanged gifts. Since Olivia couldn't go out shopping, she'd wrapped up some of her own things. The first present that Jettie opened was the hairbrush.

"Oh, Olivia, this is just so pretty. Look at that workmanship." Jettie touched the carved wooden back. Then she turned it over and ran it through her hair.

"It belonged to my mother," Olivia said quietly and saw the anticipated look of distress that passed over Jettie's face. "I didn't want to give it to you without telling you. That wouldn't have seemed right. But I really want you to have it and I'm sure she would too, in gratitude for the way you're taking care of her daughter." Olivia rose to give Jettie a hug.

"Well thank you. You just turn around and sit yourself down on this stool here and let me have at that birds' nest on your head."

Olivia sat on the footstool between Jettie's knees while Jettie brushed her hair, just the way Olivia remembered her mother doing. Then Jettie opened her other gifts: one of Nola June's bone combs and a volume of Wordsworth's poems. Olivia had kept it when she returned the library books a few weeks ago, feeling justified in confiscating it, in exchange for all her work.

"And this is for Angel." Olivia handed Jettie the last package.

Jettie unwrapped the tiny red jacket Olivia had sewn out of an old dress Jettie had cut up for rags. Jettie dressed the bewildered cat in it and danced around the room with her, singing *Joy to the World*.

Jettie gave Olivia two store-bought maternity dresses, a delicate gold necklace, and a beautiful journal. It was just like the one Olivia had bought in Detroit, bound in wine-colored leather, but his one had a metal clasp and lock. Olivia put it to her nose to breath in the fragrance of the leather and then flipped through the empty white pages.

"You like to read so much," Jettie said, "I thought you might like to put some of your own words down. Keep a memory of this time. Maybe someday you'll even feel like writing about ... that out there. Course, you do that, you got to be extra careful where you keep it. That lock ain't gonna stop nobody what wants to cut it open." She pressed the small key into Olivia's palm.

"Thank you, Jettie. It's beautiful. How do you always know what I need? I bought one exactly like it in Detroit. Filled it with pictures and stories about everything we did. It's upstairs in one of the baskets. I do like to write things down. Helps me think them through. I'm going to start right away, before I go to bed tonight. I'll write all about the lovely Christmas we had together."

"I'm glad you like it."

After a few minutes of silence Olivia asked softly, "You never talk about your sisters. Do you know where they are for Christmas?"

"My sisters? Better not to know what they're up to. They did a good job of raising me up – when they were hardly more than babies themselves – I'll give them that. But since then ... Let's just say that of the three of us, I'm the one who turned out well. So you can imagine."

"Do you know where they are?"

"I suppose still in Erie. That's where they were last time I seen 'em. Sharing two rooms near the port. Back then they used to work a few hours in the morning, cleaning for folks, and then spend the rest of the day smoking up their wages."

"They smoked that many cigarettes?"

Jettie smiled. "Opium, Honey, opium. One year I went lookin' for 'em, planning on staying a while, but turned out they had quite a few gentlemen callers."

"You don't mean they were working as prostitutes!"

"No. They were too damned stupid to charge money. It was sailors off the boats, bringing them more of the poppy juice they loved to smoke, in exchange for a visit."

"Oh." Olivia blinked, not knowing what to say.

Jettie's expression went blank and she spoke as if to herself. "Those sailors, they had a name for my big sisters. I passed some of 'em, on my way out. They had a young one with them, hardly but a boy, and they were tellin' him what a swell time he was going to have with the pair of lobster kettles at the top a them stairs."

Chapter Forty-Six

It was a hard January. Every morning Olivia high-stepped to the barn through a fresh crust of snow and was increasingly grateful that she wasn't in Uncle Scruggs' awful cabin. She spent long hours in the kitchen, the table pulled close to the stove, writing in her journal about Mourning and Jeremy and Jettie.

One morning she became lost in a frenzy of scribbling. She wrote it all down: how she'd met her new neighbors, how nosy Iola was, the way she stared at Olivia with her snake eyes, and everything about what happened in the barn. Every horrible minute. After she finished she closed the journal and sat staring into space, opening and closing her cramped hand. She'd written nothing about her night with Mourning, but had left out no sickening detail of what Filmore had done to her. It was there, on paper. That was the last entry she made in that journal. She had no stomach for writing after that.

One freezing noontime in February, Olivia was sweeping up the kitchen when Jettie stomped in, bringing a gust of cold with her.

"You are not going to believe who I saw just now, riding right up the middle of Main Street."

"If I'm not going to believe it, I guess you'd better not bother telling me," Olivia said, in no mood for gossip.

"Well, you sure do want me to tell you – it was your friend what you've been so worried about. Mr. Mourning Free."

"Mourning? Mourning's here? Are you sure it was him?"

"I wouldn't be telling you so if I warn't. I tried to catch him up and have a word, but he was on horseback. Not that broken-down old nag he used to

388

have. Pretty gray mare with speckles of white."

When Jettie first said his name Olivia had frozen, broom midair, as shocked as if a rock had thudded into her chest. Then she felt paralyzed by a muddle of feelings: surprise, relief, joy, curiosity. But the emotion that seemed to be winning out was one she had not at all anticipated: fear. Fear strong enough to make her feel sick. All this time she'd thought she'd give anything for the chance to talk to Mourning. But now ... what would she say? He would glance at her swollen belly and assume it was his and what would she say? *I think it is? Think.* She'd have to tell him who else it might belong to. Say the words, relive the story they told.

It hadn't been hard to tell Jettie. It had poured out, on its own. And now she'd written it in her journal. But she couldn't bear to say it again. Nor could she bear to burn that picture into Mourning's mind – her tied to that bed, legs forced wide apart. She began to feel shaky, stunned to realize how much easier it would be to simply rejoice in knowing he was alive. And never see him again.

She also feared seeing that old distrust on his face, him again asking her to swear she'd never claim he'd forced it on her.

And then there was Jettie. The minute she saw Olivia and Mourning together, Jettie would know. Olivia didn't doubt that. She had no idea how Jettie felt about coloreds, but imagined her doughy face forged into a slab of iron. *Nigger-loving slut. Get out of my house.* It was a face that inhabited Olivia's nightmares of what might happen if she gave birth to a black baby.

Olivia pulled out a chair and sat.

"Well, don't you look like you seen a ghost," Jettie said. "What's the matter? I thought you'd be thrilled half to pieces."

"I am. I just got a little out of breath pushing that broom is all. Of course, I'm glad to know he's all right. Really glad. I wish I could ask you to go get him, bring him back here, find out where he's been, but . . ." Olivia looked down at her belly. "He doesn't know anything about what happened."

"No, course he don't. But if you want I could go search him out, without letting on about you being here. I could pretend I'm just being friendly-like, asking where he's been."

"If you think there's any chance of Mourning Free telling some nosy white lady what he had for breakfast, you don't know him very well. He's as stubborn and keep-to-himself as they come."

"Well, I got to get back to the shop. You give a good think on whether you want me to go looking for him."

The next day Jettie went shopping at Killion's General and asked some people there if they'd seen Mourning. She came back and reported to Olivia. "When I seen him he must've already been on his way out of town. Seems the only reason he come here was to get some kind of paper from Mr. Carmichael."

"His Free Man of Color paper," Olivia said.

"Yes, that's right. That's what they called it. Mr. Carmichael offered him to stay the night in his office like he used to, but Mourning said he had to be riding on. I don't think he said a word to another soul. Just rode straight to Mr. Carmichael's office, asked for his paper, and left town as fast as he could."

"Did he tell Mr. Carmichael where he was going?"

"No. Not where he'd been and not where he was headed for."

Olivia let out a deep sigh. "Well at least I know those devils didn't kill him."

Spring came early that year. By the beginning of March the snow had melted and first buds were beginning to appear on the skeletal trees. Olivia could no longer see her breath and decided enough with sponge baths – it was time for a proper tub. She was in the kitchen, luxuriating in the hot water, when her contractions started. By the time she realized what the strange convulsions were, she barely managed to struggle to her feet. Luckily it was evening and Jettie was in the house. Olivia called for her as she stepped out of the water and reached for the towel.

"Now?" Jettie said. "It can't be now. It's not supposed to be for another three weeks."

"Well something is happening." Olivia dropped the towel and stood naked, grasping the counter with both hands as another contraction gripped her.

"I'll go fetch Doc Gaylin," Jettie said.

"Doc Gaylin!" Olivia felt the contraction release her and straightened up to grab Jettie's arm. "No. No, no, no. I haven't spent all these months in prison so you can go and ruin everything now. Help me get some clothes on and then go get a buggy. You're going to drive me back to that Doctor Murdock in Weaverton."

"Weaverton! We can't go driving all that way at night and you in labor. It's too far. There's no time. Anyway, it's too late to get a buggy, the livery's closed."

"So knock on Mr. Ferguson's door. You know he'll come out if it means putting a nickel in his pocket."

Olivia bent over as another contraction began.

"Oh listen to you. You're talking crazy. We don't got time for all that. Suppose we get all the way over there and that doctor ain't even home? We were supposed to go to a hotel next week, stay someplace where they got a doctor and wait for the baby. We can't make a drive like that now, at night, with the baby already coming."

"Get moving, Jettie. Stop wasting time arguing with me. I am *not* having this baby in Five Rocks."

"Stubborn mule just like your father. Where's your chemise?" She clumsily fought with the thin muslin garment. "Oh hell, I got it all inside out."

"I don't care if it's upside down. Never mind, give it to me. I'll get myself dressed. You go get that buggy. Now."

Jettie looked like she might faint, but finally rushed

out the back door. Freezing, with her chemise wadded up in one hand, Olivia waddled naked into the parlor where she sank down on a chair and reached for her moccasins. After waiting for another contraction to pass, she rose and made her cautious way up the stairs.

When it had first grown cold she'd asked Jettie to bring her a few sets of long johns from the store and now she pulled on pants and shirt. She pulled a dress on over them and then shrugged into the warmest sweater she owned. She took the pillowcase from her pillow and shoved $20 in gold coins, a hair brush, two towels, a second set of long johns, and a pile of clean rags into it. After throwing a pillow and two blankets to the bottom of the stairs, she clutched the pillowcase in one hand and the handrail in the other and began her descent. Halfway down she had to stop and sit on one of the steps while she waited out another contraction.

Then she sat on the bottom step, draped in her black cloak. She leaned back, smoothed the front of her dress, and spread her palms over her belly, feeling the movement. A deep calm had come over her. She knew a great deal of pain awaited her, but she was no longer frightened.

"How bad can it be?" she asked out loud, speaking to the child as she gently stroked her stomach. "I'll get through it, same as every woman does. So will you, don't worry. We're both going to be just fine. And no matter what happens, I don't care who your father is, I'm going to look out for you. I promise. None of this mess is any of your fault. You're just a sweet innocent baby and your mamma's going to look out for you. Long as I'm breathing, you'll never be alone in this world. Cross my heart."

The End

Olivia's story continues in Book 2 of the Olivia Series, **The Way the World Is**, which is available at www.amazon.com

In today's book market word-of-mouth and customer recommendations are crucial to success. If you enjoyed **Olivia, Mourning**, please consider taking the time to post even a brief review on Amazon and/or Goodreads.

Other Books by Yael Politis

- **The Lonely Tree**

- **The Way the World Is**
  (Book 2 of the Olivia Series)

- **Whatever Happened to Mourning Free?**
  (Book 3 of the Olivia Series)
  To be published toward the end of 2014
  If you would like to receive an email notification when Book 3 is released, sign up to **Follow** the author's blog at yaelpolitis.wordpress.com
  or sign up to **Stay Up to Date** regarding new releases by Yael Politis at:
  http://www.amazon.com/Yael-Politis/e/B002BOA5NU/ref=ntt_athr_dp_pel_1

Contact
yaelpolitis.wordpress.com
poliyael@gmail.com

The Way the World Is
Book 2 of the Olivia Series

After the devastating trauma she suffered in **Olivia, Mourning** and finally knowing the reality with which she must contend, Olivia strives to rebuild herself – emotionally, socially, and financially. She starts a new life in Detroit, the young and exciting city on a river where she has come to feel at home. New friends help the healing process while she continues her search for the two people she loves, who have disappeared from her life. She finds solace in helping fugitive slaves escape over the river to Canada, believing, as one of her new friends says, "In this time and place it is the most worthy thing a person can do."

What Midwest Book Review Says
"Fans of *Olivia, Mourning* will find this sequel no less engrossing, with its gritty protagonist ... a powerful saga that makes for thoroughly engrossing, compelling historical fiction at its best." *D. Donovan, Senior eBook Reviewer, Midwest Book Review*

Whatever Happened to Mourning Free?
Book 3 of the Olivia series
To be published by the end of 2014

Book 3 is not a "continuation" of Book 2 in the same sense that Book 2 continues Book1. Book 3 does answer the question asked in its title and provides a narrative account of how Olivia, Mourning, and Little Boy became reunited, but it skips three generations forward to focus on descendants of the Killion and Free families, who are still struggling with problems echoing those faced by Olivia and Mourning.

It's 1967 and Charlene Connor has just graduated from U of M, without her "Mrs." Her mother recently passed away and soon afterwards her father fled the silence to a new start elsewhere. So Charlene is going "home" to an empty house.
Two things will make this long, hot summer bearable: Reeves Valenti, the high school sweetheart she left behind, and the African-American lawyer who knocks on her door, bringing information about her great-great-great Aunt Olivia Killion. Charlene has always longed to know what happened to Olivia and her friend and partner Mourning Free; she didn't know that finally discovering the answers to her questions would bring a new person – and a fundamental change – into her life.

This book is not autobiographical. In most things Charlene Connor is my opposite. In many ways she is my fantasy of what I would like to be. I did, however, grow up as a "Foundation kid" at 32 Brookline Lane in Dearborn, Michigan, which is not far from Olivia's farm. Since 1973 I have lived in Israel.

The Lonely Tree

British Mandate Palestine and Israel – 1934-1967

Tonia's parents take her to live on Kfar Etzion, an isolated and struggling religious kibbutz south of Jerusalem. Fifteen-year-old Tonia does not believe that their dream of establishing a Jewish state will ever come to be. Life on the kibbutz is harsh and Tonia dreams of security and a little comfort, though material wealth for its own sake is not what she longs for. She wants something simple – to be able to bring up her own children under a roof of her own, in a place where they won't feel constantly threatened. She is determined to seek this different life in America – as soon as she is old enough – even though that means turning her back on her love for Amos Amrani, a handsome young Yemenite who belongs to the Jewish underground.

Much of this novel takes place in Kfar Etzion, during its establishment, siege, and fall to the Arab Legion during hostilities immediately prior to Israel's War of Independence – resulting in the massacre of its surviving defenders. A later part of the story is set in Grand Rapids, Michigan, where Tonia tries to find her new life.

This is one of very few English novels that take place in British Mandate Palestine and the only one that tells the story of Kfar Etzion. While the characters are fictional, historical events are accurately portrayed. The Lonely Tree, however, does not read like a history book. It is a character-driven love story with no political agenda.